Praise for Brad Meltzer:

'This is non-stop, well researched action . . .
The scenarios are credible, the tension excruciating
and the ending slaps you in the face'
Guardian on *The Zero Game*

'Meltzer has earned the right to belly up to the bar with
John Grisham, Scott Turow and David Baldacci'
People

'Breakneck . . . an action-packed read'
Mail on Sunday

'Meltzer's plot is well thought-out, with a
particularly vivid climax'
The Sunday Times

'Grisham had better beware for there's a new
kid on the block.'
The Irish Times

'Compulsive'
Daily Mail

'Meltzer has mastered the art of baiting and hooking readers
into a fast moving plot'
USA Today

'Meltzer's dark political thriller pulses with adrenaline
in a mean and dangerous race to the final revelation'
Oxford Times

Also by Brad Meltzer

The Tenth Justice
Dead Even
The First Counsel
The Millionaires
The Zero Game

THE BOOK OF FATE

BRAD MELTZER

HODDER

Copyright © 2006 by Brad Meltzer

First published in America in 2006 by Warner Books
First published in Great Britain in 2006 by Hodder & Stoughton
A division of Hodder Headline

This paperback edition published in 2007

The right of Brad Meltzer to be identified as the Author of the Work
has been asserted by him in accordance with the Copyright, Designs
and Patents Act 1988.

A Hodder paperback

1

All rights reserved. No part of this publication may be reproduced,
stored in a retrieval system, or transmitted, in any form or by any
means without the prior written permission of the publisher, nor
be otherwise circulated in any form of binding or cover other
than that in which it is published and without a similar
condition being imposed on the subsequent purchaser.

All characters in this publication are fictitious and any resemblance
to real persons, living or dead, is purely coincidental.

A CIP catalogue record for this title is available from the British Library

ISBN 978 0 340 82506 8

Typeset in Plantin Light by Palimpsest Book Production Limited,
Grangemouth, Stirlingshire

Printed and bound by Mackays of Chatham Ltd, Chatham, Kent

Hodder Headline's policy is to use papers that are natural, renewable
and recyclable products and made from wood grown in sustainable
forests. The logging and manufacturing processes are expected to
conform to the environmental regulations of the country of origin.

Hodder & Stoughton Ltd
A division of Hodder Headline
338 Euston Road
London NW1 3BH

For Lila,
my girl,
who took my heart,
and with her sweet smile,
doubled its size

ACKNOWLEDGEMENTS

It's been almost ten years since *The Tenth Justice* was published. I am thankful to everyone – especially you, our amazing readers – who offers the support that allows me to continue talking to my imaginary friends: First, always, my First Lady, Cori, for believing even before page one, and for somehow still loving me. Her brainpower, opinions, and editing are the true seeds in each book's bloom. Every day, I'm humbled by her. Every day, I wonder how I was so lucky to find her. Jonas and Lila, I find words for a living, yet there aren't words enough to define my love for you. You are my life's sweetest blessings and greatest joys. Jill Kneerim, wonderful agent, beautiful friend, whose guidance and insight have been there from the first photocopies; Elaine Rogers, forever the first; Ike Williams, Hope Denekamp, Cara Shiel, and all our friends at the Kneerim & Williams Agency.

For this book especially, I want to thank my parents: my father, whose experience became the launching pad for Wes, and my mother, for showing me the unquestioning support that went with it; my sister, Bari, whose strength I always draw upon; Dale Flam, for steering the rest of the ship into so many amazing new places; Bobby, Matt, Ami, Adam, and Will, for their vital input and unwavering love; Noah Kuttler, who, after my wife, is the person I lean on most. His constant input and vital feedback are two of the key reasons this book is in your hands. I love him like family. Thank you, Calculator. Ethan Kline is just as valuable to this craft, and his insights into early drafts always shape the outcome; Steve 'Scoop' Cohen, for giving me Dreidel and so much more; Edna Farley, Kim from L.A., and Dina Friedman, who do so much of the heavy lifting; Paul Brennan, Matt Oshinsky, Paulo Pacheco, Joel Rose, Chris Weiss, and Judd Winick, always my brothers, my Rogos, whose friendship inspires so much of my writing in ways they can never prove in a court of law.

Every novel is a lie that tries to sound like the truth. I owe the following people enormous thank-yous for giving me the truths that are weaved throughout this book. Without a doubt, I would've never been able to explore this world without the help of President George H. W. and Mrs Barbara Bush and President Bill Clinton. The Bushes didn't need to open their world to me. Yet their generosity gave me so many of the details that made this book (which is all fiction!) come to life. I only hope they know how much I respect them. That same level of respect and thanks also goes to President Clinton, whose support I have treasured since my first novel. I don't care what side of the aisle you're on. Years later, it's still clear why we elected both of them. Staying with that theme, Jean Becker answered every one of my silly questions, but it's her friendship I cherish; Doug Band, Kris Engskov, Tom Frechette, and Andrew Friendly answered the rest of my inane queries, and in the process displayed why they were chosen to stand beside the most powerful men in the world; Thom Smith informed me on all things Palm Beach; Mary Louise Knowlton, Nancy Lisenby, Laura Cather Pears, Linda Casey Poepsel, and Michele Whalen are the best A-listers (and nicest people) in any presidency; Paul Bedard, Jessica Coen, Chuck Conconi, Joan Fleischman, Paula Froelich, Ann Gerhart, Ed Henry, Perez Hilton, Lorrie Lynch, John McCaslin, Roxanne Roberts, Liz Smith, Linton Weeks, and Ben Widdicombe taught me everything I know about gossip and are therefore all a part of Lisbeth's character. They are the best at what they do, and their kindness and class cannot be overstated. Mike Calinoff made me the second Jew in NASCAR and offered a wonderful friendship in the process; my friends Matthew Bogdanos, Eljay Bowron, Jo Ayn 'Joey' Glanzer, Dave Leavy, Erik Oleson, Peter Oleson, Ken Robinson, Farris Rookstool, Adam Rosman, Alex Sinclair, and John Spinelli helped on all the law enforcement details – I hope they know how much I respect the work they do; Barry Kowitt brought Rogo's profession to life (www.ungerandkowitt.com); Mary Weiss gave me the 65 Roses Ball (www.cff.org); Dana Milbank helped with White House press; Shelly Jacobs answered more presidential library questions than she ever anticipated; Rags Morales, as always, drew his heart out; Dr. Lee Benjamin, Dr. Thomas Scalea, and Dr. Ronald K. Wright for their medical advice; Richard Ben Cramer's *What It Takes*, Max Skidmore's *After the White House*, and the works of Samantha Power were invaluable tools; Greg Apparcel, Steve Chaconas, Ron Edmonds, Sara Fritz, Mark Futch, Al Guthrie, Tim Krische, Jim Ponce, Walter Rodgers, Will Shortz, Laura Spencer, and Tiffini Theisen filled in all the rest of the details; my mentor and fellow schemer – and the true reason I am here – Rob Weisbach, for being the first with faith all those years ago; and the rest of my family and friends, whose names once again inhabit these pages. I also want to thank Eli Segal, who gave me my very first shot. And my second shot. When I was a twenty-two-year-old kid, Eli treated me as an equal. It meant everything. I wouldn't be writing today without you, Eli.

Finally, I owe a huge thank-you to everyone at Warner Books: David Young, Larry Kirshbaum, Maureen Egen, Emi Battaglia, Tina Andreadis, Chris Barba, Martha Otis, Jen Romanello, Karen Torres, Becka Oliver, Evan Boorstyn, the nicest and hardest-working sales force in show business, and all the truly nice people who, through all these years, have become part of our family. Let me just say it as honestly as I can: They do the real work, and we'd be lost without them. I also want to stand on my desk and yell 'O Captain! My Captain!' to my editor, Jamie Raab. I think the hardest part of being an editor is understanding your authors. Jamie has always understood me, watched out for me, taken care of me. No author is more blessed. So thank you, Jamie, for your encouragement, and most important, for your faith.

Whatever limits us, we call Fate.
Ralph Waldo Emerson

God does not roll dice.
Albert Einstein

1

Six minutes from now, one of us would be dead. That was our fate. None of us knew it was coming.

'*Ron, hold up!*' I called out, chasing after the middle-aged man in the navy-blue suit. As I ran, the smothering Florida heat glued my shirt to my chest.

Ignoring me, Ron Boyle darted up the tarmac, passing Air Force One on our right and the eighteen cars of the motorcade that idled in a single-file line on our left. As deputy chief of staff, he was always in a rush. That's what happens when you work for the most powerful man in the world. I don't say that lightly. Our boss was the Commander in Chief. The President of the United States. And when he wanted something, it was my job to get it. Right now President Leland 'The Lion' Manning wanted Boyle to stay calm. Some tasks were beyond even me.

Picking up speed as he weaved through the crowd of staffers and press making their way to their assigned cars, Boyle blew past a shiny black Chevy Suburban packed with Secret Service agents and the ambulance that carried extra pints of the President's blood. Earlier today, Boyle was supposed to have a fifteen-minute sit-down with the President on Air Force One. Because of my scheduling error, he was now down to a three-minute drive-by briefing sometime this afternoon. To say he was annoyed would be like calling the Great Depression *a bad day at the office*.

'Ron!' I said again, putting a hand on his shoulder and trying to apologize. 'Just wait. I wanted to—'

He spun around wildly, slapping my hand out of the way. Thin and pointy-nosed with a thick mustache designed to offset both, Boyle had graying hair, olive skin, and striking brown eyes with a splash of light blue in each iris. As he leaned forward, his cat's eyes glared down at me. 'Don't touch me again unless you're shaking my hand,' he threatened as a flick of spit hit me in the cheek.

Gritting my teeth, I wiped it away with the back of my hand. Sure, the scheduling hiccup was my fault, but that's still no reason t—

'Now, what the hell's so damn important, Wes, or is this another vital reminder that when we're eating with the President, we need to give you our lunch orders at least an hour in advance?' he added, loud enough so a few Secret Service agents turned.

Any other twenty-three-year-old would've taken a verbal swing. I kept my cool. That's the job of the President's aide . . . a.k.a. the body person . . . a.k.a. the buttboy. Get the President what he wants; keep the machine humming.

'Lemme make it up to you,' I said, mentally canceling my apology. If I wanted Boyle quiet – if we didn't want a scene for the press – I needed to up the ante. 'What if I . . . what if I squeezed you into the President's limo right now?'

Boyle's posture lifted slightly as he started buttoning his suit jacket. 'I thought you— No, that's good. Great. Excellent.' He even painted on a tiny smile. Crisis averted.

He thought all was forgiven. My memory's way longer than that. As Boyle triumphantly turned toward the limo, I jotted down another mental note. Cocky bastard. On the way home, he'd be riding in the back of the press van.

Politically, I wasn't just *good*. I was great. That's not ego; it's the truth. You don't apply for this job, you're invited to interview. Every young political gunner in the White House would've killed to clutch this close to the leader of the free world. From here, my predecessor had gone on to become the number two guy in the White House Press Office. *His* predecessor in the last White House took a job managing four thousand people at IBM. Seven months ago, despite my lack of connections, the President picked me. I beat out a senator's son and a pair of Rhodes scholars. I could certainly handle a tantrum-throwing senior staffer.

'Wes, let's go!' the Secret Service detail leader called out, waving us into the car as he slid into the front passenger seat, where he could see everything coming.

Trailing Boyle and holding my leather shoulder bag out in front of me, I jumped into the back of the armored limo, where the President was dressed casually in a black windbreaker and jeans. I assumed Boyle would immediately start talking his ear off, but as he passed in front of the President, he was strangely silent. Hunched over as he headed for the back left seat, Boyle's suit jacket sagged open, but he quickly pressed his hand over his own heart to keep it shut. I didn't realize until later what he was hiding. Or what I'd just done by inviting him inside.

Following behind him, I crouched toward one of the three fold-down seats that face the rear of the car. Mine was back-to-back with the driver and across from Boyle. For security reasons, the President always sat in the back right seat, with the First Lady sitting between him and Boyle.

The jump seat directly across from the President – the hot seat – was already taken by Mike Calinoff, retired professional race car driver, four-time Winston Cup winner, and special guest for today's event. No surprise. With only four months until the election, we were barely three points ahead in the polls. When the crowd was that fickle, only a fool entered the gladiator's ring without a hidden weapon.

'So she's fast, even with the bulletproofing?' the racing champ asked, admiring the midnight-blue interior of Cadillac One.

'Greased lightning,' Manning answered as the First Lady rolled her eyes.

Finally joining in, Boyle scootched forward in his seat and flipped open a manila folder. 'Mr President, if we could—?'

'Sorry – that's all I can do, sir,' Chief of Staff Warren Albright interrupted as he hopped inside. Handing a folded-up newspaper to the President, he took the middle seat directly across from the First Lady, and more important, diagonally across from Manning. Even in a six-person backseat, proximity mattered. Especially to Boyle, who was still turned toward the President, refusing to give up his opening.

The President seized the newspaper and scrutinized the crossword puzzle he and Albright shared every day. It had been their tradition since the first days of the campaign – and the reason why Albright was always in that coveted seat diagonally across from the President. Albright started each puzzle, got as far as he could, then passed it to the President to cross the finish line.

'Fifteen down's wrong,' the President pointed out as I rested my bag on my lap. '*Stifle.*'

Albright usually hated when Manning found a mistake. Today, as he noticed Boyle in the corner seat, he had something brand-new to be annoyed by.

Everything okay? I asked with a glance.

Before Albright could answer, the driver rammed the gas, and my body jerked forward.

Three and a half minutes from now, the first gunshot would be fired. Two of us would crumble to the floor, convulsing. One wouldn't get up.

'Sir, if I could bend your ear for a second?' Boyle interrupted, more insistently than before.

'Ron, can't you just enjoy the ride?' the First Lady teased, her short brown hair bobbing as we hit a divot in the road. Despite the sweet tone, I saw the glare in her leaf-green eyes. It was the same glare she used to give her students at Princeton. A former professor with a PhD in chemistry, Dr. First Lady was trained to be tough. And what Dr. First Lady wanted, Dr. First Lady fought for. And got.

'But, ma'am, it'll just take—'

Her brow furrowed so hard, her eyebrows kissed. 'Ron. *Enjoy the ride.*'

That's where most people would've stopped. Boyle pushed even harder, trying to hand the file directly to Manning. He'd known the President since they were in their twenties, studying at Oxford. A professional banker, as well as a collector of antique magic tricks, he later managed all of the Mannings' money, a magic trick in itself. To this day, he was the only person on staff who was there when Manning married the First Lady. That alone gave him a free pass when the press discovered that Boyle's father was a petty con man who'd been convicted (twice) for insurance fraud. It was the same free pass he was using in the limo to test the First Lady's authority. But even the best free passes eventually expire.

Manning shook his head so subtly, only a trained eye could see it. First Lady, one; Boyle, nothing.

Closing the file folder, Boyle sank back and shot me the kind of look that would leave a bruise. Now it was my fault.

As we neared our destination, Manning stared silently through the light green tint of his bulletproof window. 'Y'ever hear what Kennedy said three hours before he was shot?' he asked, putting on his best Massachusetts accent. '*You know, last night would've been a hell of a night to kill a President.*'

'*Lee!*' the First Lady scolded. 'See what I deal with?' she added, fake laughing at Calinoff.

The President took her hand and squeezed it, glancing my way. 'Wes, did you bring the present I got for Mr Calinoff?' he asked.

I dug through my leather briefcase – the bag of tricks – never taking my eyes off Manning's face. He tossed a slight nod and scratched at his own wrist. *Don't give him the tie clip . . . go for the big stuff.*

I'd been his aide for over seven months. If I was doing my job right, we didn't have to talk to communicate. We were in a groove. I couldn't help but smile.

That was my last big, broad grin. In three minutes, the gunman's third bullet would rip through my cheek, destroying so many nerves, I'd never have full use of my mouth again.

That's the one, the President nodded at me.

From my overpacked bag, which held everything a President would ever need, I pulled out a set of official presidential cuff links, which I handed to Mr Calinoff, who was loving every split second in his folded-down, completely uncomfortable hot seat.

'Those are real, y'know,' the President told him. 'Don't put 'em on eBay.'

It was the same joke he used every time he gave a set away. We all still laughed. Even Boyle, who started scratching at his chest. There's no better place to be than in on an inside joke with the President of the United States. And on July 4th in Daytona, Florida, when you'd flown in to yell, '*Gentlemen, start your engines!*' at the legendary Pepsi 400 NASCAR race, there was no better backseat in the world.

Before Calinoff could offer a thank-you, the limo came to a stop. A red lightning bolt flashed by us on the left – two police motorcycles with their sirens blaring. They were leapfrogging from the back of the motorcade to the front. Just like a funeral procession.

'Don't tell me they closed down the road,' the First Lady said. She hated it when they shut traffic for the motorcade. Those were the votes we'd never get back.

The car slowly chugged a few feet forward. 'Sir, we're about to enter the track,' the detail leader announced from the passenger seat. Outside, the concrete openness of the airport runway quickly gave way to rows and rows of high-end motor coaches.

'Wait . . . we're going out on the track?' Calinoff asked, suddenly excited. He shifted in his seat, trying to get a look outside.

The President grinned. 'Did you think we'd just get a couple seats in front?'

The wheels bounced over a clanging metal plate that sounded like a loose manhole cover. Boyle scratched even more at his chest. A baritone rumble filled the air.

'That thunder?' Boyle asked, glancing up at the clear blue sky.

'No, not thunder,' the President replied, putting his own fingertips against the bulletproof window as the stadium crowd of 200,000 surged to its feet with banners, flags, and arms waving. 'Applause.'

'*Ladies and gentlemen, the President of the United States!*' the announcer bellowed through the P.A. system.

A sharp right-hand turn tugged us all sideways as the limo turned onto the racetrack, the biggest, most perfectly paved highway I'd ever seen in my life.

'Nice roads you got here,' the President said to Calinoff, leaning back in the plush leather seat that was tailor-made to his body.

All that was left was the big entrance. If we didn't nail that, the 200,000 ticket holders in the stadium, plus the ten million viewers watching from home, plus the seventy-five million fans who're committed to NASCAR, would all go tell their friends and neighbors and cousins and strangers in the supermarket that we went up for our baptism and sneezed in the holy water.

But that's why we brought the motorcade. We didn't *need* eighteen cars. The runway in the Daytona Airport was actually adjacent to the racetrack. There were no red lights to run. No traffic to hold back. But to everyone watching . . . Have you ever seen the President's motorcade on a racetrack? Instant American frenzy.

I didn't care how close we were in the polls. One lap around and we'd be picking out our seats for the inauguration.

Across from me, Boyle wasn't nearly as thrilled. With his arms crossed against his chest, he never stopped studying the President.

'Got the stars out too, eh?' Calinoff asked as we entered the final turn and he saw our welcoming committee, a small mob of NASCAR drivers all decked out in their multicolor, advertising-emblazoned jumpsuits. What his untrained eye didn't notice were the dozen or so 'crew members' who were standing a bit more erect than the rest. Some had backpacks. Some carried leather satchels. All had sunglasses. And one was speaking into his own wrist. Secret Service.

Like any other first-timer in the limo, Calinoff was practically licking the glass. 'Mr Calinoff, you'll be getting out first,' I told him as we pulled into the pit stalls. Outside, the drivers were already angling for presidential position. In sixty seconds, they'd be running for their lives.

Calinoff leaned toward my door on the driver's side, where all the NASCAR drivers were huddled.

I leaned forward to block him, motioning to the President's door on the other side. '*That* way,' I said. The door right next to him.

'But the drivers are over *there*,' Calinoff objected.

'Listen to the boy,' the President chimed in, gesturing toward the door by Calinoff.

Years ago, when President Clinton came for a NASCAR race, members of the crowd booed. In 2004, when President Bush arrived with legendary driver Bill Elliott in his motorcade, Elliott stepped out first and the crowd erupted. Even Presidents can use an opening act.

With a click and a thunk, the detail leader pushed a small security button under the door handle which allowed him to open the armor-lined door from the outside. Within seconds, the door cracked open, twin switchblades of light and Florida heat sliced through the car, and Calinoff lowered one of his handmade cowboy boots onto the pavement.

'And please welcome four-time Winston Cup winner . . .

Mike Caaaalinoff!' the announcer shouted through the stadium.

Cue crowd going wild.

'Never forget,' the President whispered to his guest as Calinoff stepped outside to the 200,000 screaming fans. '*That's* who we're here to see.'

'And now,' the announcer continued, 'our grand marshal for today's race – Florida's own . . . President Leeeee Maaaaanning!'

Just behind Calinoff, the President hopped out of the car, his right hand up in a wave, his left hand proudly patting the NASCAR logo on the chest of his windbreaker. He paused for a moment to wait for the First Lady. As always, you could read the lips on every fan in the grandstands. *There he is . . . There he is . . . There they are . . .* Then, as soon as the crowd had digested it, the flashbulbs hit. *Mr President, over here! Mr President . . . !* He'd barely moved three steps by the time Albright was behind him, followed by Boyle.

I stepped out last. The sunlight forced me to squint, but I still craned my neck to look up, mesmerized by the 200,000 fans who were now on their feet, pointing and waving at us from the grandstands. Two years out of college, and this was my life. Even rock stars don't have it this good.

Putting his arm out for a handshake, Calinoff was quickly enveloped by the waiting crowd of drivers, who smothered him with hugs and backslaps. At the front of the crowd was the NASCAR CEO and his surprisingly tall wife, here to welcome the First Lady.

Approaching the drivers, the President grinned. He was next. In three seconds, he'd be surrounded – the one black windbreaker in a Technicolor sea of Pepsi, M&M's,

DeWalt, and Lone Star Steakhouse jumpsuits. As if he'd
won the World Series, the Super Bowl, and the—

Pop, pop, pop.

That's all I heard. Three tiny pops. A firecracker. Or a
car backfiring.

'Shots fired! Shots fired!' the detail leader yelled.

'*Get down! Get back!*'

I was still smiling as the first scream tore through the
air. The crowd of drivers scattered – running, dropping,
panicking in an instant blur of colors.

'*God gave power to the prophets . . .*' a man with black
buzzed hair and a deep voice shouted from the center of
the swirl. His tiny chocolate eyes seemed almost too close
together, while his bulbous nose and arched thin eyebrows
gave him a strange warmth that for some reason reminded
me of Danny Kaye. Kneeling down on one knee and
holding a gun with both hands, he was dressed as a driver
in a black and bright yellow racing jumpsuit.

Like a bumblebee, I thought.

'*. . . but also to the horrors . . .*'

I just kept staring at him, frozen. Sound disappeared.
Time slowed. And the world turned black-and-white, my
own personal newsreel. It was like the first day I met the
President. The handshake alone felt like an hour. Living
between seconds, someone called it. Time standing still.

Still locked on the bumblebee, I couldn't tell if he was
moving forward or if everyone around him was rushing
back.

'*Man down!*' the detail leader shouted.

I followed the sound and the hand motions to a man
in a navy suit, lying facedown on the ground. Oh, no.
Boyle. His forehead was pressed against the pavement,
his face screwed up in agony. He was holding his chest,

and I could see blood starting to puddle out from below him.

'*Man down!*' the detail leader shouted again.

My eyes slid sideways, searching for the President. I found him just as a half dozen jumpsuited agents rushed at the small crowd that was already around him. The frantic agents were moving so fast, the people closest to Manning were pinned against him.

'Move him! *Now!*' an agent yelled.

Pressed backward against the President, the wife of the NASCAR CEO was screaming.

'You're crushing her!' Manning shouted, gripping her shoulder and trying to keep her on her feet. 'Let her *go!*'

The Service didn't care. Swarming around the President, they rammed the crowd from the front and right side. That's when momentum got the best of them. Like a just-cut tree, the crush of people tumbled to the side, toward the ground. The President was still fighting to get the CEO's wife out. A bright light exploded. I remember the flashbulb going off.

'. . . *so people could test their faith* . . .' the gunman roared as a separate group of agents in jumpsuits got a grip on his neck . . . his arm . . . the back of his hair. In slow motion, the bumblebee's head snapped back, then his body, as two more pops ripped the air.

I felt a bee sting in my right cheek.

'. . . *and examine good from evil!*' the man screamed, arms spread out like Jesus as agents dragged him to the ground. All around them, other agents formed a tight circle, brandishing semiautomatic Uzis they had torn from their leather satchels and backpacks.

I slapped my own face, trying to kill whatever just bit me. A few feet ahead, the crowd surrounding the President collided with the asphalt. Two agents on the far side grabbed the First Lady, pulling her away. The rest never stopped shoving, ramming, stepping over people as they tried to get to Manning and shield him.

I looked as the puddle below Boyle grew even larger. His head was now resting in a milky white liquid. He'd thrown up.

From the back of the President's pile, our detail leader and another suit-and-tie agent gripped Manning's elbows, lifted him from the pile, and shoved him sideways, straight at me. The President's face was in pain. I looked for blood on his suit but didn't see any.

Picking up speed, his agents were going for the limo. Two more agents were right behind them, gripping the First Lady under her armpits. I was the only thing in their way. I tried to sidestep but wasn't fast enough. At full speed, the detail leader's shoulder plowed into my own.

Falling backward, I crashed into the limo, my rear end hitting just above the right front tire. I still see it all in some out-of-body slow motion: me trying to keep my balance . . . slapping my hand against the car's hood . . . and the splat from my impact. Sound was so warped, I could hear the liquid squish. The world was still black-and-white. Everything except for my own red handprint.

Confused, I put my hand back to my cheek. It slid across my skin, which was slick and wet and raw with pain.

'Go, go, *go!*' someone screamed.

Tires spun. The car lurched. And the limo sped out from under me. Like a soda can forgotten on the roof, I tumbled backward, crashing on my ass. A crunch of rocks bit into my rear. But all I could really feel was the tick-tock tick-tock pumping in my cheek.

I looked down at my palm, seeing that my chest and right shoulder were soaked. Not by water. Thicker . . . and darker . . . dark red. *Oh, God, is that my—?*

Another flashbulb went off. It wasn't just the red of my blood I was seeing. Now there was blue . . . on my tie . . . and yellow . . . yellow stripes on the road. Another flashbulb exploded as knives of color stabbed my eyes. Silver and brown and bright green race cars. Red, white, and blue flags abandoned in the grandstands. A screaming blond boy in the third row with an aqua and orange Miami Dolphins T-shirt. And red . . . the dark, thick red all over my hand, my arm, my chest.

I again touched my cheek. My fingertips scraped against something sharp. Like metal – or . . . is that bone? My stomach nose-dived, swirling with nausea. I touched my face again with a slight push. That thing wouldn't budge . . . *What's wrong with my fa—?*

Two more flashbulbs blinded me with white, and the world flew at me in fast-forward. Time caught up in a fingersnap, blurring at lightspeed.

'I'm not feeling a pulse!' a deep voice yelled in the distance. Directly ahead, two suit-and-tie Secret Service agents lifted Boyle onto a stretcher and into the ambulance from the motorcade. His right hand dangled downward, bleeding from his palm. I replayed the moments before the limo ride. He would've never been in there if I hadn't—

'He's cuffed! Get the hell off!' A few feet to the left, more agents screamed at the dogpile, peeling layers away to get at the gunman. I was on the ground with the rest of the grease stains, struggling to stand up, wondering why everything was so blurry.

Help . . . ! I called out, though nothing left my lips.

The grandstands tilted like a kaleidoscope. I fell backward, crashing into the pavement, lying there, my palm still pressed against the slippery metal in my cheek.

'*Is anyone——?*'

Sirens sounded, but they weren't getting louder. Softer. They quickly began to fade. Boyle's ambulance . . . *Leaving . . . They're leaving me . . .*

'*Please . . . why isn't . . . ?*'

One woman screamed in a perfect C minor. Her howl pierced through the crowd as I stared up at the clear Florida sky. *Fireworks . . . we were supposed to have fireworks. Albright's gonna be pissed . . .*

The sirens withered to a faint whistle. I tried to lift my head, but it didn't move. A final flashbulb hit, and the world went completely white.

'*Wh-Why isn't anyone helping me?*'

That day, because of me, Ron Boyle died.

Eight years later, he came back to life.

2

Eight years later,
Kuala Lumpur, Malaysia

Some scars never heal.

'Ladies and gentlemen, the *ex*-President of the United States, Leland Manning,' our host, the deputy prime minister of Malaysia announces. I cringe as I hear the words. Never call him *ex*. It's *former*. *Former* President.

The deputy prime minister repeats it again in Mandarin, Cantonese, and Malay. The only words I understand each time are: Leland Manning . . . Le*land* Manning . . . Leland *Manning*. From the way Manning tugs on his earlobe and pretends to glance backstage, it's clear that the only words he hears are *ex-President*.

'Here you go, sir,' I say, handing him a letter-sized leather box that holds the pages of his speech. I've got a 101 fever and just stepped off an eleven-hour flight to Kuala Lumpur during which I didn't sleep a minute. Thanks to the time difference, it feels like three in the morning. It doesn't slow Manning down. Presidents are built to run all night. Their aides, however, aren't. 'Good luck,' I add as I pull the burgundy curtain aside, and he bounds out from the right-hand side of the stage.

The crowd rises to a standing ovation, and Manning waves the speechbox in the air as if he's got the nuclear codes in there. We used to actually have them. A military aide would follow us everywhere, carrying the codes in a leather briefcase known as *the Football*.

These days, we don't have a mil aide . . . or the Football . . . or a motorcade . . . or a staff of thousands who will fly fax machines and armored limos around the world for us. These days, beyond a few Secret Service agents, I have the President, and the President has me.

Four months after the assassination attempt, President Manning lost his bid for reelection, and we all got tossed from the White House. The *leaving* was bad enough – they took everything from us . . . our jobs, our lives, our pride – but the *why* . . . the *why* is what haunts.

During the congressional investigations after the assassination attempt, Capitol Hill nitpickers were all too eager to point out every possible security flaw made on the racetrack trip, from the Secret Service agent in the local Orlando field office who had been stopped for a DUI two days before the President's visit . . . to the unexplainable holes that allowed the gunman to sneak through security . . . to the fact that the President's personal physician had accidentally ordered the wrong blood type for the ambulance on the day of the event. None of those mistakes mattered. But there was one that did.

After John Hinckley took a shot at President Reagan in 1981, Reagan's approval ratings shot up to 73 percent, the highest they reached during his eight years in office. After that day at the speedway, Manning's approval ratings kamikazed to a dismal 32 percent. The only thing to blame is the photo.

Pictures endure after every crisis. Even in the midst of the chaos, photographers manage to click their shutters and snap a shot. Some photos, like the one of Jackie Kennedy at the moment of JFK's shooting, show unapologetic terror.

Others, like the one of Reagan, caught mid-blink during his shooting, show just how little time anyone has to react. It's the one thing politicians can't spin. They can manipulate their policies, their votes . . . even their personal backgrounds – but photographs . . . photographs rarely lie.

So when we heard about the photo in question – a crisp digital print of President Manning in mid-yell . . . standing behind the NASCAR CEO's wife . . . his hand on her shoulder as he was tugged backward by the Service . . . and best of all, trying to help push her out of the crushing crowd – we thought we'd have Reagan numbers. America's Lion in mid-roar.

Then we *saw* the photo. So did America. And they didn't see Manning pushing the CEO's wife *forward*, out of the way. They saw the President pulling her *back*, in front of him . . . cowering down behind his own personal shield. We trotted out the CEO's wife, who tried to explain that it wasn't how it looked. Too late. Five hundred front pages later, the Cowardly Lion was born.

'Roar,' Manning whispers into the microphone with a wry smile as he grips the sides of the podium onstage.

When former President Eisenhower was lying on his deathbed, he looked at his son and one of his doctors and said, 'Pull me up.' They propped him up in bed. 'Two big men,' Ike groused. 'Higher.' They propped him even more. He knew what was coming. He died minutes later. All Presidents want to go out strong. Manning's no different.

He roars again, this time even softer. It took three years before he could make that joke. Today, it gets easy laughs and applause, which is why he opens every paid speech with it.

It's okay to make jokes now. The public even expects it – they can't get over it until you do. But as I learned during my first week on the job, just because the President is laughing doesn't mean he's laughing. Manning lost far more than the presidency that day at the speedway. He also lost one of his dearest friends. When the shots were fired, the President . . . myself . . . Albright and everyone else – we all went down. Boyle was the only one who never got back up.

I still see the milky pink puddle seeping out below him as he lay there facedown, his face pressed against the pavement. I hear the doors of his ambulance slam shut like a bank vault . . . the sirens fading into a muffled black hole . . . and the gasping, stuttering sobs of Boyle's daughter, struggling to get through the eulogy at her father's funeral. That was the one that cut deepest, and not just because her voice was shaking so much she could barely get the words out. His daughter, barely entering high school, had the same intonation as her dad. Boyle's whistling *s*'s and short Florida *o*'s. When I closed my eyes, it sounded like Boyle's ghost speaking at his own memorial. Even the critics who once used his father's arrests to call him a *moral black eye on the administration* kept their mouths shut. Besides, the damage had already been done.

The funeral was televised, of course, which for once I appreciated, since the surgeries and the damage in my face meant I was watching it all from my hospital room. In a warped way, it was even worse than actually being there, especially as the President stood up to deliver the final eulogy.

Manning always memorized the opening lines of his speeches – better to look the audience in the eye. But that day at the funeral . . . That was different.

No one else even saw it. At the podium, the President

had his chest out and his shoulders back in a conscious display of strength. He looked out at the reporters who lined the back walls of the crowded church. At the mourners. At his staff. And at Boyle's wife and now-bawling young daughter.

'C'mon, boss,' I whispered from my hospital room.

The Cowardly Lion pictures were already published. We all knew it was the death of his presidency, but at that moment, it was just about the death of his friend.

Hold it together, I begged in my own silent prayer.

Manning pursed his lips. His velvet-gray eyes narrowed. I knew he'd memorized the opening line. He memorized every opening line.

You can do it . . . I added.

And that's when President Manning looked down. And read the first line of his speech.

There was no gasp from the audience. Not a single story was written about it. But I knew. And so did the staff, who I could see huddling imperceptibly closer whenever the cameras cut away to the crowd.

That same day, to add another knife in our necks, the man who killed Boyle – Nicholas 'Nico' Hadrian – announced that although he had taken multiple shots at the President, he never intended to hit him, and that it was just a warning for what he called 'the secret Masonic cult intent on seizing control of the White House in the name of Lucifer and his hordes in Hell.' Needless to say, one insanity plea later, Nico was institutionalized at St. Elizabeths Hospital in Washington, D.C., where he remains to this day.

In the end, Boyle's death was the worst crisis we'd ever faced . . . a moment where something was finally bigger than the White House. The communal tragedy pulled everyone closer. And I watched it alone in a hospital room, through the one eye I could see out of.

'He's quite funny,' says the Malaysian deputy prime minister, a man in his fifties with a slight acne problem. He sounds almost surprised as he joins me and Mitchel, one of our Secret Service agents, backstage. He eyes Mitchel, then cuts in front of me, turning back to study the profile of the President at the podium. After all this time as an aide, I don't take it personally.

'You've worked with him long?' the deputy prime minister asks, still blocking my view.

'Almost nine years,' I whisper. It sounds like a long time to be just an assistant, but people don't understand. After what happened . . . after what I did . . . and what I *caused* . . . I don't care what my counselors said. If it weren't for me, Boyle would've never been in the limo that day. And if he hadn't been there . . . I clamp my eyes shut and refocus by visualizing the oval lake at my old summer camp. Just like my therapist taught me. It helps for a second, but as I learned in the hospital, it doesn't change the truth.

Eight years ago, when Boyle was yelling in my face, I *knew* the President would never be able to meet with him during a four-minute limo ride. But instead of taking the verbal lashing and simply rescheduling him, I avoided the whole headache and threw him the one bone I knew he'd go running for. I was so damn smug about it too. Dangling the President in front of him just to make my job easier. That decision took Boyle's life. And destroyed my own.

The only good news, as always, came from Manning. When most aides leave the job, they have half a dozen job offers. I had none. Until Manning was kind enough to invite me back on board. Like I said, people don't understand. Even out of the White House, this is still a once-in-a-lifetime opportunity.

'By the way, Wes,' Mitchel interrupts, 'you ever find out if they got the honey for the President's tea? You know he needs it for his throat.'

'Already on it,' I reply, wiping my forehead with the palm of my hand. Between the heat from the lights and my fever, I'm ready to pass out. Doesn't matter. The President needs me. 'It should be waiting in the car when we're done.' Double-checking, I pull my satellite phone from my pocket and dial the number for our Secret Service driver outside. 'Stevie, it's Wes,' I say as he picks up. 'That honey get there yet?'

There's a short pause on the other line. 'You're kidding, right?'

'Is it there or not?' I say, deadly serious.

'Yes, Wes – the all-important honey has arrived. I'm guarding it right now – I hear there's a gang of bumble-bees in the neighborhood.' He pauses, hoping I'll join him in the joke.

I stay silent.

'Anything else, Wes?' he asks dryly.

'No . . . that's all for now.'

I can practically hear his eyes rolling as I hang up the phone. I'm not an imbecile. I know what they say about me. But they're not the ones who still see the puddle of blood under Boyle every time I hear an ambulance pass. Manning lost the presidency and his best friend. I lost something far more personal. It's no different than a trapeze artist who takes a bad fall during a triple back-flip. Even when the bones are healed and everything's back in place . . . even when they put you back in the big top . . . you can swing as hard as you want, but it takes time before you'll ever fly as high again.

'. . . though I still make 'em call me *Mr President*,' Manning jokes from onstage.

A swell of laughter gushes up from the audience, which is comprised of seven hundred of the top employees of the Tengkolok Insurance Corporation, the forty-third largest company in Malaysia. The good news is, they're paying $400,000 and private jet travel for the fifty-seven-minute speech . . . plus a short Q&A, of course. As a *Newsweek* reporter once told me, the post-presidency is like a prime-time hit in syndication: less visible, but far more profitable.

'They like him,' the deputy prime minister tells me.

'He's had some practice in front of crowds,' I reply.

He keeps his eyes locked on the President's silhouetted profile, refusing to acknowledge the joke. From this angle, the way Manning jabs a determined finger out toward the audience, he looks like he's back in fighting shape. The spotlight gives him an angelic glow . . . thinning out his extra fifteen pounds and softening every feature, from his sharp chin to his leathered skin. If I didn't know better, I'd think I was back in the White House, watching him through the tiny peephole in the side door of the Oval. Just like he watched over me in my hospital room.

I was there almost six months. For the first few, someone from the White House called every day. But when we lost the election, the staff disappeared, as did the phone calls. By then, Manning had every reason to do the same and forget about me. He knew what I'd done. He knew why Boyle was in the limo. Instead, he invited me back. As he taught me that day, loyalty mattered. It still does. Even after the White House. Even in Malaysia. Even at an insurance conference.

A yawn leaps upward in my throat. I grit my teeth and fight, trying to swallow it whole.

'Is boring for you?' the deputy prime minister asks, clearly annoyed.

'N-No . . . not at all,' I apologize, knowing the first rule of diplomacy. 'It's just . . . the time zone . . . we just flew in, so still adjusting . . .' Before I can finish, he turns my way.

'You should—'

Seeing my face, he cuts himself off. Not for long. Just enough to stare.

Instinctively, I try to smile. Some things you can't unlearn. The left half of my lip goes up, the right half stays flat, dead on my face.

Boyle went down that day at the racetrack. But he wasn't the only one hit.

'—should take melatonin,' the deputy prime minister stammers, still staring at the faded slash marks on my cheek. The scars crisscross like interconnecting railroad tracks. When it first happened, they were dark purple. Now they're a shade redder than my pale chalky skin. You still can't miss them. 'Melatonin,' he repeats, now locking on my eyes. He feels stupid for gawking. But he can't help himself. He peeks again, then takes a second to glance down at my mouth, which sags slightly on my right side. Most people think I had a mini-stroke. Then they see the scars. 'Very best for jet lag,' he adds, again locking eyes.

The bullet that tore through my cheek was a Devastator – specially designed to fracture on impact and tumble into the skin instead of going straight through it. And that's exactly what happened when it ricocheted off the armored hood of the limo, shattering into pieces and plowing into my face. If it had been a direct hit, it might've been cleaner, the doctors agreed, but instead, it was like a dozen tiny missiles burrowing into my cheek. To maximize the pain, Nico even stole a trick from Mideast suicide bombers, who dip their bullets and bombs in rat poison, since it acts as a blood thinner and keeps you bleeding as long as possible. It worked. By the time the Service got to me, I was so bloody, they covered me, thinking I was dead.

The wound played punching bag with my facial nerve, which I quickly found out has three branches: the first gives nerve function to your forehead . . . the second controls your cheeks . . . and the third, where I got hit, takes care of your mouth and lower lip. That's why my mouth sags . . . and why my lips purse slightly off-center when I talk . . . and why my smile is as flat as the smile of a dental patient on Novocain. On top of that, I can't sip through straws, whistle, kiss (not that I have any takers), or bite my top lip, which requires more manipulation than I ever thought. All that, I can live with.

It's the staring that tears me apart.

'Melatonin, huh?' I ask, turning my head so he loses his view. It doesn't help. A face is what we hold in our memories. It's our identity. It shows us who we are. Worst of all, two-thirds of face-to-face communication comes from facial expressions. Lose those – which I have – and in the researchers' words, it's socially devastating. 'I tried it years ago . . . maybe I'll give it another shot.'

'I think you like it,' the deputy prime minister says. 'Help you feel good.' He turns back to the lit silhouette of the President, but I already hear the shift in his voice. It's subtle but unmistakable. You don't need a translator to understand pity.

'I should . . . I'm gonna go check on that honey and tea,' I say, stepping back from the deputy prime minister. He doesn't bother turning around.

Making my way through the backstage darkness of the Performing Arts Center, I sidestep between a papier-mâché palm tree and an enormous jagged rock made of plastic and foam – both pieces from the *Lion King* set which sits further behind the curtain.

'. . . and countries look to the United States in ways that we still cannot underestimate . . .' Manning says as he finally segues into the more serious part of his speech.

'. . . even now, when we're hated in so many corners of the world,' I whisper to myself.

'. . . even now, when we're hated in so many corners of the world . . .' the President goes on.

The line tells me he's got forty-one minutes to go in the fifty-seven-minute speech, including the moment thirty seconds from now when he'll clear his throat and take a three-beat pause to show he's extra-serious. Plenty of time for a quick break.

There's another Secret Service agent near the door at the back of the stage. Jay. He's got a pug nose, squatty build, and the most feminine hands I've ever seen.

Nodding hello, he reads the sheen of sweat on my face. 'You okay there?' Like everyone, he gives my scars a quick glance.

'Just tired. These Asia flights take it outta me.'

'We've all been up, Wes.'

Typical Service. No sympathy. 'Listen, Jay, I'm gonna go check on the President's honey, okay?'

Behind me, onstage, the President clears his throat. One . . . two . . . three . . .

The moment he starts speaking, I shove open the metal

soundproof door and head down a long, fluorescent-lit, cement-block hallway that runs back past the dressing rooms. Jay's job is to fight every perceived and unperceived threat. With forty minutes left to go, the only thing I need to fight is my own exhaustion. Lucky me, I'm in the perfect place for a rumble.

On my right in the empty hallway, there's a room marked *Dressing Room 6*. I saw it when we came in. There's gotta be a couch, or at least a chair in there.

I grip the doorknob, but it doesn't turn. Same with dressing room 5 right across from it. *Crapola*. With so few agents, they must've locked them for security.

Zigzagging up the hallway, I bounce to dressing rooms 4 . . . 3 . . . 2. Locked, locked, and locked. The only thing left is the big number 1. The bad news is the sign taped to the door:

EMERGENCY USE ONLY

Emergency Use Only is our code for the President's private holding room. Most people think it's a place to relax. We use it to keep him away from the handshaking and photographing crowds, including the hosts, who're always worst of all. *Please, just one more picture, Mr President*. Plus the room's got a phone, fax, fruit, snacks, half a dozen bouquets of flowers (which we never ask for but they still send), seltzer water, Bailao tea, and . . . as they showed us during the walk-through . . . a connecting anteroom with a sofa and two ultra-cushy pillows.

I look at the other dressing rooms, then back to the closed metal door that leads to the stage. Jay's on the other side. Even if I ask, there's no way he'll unlock the other dressing rooms. I turn back to the *Emergency* sign on dressing room 1. My head's burning; my body's drenched. No one'll ever notice (thank you, soundproofing). Plus I've got over a half hour until the President's speech is – No. No, no, no. Forget it. This's the President's private space. I don't care if he won't notice. Or hear. It's just . . . going into his room like that . . . It's not right.

But as I turn to leave, I catch a flutter of light under the door. It goes dark, then white. Like a passing shadow. The problem is, the room's supposed to be empty. So who the hell would—?

Going straight for the doorknob, I give it a sharp twist. If this is that autograph nut from the parking lot . . . With a click, the door pops open.

As it swings wide, I'm hit with the smell of freshly cut flowers. Then I hear the cackling clang of metal against glass. Chasing the sound, I turn toward the small glass-top coffee table on the left side of the room. An older bald man in a suit but no tie rubs his shin from where he banged it. He's in mid-hop, but he doesn't stop moving. He's rushing right at me.

'Sorry . . . wrong room,' he says with a slight hint of an accent I can't quite place. Not British, but somehow European. His head is down, and from the tilt of his shoulder, he's hoping to squeeze past me in the doorway. I step in front of him, cutting him off.

'Can I help y—?'

He slams into me at full speed, ramming my shoulder with his own. He's gotta be fifty years old. Stronger than he looks. Stumbling slightly back, I grab the doorjamb and try to stay in front of him. 'You nuts?' I ask.

'Sorry . . . this was . . . I-I'm in the wrong place,' he insists, keeping his head down and stepping back for another pass. The way he stutters and keeps shuffling in place, I start thinking he's got more problems than just being in the wrong room.

'This is a private room,' I tell him. 'Where'd you—?'

'The bathroom,' he insists. 'Looking for the bathroom.'

It's a quick excuse, but not a good one. He was in here way too long. 'Listen, I need to call the Secret Ser—'

Springing forward, he barrels at me without a word. I lean forward to brace myself. That's exactly what he's counting on.

I expect him to ram into me. Instead, he turns his foot sideways, pounds his heel down on the tips of my left toes, and grabs me by my wrist. I'm already falling forward. He tugs my wrist even harder, ducking down and letting momentum take care of the rest. Like a freshly spun top, I whip backward into the room, completely off balance. Behind me . . . the table . . .

The backs of my calves hit the metal edge, and gravity sends me plunging back toward the wide glass top. I paddle my arms forward to stop the fall. It doesn't help.

As my back hits the glass, I grit my teeth and brace for the worst. The glass crackles like the first few kernels of popcorn . . . then shatters like a thunderstorm of raining glass. The coffee table's smaller than a bathtub, and as I tumble in backward, my head hits the outer metal edge. A jolt of pain runs down my spine, but my eyes are still on the door. I crane my neck up for a better look. The stranger's already gone . . . and then . . . as I stare at the empty doorway . . . he sticks his head back in. Almost as if he's checking on me.

That's when our eyes lock. Contact.

Oh, God. My stomach sinks down to my kneecaps. Th-That's . . .

His face is different . . . his nose rounded . . . his cheeks more chiseled. I grew up in Miami. I know plastic surgery when I see it. But there's no mistaking those eyes – brown with a splash of light blue . . . He . . . he died eight years ago . . .

That was Boyle.

3

'Wait!'

He takes off in an eyeblink, darting to the left down the hallway – away from the doorway where Jay is. Boyl – whoever he is, he's smart.

I grab the edges of the coffee table and try to boost myself out. My hip and knees grind against the shards of glass as I twist into place. Stumbling to my feet, I rush forward, completely hunched over. I'm so off balance, I practically fall through the doorway, back into the hall, which is completely empty.

He barely had a five-second head start. It's more than enough.

Up ahead, the far end of the hallway bends around to the left. In the distance, a metal door slams shut. Damn. I run as fast as I can, gritting my teeth just to keep myself from hyperventilating. But I already know what's coming. Turning the corner, the hallway dead-ends at two more soundproof metal doors. The one on the right leads to an emergency set of stairs. The one straight ahead leads outside. If we were in the White House, we'd have two Secret Service guys standing guard. As a Former, we've barely got enough to cover the entrances that lead to the stage.

I shove open the door on my right. As it crashes into the wall, a low thud echoes up the concrete stairwell. I

hold my breath and listen for footsteps . . . movement . . .
anything. All I get is silence.

Spinning back, I slam into the metal bar of the remaining
door, which whips open and flings me out into the sweet,
steamy Malaysian air. The only light in the alley comes
from the headlights of a black Chevy Suburban, a metal
Cheshire cat with a glowing white stare. Behind the
Suburban is a gaudy, white twelfth-grade-prom stretch
limousine. Our ride back to the hotel.

'Everything okay?' an agent with cropped brown hair
calls out as he steps around to the front of the Suburban.

'Yeah . . . of course,' I say, swallowing hard and knowing
better than to put him in panic. Jumping down the last
three steps, my heart's racing so fast, I feel like it's about
to kick through my chest. I continue to scan the alleyway.
Nothing but empty dumpsters, a few police motorcycles,
and the mini-motorcade.

The stairs . . .

I spin back to the doorway, but it's already too late.
The door slams shut with a sonic boom, locking from the
inside.

'Relax,' the agent calls out. 'I got the key right here.'

He jogs up the stairs and flips through his key ring.
'Manning still on time?' he asks.

'Yeah . . . he's perfect . . . right on time . . .'

The agent studies me carefully, fishing through his keys.
'Sure you're okay, Wes?' he asks, pulling the door open as
I run back inside. 'You look like you've seen a ghost.'

4

He's long gone.

A half hour later, after the final question in the President's Q&A ('*Do you miss the White House?*'), I'm sitting in the back of the prom limo, trying to read the President's mood.

'The crowd was good,' Manning offers.

That means *they were flat.*

'I agree,' I tell him.

That means *I understand.* Foreign speeches are always tough – the audience misses half the jokes, and Manning feels sorry for himself because the whole country no longer stops at his arrival.

In the front of the car, two of our Secret Service guys are dead silent, not even whispering into their radios. That means they're nervous. Back at the Arts Center, I reported the fact that I saw someone by the dressing rooms. When they asked for a description, I gave them everything I saw, though I left out his eye color and the fact it looked like Boyle. *Uh, yeah, it was our dead deputy chief of staff we buried eight years ago.* There's a fine line between being careful and looking like a whackjob.

As our car lurches to a stop in front of the Palace of the Golden Horses – Asia's most luxurious and overdecorated horse-themed hotel – three different valets open the limo's door. 'Welcome back, Mr President.'

Well accustomed to dealing with VIPs, the Palace has eighteen elevators and seventeen different staircases to sneak inside. Last time we were here, we used at least half of them. Today, I asked the Service to take us straight through the front door.

'*There he is . . . There he is . . .* ' simultaneous voices call out as we hit the lobby. A pack of American tourists are already pointing, searching for pens in their fanny packs. We've been spotted, which was the goal. Secret Service looks to me. I look to Manning. It's his call, though I already know the answer.

The President nods slightly, pretending he's doing a favor. But no matter how fast he buries it, I see the grin underneath. Anytime former Presidents travel abroad, the CIA arranges a quick briefing, which once again lets the Former feel like he's back in the thick of it. That's why all Formers love foreign trips. But when you're in a far-off land missing the adrenaline of attention, there's no better sugar rush than a quick fix of adoring fans.

Like the Red Sea before Moses, the agents step aside, leaving a clear path across the marble floor to the President. I pull a dozen glossy photos and a Sharpie marker from the bag of tricks and hand them to Manning. He needed this one. Welcome home, boss.

'Can you make it out to *Bobby-boy*? Just like that – *Bobby-boy*?' a man with oversize glasses asks.

'So where're you from?' Manning says, doing what he does best.

If I wanted to, I could stay at the President's side and help the Service keep the line orderly. Instead, I step back, slip away from the crowd, and head for the front desk, just beneath the enormous golden dome with its hand-painted running horses.

It's been gnawing at me since the moment Boyle disappeared down that corridor. I'm not sure how he got backstage, but if he's trying to get near the President, there's only one other place to make the attempt.

'How can I help you today, sir?' a beautiful Asian woman asks in flawless English. To her credit, she glances at my scars but doesn't linger.

'I'm with President Manning,' I tell her, hoping to grease the wheels.

'Of course, you are, Mr Holloway.'

I know we leave a hell of a calling card, but I'm still impressed.

'How can we help you?' she asks.

'Actually, I'm trying to track down one of the President's friends. He's supposed to be meeting us tonight, and I just wanted to see if he checked in yet . . . last name *Boyle*.'

Clicking at her keyboard, she doesn't even pause at his name. Fancy Malaysian hotels are good, but they're not that good.

'I'm sorry, sir, but we have no one under name *Boyle*.'

I'm not surprised. 'How about *Eric Weiss*?' I ask. It was Boyle's fake name from our White House days when he didn't want reporters tracking us in hotels.

'Eric Weiss?' she repeats.

I nod. It's Houdini's real name – a dumb joke by Boyle, who collected old magician posters. But coming back from the dead? Even Eric Weiss couldn't pull off that trick.

'Sorry, no Eric Weiss,' she says.

I glance over at the President. He's still got at least three more tourist autographs to get through.

'Actually, can you try one more: last name *Stewart*, first name *Carl*.'

'Carl Stewart,' she repeats, tapping at her keyboard. It's a long shot, no doubt – the first and middle names of the President's father, and the hotel codename we used to use for the President when I first started in the White House . . . right before Boyle was—

'Carl Stewart,' the front desk clerk says proudly. 'I have him right here.'

I feel the blood seep from my face. That codename was assigned to the President during our old trips as a way to hide what room he was in. No one knew that codename. Not even the First Lady. 'You do?'

She squints at the screen. 'But according to this, he checked out about an hour ago. I apologize, sir – looks like you just missed him.'

'D'you have his address? Did he pay by credit card?' My questions tumble out before I can even catch myself. 'I mean . . . we . . . were hoping to pay his bill for him,' I add, finally slowing down. 'Y'know . . . the . . . President's treat.'

She stares straight at me. Now she thinks I'm nuts. Still, she checks her screen. 'I apologize again, sir. It appears he paid by cash.'

'What about his home address? I just want to make sure we have the right Carl Stewart.' I add a laugh to put her at ease. That's when I realize Malaysians don't enjoy being laughed at.

'Sir, our guests' personal information . . .'

'It's not for me, it's for *him*.' I point back at the former President of the United States and his three armed body-guards. It's a hell of a trump card.

The clerk forces an uneasy smile. She looks over her shoulder. There's no one around but us. Reading from the screen, she says, 'Mr Stewart lives at . . . 3965 Via Las Brisas – Palm Beach, Florida.'

My legs go numb. I grip the marble counter to keep from falling over. That's no codeword. That's President Manning's private home address. Only family has that. Or old friends.

'Sir, are you okay?' the desk clerk asks, reading my complexion.

'Yeah . . . just perfect,' I say, forcing some peppy into my voice. It doesn't make me feel any better. My head's spinning so fast, I can barely stand up. Boyle . . . or whoever he was . . . he wasn't just in that dressing room . . . he was *here* last night. Waiting for us. For all I know, he would've been waiting for the President if I hadn't seen him first.

I replay the moments backstage at the speech. The metal clang as he banged into the coffee table. The panicked look on his face. Up till now, I assumed that when I saw him, he was in the process of breaking in. But now . . . him being here last night . . . and using that decade-old codename . . . Boyle's no idiot. With all the fake names to choose from, you don't use that name to hide. You use it so someone can find you. I twist the kaleidoscope and a new picture clicks into place. Sure, Boyle could've been breaking in. But he could've just as easily been invited. The problem is, considering that the only people on this trip are me and three Secret Service agents who never even worked in the White House, there's only one person left who would've recognized that old codename. One person who could've known Boyle was coming – and invited him inside.

I glance back at the President just as he finishes his final autograph. There's a wide smile across his face.

A knot of pain tugs the back of my neck. My hands start shaking at my sides. Why would . . . how could he do that? Ten feet away, he puts his arm around an Asian woman and poses for a photo, grinning even wider. As the flash explodes, the knot in my neck tightens like a noose. I clamp my eyes, straining to find the lake from summer camp . . . grasping for my focal point. But all I see is Boyle. His shaved head. The fake accent to throw me off. Even the sobs of his daughter, who I apologize to every time I see her grieving during the anniversaries of the event.

For eight years, his death has been the one wound that would never mend, festering over time with my own isolation. The guilt . . . everything I caused . . . Oh, Lord, if he's actually back . . .

I open my eyes and realize they're filled with tears. Quickly wiping them away, I can't even look at Manning.

Whatever Boyle was doing there, I need to figure out what the hell is going on. In the White House, we had access to the entire military. We don't have the military anymore. But that doesn't mean I don't have my own personal reserves.

I pull out my satellite phone and dial the number from memory. The sun should just be coming up in Washington.

Accustomed to emergencies, he picks up on the first ring. Caller ID tells him who it is.

'Let me guess, you're in trouble,' Dreidel answers.

'This one's serious,' I tell him.

'It involve your boss?'

'Doesn't everything?' Dreidel's my closest friend from the White House, and more important, knows Manning better than anyone. By his silence, it's clear he understands. 'Now you got a second? I need some help.'

'For you, my friend, anything . . .'

5

Paris, France

'With mayonnaise?' the thin woman with the red bifocals asked in a heavy French accent.

'Oui,' Terrence O'Shea replied, nodding respectfully, but disappointed that she even asked. He thought his French was flawless – or as flawless as FBI training could make it – but the fact she asked the question in English and referred to the garlicky *aïoli* as 'mayonnaise' . . . 'Excusez-moi, madame,' O'Shea added, 'pourquoi m'avez vous demandé cela en anglais?' *Why did you ask me in English?*

The woman pursed her lips and smiled at his largely Swiss features. His thin blond hair, pink skin, and hazel eyes came from his mother's family in Denmark, but his fat, buckled nose was straight from his father's Scottish side – made only worse by a botched hostage rescue back from his days doing fieldwork. As the woman handed O'Shea the small container of french fries drenched with mayo, she explained, 'Je parle très mal le danois.' *My Danish is terrible.* Reading O'Shea's thin grin, she added, 'Vous venez de Danemark, n'est-ce pas?' *You are from Denmark, yes?*

'Oui,' O'Shea lied, taking a strange joy in the fact she didn't spot him as American. Then again, blending in was part of the job.

'J'ai l'oeiul pour les choses,' the woman added.

'J'ai l'oeiul pour les choses,' O'Shea repeated, dropping a few coins into the glass tip jar on the edge of the woman's sausage-and-french-fry pushcart. *Sometimes you just know.*

Heading further up Rue Vavin, O'Shea felt his cell phone vibrate in his pocket for the third time. He'd already convinced the pushcart woman that he wasn't American, and even though it didn't matter, he wasn't going to reveal himself by interrupting their conversation and picking up on the first ring.

'This is O'Shea,' he finally answered.

'What're you doing in France?' the voice on the other line asked.

'Interpol conference. Some nonsense on trends in intelligence. Four whole days away from the pit.'

'Plus all the mayo you can eat.'

Just as he was about to bite his first mayo-dipped fry, O'Shea paused. Without another word, he pitched the basket of fries into a nearby trash can and crossed the street. As a Legat – a Legal Attaché – for the FBI, O'Shea had spent almost a decade working with law enforcement officials in seven foreign countries to help deter crime and terrorism that could harm the United States. In his line of work, the surest way to get yourself killed was being obvious and predictable. Priding himself on being neither, he buttoned his long black coat, which waved out behind him like a magician's cape.

'Tell me what's going on,' O'Shea said.

'Guess who's back?'

'I have no idea.'

'Guess . . .'

'I don't know . . . that girl from Cairo?'

'Let me give you a hint: He was killed at the Daytona Speedway eight years ago.'

O'Shea stopped midstep in the middle of the street. Not in panic. Or surprise. He'd been at this too long to be fazed by bad intel. Better to confirm. 'Where'd you get it?'

'Good source.'

'How good?'

'Good enough.'

'That's not—'

'As good as we're gonna get, okay?'

O'Shea knew that tone. 'Where'd they spot him?'

'Malaysia. Kuala Lumpur.'

'We have an office there . . .'

'He's already gone.'

No surprise, O'Shea thought. Boyle was too smart to linger. 'Any idea why he's out?'

'You tell me: It was the same night President Manning was there for a speech.'

A red Fiat honked its horn, trying to blast O'Shea out of the way. Offering an apologetic wave, O'Shea continued toward the curb. 'You think Manning knew he was coming?'

'I don't even wanna think about it. Y'know how many lives he's risking?'

'I told you when we first tried to bring him in – the guy's poison. We should've never tried to flip him all those years ago.' Watching the rush of Paris traffic, O'Shea let the silence sink in. Across the street, he watched the thin woman with the red bifocals dole out another basket of fries with *aïoli*. 'Anyone else see him?' O'Shea finally asked.

'President's aide apparently got a look – y'know . . . that kid with the face . . .'

'He have any idea who he was looking at?'

'That's the question, isn't it?'

O'Shea stopped to think about it. 'What about the thing in India next week?'

'India can wait.'

'So you want me on a plane?'

'Say good-bye to Paris, sweetheart. Time to come home.'

6

St. Elizabeths Mental Hospital,
Washington, D.C.

'Make it quick, Nico – no futzing around,' said the tall orderly with the sweet onion breath. He didn't shove Nico inside or stay with him while he undid his pants. That was only for the first few months after Nico's assassination attempt on the President – back when they were worried he'd kill himself. These days, Nico had earned the right to go to the bathroom alone. Just like he'd earned the right to use the telephone and to have the hospital stop censoring his mail. Each was its own victory, but as The Three had promised him, every victory brought its own cost.

For the telephone, the doctors asked him if he still had anger toward President Manning. For the mail, they asked him if he was still fixated on the crosses – the crucifix around his nurse's neck, the one the overweight lady wore in the law firm commercial on TV, and most important, the hidden ones only he knew were there: the ones created by window-panes and telephone poles . . . in intersecting sidewalk cracks, and the T-shaped slats of park benches, and in perpendicular blades of grass, and – when they stopped letting him go outside because the images were too overwhelming – in crisscrossing shoelaces and phone cords and wires and discarded socks . . . in the seams of the shiny tile floor and the closed doors of the refrigerator . . . in horizontal shades

and their vertical pull cords, in banisters and their railings . . .
and of course, in the white spaces between the columns of
the newspaper, in the blank spaces between the push buttons
of the telephone, and even in cubes, especially when
is unfolded to its two-dimensional version

,

which then allowed him to include dice, luggage, short
egg cartons, and of course, the Rubik's Cube that sat on
the edge of Dr. Wilensky's desk, right beside his perfectly
square Lucite pencil cup. Nico knew the truth – symbols
were always signs.

No more drawing crosses, no more carving crosses, no
more doodling crosses on the rubber trim of his sneakers
when he thought no one was looking, his doctors had told
him. If he wanted full mail privileges, they needed to see
progress.

It still took him six years. But today, he had what he
wanted. Just like The Three promised. That was one of
the few truths besides God. The Three kept their promises . . . even back when they first welcomed him in. He
had nothing then. Not even his medals, which were lost
– *stolen!* – in the shelter. The Three couldn't bring them
back, but they brought him so much more. Showed him
the door. Showed him what no one else saw. Where God
was. And where the devil was hiding. And waiting. Almost
two hundred years, he'd been there, tucked away in the
one place the M Men hoped people would never look –
right in front of their own faces. But The Three looked.

They searched. And they found the devil's door. Just as the Book had said. That's when Nico played his part. Like a son serving his mother. Like a soldier serving country. Like an angel serving God's will.

In return, Nico just had to wait. The Three had told him so on the day he pulled the trigger. Redemption was coming. Just wait. It'd been eight years. Nothing compared to eternal salvation.

Alone in the restroom, Nico closed the toilet seat and kneeled down to say a prayer. His lips mouthed the words. His head bobbed up and down slightly . . . sixteen times . . . always sixteen. And then he closed his left eye on the word *Amen*. With a tight squeeze of his fingertips, he plucked an eyelash from his closed eye. Then he plucked another. Still down on his knees, he took the two lashes and placed them on the cold white slab of the closed toilet seat. The surface had to be white – otherwise, he wouldn't see it.

Rubbing the nail of his right pointer finger against the grout in the floor, he filed his nail to a fierce, fine point. As he leaned in close like a child studying an ant, he used the sharpened edge of his nail to push the two eyelashes into place. What the doctors took away, he could always put back. As The Three said, it's all within him. And then, as Nico did every morning, he slowly, tenderly gave a millimeter's push and proved it. There. One eyelash perfectly intersecting with the other. A tiny cross.

A thin grin took Nico's lips. And he began to pray.

7

Palm Beach, Florida

See that redheaded mummy in the Mercedes?' Rogo asks, motioning out the window at the shiny new car next to us. I glance over just in time to see the fifty-something redhead with the frozen face-lift and an equally stiff (and far more fashionable) straw hat that probably costs as much as my crappy little ten-year-old Toyota. 'She'd rather die than call,' he adds.

I don't respond. It doesn't slow him down. 'But that guy driving that midlife crisis?' he adds, pointing at the balding man in the cherry-red Porsche that pulls out around us. 'He'll call me right after he gets the ticket.'

It's Rogo's favorite game: driving around, trying to figure out who'll be a potential client. As Palm Beach's least-known but most aggressive speeding ticket lawyer, Rogo is the man to call for any moving violation. As my roommate and closest friend since eighth grade, when he and his mom moved from Alabama to Miami, he's also the only person I know who loves his job even more than the President does.

'Oooh, and that girl right there?' he asks as he motions across two lanes of traffic to the sixteen-year-old with braces driving a brand-new Jeep Cherokee. 'Pass the bread, 'cause that's my *butter*!' Rogo insists in a wet lick of a Southern accent. 'New car and braces? Choo, choo – here comes the *gravy train*!'

He slaps me on the shoulder like we're watching a rodeo.

'Yee-hah,' I whisper as the car climbs up the slight incline of Royal Park Bridge and across the Intracoastal Waterway. On both sides of us, the morning sun ricochets off glossy waves. The bridge connects the communities of working-class West Palm Beach with the millionaire haven known as Palm Beach. And as the car's tires rumble and we cross to the other side, the well-populated, fast-food-lined Okeechobee Boulevard gives way to the perfectly manicured, palm-tree-lined Royal Palm Way. It's like leaving a highway rest stop and entering Oz.

'Do you feel rich? 'Cause I feel *silver dollar*!' Rogo adds, soaking up the surroundings.

'Again, yee-hah.'

'Don't get all sarcastic,' Rogo warns. 'If you're not nice, I'm not gonna let you drive me to work for the next week while my car's in the shop.'

'You said it'd only be in the shop for a day.'

'Ah, the negotiation continues!' Before I can argue, he does a double take on the braces girl, who's now right next to us. 'Wait, I think she *was* a client!' he shouts, rolling down his window. 'Wendy!' he yells, leaning over and honking my horn.

'Don't do that,' I tell him, trying to push his hand away. When we were fourteen, Rogo was short. These days, at twenty-nine, he's added bald and fat to his repertoire. And strong. I can't move him.

'Braces Girl!' he shouts, honking again. 'Hey, Wendy, is that you!?'

She finally turns and rolls down her own window, struggling to keep her eyes on the road.

'Your name Wendy?' he yells.

'No,' she calls back. 'Maggie!'

Rogo seems almost hurt by his own misinformation. It never lasts long. He's got a smile like a butcher's dog. 'Well, if you get a speeding ticket, go to down-withtickets.com!'

Rolling up his window, he scratches at his elbow, then readjusts his crotch, proud of himself. It's vintage Rogo – by the time he's done, I can't even remember what the argument's about. It's the same way he bulldozed into the legal profession. After two bad sets of LSAT scores, Rogo flew to Israel for his third attempt. Not even close to being Jewish, he'd heard that in Israel, they took a more relaxed approach to the concept of a *timed* exam. 'What, an extra twenty minutes? Who's it gonna kill?' he asked for a full month, imitating his proctor in full Israeli accent. And with those twenty minutes, Rogo finally got a score that would get him into law school.

So as he found a home in speeding tickets and for the first time had some money in his pocket, the last thing he needed was a boring roommate who'd have trouble making the rent. Back then, my only job prospect was staying with the President, who'd moved to P.B. after the White House. P.B. being what the locals call Palm Beach, as in, 'We'll be in P.B. all winter.' I was living with my parents in Boca Raton; because of the low salary, I couldn't afford the tony neighborhood near the President's Palm Beach compound. With a roommate, though, I'd at least be able to live closer. It was right after the shooting. The scars were still purple on my face. Eighth grade goes a long way. Rogo didn't even hesitate.

'I still don't understand why you have to be in so early,' Rogo adds in mid-yawn. 'It's barely seven. You just got back from Malaysia last night.'

'The President's—'

'—an early riser . . . the world's greatest guy . . . can heal the sick while cooking a six-course meal. Jesus and Emeril all in one body. I know how the cult works, Wes.' He points out the window at a hidden cop car about two blocks up. 'Careful, speed trap.' Right back into it, he adds, 'I'm just saying he should let you sleep in.'

'I don't need to sleep in. I'm good. And FYI, it's not a cult.'

'First of all, it *is* a cult. Second, don't say *FYI*. My mother says *FYI*. So does yours.'

'That doesn't mean it's a cult,' I push back.

'Really? So it's healthy that almost eight years after you left the White House, you're still running errands like some overhyped intern? What happened to grad school, or that event coordinator job, or even that threat of being a chef you made a few years back? Do you even enjoy work anymore, or d'you just stay there because it's safe and they protect you?'

'We do more good for the community than you'd ever know.'

'Yeah, if you're chief of staff. You, on the other hand, spend half your day wondering whether he wants iceberg or romaine lettuce in his salad!'

I grip the steering wheel and stare straight ahead. He doesn't understand.

'Don't do that!' Rogo threatens. 'Don't save your confidence for Manning. I just attacked you – you're supposed to fight back!'

There's a curdle in his voice that he usually saves just for traffic cops. He's getting riled, which isn't saying much for Rogo. In high school, he was the kid who threw his cards when he lost at Monopoly . . . and threw his tennis racket when he missed a shot. Back then, that temper got him in way too many fights, which was only made worse by the fact that he didn't have the physical size to back it up. He says he's 5'7". He's 5'6" if he's lucky.

'You know I'm right, Wes. Something internally bad happens when you give your entire existence to a single person. You feel me?'

He may be the smartest dumbest friend I have, but for once, he's reading me all wrong. My silence isn't from acquiescence. It's from my mental picture of Boyle, still staring at me with those brown and blue eyes. Maybe if I tell Rogo—

My phone vibrates in my pocket. This early in the morning, it's only bad news. I flip open the phone and check caller ID. I'm wrong. Here comes the cavalry.

'Wes here,' I say as I answer.

'Got time to chat?' Dreidel asks on the other end.

I glance over at Rogo, who's back to hunting for potential clients. 'Let me call you right back.'

'Don't bother. How about meeting for breakfast?'

'You're in town?' I ask, confused.

'Just for a quick business meeting. I tried to tell you when you called from Malaysia. You were too busy panicking,' he points out in his usual perfect calm. 'So breakfast?'

'Gimme an hour. I got one thing to do at work.'

'Perfect. I'm at the Four Seasons. Call me from the lobby. Room 415.'

I shut the phone and for the first time enjoy the passing palm trees. Today's suddenly looking up.

8

Miami, Florida

O'Shea carried two passports. Both of them legal. Both
with the same name and address. One was blue, like any
other U.S. citizen's. The other was red . . . and far more
powerful. For diplomats only. Fingering the embossed letters
of the passports in his breast pocket, he could tell the red
was on top. With a flick of his wrist, he could easily pull it
out. And once the airport agents saw it, he'd no longer be
stuck in the customs line that swerved through the back
corridors of Miami International Airport. After the nine-
and-a-half-hour flight from Paris to Florida, he'd walk right
to the front. With a flick of his wrist, he'd be gone.

Of course, he'd also leave a trail of paperwork that
tracked red passports everywhere. And as his FBI training
taught him, all trails were eventually followed. Still, in most
cases, that trail would be manageable. But in this one –
between Boyle and The Three . . . and all they'd done –
nothing was worth the risk. Not with so much at stake.

'Next!' a Latino customs clerk called out, waving O'Shea
up to the small bulletproof booth.

O'Shea readjusted the U.S. Open baseball cap that he
wore to blend in. His sandy-blond hair still peeked out,
curling up under the edges. 'How's everything going?' he
asked, knowing the small talk would keep the clerk from
making eye contact.

'Fine,' the clerk responded, his head down.

Pulling out his blue passport, O'Shea handed it to the clerk.

For no reason, the clerk looked up. O'Shea had a smile waiting for him, just to keep things calm. As usual, the clerk immediately grinned back. 'Coming back from work?' he asked.

'Lucky me, no. Vacation.'

Nodding to himself, the clerk studied O'Shea's passport. Even tilted it slightly to inspect the new holograms that they recently added to crack down on forgeries.

O'Shea readjusted his U.S. Open cap. If he'd pulled the red passport, he wouldn't be waiting here.

'Have a great one,' the clerk said, stamping O'Shea's passport and handing it back. 'And welcome home.'

'Thanks,' O'Shea replied, tucking the passport back into his breast pocket. Right next to his FBI badge and ID.

Within a minute, O'Shea cut past the baggage carousels and headed for the signs marked *Nothing to Declare/Exit*. As his foot hit the sensor mat, two frosted-glass doors slid open, revealing a mob of family and friends pressed against short metal barriers, waiting for their loved ones despite the early hour. Two little girls jumped, then sagged, when they realized O'Shea wasn't their dad. He didn't notice. He was too busy dialing a number on his cell phone. It rang three times before his partner answered.

'Welcome, welcome,' Micah said, finally picking up. From the soft humming in the background, it sounded like he was in a car.

'Tell me you're in Palm Beach,' O'Shea replied.

'Got here last night. It's nice down here. Fancy. Y'know they got tiny water fountains on the sidewalks just for spoiled little dogs?'

'What about Wes?'

'Three cars in front of me,' Micah said as the humming continued. 'Him and his roommate just crossed the bridge a minute ago.'

'I assume he hasn't seen you yet?'

'You said to wait.'

'Exactly,' O'Shea replied, stepping outside the airport and spotting his name on a handwritten sign. The private driver nodded hello and tried to grab O'Shea's small black piece of luggage. O'Shea waved him off and headed for the car, never taking the phone from his ear.

'He's dropping the roommate off right now,' Micah added. 'Looks like Wes is headed into work.'

'Just stay with him,' O'Shea replied. 'I'll be there as quick as I can.'

9

Washington, D.C.

The phone shrieked through the small office, but he didn't pick it up. Same on the second ring. He knew who it was – on this line, there was only one person it could be – but he still didn't move. Not until he knew for sure. Leaning both elbows on his desk, Roland Egen studied his phone's digital screen, waiting for caller ID to kick in. Black electronic letters popped into place: *Offices of Leland Manning*.

'You're early,' The Roman said as he pressed the receiver to his ear. He had pale, rosy skin, bright blue eyes, and a shock of black hair. *Black Irish*, his fishing buddies called it. But never to his face.

'You said to make sure no one was here.'

The Roman nodded to himself. Finally, someone who followed directions. 'So the President's not in yet?'

'On his way. He sleeps late after overnight trips.'

'And the First Lady?'

'I'm telling you, it's just me. Now can we hurry up? People'll be here any second.'

Sitting at his desk and squinting out the window, The Roman watched as the light snow tumbled from the early morning sky. It may've been eighty degrees in Florida, but in D.C., winter was just unpacking its first punch. He didn't mind. When he was little, his grandmother had taught him to enjoy the quiet that came with the cold. Just

as his grandfather had taught him to appreciate the calm
that came to the waters of the Potomac. As any fisherman
knew, winter chased away the jet skiers and pleasure
boaters. And that was always the best time to put your
line in the water. Especially when you had the right bait.

'What about Wes?' The Roman asked. 'You get everything I sent?'

'Yeah . . . right here . . .'

He could hear the hesitation in his associate's voice.
No one liked being the bad guy – especially in politics.
'And you found something to put it in?' The Roman asked.

'We have a – That's why I came in early. We have this
lapel pin—'

'You can get him to wear it . . .'

'I-I think so.'

'It wasn't a question. Get him to wear it,' The Roman
shot back.

'You sure Wes'll even come in?' his associate asked.
'Agents here said he was sick as a hound the entire flight
back. Puked his lungs all over his pants.'

Outside, a crack of blue light slit through the tired, gray
sky. 'I'm not surprised,' The Roman said as the snow
continued to fall. 'If I were him right now, I'd be wrecking
my pants too. Now about that pin . . .'

'Don't worry,' his associate said. 'Wes won't even look
twice at it . . . especially when it's served by a friendly face.'

10

Palm Beach, Florida

'Hold it!' I yell, darting around the corner of the lobby and heading for the elevator's closing doors. Inside the elevator, a blond woman looks away, pretending she didn't hear me. That's why I hate Palm Beach. As the doors are about to pucker in a tight kiss, I leap forward and squeeze through. Now stuck with me, the blonde turns to the floor selection panel and pretends she's searching for *Door Open*. I should call her on it and tell her off.

'Thanks,' I say, bent over as I catch my breath.

'What floor?'

'Four.'

'Oh, you're with—'

'Yeah,' I say, finally looking up to see her.

She stares at my face, then quickly glances up at the electronic floor indicator. If she could run and scream 'Monster!' she would. But like the best Palm Beach hostesses, she'll overlook anything if it means a good social climb. 'Must be wild to work for him,' she adds, my new best friend, even though she refuses to make eye contact. I'm used to it by now. I haven't had a date in two years. But every pretty girl wants to talk to the President.

'Wilder than you know,' I say as the doors open on the fourth floor. Heading left toward a set of closed double doors, I sprint out as fast as I can. Not because of the blonde, but because I'm already—

'Late!' a scratchy voice scolds behind me. I spin back toward the open double doors of the Secret Service's suite, where a man with a neck as thick as my thigh sits behind a glass partition that looks like a bank teller's window.

'How late?' I call out, turning back toward the closed doors on the opposite side of the beige-carpeted hallway. Along with the Service's, they're the only doors on the whole floor – and unlike the law firm or the mortgage company just below, these doors aren't oak and stately. They're black and steel-lined. Bulletproof. Just like our windows.

'Late enough,' he says as I pull my ID badge from my pocket. But just as I'm about to swipe it through the card reader, I hear a quiet thunk, and the closed doors unlock.

'Thanks, A.J.!' I call out, pulling the door open.

Inside, I check the left-hand wall for the Secret Service agent who usually stands guard. He's not there, which means the President's not in yet. Good. I check the reception desk. The receptionist is gone too. Bad.

Crap. That means they already . . .

Sprinting across the enormous presidential seal that's woven into the bright blue carpet, I cut to my left, where the hallway is lined with bad paintings and poor sculptures of the President. They've arrived every single day since we left office – all from strangers, fans, supporters. They draw, paint, pencil, sketch, bronze, and sculpt him in every possible permutation. The newest ones are a set of Florida toothpicks with his profile carved into each one, and a bright yellow ceramic sculpture of the sun, with his face in the middle. And that's not even including what the corporations send: every CD, every book, every DVD that's released, they all want the former President to have it, though all we do is ship it to his Presidential Library. Knocking over a beechwood walking cane with his childhood photos glued to it, I trip down the hall and head for the second-to-last office that's—

'Nice of you to join us,' a raspy female voice announces as the entire room turns at my arrival. I do a quick head count just to see if I'm last – two, three, four, five . . .

'You're last,' Claudia Pacheco, our chief of staff, confirms as she leans back in her seat behind her messy mahogany desk. Claudia's got brown, graying hair that's pulled back in an almost military-tight bun and smoker's lips that reveal exactly where the raspy voice comes from. 'President with you?' she adds.

I shake my head, forgoing my one excuse for being late.

Out of the corner of my eye, I spot Bev and Oren smirking to themselves. Annoying and annoyinger. They both eye the small gold lapel pin that sits on the corner of Claudia's desk. Sculpted in the shape of the White House, the gold pin was no bigger than a hotel piece from Monopoly, but what made it memorable were the two gold poorly sculpted heads of the President and First Lady, pressed together and joined by one connecting ear, that dangled like charms just below it. The President bought it for Claudia years ago as a gag gift from a street vendor in China. Today, it's part of her leftover White House tradition: whoever's the last to arrive at the Monday morning staff meeting wears the pin for the next week. If you miss the meeting, you wear it for a month. But to my surprise, Claudia doesn't reach for it.

'What happened with the break-in backstage?' she asks in her barreling Massachusetts accent.

'Break-in?'

'In Malaysia . . . the guy in the President's holding room . . . the shattered glass table. My speaking Spanish here?'

In high school, Claudia was the girl who organized all the extracurricular events but never had any fun at them. It was the same when she ran Oval Office Operations, easily one of the most thankless jobs in the White House. She's not in it for the credit or the glory. She's here because she's dedicated. And she wants to make sure we are too.

'No . . . of course . . .' I stutter. 'But it wasn't— That wasn't a break-in.'

'That's not what the report said.'

'They sent you a report?'

'They send us everything,' Bev says from the two-person love seat perpendicular to Claudia's desk. She should know. As head of correspondence, she answers all the President's personal mail and even knows what inside jokes to put at the bottom of his friends' birthday cards. For a man with a good ten thousand 'friends,' it's tougher than it sounds, and the only reason Bev pulls it off is because she's been with the President since his first run for Congress almost twenty-five years ago.

'And they called it a *break-in*?' I ask.

Claudia holds up the report as Bev pulls the lapel pin from the corner of the desk. 'Break. In,' Claudia says, pointing to the words.

My eyes stay with the pin as Bev fidgets with it, running her thumb over the President's and First Lady's faces.

'Was there anything even worth stealing in the holding room?' Bev asks, brushing her dyed-black hair over her shoulder and revealing a V-neck sweater that shows off decade-old breast implants, which she got, along with the name *Busty Bev*, the year we won the White House. In high school, Bev was the girl voted Fabulous Face, and even now, at sixty-two, it's clear that appearances still matter.

'No one stole anyth— Trust me, it wasn't a break-in,' I say, rolling my eyes to downplay. 'The guy was drunk. He thought he was in the bathroom.'

'And the broken glass table?' Claudia asks.

'We're lucky it was just broken. Imagine if he thought it was a urinal,' Oren interrupts, already laughing at his own joke and scratching at his messy-prep eight a.m. shadow. At 6'1', Oren is the tallest, handsomest, toughest-looking gay man I've ever met in my life, and the only one close to my age in the office. From his seat across from Claudia's desk, it's clear he was the first one here. No surprise. If Bev was Fabulous Face, Oren was the smart kid who sent the dumb ones to buy beer. A born instigator, as well as our director of travel, he's also got the softest political touch in the entire office, which is why, with one simple joke, the room quickly forgets its obsession with the table.

I nod him a thank-you and—

'What about the table?' Bev asks, still fidgeting with the pin.

'That was me,' I say way too defensively. 'Read the report – I tripped into it as he was running out.'

'Wes, relax,' Claudia offers in her chief of staff monotone. 'No one's accusing you of—'

'I'm just saying . . . if I thought it was serious, I'd still be hunting for the guy myself. Even the Service thought he was just a wanderer.' On my left, Oren playfully taps his own lapel, hoping I don't notice. Motioning to Bev, he's trying to get her attention. He's only worn the pin once –

on a day I told him, 'Wait in your office, the President wants to see you.' The President wasn't even in the building. It was an easy trick. This is just fourth-grade payback. He again motions to Bev. Lucky me, she doesn't notice.

'Listen, I'm sorry to do this, but are we done?' I ask, looking down at my watch and realizing I'm already late. 'The President wants me to—'

'Go, go, go,' Claudia says, closing her datebook. 'Just do me a favor, Wes. When you're at tonight's cystic fibrosis event – I know you're always careful – but with the break-in . . .'

'It wasn't a break-in.'

'. . . just keep your eyes open a little bit wider, okay?'

'I always do,' I say, dashing for the door and narrowly escaping the—

'What about the pin?' a rusty voice interrupts from his usual swivel chair in the back corner.

'Aaaaand you're screwed,' Oren says.

'Red light, red light!' Claudia calls out. It's the same thing she yells at her kids. I stop right there. 'Thanks, B.B.,' she adds.

'Jes' doin' mah duty,' B.B. says, the words tumbling out of the side of his mouth in a slow Southern crawl. With a shock of messy white hair and a rumpled button-down shirt with the President's faded monogrammed initials on the cuffs, B.B. Shaye has been by the President's side even longer than the First Lady. Some say he's Manning's distant cousin . . . others say he's his senile old sergeant from Vietnam. Either way, he's been the President's shadow for almost forty years – and like any shadow, he'll creep you out if you stare at him too long. 'Sorry, kiddo,' he offers with a yellow-toothed grin as Bev hands me the gold White House with the dangling heads.

For authenticity, the sculptor used two flakes of green glitter for the First Lady's eye color. Since gray glitter is harder to come by, the President's eyes are blank.

'Just tell people they're your grandchildren,' Oren says as I open the clasp and slide it into my lapel. Shoving too hard, I feel a sharp bite in my fingertip as the pin punctures my skin. A drop of blood bubbles upward. I've taken much worse.

'By the way, Wes,' Claudia adds, 'one of the curators from the library said he wants to talk to you about some exhibit he's working on, so be nice when he calls . . .'

'I'm on my cell if you need me!' I call out with a wave. Rushing to the door, I lick the drop of blood from my finger.

'Careful,' B.B. calls out behind me. 'It's the small cuts that'll kill ya.'

He's right about that. Out in the hallway, I blow past an oversize oil painting of President Manning dressed as a circus ringmaster. Dreidel said he had info on Boyle. Time to finally find out what it is.

11

'Welcome back, Mr Holloway,' the valet at the Four Seasons says, knowing my name from countless visits with the President. Unlike most, he stays locked on my eyes. I nod him a thank-you just for that.

As I step inside the hotel, a blast of air-conditioning wraps me in its arms. Out of habit, I look over my shoulder for the President. He's not here. I'm on my own.

Cutting across the beige marble floor of the lobby, I feel my heart kicking inside my chest. It's not just Boyle. For better or worse, that's always been Dreidel's effect on me.

As Manning's original buttboy, Gavin 'Dreidel' Jeffer isn't just my predecessor – he's also the one who put me on the President's radar and recommended me for the job. When we met a decade ago, I was a nineteen-year-old volunteer in the Florida campaign office, answering phones and putting out yard signs. Dreidel was twenty-two and Manning's right- and left-hand man. I actually told Dreidel it was an honor to meet him. And I meant it. By then, we'd all heard the story.

Back during primary season, Dreidel was just some unaffiliated local kid setting up folding chairs during the first primary debate. Like any other roadie, when the show was over, he tried to get closer to the action by sneaking backstage. Where he found himself was the heart of the spin room, where the best liars in America were telling tall tales about why their candidate had just won. In a sloppy oxford shirt, he was the one silent kid in a room full of yammering adults. The CBS reporter spotted him instantly, shoving a microphone in his face. 'What'd you think, son?' the reporter asked.

Dreidel stared blankly into the red light of the camera, his mouth dangling open. And without even thinking about it, he gave the God's honest response that would forever change his life: 'When it was over, Manning's the only one who didn't ask his staff, *How'd I do?*'

That question became Manning's mantra for the next year and a half. Every news organization picked up the clip. Every major paper ran with the quote. They even passed out printed-up buttons saying *How'd I do?*

Three words. When Dreidel retold the story at his wedding a few years back, he said he didn't even realize what had happened until the reporter asked how to spell his name. It didn't matter. Three words, and Dreidel – the little Jewish spinner, as the White House press nicknamed him – was born. Within a week, Manning offered him a job as buttboy, and throughout the campaign, hundreds of young volunteers rolled their eyes. It's not that they were jealous, it's just . . . Maybe it's his smug smile, or the ease with which he stumbled into the job, but in the school yard, Dreidel was the kid who used to have the best birthday party, with the best presents, with the best favors for anyone lucky enough to be invited. For a few years, it puts him in the *in* crowd, but as cockiness sets in, he doesn't even realize he's on the outs.

Still, he's always been Manning's good luck charm. And today, hopefully mine.

'Good day, Mr Holloway,' the concierge calls out as I

slide past him and head toward the elevators. It's the second person who knows my name, instantly reminding me of the need to be discreet. Of course, that's why I called Dreidel in the first place. The President would never admit it, but I know why he and the First Lady attended Dreidel's wedding and wrote his recommendation for Columbia Law School – and asked me to pick out a gift when Dreidel's daughter was born: rewards for years of good service. And in White House terms, *good service* means keeping your mouth shut.

As the elevator doors open on the fourth floor, I follow the directional arrows and start counting room numbers: 405 . . . 407 . . . 409 . . . From the distance between doors, I can tell these're all suites. Dreidel's moving up in the world.

The hallway dead-ends at room 415, a suite so big it's got a doorbell on it. There's no way I'm giving him the pleasure of ringing it.

'Room service,' I announce, rapping my knuckles against the door.

No one answers.

'Dreidel, you in there?' I add.

Still no response.

'It's me, Wes!' I yell, finally giving up and ringing the doorbell. 'Dreidel, are you—?'

There's a loud thunk as the lock flicks open. Then a jingling of metal. He's got the door chain on too.

'Hold on,' he calls out. 'I'm coming.'

'What're you doing? Stealing the wood hangers?'

The door cracks open, but only a few inches. Behind it, Dreidel sticks his head out like an anxious housewife surprised by a salesman. His usually perfectly parted hair is slightly mussed, draping boyish bangs across his forehead.

He pushes his circular wire-rim glasses up on his thin sculpted nose. From the little I can see, he's not wearing a shirt.

'No offense, but I'm not having sex with you,' I say with a laugh.

'I said to call from downstairs,' he shoots back.

'What're you getting so upset about? I figured you'd like showing off your big room and—'

'I'm serious, Wes. Why'd you come up here?' There's a new tone in his voice. Not just annoyance. Fear. 'Did anyone follow you?' he adds, opening the door a bit more to check the hallway. He's got a towel around his waist.

'Dreidel, is everything—?'

'I said call from *downstairs!*' he insists.

I step back, completely confused.

'Honey,' a female voice calls out from within the room, 'is everything—' The woman stops midsentence. Dreidel turns, and I spot her over his shoulder, just turning the corner inside the room. She's dressed in one of the hotel's white overfluffed bathrobes – a thin African-American woman with gorgeous braids. I have no idea who she is, but the one thing I'm sure of is, she's not Dreidel's wife. Or his two-year-old daughter.

Dreidel's face falls as he reads my reaction. This is the part where he says it's not how it looks.

'Wes, it's not what you think.'

I stare at the woman in the bathrobe. And Dreidel in his towel. 'Maybe I should . . . I'll just go downstairs,' I stutter.

'I'll meet you there in two minutes.'

Stepping back, I study the woman, who's still frozen in place. Her eyes are wide, silently apologizing.

12

'Where's he now?' O'Shea asked, pressing his palm against the window of the black sedan and feeling the warmth of the Florida sun. It was freezing in France. But somehow, even with the Palm Beach heat and the liquid-blue sky, he wasn't any warmer.

'He just took the elevator upstairs in the hotel,' Micah replied.

'Elevator? You let him ride alone?'

'Better than me jumping in with him. Relax – there're only four floors. He's not getting far.'

O'Shea rolled his tongue inside his cheek. 'So what're you still doing in the lobby?'

'Waiting for one of the—'

Through the phone, O'Shea heard a slight ping followed by a low rumble. Micah's elevator had finally arrived. 'I'll have him in—'

Micah's voice went silent. But from the background noise, O'Shea could tell Micah was still on the line.

'Micah, what happened?' he asked.

No response.

'Micah, you okay!?'

There was another low rumble. Elevator doors closing. Then a rough swishing. Like two windbreakers being rubbed together. Micah was moving. The swishing continued. At that pace, he was clearly not in the elevator,

O'Shea thought. But if he wasn't in the elevator, that meant . . .

'Wes just stepped out, didn't he?' O'Shea asked as his sedan made a sharp left onto a well-manicured drive.

'Not bad, Watson,' Micah whispered. 'You should do this professionally.'

'Anyone with him?'

'Nope. All alone,' Micah said. 'Something happened up there, though. Kid's got his tail between his legs. Like he got dumped.'

'Is he leaving the hotel?'

'Nope again. Headed for the restaurant in back. I'm telling you, he really looks terrible . . . I mean, even more than those Frankenstein marks in his face.'

'That's a shame,' O'Shea said as his car curved into the horseshoe driveway of the main entrance. ''Cause his day's about to get a whole lot worse.' On his right, the car door sprang open and a valet with blond hair offered a slight tip of his hat.

'Welcome to the Four Seasons, sir. Are you checking in with us today?'

'No,' O'Shea offered as he stepped out of the car. 'Just grabbing a little something for breakfast.'

13

Hunched forward in a big wicker armchair, I stir my coffee with a silver spoon and watch my reflection swirl into oblivion.

'Is it really that bad?' a voice teases behind me.

I turn just in time to see Dreidel enter the hotel's open-air restaurant. His black hair is gelled and parted. The boyish bangs are long gone. Combined with his monogrammed white shirt and antique wire-rim glasses, it's clear he's mastered the art of sending a message without saying a word. Right now he's selling confidence. Too bad I'm not buying.

Ignoring the foamy waves of the Atlantic Ocean on our left, he puts a hand on my shoulder and crosses around to the oversize wicker seat next to me. As he moves, his hand runs from my shoulder to the back of my neck, always holding tight enough to reassure.

'Don't use his moves on me,' I warn.

'What're you—?'

'His *moves*,' I repeat, pulling away so his hand's no longer on my neck.

'You think I'm—? You think I'd pull a Manning on you?'

Dreidel was with him for almost four years. I'm going on nine. I don't even bother to argue. I just stare back down at my overpriced, still-swirling coffee and let the silence sink in. This is why the in crowd turns on him.

'Wes, what you saw up there—'

'Listen, before you say it, can we just spare ourselves the awkwardness and move on? My bad . . . my fault . . . clearly none of my business.'

He studies me carefully, picking apart every syllable and trying to figure out if I mean it. When you shadow a President, you become fluent in reading between the lines. I'm good. Dreidel's better.

'Just say it already, Wes.'

I stare out across the open terrace and watch the waves kamikaze into the beach.

'I know you're thinking it,' he adds.

Like I said, Dreidel's better. 'Does Ellen know?' I finally ask, referring to his wife.

'She should. She's not stupid.' His voice creaks like a renegade floorboard. 'And when Ali was born . . . marriage is hard, Wes.'

'So that girl up there . . .'

'Just someone I met at the bar. I flashed my room key. She thinks I'm rich because I can afford to stay here.' He forces a grin and tosses his room key on the table. 'I didn't realize you had so many money addicts in Palm Beach.'

This time, I'm the one who's silent. A waiter approaches and fills Dreidel's cup with coffee.

'You guys talked about divorce?' I ask.

'Can't.'

'Why not?'

'Why do you think?' he challenges.

I look over at the file folder that's lying between us on the table. The handwritten tab says *Fundraising*.

'I thought you said you were down here on business.'

'And that's not business?' he asks.

A few months back, Dreidel called the President to tell him he was running for State Senate in the 19th District in his home state of Illinois. But when it comes to impending elections, 'happily married father' polls far better than 'recently divorced dad.'

'See, and you thought you were the only one with problems,' Dreidel adds. 'Now assuming that was Boyle, you want to hear how he cheated death, or not?'

14

I sit up straight in my chair. 'You actually found something?'

'No, I called you here to waste your time.' With a deep sip of coffee, Dreidel's a different man. Like anyone in the White House, he's always better when he's in control. 'So back to the beginning . . . the real beginning . . . On the day the two of you got shot at the speedway, you remember how long the drive was to get you to the hospital?'

A simple question, but I don't give him an answer.

'Just guess,' he says.

I grit my teeth, surprised by how hard the memory hits. I can still see the ambulance doors closing on Boyle . . .

'Wes, I know you don't want to relive it, I just need—'

'I passed out,' I blurt. 'From what they said, the ambulance took about four minutes . . .'

'It was three minutes.'

'Pretty fast.'

'Actually, pretty slow considering Halifax Medical Center is only a mile and a half from the speedway. Now guess how long it took for the ambulance that drove there with Boyle, who was – no offense – a whole lot more important than you were to the administration, not to mention far more injured?'

I shake my head, refusing to play along.

'Twelve minutes,' Dreidel blurts.

We sit in silence as I take it in.

'So?' I ask.

'C'mon, Wes. *Twelve minutes* for a speeding ambulance with a critically injured White House senior staff member to travel a mile and a half? The average person *walks* faster. My grandmother walks faster. And she's dead.'

'Maybe they got stuck in the panicking riot outside.'

'Funny, that's exactly what *they* said.'

'They?'

From the briefcase that's leaning against the side of his chair, Dreidel pulls out a bound document about half as thick as a phone book. He drops it on the table with a thud that sends our spoons bouncing. I recognize the congressional logo immediately. *Investigation into the Assassination Attempt on President Leland F. Manning.* Congress's official investigation into Nico's attack. Dreidel leaves it on the table, waiting to see if I pick it up. He knows me better than I thought.

'You never read it, did you?' he asks.

I stare at the book, still refusing to touch it. 'I flipped through it once . . . It's just . . . it's like reading your own obituary.'

'More like Boyle's obituary. You lived, remember?'

I brush my hand against my face. My fingertips rise and fall in the craters of my scars. 'What's your point?'

'Play the numbers, Wes. Two trains leave the station at almost the exact same time. Both race for the hospital. It's a matter of life and death. One takes three minutes. The other takes twelve. You don't see a problem there? And if that weren't enough, remember what the real security screwup was that Congress ripped our doctors apart for?'

'You mean bringing the President's wrong blood type?'

'See, that's where they always got it wrong. When Congress did their investigation, they tore out what little hair they had left in their heads because they found pints of O-negative blood along with the President's B-positive. Naturally, they assumed someone made a mistake and brought the wrong blood. But knowing who you saw at the speech that night – well, guess who else happened to be O-negative?'

'Boyle?'

'And that's how he pulled off his big magic trick.'

'It wasn't a magic trick,' I insist.

'No, you're right. But it *was* an illusion.' Waving his left hand back and forth in front of me, he adds, 'You're so busy watching the moving hand, you completely ignore the sly hand's misdirection.' From his right hand, he drops a quarter on the table.

'Way to be melodramatic,' I point out.

He shakes his head as if I'm missing the point. 'Do you have any idea what you've stumbled onto? This thing was more fixed than a Harlem Globetrotters game. You, me, Congress, the whole world . . . we got—' He leans in close, lowering his voice. 'We got *fooled*, Wes. They lied. I mean, if that was really Boyle—'

'It was him! I saw him!'

'I'm not saying you didn't. I just . . .' He looks around, his voice getting even quieter. 'This isn't one of those petty news stories they save until the end of the broadcast.'

He's right about that. 'I don't understand, though – why would the President's ambulance be hauling around Boyle's blood?'

'I know. That's the question, isn't it?' Dreidel asks. 'But

when you pick it apart, only one explanation makes sense. They only carry around blood . . .'

'. . . when they think someone's life is in danger.' I pick up the quarter and tap it against the white tablecloth. 'Oh, God. If they were expecting it . . . you think Boyle was wearing a vest?'

'Had to,' Dreidel says. 'He took two shots in the chest . . .'

'But all that blood—'

'. . . and one shot that went through the back of his hand and straight into his neck. Read the report, Wes. Nico was an army-trained sniper who specialized in heart shots. Boyle went facedown the moment it happened. That shot to the neck . . . I'll bet that's what you saw pooling below him.'

I close my eyes and hear myself offering to put Boyle in the limo. There's a jagged piece of metal in my cheek. The bumblebee's still screaming . . . 'But if he was wearing a vest . . .' I look out toward the ocean. The waves are deafening. '. . . th-they knew. They had to've known . . .'

'Wes, will you stop—' Dreidel cuts himself off and lowers his voice. We don't need anyone staring. 'They didn't know,' he whispers. 'They could've had an open threat on Boyle's life. He could've been wearing that vest for a month. In fact, according to the report, the President *wasn't* wearing *his* vest that day. Didja hear that?' He waits until I nod, just to make sure I'm focused. 'If they'd known there was a gunman, Manning never would've been there, much less been allowed to go without that vest.'

'Unless he *was* wearing one and that's just part of their story,' I point out.

'Listen, I know you're close to this—'

'Close to it? It ruined my life! D'you understand that?'

I finally explode. 'This wasn't just some crappy afternoon. Little kids point at me and hide behind their moms! I can't fucking smile anymore! Do you have any idea what that's like?'

The restaurant goes silent. Every single person is looking at us. The preppy family with two twin girls. The sandy-haired man with the U.S. Open cap. Even our waiter, who quickly approaches, hoping to calm things down.

'Everything okay, sir?'

'Yeah . . . sorry . . . we're fine,' I tell him as he fills our coffee cups that don't need refilling.

As the waiter leaves, Dreidel watches me closely, giving me a moment. It's how he taught me to deal with the President when he loses his cool. Put your head down and let the fire burn itself out.

'I'm okay,' I tell him.

'I knew you would be,' he says. 'Just remember, I'm here to help.'

I take a deep breath and bury it all away. 'So assuming there was a threat on Boyle's life at the time, why not just take him to the hospital?'

'That's the nail I keep stepping on. They caught Nico . . . Boyle was injured, but obviously alive . . . why pretend you're dead and walk away from your life and your entire family? Maybe that's what they were talking about during those twelve minutes in the ambulance. Maybe that's when Boyle made his decision to hide.'

I shake my head. 'In twelve minutes? You can't just shuck your whole life in twelve minutes – especially when you're bleeding out of your neck. They had to've made plans before that.'

'*They?*' Dreidel asks.

'C'mon, this isn't like hiding from your little brother

in a pillow fort. To pull something this big off, you need the Service, plus the ambulance driver, plus the doctor who took care of his neck.' I pause for a moment to make the point clear. 'Plus someone to authorize it.'

Dreidel lowers his chin, looking at me from just above the rounded rim of his glasses. He knows what I'm getting at. 'You really think he'd—? You think he'd do that?'

It's the question I've been fighting with since the moment I saw Boyle's fake name back at that hotel. You don't use that name to hide. You use it so someone can find you. 'I just . . . I don't see how the President *wouldn't* know. Back then, Manning couldn't pee in a bush unless someone checked it first. If Boyle was wearing a vest – which he clearly had to've been – there had to be a credible threat. And if there was a credible threat . . . and extra blood in the ambulance . . . and contingencies in place to make sure Boyle was safe . . . Manning had to've signed off on that.'

'Unless Albright signed off for him,' Dreidel counters, referring to our old chief of staff and the one other person in the limo with us that day at the speedway.

It's a fair point, but it doesn't bring us any closer to an answer. Albright died of testicular cancer three years ago. 'Now you're blaming it all on a corpse?'

'Doesn't make it any less credible,' Dreidel challenges. 'Albright used to sign off on security details all the time.'

'I don't know,' I say, shaking my head. 'Manning and Boyle had known each other since college. If Boyle was planning on disappearing, that's a hell of a prank to pull on a friend, much less the President of the United States.'

'You joking? Boyle walked away from his family, his wife . . . even his own daughter. Look at the full picture, Wes: Nico the nutjob takes a potshot at the President.

Instead, he hits Boyle square in the chest. But instead of going to the hospital to get patched up, Boyle takes that exact moment to fake his own death and disappear off the face of the earth. You do something like that, you've obviously got a damn good reason.'

'Like father, like son?' I ask.

'Yeah, I thought about that. Problem is, Boyle's dad was just a petty scumbag. This is . . . this is big-league. With a capital *big*.'

'Maybe Boyle hired Nico. Maybe the shooting was a giant smoke screen to give Boyle a way to get out.'

'Way too *Mission: Impossible* sequels,' Dreidel says. 'If Nico misses, you're risking a head shot. More important, if the Service was helping, they're not putting the President, and his staff, and 200,000 spectators in danger while entrusting it all to some whacked looney tune. You've seen Nico in the interviews – he's Stephen King–movie crazy. If Boyle wanted to do this to himself, he'd fake a heart attack at home and be done with it.'

'So you think when Nico fired those shots, Boyle and the Service just used the instant chaos to sneak him out of there?' I ask, trying hard to keep it to a whisper.

'I don't know what to think. All I know is, for Boyle to put on a bulletproof vest, he must've been expecting something. I mean, you don't bring an umbrella unless you think it's gonna rain, right?'

I nod, unable to argue. Still, it doesn't get us any closer to the *why*. Why was Nico taking shots at Boyle? Why was Manning's motorcade traveling around with Boyle's blood? And why would Boyle walk away from his life, his wife, and his teenage daughter? I mean, what could possibly tempt – or terrify – a man so much that he'd throw his entire life away?

'Maybe you should just ask,' Dreidel blurts.

'Who, Manning? Oh, right – I'll just run up and say, "By the way, sir, I just saw your dead buddy – yeah, the one whose assassination wrecked your entire presidency. Oh, and since he's alive, while I've been slaving for your ass every single day since I got out of the hospital, why'd you lie to me for over eight years about the single worst moment of my life?" Yeah, that'd be genius.'

'What about the Service?'

'Same difference. Boyle could've never disappeared all those years ago if he didn't have their help. The last thing I need is to shout from the roof that I'm the one to blow it all open. Until I know what's going on, better to keep things quiet.'

Dreidel leans back in his wicker chair. 'When you saw Boyle backstage in that dressing room, you think he was trying to kill Manning?'

'Kill him?'

'Why else would he come out of hiding after almost eight years? Just to say hello?'

'I guess, but . . . to kill him? Isn't that—?'

'Kaiser Soze,' Dreidel interrupts. '*Greatest trick the devil pulled off: convincing the world he didn't exist.*' He looks back up at me, and I swear there's almost a smile on his face. 'Man, can you imagine? Being legally dead but still alive? Y'know how much freedom that gives you?'

I stare down at Dreidel's room key and try hard not to picture the fluffy white bathrobe that comes with it.

'Maybe that's what Boyle wanted all those years ago,' he adds. 'Just a way out.'

I shake my head but still catch the deeper point. The only way to understand what's going on is to understand Boyle. 'So where does that leave us?' I ask.

'*Us?* This ain't *my* disaster.' He laughs as he says it, but he's definitely not joking. 'C'mon, Wes, you know I'm just joking,' he adds, knowing I get the point. Like any great political trickster, his first move is to remove his own fingerprints. It's why I called him in the first place. He spent almost four years by the President's side, but you'll never find him in the background of a single photograph. No one's better at being invisible, which is, right now, the number one thing I need if I plan on finding out the truth.

'Got any connections with law enforcement?' he adds, already two moves ahead. 'If they can take a peek at Boyle's background—'

'I've got someone perfect for that,' I tell him. But he's glancing over my shoulder, back toward the entrance to the restaurant. Following his stare, I turn around to find the black woman with the braids. She's traded the bathrobe for the other Palm Beach uniform: white slacks with a pale orange designer T-shirt. All set for a day on the town.

'Listen, I should run,' Dreidel says, already out of his seat. 'Just be smart about this.'

'Smart?'

'Careful. Be careful. Because if Manning *is* in on this . . .' He takes another look around, then leans in close. 'You thought America turned on him before? They'll crucify him, Wes. Seriously. Crucify.'

I nod. Across the restaurant, his girlfriend shoots us a look. 'And while we're on the subject, Wes. I'm happy to keep your secret – just promise me you'll keep mine.'

'O-Of course. I'd never say a word.'

He turns to go, leaving me with the bill. 'By the way, you interested in forking over five hundred bucks and coming to my fundraiser tonight?'

I shake my head in disbelief. 'Dreidel, how much did your soul cost when you finally sold it?'

'You coming or not?'

'I would, but I've got a Manning event tonight.'

Dreidel nods and doesn't linger. He knows who always comes first.

As he heads for the door, I decide not to turn and stare at the girl. Instead, I hold up my spoon and use the bottom of it as my own little fun-house mirror. Over my shoulder, I spot Dreidel just as he approaches her. He doesn't reach out to hold her hand until he thinks they're out of sight.

'Excuse me,' someone says over my left shoulder. I turn, expecting to see the waiter. Instead, it's a blond guy in a black T-shirt. And a U.S. Open baseball hat.

'Wes Holloway?' he asks, opening his wallet to show me an FBI badge. 'Terrence O'Shea. You have a few seconds to chat?'

15

St. Elizabeths Mental Hospital,
Washington, D.C.

'Breakfast bell's ringing, Nico. French toast or western omelet?' asked the petite black food service woman with the vinegar smell and the pink rhinestones set into her pink fingernails.

'What's for dinner?' Nico asked.

'You listening? We're on breakfast. French toast or western omelet?'

Putting on his shoes and kneeling just in front of his narrow bed, Nico looked up at the door and studied the rolling cart with the open tray slots. He'd long ago earned the right to eat with his fellow patients. But after what happened to his mother all those years ago, he'd rather have his meals delivered to his room. 'French toast,' Nico said. 'Now what's for dinner?'

Throughout St. Elizabeths, they called Nico an NGI. He wasn't the only one. There were thirty-seven in total, all of them living in the John Howard Pavilion, a red brick, five-story building that was home to Nico and the other thirty-six patients *n*ot *g*uilty by reason of *i*nsanity.

Compared to the other wards, the NGI floors were always quieter than the rest. As Nico heard one doctor say, 'When there're voices in your head, there's no need to talk to anyone else.'

Still down on one knee, Nico yanked hard to fasten the Velcro on his sneakers (they took away the laces long ago) and carefully watched as the food service woman carried a pink plastic tray filled with French toast into his small ten-by-fifteen room, which was decorated with a wooden nightstand and a painted dresser that never had anything but a Bible and a set of vintage red glass rosary beads on it. The doctors offered to get Nico a sofa, even a coffee table. Anything to make it feel more like home. Nico refused, but never said why. He wanted it this way. So it looked like her room. His mom's room. In *her* hospital.

Nodding to himself, he could still picture the stale hospital room where his mother lay silent for almost three years. He was only ten when the Creutzfeldt-Jakob disease hit . . . when one faulty gene in her brain ignited the CJD protein that eventually kick-started her coma. When the diagnosis first came back, she didn't complain – not even when young Nico asked why God was taking her. She smiled, even then, and respectfully told him that's how it was written in the Book. The Book of Fate. Her head was shaking, but her voice was strong as she told him never to argue with it. The Book had to be respected. Had to be heeded. Let it guide you. But it wasn't just respect. She took strength from it. Security. No doubt, his mother knew. She wasn't afraid. How could anyone be afraid of God's will? But he still remembered his father standing behind him, squeezing his shoulders and forcing him to pray every day so Jesus would bring his mom back.

For the first few weeks, they prayed in the hospital chapel. After six months, they visited every day but Sunday, convinced that their Sunday prayers would be more effective if they came from church. It was three years later that Nico changed his prayers. He did it only once. During a frozen snow day in the fist of Wisconsin's winter. He didn't want to be in church that day, didn't want to be in his nice pants and church shirt. Especially with all the great snowball fights going on outside. So on that Sunday morning, as he lowered his head in church, instead of praying for Jesus to bring his mom back, he prayed for him to take her. The Book had to be wrong. That day, his mother died.

Staring at the plastic tray of French toast and still kneeling by his bed, Nico, for the third time, asked, 'What's for dinner?'

'It's meat loaf, okay?' the delivery woman replied, rolling her eyes. 'You happy now?'

'Of course, I'm happy,' Nico said, flattening the Velcro with the heel of his hand and smiling to himself. Meat loaf. Just like his mom was supposed to have on *her* last night. On the day she died. The Three told him so. Just like they told him about the M Men . . . the Masons . . .

Nico's father had been a Freemason – proud of it too. To this day, Nico could smell the sweet cigar smoke that wafted in the door with his dad when he came back from Lodge meetings.

Nothing more than a social club, Nico had told them. All the Masons did was sell raffle tickets to raise money for the hospital. Like the Shriners.

The Three were patient, even then. They brought him the maps – taught him the history. How the Freemasons had grown worldwide hiding under the cover of charity. How they'd perfected their deceptions, telling people they were born out of the master stonemason guilds in the Middle Ages – a harmless organization where members could gather and share trade secrets, artisan-to-artisan. But The Three knew the truth: The Masons' craftwork had built some of the most holy and famous places in the world

– from King Solomon's Temple to the Washington Monument – but the secrets the Masons protected were more than just inside tips for how to build archways and monuments. The night before Martin Luther King Jr. was killed, he was in a Mason Temple in Memphis. 'I might not get there with you,' King said that night to his followers. Like he knew that bullet was coming the next day. And the fact he was in a Masonic Temple . . . it was no coincidence. Fate. Always fate. At their highest levels, the Masons' ancient goal had never changed.

Even the church stood against the Masons at their founding, The Three explained.

It was a fair point, but Nico wasn't stupid. In the Middle Ages, there was much the church opposed.

The Three still didn't waver. Instead, they hit him with the hardest truth of all: what really happened to his mother the night she died.

16

'But you can't tell anyone I told you,' the woman whispered through the receiver.

Brushing a stray strand of red hair behind her ear, Lisbeth reached for the tiny tape recorder on her desk, double-checked it was plugged into the phone, and hit *Record*. 'You have my word,' Lisbeth promised. 'Our secret.'

As a reporter for the *Palm Beach Post*, Lisbeth was well aware that Florida law made it illegal to record private conversations unless the person recording first asked the other party. But as the gossip columnist for Below the Fold – the *Post*'s most popular section of the paper – Lisbeth also knew that the moment she asked permission, her source would freeze and fall silent. Plus she had to get the quote right. Plus she had to have proof for when the paper's lawyers gave her their usual libel thumbwrestle. It's the same reason why she had a mini-refrigerator stocked with wine and beer in the corner of her tiny beige cubicle, and a fresh bowl of peanuts on the corner of her desk. Whether it was her fellow reporters coming by to chat or a stranger calling on the phone, it was the sacred rule she learned when she took over the column six years ago: Always keep 'em talking.

'So about your story, Mrs . . . ?'

'I'm just passing this along,' the woman insisted. 'Free of charge.'

Making a note to herself, Lisbeth wrote the word *Pro?* in her spiral notepad. Most people fall for the name trap.

'Again, you didn't hear it from me . . .' the woman continued.

'I promise, Mrs . . .'

'. . . and I'm not falling for your little trick the second time either,' the woman said.

Lisbeth crossed out the question mark, leaving only *Pro*.

Excited by the challenge, Lisbeth started spinning her phone cord like a mini–jump rope. As the cord picked up speed, the sheets of paper thumbtacked to the right-hand wall of her cubicle began to flutter. When Lisbeth was seventeen, her dad's clothing store had shut down, forcing her family into bankruptcy. But when her local newspaper in Battle Creek, Michigan, reported the story, the smartass reporter who wrote it up threw in the words *alleged poor sales*, implying a certain disingenuousness to her dad's account. In response, Lisbeth wrote an op-ed about it for her school newspaper. The local paper picked it up and ran it with an apology. Then the *Detroit News* picked it up from there. By the time it was done, she got seventytwo responses from readers all across Michigan. Those seventy-two letters were the ones that lined every inch of her cubicle walls, a daily reminder of the power of the pen – and a current reminder that the best stories are the ones you never see coming.

'Regardless,' the woman said, 'I just thought you'd want to know that although it won't officially be announced until later this afternoon, Alexander John – eldest son of the Philadelphia Main Line Johns, of course – will be awarded a Gold Key in the National Scholastic Art Awards.'

Lisbeth was writing the words *National Schola-* when she lifted her pen from the page. 'How old is Alexander again?'

'Of course – seventeen – seventeen on September ninth.'

'So . . . this is a high school award?'

'And national – not just statewide. Gold Key.'

Lisbeth scratched at her freckled neck. She was slightly overweight, which she tried to offset with lime-green statement glasses that a rail-thin salesclerk promised would also shave some time off her thirty-one years. Lisbeth didn't believe the clerk. But she did buy the glasses. As she continued to scratch, a strand of red hair sagged from its ear perch and dangled in front of her face. 'Ma'am, do you happen to be *related* to young Alexander?'

'What? Of course not,' the woman insisted.

'You're sure?'

'Are you suggesting—? Young lady, this award is an honor that is—'

'Or are you in the employ of young Alexander's family?'

The woman paused. 'Not full-time, of course, but—'

Lisbeth hit the *Stop* button on her tape recorder and chucked her pen against her desk. Only in Palm Beach would a mother hire a publicist for her eleventh grader's elbow macaroni art masterpiece. 'It's a national award,' Lisbeth muttered to herself, ripping the sheet of paper from her notepad. But as she crumpled it up, she still didn't hang up the phone. Sacred Rule #2: A crappy source today might be a great one tomorrow. Sacred Rule #3: See Sacred Rule #2.

'If I have space, I'll definitely try to get it in,' Lisbeth added. 'We're pretty full, though.' It was an even bigger lie than the thinning and de-aging effects of her lime-green glasses. But as Lisbeth hung up the phone and tossed the crumpled paper into the trash, she couldn't help but notice the near-empty three-column grid on her computer screen.

Twenty inches. About eight hundred words. That's what it took every day to fill Below the Fold. Plus a photo, of course. So far, she had five inches on a local socialite's daughter marrying a professional pool player (B+, Lisbeth thought to herself), and four inches on a week-old cursing match between some teenager and the head of the DMV (C– at best). Eyeing the balled-up paper in the plastic garbage can, Lisbeth glanced back at her still mostly empty screen. No, she told herself. It was still too early in the day to be desperate. She hadn't even gotten the—

'Mail!' a voice called out as a hand reached over the top edge of the cubicle, wagging a short pile of envelopes in the air. Looking up, Lisbeth knew that if she reached for the stack, he'd just pull it away, so she waited for the hand . . . and its owner . . . to turn the corner. 'Morning, Vincent,' she said before he even appeared.

'Tell me you got something good today,' Vincent said, his salt-and-pepper mustache squirming like a caterpillar on his lip. He tossed the pile of mail on Lisbeth's already oversubscribed desk. It wasn't until it fanned out accordion-style in front of her that Lisbeth saw the tear in each envelope.

'You opened my mail?' she asked.

'I'm your editor. That's my job.'

'Your job is opening my mail?'

'No, my job is to make sure your column is the best it can be. And when it is, and when every person in this town is whispering to their neighbors about whatever scandal you so cleverly unearthed, we usually get about twenty to thirty letters a day, plus the usual press releases and invitations. Know what you got this morning? Six. And that's including the invites.' Peering over her shoulder and reading from the mostly empty grid on Lisbeth's computer screen, Vincent added, 'You spelled *DMV* wrong.'

Lisbeth squinted toward the screen.

'Made you look,' Vincent added, laughing his little huffing laugh. With his navy and red Polo-knockoff suspenders and matching bow tie, Vincent dressed like Palm Beach royalty on an editor's salary.

Annoyed, Lisbeth pulled his left suspender back like a bowstring and let it snap against his chest.

'Ow . . . that . . . that actually hurt,' he whined, rubbing his chest. 'I was making a point.'

'Really? And what was that? That I should find more stories about handjobs in hot tubs?'

'Listen, missy, that was a fun story.'

'*Fun?* I don't want fun. I want *good*.'

'Like what? Like your supposed top-secret source who whispered all those promises in your ear, then jumped off the face of the earth? What was her name again? Lily?'

'Iris.' As Lisbeth said the word, she could feel the blood rush to her ears. Four months ago, a woman identifying herself only as Iris cold-called Lisbeth on the office's main line. From the shakiness in Iris's voice, Lisbeth could hear the tears. And from the hesitation . . . she knew what fear sounded like. For twenty minutes, Iris told her the story: about how, years ago, she used to do Thai massages at a local bathhouse . . . that it was there she first met the man she called Byron . . . and the thrill of secretly dating one of Palm Beach's most powerful men. But what got Lisbeth's attention was Iris's graphic detail of how, on a number of occasions, he lashed out physically, eventually breaking her collarbone and jaw. For Lisbeth, that was a story that mattered. And that was what the letters on her wall were there for. But when she asked for Byron's real name – and Iris's, for that matter – the line went dead.

'She was yanking your ya-ya,' Vincent said.

'Maybe she was scared.'

'Or maybe she just wanted some attention.'

'Or maybe she's now married, and therefore terrified her husband will dump her the instant he finds out his lovely wife used to be a bathhouse girl. Think, Vincent. Sources only stay quiet when they have something to lose.'

'Y'mean like their job? Or their career? Or their supposedly well read gossip column?'

Lisbeth stabbed him with a cold, piercing stare. Vincent stabbed her right back.

'Six,' he said as he turned to leave. 'Six letters in the stack.'

'I don't care if it's one.'

'Yes, you do. You're a great writer but a terrible liar, sweetie.'

For once, Lisbeth stayed silent.

'By the way,' Vincent added, 'if a publicist calls for some art award for the John family . . . don't be such a snob. Think Page Six. Good bold names are good bold names.'

'But if the story's crap—'

'I hate to break it to you, pumpkin,' Vincent called out, already halfway down the hallway, 'but there's no Pulitzer for gossip.'

Alone in her cubicle, Lisbeth studied the empty grid on her screen, then looked down at the crumpled sheet of paper in her trash. She bent down below her desk to pull it from the garbage, and the phone rang above her. At the noise, she bolted upward, smashing the back of her head against the corner of her desk.

'Aaahh,' she yelled, rubbing her head fiercely as she reached for the phone. 'Below the Fold. This is Lisbeth.'

'Hi, I . . . uh . . . I work over at the Four Seasons,' a male voice began. 'Is this the place you call for—?'

'Only if it's a good one,' Lisbeth said, still rubbing, but all too aware what he was asking. It was the deal she made with all local hotel employees. A hundred bucks for any tip she used in the column.

'Well . . . uh . . . I was serving some of President Manning's old employees,' he said. 'And . . . I don't know if they count as celebrities, but if you're interested . . .'

'No, I'm definitely interested.' She hit the *Record* button and scrambled for a pen. Even on her best days, there was no bigger bold name than *Manning*. 'Those're exactly the type of people we love to write about.'

17

'Maybe it'd be better if we stepped outside,' O'Shea suggests, towering over me in the restaurant. He's got a buckled nose that makes it clear he's not afraid to take a punch. He tries to hide it with his sunglasses, but some things are hard to miss. The moment he flashed an FBI badge, people turned to stare.

'Yeah . . . that'd be great,' I reply, calmly standing from my seat and following him through the open-air walkway that leads to the pool area outside. If I plan on keeping this quiet, the last thing I need is to be spotted with the FBI in a public place.

Surrounded by palm trees on all sides, the pool is a picture of privacy – this early in the morning, all the lounge chairs are empty – but for some reason, O'Shea doesn't slow down. It's not until we pass one of the many over-size potted plants that I see what he's looking at: two guys in a small wooden cabana folding towels, getting ready for the day. O'Shea keeps walking. Whatever he wants, he wants it in private.

'Listen, can you tell me where we're—?'

'How was your trip to Malaysia?' As he asks the question, I'm staring at the back of O'Shea's head. He doesn't even turn around to see my reaction.

'Um . . . it was fine.'

'And the President had a good time?'

'I don't see why he wouldn't,' I reply, annoyed.

'Anything else of note happen?' O'Shea asks, heading down a short path that's covered with water. A wave crashes in the distance, but it's not until a cascade of sand fills my loafers that I realize we're on the private beach behind the pool. Empty lounge chairs, empty lifeguard stands. The vacant beach goes on for miles.

As we pass a tiny hut that's used for snorkeling gear rentals, a man with finely combed brown hair steps out from behind it and pats me on the back. He's got a small nick that's missing from the top of his left ear.

'Say hi to my partner. Micah,' O'Shea explains.

I turn back to the hotel, but thanks to the wall of palm trees, I can only make out a few terraces on the top floors of the building. Not a soul in sight. It's at that same moment I realize Micah has slowed his pace, so he's now slightly behind me.

'Maybe you should take a seat,' O'Shea adds, motioning to one of the lounges.

'It'll only take a second,' Micah adds behind me.

Spinning around, I start back toward the path. 'I should really get—'

'We saw the report you filed with the Service, Wes. We know who you saw in Malaysia.'

I stop right there, almost tripping in the sand. As I find my balance and turn to face them, O'Shea and Micah have the ocean at their backs. The waves pound ruthlessly. Subtlety isn't their strong point.

'What're you talking about?' I ask.

'The report,' O'Shea says. 'Fifty-something guy with Boyle's height, Boyle's weight, Boyle's shaved bald head, though for some reason you left out his eye color – and the fact you thought it was him.'

'Listen, I don't know *what* I saw that night . . .'

'It's okay, Wes,' Micah says with a singsong quality to his voice. 'Boyle *was* in Malaysia. You're not crazy.'

Most people would be relieved. But I've been around law enforcement long enough to know their tricks and treats. This one's called *tone matching*. Designed to subconsciously affect a target's mood, it's built on the fact that you tend to match the tone that's aimed at you. When someone yells, you yell back. Whisper, you whisper back. Usually, they use it to strengthen a witness who's depressed, or bring down a target who's cocky. Micah just sang to me, hoping I'd sing back. There's only one problem. FBI agents don't sing – and I don't either. If they're using mind games, there's something they're not saying.

'Boyle's really alive?' I ask, refusing to admit anything.

O'Shea studies me carefully. For the first time, he's staring at my scars. 'I know this is personal for you—'

'That's *not* what this is about!' I shoot back.

'Wes, we're not here to attack,' Micah says softly.

'And enough with the damn voice tricks! Just tell me what the hell is going on!'

The wind rockets across the shore, blowing Micah's tightly combed hair out of place. O'Shea shifts his weight, uncomfortable in the sand and well aware he picked the wrong button to press. It's not just their suits that make them stand out. The two agents exchange a glance. O'Shea offers a small nod.

'Boyle ever mention a group he called *The Three*?' Micah finally asks.

I shake my head no.

'What about *The Roman*?'

'Is that a group too?'

'It's a person,' O'Shea says, watching my reaction.

'Am I supposed to know him?' I ask.

For the second time, the two agents share a glance. O'Shea squints against the morning sun as it burns through the clouds. 'You have any idea how long we've been hunting Boyle?' O'Shea asks. 'Y'think this all started with his miraculous "death"? We were chasing him back in the White House, just waiting for him to screw up. And then when he did . . . poof . . . world's greatest get-out-of-jail-free card.'

'So when he was shot . . .'

'. . . we got snookered. Just like the rest of America. Even closed the case and filed the files. Three years later, he made his first mistake and got spotted in Spain by some local ex-pat who was just enough of a political junkie to recognize him. Lucky us, he calls it in, but before we could even do follow-up, the witness's car mysteriously blows up in front of his house. Pro job too – Semtex-H with a pressure-touch switch. Lucky us again, no one's hurt, but the message is sent. Witness decides he never saw anything.'

'And you think Boyle knows Semtex-H? I mean . . . he's an accountant.'

'Which means he knows how to pay people and manipulate and keep his fingerprints off everything no matter what he touches.'

'But he . . .'

'. . . makes his living preying on people. That's what he does, Wes. It's what he did in the White House . . . and with our agents . . . and especially with the Service.'

Reading the confusion on my face, he adds, 'C'mon, you must've figured this one out. The twelve minutes in the ambulance . . . the extra blood . . . Why do you think Manning and the Service helped him? Out of the kindness of their hearts? He's a termite, Wes – digging into the vulnerable, then exploiting their weaknesses. D'you understand what I'm saying? He thrives on weaknesses. All weaknesses.'

The way he studies me . . . the way his glowing blue eyes lock onto mine . . . 'Wait, are you saying *I*—?'

'We checked your file, Wes,' O'Shea adds, pulling a folded sheet of paper from inside his jacket. 'Seven months with a Dr. Collins White, who it says here is a *critical incident specialist.* Sounds pretty technical.'

'Where'd you get that?' I ask.

'And the analysis: panic disorder and post-traumatic stress comorbidity . . .'

'That was eight years ago!' I tell them.

'. . . triggering compulsive behavior involving light switches, locking and unlocking doors . . .'

'That's not even—'

'. . . and a full-fledged obsession with the need for repetitive praying,' O'Shea continues, unconcerned. 'That true? What, was that your way of dealing with the shooting? Saying the same prayers over and over?' He flips over to the second page. 'Not even religious, are you? That's a real Nico reaction.'

To my own surprise, my eyes well up and my throat tightens. It's been a long time since anyone—

'I know it was hard for you, Wes,' O'Shea adds. 'Even harder than the way you stapled your fingers with Boyle. But if he has something over you, we can help you out of it.'

Help me out of it? 'You think I'd—?'

'Whatever he offered you, you'll only get burned.'

'He didn't offer me *anything*,' I insist.

'Is that why you were fighting?'

'Fighting? What're you—?'

'The broken coffee table? The shattered glass from where you hit it? We saw the report,' Micah interrupts, his singsong voice long gone.

'I didn't know he was back there!'

'Really?' Micah asks, his voice picking up speed. 'In the middle of a speech in a foreign country, you leave the President's side – where you were supposed to be . . .'

'I swear—'

'. . . and disappear backstage to the one room where Boyle happens to be hiding—'

'I didn't know!' I yell.

'We have agents who were there!' Micah explodes. 'They found the fake name Boyle used in the hotel! When they interviewed the desk clerks on duty that night, one of them picked out *your photo*, saying *you* were the one looking for *him*! Now do you wanna start over, or do you wanna bury yourself even deeper? Just tell us why Manning sent you instead of the Service to meet him.'

It's the second time they've confirmed Manning and the Service being involved – and the first time I realize I'm not the one they're after. Big hunters want big game. And why take a cub when you can bag the Lion?

'We know Manning's been good to you—'

'You don't know anything about him.'

'Actually, we do,' O'Shea says. 'Just like we know Boyle. Believe me, Wes, when they were in power, you didn't see half of what they—'

'I was with them every day!'

'You were with them for the last eight months, when all they cared about was reelection. You think that's reality? Just because you know what they like on their turkey sandwiches doesn't mean you know what they're capable of.'

If I were Rogo, I'd rush forward and bury my fist in his jaw. Instead, I dig my foot in the sand. Anything to help me keep standing. From what they're saying, Manning definitely has some pretty dark dirt on his hands. Maybe they're just fishing. Maybe it's the truth. Either way, after everything Manning's done for me . . . after taking me back in and being by my side all these years . . . I'm not biting that hand until I know the facts myself.

'Ever see a three-car collision?' Micah asks. 'Y'know which car suffers the most damage? The one in the middle.' He pauses just long enough to let it all sink in. 'Manning, you, Boyle. Which car d'you think *you* are?'

I grind my leg even deeper into the sand. 'That's . . . that's not—'

'By the way, where'd you get the nice timepiece?' Micah interrupts, motioning to my vintage Franck Muller watch. 'That's a ten-thousand-dollar bauble.'

'What're you—? It was a gift from the president of Senegal,' I explain. At home, I've got at least a half dozen more, including a platinum Vacheron Constantin given by the Saudi crown prince. When we were in office, they became gifts of the White House. Today, there're no rules on giving to former Presidents and his staff. But before I can tell him—

'Mr Holloway,' a voice calls out behind me.

I turn just in time to see my waiter from breakfast. He's up by the pool area, holding my credit card in his hand.

'Sorry . . . didn't want you to forget this,' he calls out, now scrambling toward us on the beach.

O'Shea turns toward the ocean so the waiter can't hear. 'Focus, Wes – are you really that blindly devoted? You know they lied to you. You keep covering for them and you're just gonna be someone who needs a lawyer.'

'Here you go, sir,' the waiter says.

'Thanks,' I reply, forcing a half-smile.

O'Shea and Micah aren't nearly as kind. From the angry glares they drill my way, they still want more. The problem is, I don't have anything to give them. At least not yet. And until I do, I've got nothing to barter for protection.

'Wait up . . . I'll walk out with you,' I say, pivoting in the sand and falling in line behind the waiter.

Years ago, I used to bite at a small callus on the side of my pointer finger. When I got to the White House, Dreidel made me stop, saying it looked bad in the background of the President's photos. For the first time in a decade, I start gnawing at it.

'See you soon,' O'Shea calls out.

I don't bother to answer.

As we reach the pool area, there's a young family getting an early start on the day. Dad unpacks a newspaper, Mom unpacks a paperback, and their three-year-old boy with a bowl haircut is on his hands and knees, playing with two Matchbox cars, ramming them head-on, over and over, into each other.

I look over my shoulder and glance back at the beach. O'Shea and Micah are already gone.

They're right about one thing: I definitely need a lawyer. Fortunately, I know exactly where to find one.

18

Washington, D.C.

'*You know they lied to you. You keep covering for them and you're just gonna be someone who needs a lawyer.*'

'*Here you go, sir.*'

'*Thanks,*' Wes's voice said, coming through the small speaker on the edge of the short metal file cabinet. '*Wait up . . . I'll walk out with you.*'

Adjusting the volume, The Roman turned the knob slightly, his thick, steely hands almost too big for the job. When he was little, he only fit into his grandfather's gloves. But after years of tying lures onto fishing string, he'd mastered the art of a soft touch.

'*Have a wonderful day, Mr Holloway,*' a voice squawked through the speaker.

Getting a small enough microphone was the easy part. So was getting a transmitter that ran on a satellite signal so it would broadcast halfway across the country. Protecting the President was the Secret Service's specialty, but with jurisdiction over counterfeiting and financial crimes, their Intelligence Division had one of the most formidable surveillance operations in the world. Indeed, the only hard part was figuring out a place to hide it. And someone to put it there.

The phone rang on the corner of his desk, and The Roman glanced down at caller ID. Dark digital letters read

Offices of Leland Manning. The Roman smiled to himself, brushing his black hair from his chalky skin. If only the bass were this predictable.

'Any problems?' The Roman asked as he picked up the phone.

'Not a one. I did it first thing this morning. Put it in that lapel pin just like you said.'

'So I gathered from his last two hours of conversation.'

Reaching down, The Roman tugged open the bottom drawer of the file cabinet, and his fingertips tap-danced to the last file in back. The only unmarked one in there.

'Wes say anything interesting yet?' his associate asked.

'He's getting there,' The Roman replied, flipping open the file on his desk and revealing a small stack of black-and-white photos.

'What about you? If your investigation's so vital . . . I thought you were coming down here.'

'I'll be there,' The Roman said as he stared down at the pictures. Graying from age, all of them were from the day at the speedway. One of Nico with the Service tackling him to the ground, one of the President being shoved inside his limo, and of course, one of Boyle, in mid-clap moments before he was shot. The smile on Boyle's face looked unbreakable . . . his cheeks frozen, teeth gleaming. The Roman couldn't take his eyes off it. 'I just have to take care of one thing first.'

19

Palm Beach, Florida

'Where is he?' I ask, rushing through the welcome area of the small office with its dozens of potted plants and orchids.

'Inside,' the receptionist says, 'but you can't—'

She's already too late. I cut past her cheap Formica desk that looks suspiciously like the one I threw away a few weeks ago and head for the door covered with old Florida license plates. Beyond the plants, which were the standard thank-you gift from clients, the office had all the design sense of a fifteen-year-old boy. It didn't matter. Moving over the bridge a year ago, Rogo took this office so he'd have a proper Palm Beach address. When you're targeting the rich, and 95 percent of your business is done by mail, that's all you need.

'Wes, he's busy in there!' the receptionist calls out.

I twist the doorknob, shove open the door, and send it slamming into the wall. Standing at his desk, Rogo jumps at the sound. 'Wes, that you?' His eyes are closed. As he tries to make his way toward me, he taps his blotter and pencil cup and keyboard like a blind man feeling his way.

'What happened to your eyes?' I ask.

'Eye doctor. Dilated,' Rogo says, patting a picture frame of his childhood dog. The frame falls and he fumbles to pick it up. 'Being blind sucks,' he says.

'I need to talk to you.'

'Meanwhile, ready for new levels of pathetic? When I was at the doctor, I *cheated* on my eye exam. Before he got in there, he left the eye chart up – y'know with the giant *E* and the little *N3QFD* at the bottom? I memorized it, then spit it right back at him. Suckaaaaaa!'

'Rogo . . .'

'I mean, that's even more sad-sack than—'

'Boyle's alive.'

Rogo stops patting the picture frame and turns straight at me. 'Wha wha?'

'I saw him. Boyle's alive,' I repeat. I slowly slink toward one of the chairs across from his desk. Rogo turns his head, following me perfectly.

'You can see, can't you?' I ask.

'Yeah,' he replies, still in shock.

'And is that my old desk out there in your reception area?'

'Yeah. I picked it up when you threw it away.'

'Rogo, I left that desk for charity.'

'And I thank you for that. Now would you like to tell me what the hell you're talking about with your dead former coworker?'

'I swear to you – I saw him . . . I spoke to him.'

'Did he look—?'

'He got plastic surgery.'

'Well, who wouldn't?'

'I'm serious. The shooting . . . that day at the speedway . . . it was . . . it wasn't how it looked.'

It takes me almost a half hour to fill him in on the rest of the details, from backstage in Malaysia, to Dreidel's info about the O-negative blood, to the FBI cornering me on the beach and asking me about The Roman and The

Three. Forever a lawyer, he never interrupts. Forever Rogo, his reaction is instantaneous.

'You told Dreidel before *me*?'

'Oh, please . . .'

'I was in the car with you this morning. What, you were so enraptured by classic hits from the eighties, nineties, and today that you forget to mention, "Oh, by the way, that guy who died and cratered my life? Well, he must be on some all-bran diet, because he's actually *living*"?'

'Rogo . . .'

'Can I just say one more thing?'

'Is it about Dreidel?'

He crosses his arms against his chest. 'No.'

'Okay, then just—'

'You're in trouble, Wes.'

I blink about four times trying to digest the words. Coming from Rogo, they hit even harder than the waves on the beach.

'I'm serious,' Rogo continues. 'They pinned you. Just by seeing Boyle, the FBI now thinks you're part of this. You don't help them and they stick you as an accessory to whatever Boyle and Manning were up to. You do help 'em and . . .'

'. . . I kiss away whatever life I have left. What d'you think I'm doing here? I need help.'

When I asked Dreidel, he hesitated, weighing the personal and political consequences. Rogo's always been built a little bit differently. 'Just tell me who to punch.'

For the first time in the last forty-eight hours, I actually half smile.

'What,' he asks, 'you think I'm letting you get beat up all by yourself?'

'I was thinking of going to Manning,' I tell him.

'And I was thinking you should start worrying about yourself for once.'

'Will you stop with that?'

'Then stop being the buttboy. Didn't you hear what the FBI said? The President was in on it, whatever the hell *it* is! I mean, how else do you explain Nico getting that close and sneaking a gun past all those Secret Service agents? Y'smell that? That's the whiff of an inside job.'

'Maybe that's where The Roman and The Three come in.'

'And those're the names the FBI mentioned?'

'That's why I want to go to Manning first. Maybe he'll—'

'Do you even hear yourself when you speak!? You go to Manning and you risk alerting the one person who has the best reason of all to put you in the guillotine. Now I'm sorry if that ruins the tiny safe haven you've built for yourself over the past eight years, but it's time to pay attention. The scars on your face, despite what you think, are *not penance*. You don't owe anybody anything.'

'That's not the point.'

'No, the point is: Leland Manning is a good man. Even a great man. But like any other man – especially one who runs for office – he will lie *straight to your face* when he needs to. Just do the math, Wes: How many U.S. Presidents you ever seen in jail? Now how many lower-level aides who swear they're innocent?'

For the first time, I don't answer.

'Exactly,' Rogo continues. 'Taking down a President is like demolishing a building – very little explosion and lots of gravity. Right now you're too damn close to getting sucked in the hole.'

'That doesn't mean he's a monster.'

'Please, you wouldn't even be here if you didn't think there were crawdads in your bed.'

Sitting across from him, I keep my eyes on the carpet. During our final week in office, former Presidents Bush, Clinton, all of them called. But it was Bush Senior who gave Manning the best advice. He told him that 'when you get off Air Force One, wave from the top of the steps . . . and when the lonely TV interviewer standing on the tarmac asks, "How does it feel to be home?" you go, "Great to be back!" And you look ahead and you try not to think what it used to be like just four or five hours before.' When our plane touched down, Manning did just that. He told that lie with ease and a perfect grin.

Rogo watches me carefully as I bite at the callus on my hand.

'I know what he means to you, Wes.'

'No. You don't.' I shove my hand under my thigh. 'Just tell me what you think I should do.'

'You already know what I think,' Rogo says with a grin. Even when he used to get his ass kicked, he's always loved a good fight. He pulls a notepad from his desk and starts hunting for a pen. 'Y'know why I get a 96 percent dismissal rate on speeding tickets? Or 92 percent on illegal U-turns? Because I dig, dig, dig, and dig some more. Check the details, Wes: If the cop puts the wrong statute number on the ticket, dismiss. If he doesn't bring his ticket log, dismiss. Always comes down to the details – which is why I wanna know who the hell The Three and this guy The Roman are.'

'You still have that buddy at the police station?'

'How else you think I get the list of speeding ticket violators two hours before anyone else? He'll run whoever we need.'

'Dreidel said he'd look up some of the other stuff too. He's always good at—'

My phone vibrates in my pocket. Flipping it open, I spot a familiar number. Perfect timing.

'Any news?' I ask, picking up.

'Did you tip her?' Dreidel blurts, his voice racing.

'Excuse me?'

'The reporter – Lisbeth something – from the *Palm Beach Post* . . .' He takes a breath to stay calm. All it does is tell me something's wrong. 'Did you call her this morning?'

'I don't know what you're—'

'It's okay if you did . . . I'm not mad . . . I just need to know what you said.'

It's the second time he's cut me off. And like any other young politician, the moment he says he's not mad is the exact same moment he'll rip your tongue out.

'Dreidel, I swear, I didn't—'

'Then how'd she know we were meeting!? She had that I drank coffee and ate some of your toast! Who'd you . . . ?' Catching himself, he again lowers his voice. 'Just . . . who else did you tell?'

I look over at Rogo. 'No one. No one that could've called her. I swear . . .'

'Okay, it's okay,' he tells himself more than me. 'I just . . . I need you to kill the story, okay? She's calling you now for a quote. Can you do me that favor and kill it?' I've known Dreidel for almost a decade. Last time I heard him this panicked, he had the First Lady screaming at him. 'Please, Wes.'

'Fine . . . that's fine . . . but why're you so nervous about some dumb breakfast?'

'No, not a breakfast. A breakfast in Palm Beach.

Florida . . . when my wife thought I was still checking out of my hotel from the meeting I had yesterday. In *Atlanta*.'

He gives me a minute to connect the dots.

'Wait, so that woman . . . You didn't just meet her at a bar . . .'

'Jean. Her name's Jean. And yes, I left Atlanta and flew in early for her. I met her a few months ago. Okay? You happy? Now you got all the juice. All I'm asking is that you keep it away from this gossip woman, because if that story runs tomorrow and Ellen sees it—'

There's a click on my phone.

'That's her,' Dreidel says. 'All you have to do is bury it. Trade her something . . . give her ten minutes with Manning. Please, Wes – my family – just think of Ali,' he adds, referring to his daughter. 'And my State Senate race.'

Before I can even react, there's another click. I hit the *Send* button on my phone and pick up the other line.

'Wes here,' I answer.

'Mr Holloway, Gerald Lang here,' he says, his tone dry and professorial. 'From the curator's office,' he explains, referring to the Manning Presidential Library. 'Claudia suggested I ring you and—'

'Now's not actually the best time.'

'It'll only take a moment, sir. See, we're putting together a new exhibit about presidential service, with a particular focus on the long history of the young men who have served as presidential aides. Sort of a . . . true retrospective, if you can imagine . . . everyone from Meriwether Lewis, who served under Thomas Jefferson, to Jack Valenti, who worked with LBJ, to eventually, hopefully, well . . . yourself.'

'Wait . . . this exhibit's about . . . *me?*'

'Actually, more the others, of course. A true retrospective.'

He's already backpedaling, which means he knows the rules. My job is to be the closest man to the President. Right beside him. But never in front of him. 'I appreciate the offer, Mr Lang . . .'

'Gerald.'

'And I'd love to help, Gerald, but—'

'President Manning said it was okay,' he adds, pulling the trump card. 'Claudia too. A true retrospective. So when do you think we can sit down and—?'

'Later, okay? Just . . . call me later.' Rushing off the phone, I click back to Dreidel.

'What'd she say? Does she know?' Dreidel asks, still panicking.

Before I can answer, my phone clicks again. Clearly, my curator friend didn't get the point. 'Let me just get rid of this guy,' I tell Dreidel, once again clicking over. 'Gerald, I already told you—'

'Who's Gerald?' a female voice interrupts.

'E-Excuse me?'

'Hiya there, Wes, this is Lisbeth Dodson from the *Palm Beach Post*. How'd you like to have your name in bold?'

20

Washington, D.C.

The left front tire dove into the pothole at full speed, slicing through the puddle of melted snow and unleashing a jarring punch that shook the black SUV. With a twist of the steering wheel, the car jerked to the right. A second punch pummeled the car. The Roman cursed to himself. D.C. roads were bad enough. But southeast Washington was always the worst.

Flicking on his wipers, he brushed a light dust of snow from the windshield and made a sharp left onto Malcolm X Avenue. The burned-out cars, overpiled trash cans, and boarded-up buildings told him this wasn't a neighborhood to be lost in. Fortunately, he knew exactly where he was going.

Within a mile, the car bucked to a halt at the light where Malcolm X intersected with Martin Luther King Jr. Avenue. The Roman couldn't help but grin to himself. For eight years, he'd relied a great deal on peaceful co-existence. But now, with Boyle's reappearance . . . with Wes as a witness . . . even with O'Shea and Micah closing in . . . sometimes there was no choice left but the tough one.

It was no different eight years ago when they first approached Nico. Of course, not all three of them were there. For safety, only one went. Naturally, Nico was hesitant – even belligerent. No one likes seeing his family attacked. But that's when Nico was shown the proof: the records from his mother's stay in the hospital.

'What's this?' Nico had asked, scanning the sheet of paper filled with room numbers and delivery times. The single word *Dinner* was handwritten across the top.

'It's the hospital's meal delivery log,' Number Three explained. 'From the day your mother died.'

Sure enough, Nico saw his mother's name. *Hadrian, Mary.* And her old room number. *Room 913.* And even what she ordered. *Meat loaf.* But what confused him was the handwritten notation in the column marked *Attempted Delivery.* On the sheet, every patient had a different delivery time: *6:03 p.m. . . . 6:09 p.m. . . . 6:12 p.m. . . .* Except for Nico's mom, where it simply said *patient deceased.*

Nico looked up, clearly confused. 'I don't understand. This is from her final Sunday . . . from the day she died?'

'Not exactly,' he told him. 'Look at the date in the corner. September 16th, right?' As Nico nodded, he quickly explained, 'September 16th was a Saturday, Nico. According to these records, your mom died on a Saturday.'

'No,' Nico insisted. 'She died Sunday. Sunday, September 17th. I remember, I was – We were in church.' Staring down at the meal delivery log, he added, 'How could this happen?'

'No, Nico. The real question is, why would someone do that?'

Nico shook his head furiously. 'No, there's no way. We were in church. In the second row. I remember my father coming in and—'

Nico froze.

'That's the great thing about church, isn't it, Nico? When the whole town's packed into the pews and watching your concerned father praying with his two young kids . . . it really is the perfect alibi.'

'Wait . . . you're saying my dad killed my—'

'What was it, three years since she'd lapsed into that coma? Three years with no mom. No one running the house. Every day – all those prayers and visits – her illness consuming your lives.'

'He'd never do that! He loved her!'

'He loved you *more*, Nico. You'd already lost three years of your childhood. That's why he did it. For you. He did it *for you.*'

'B-But the doctors . . . wouldn't the coroner . . . ?'

'Dr. Albie Morales – the neurologist who pronounced her dead – is the *worshipful master* in charge of your father's Masonic Lodge. Coroner Turner Sinclair – who filed the rest of the paperwork – is the deacon of that same Lodge. That's what Masons do, Nico. That's what they've done throughout histor—'

'You're lying!' Nico exploded, cupping his hands over his ears. 'Please be lying!'

'He did it for you, Nico.'

Nico was rocking fast – forward and back – as his tears rained down in thick drops to the sheet of paper that held his mother's final dinner order. 'When she died . . . that was . . . she died for *my* sins! *Not his!*' he wailed like a ten-year-old boy, his entire belief system shattered. 'She was supposed to die for *my sins!*'

And that's when The Three knew they had him.

Of course, that's also why they picked him in the first place. It wasn't difficult. With The Roman's access to military files, they focused on the records of Fort Benning and Fort Bragg, which housed two of the army's top sniper schools. Add the words *dishonorable discharge* and *psychological problems*, and the list narrowed quickly. Nico was actually third. But when they did some more digging – when they saw his religious devotion and found his father's group affiliation – Nico went right to the top of the list.

From there, all they had to do was find him. Since all transitional housing and homeless shelters receiving government funds must submit the names of those using the facility, that part was easy. Then they had to prove he could be controlled. That's why they took him back to his dad's mobile home. And gave him the gun. And told him that there was only one way to set his mother's spirit free.

During sniper training, Nico was taught to shoot between heartbeats to reduce barrel motion. Standing over his father, who was sobbing for mercy on the peeling linoleum floor, Nico pulled the trigger without hesitation.

And The Three realized they had their man.

All thanks to nothing more than a single sheet of paper with a fake hospital meal log.

As the traffic light blinked green, The Roman turned left and slammed the gas, sending his back wheels spinning and bits of slush spraying through the air. The car fishtailed on the never-plowed road, then quickly settled under The Roman's tight grip. He'd put in far too much time to lose control now.

In the distance, the old storefronts and buildings gave way to rusted black metal gates that fenced in the wide-open grounds and were supposed to make the neighborhood feel safer. But with twenty-two patients escaping in the last year, most neighbors understood that the gates weren't exactly living up to their expectations.

Ignoring the chapel and another towering brick building just beyond the gates, The Roman made a sharp right and stayed focused on the small guardhouse right inside the main entrance. It'd been almost eight years since the last time he was here. And as he rolled down his window and saw the peeling paint on the black and yellow gate arm, he realized nothing had changed, including the security procedures.

'Welcome to St. Elizabeths,' a guard with winter-grizzled lips said. 'Visitor or delivery?'

'Visitor,' The Roman replied, flashing a Secret Service badge and never breaking eye contact. Like every agent before him, when Roland Egen first joined the Service, he didn't start in Protective Operations. With the Service's authority over financial crimes, he first spent five years investigating counterfeit rings and computer crime in the Houston field office. From there, he got his first protective assignment, assessing threats for the Intelligence Division, and from there – thanks to his flair for criminal investigations – he rose through the ranks in the Pretoria and Rome offices. It was raw determination that helped him claw his way up through the Secret Service hierarchy to his current position as deputy assistant director of Protective Operations. But it was in his after-hours work as *The Roman* where he reaped his best rewards. 'I'm here for Nicholas Hadrian.'

'Nico's in trouble, huh?' the guard asked. 'Funny, he always says someone's coming. For once, he's actually right.'

'Yeah,' The Roman said, glancing up at the tiny cross on the roof of the old brick chapel in the distance. 'Pretty damn hysterical.'

21

Palm Beach, Florida

'Anyway, it's just a cute little squib with you and Dreidel eating at the Four Seasons,' Lisbeth says as Rogo squeezes in next to me and puts his ear to the phone. 'Sorta making the restaurant like a White House reunion in the sunny South. The President's boys and all that.'

'Sounds fun,' I tell her, hoping to keep her upbeat. 'Though I'm not sure that's actually news.'

'Amazing,' she says sarcastically. 'That's exactly what Dreidel said. You guys separated at birth, or does it just come naturally with the job?'

I've known Lisbeth since the day she took over the *Post*'s gossip column. We have a clear understanding. She calls and politely asks for a quote from the President. I politely tell her we're sorry, but we don't do those things anymore. It's a simple waltz. The problem is, if I don't play this carefully, I'll be giving her something to jitterbug to.

'C'mon, Lisbeth, no one even knows who me and Dreidel are.'

'Yep, Dreidel tried that one too. Right before he asked if he could call me back, which I also know is a guaranteed sign I'll never hear from him again. I mean, considering he's got that little fundraiser tonight, you'd think he'd want his name in the local paper. Now do you just wanna give me a throwaway quote on how great it was for you and your friend to reminisce about your old White House days, or do you want me to start worrying that there's something wrong in Manningville?' She laughs as she says the words, but I've been around enough reporters to know that when it comes to filling their columns, nothing's funny.

Careful, Rogo writes on a scrap of paper. *Girl ain't stupid.*

I nod and turn back to the phone. 'Listen, I'm happy to give you whatever quote you want, but honestly, we were only in the restaurant for a few minutes—'

'And that's officially the third time you've tried to down-play this otherwise yawn of a story. Know what they teach you in journalism school when someone tries to down-play, Wes?'

On the scrap of paper, Rogo adds an exclamation point next to *Girl ain't stupid.*

'Okay, fine. Wanna know the real story?' I ask.

'No, I'd much prefer the fake runaround.'

'But this is off the record,' I warn. She stays silent, hoping I'll keep talking. It's an old reporter's trick so she can say she never agreed. I fell for it my first week in the White House. That was the last time. 'Lisbeth . . .'

'Fine . . . yes . . . off the record. Now what's the big hubbub?'

'Manning's birthday,' I blurt. 'His surprise sixty-fifth, to be exact. Dreidel and I were in charge of the surprise part until you called this morning. I told Manning I had some errands to run. Dreidel was in town and told him the same. If Manning reads in tomorrow's paper that we were together . . .' I pause for effect. It's a crap lie, but her silence tells me it's doing the trick. 'You know we never ask for anything, Lisbeth, but if you could keep us out just this once . . .' I pause again for the big finale. 'We'd owe you one.'

I can practically hear her smile on the other line. In a city of social chits, it's the best one to bargain with: a favor owed by the former President of the United States.

'Gimme ten minutes face-to-face with Manning on the night of the surprise party,' Lisbeth says.

'Five minutes is the most he'll sit for.'

Rogo shakes his head. *Not enough*, he mouths silently.

'Deal,' she says.

Rogo makes a double okay sign with his fingers. *Perfect*, he mouths.

'So my breakfast with Dreidel . . . ?' I ask.

'Breakfast? Come now, Wes – why would anyone care what two former staffers had on their morning toast? Consider it officially dead.'

22

'You know we never ask for anything, Lisbeth, but if you could keep us out just this once . . .'

As she listened to Wes's words, Lisbeth sat up in her seat and began to spin the phone cord, jump-rope-style. From the forced pause on the other line, Wes sounded like he was ready to trade. 'We'd owe you one,' he offered, right on cue. Lisbeth stopped the phone cord's spinning. Sacred Rule #4: Only the guilty trade. Sacred Rule #5: And the opportunists.

'Gimme ten minutes face-to-face with Manning on the night of the surprise party,' she said, knowing that like any good publicist, he'd knock the time in half.

'Five minutes is the most he'll sit for.'

'Deal,' she said as she started rifling through the thick stack of invites on the far corner of her desk. Opening concert at the opera. The annual craft bazaar at the Sail-fish Club. Baby naming at the Whedons. It had to be here somewhere . . .

'So my breakfast with Dreidel . . . ?' Wes asked.

Still flipping through the stack, Lisbeth was barely paying attention. 'Breakfast? Come now, Wes – why would anyone care what two former staffers had on their morning toast? Consider it officially dead.'

Manning's surprise party – and her promised five minutes – weren't for at least another month. But that didn't mean she had to stay away until then. Especially when there were so many other ways to get in close. Slamming down the phone, Lisbeth never took her eyes off the stack. Reception for the Leukemia Society, Historical Society, Knesset Society, Palm Beach Society, Renaissance Society, Alexis de Tocqueville Society . . . and then . . . there . . .

Lisbeth yanked the rectangular card from the middle of the stack. Like every other invite, the design was understated, the printing was meticulous, and the envelope had her name on it. But this one, with its cream-colored card stock and twirling black calligraphy, also had something more: *An Evening with President Leland F. Manning. Benefiting 65 Roses – the Cystic Fibrosis Foundation.* Tonight.

She didn't mind the fake stalling from Wes and Dreidel. Or the nonsense about Manning's so-called surprise party. But once Wes asked her to kill the piece . . . Sacred Rule #6: There were only two kinds of people in a gossip column – those who want to be in there, and those who don't. Wes just put himself on the *don't* side. And without a doubt, the *don'ts* were always far more interesting.

Picking up the phone, Lisbeth dialed the number on the invite.

'This is Claire Tanz,' an older woman answered.

'Hi, Claire, this is Lisbeth Dodson from Below the Fold. I hope it's not too late to RSVP—'

'For tonight? No, no . . . oh, we read you every day,' the woman said just a bit too excited. 'Oooh, and I can call the President's staff and let them know you'll be there . . .'

'That's okay,' Lisbeth said calmly. 'I just got off the phone with them. They're already thrilled I'm coming.'

23

Three and a half minutes, Nico told himself as he watched the gray Acura cut through the snow and pass along the service road just outside his second-story shatterproof window. Pulling up the sleeve of his faded brown sweat-shirt, he glanced down at the second hand on his watch, counting to himself. *One minute . . . two . . . three . . .* Nico closed his eyes and began to pray. His head bobbed sixteen times. *Three and a half . . .* Rocking slowly, he opened his eyes and turned to the door of his room. The door didn't open.

Perched atop the rusted radiator just inside his window, Nico continued to rock slowly, turning back to the falling snow and bowing the A-string of his well-worn maple violin. The violin had a tiny four-leaf clover inlay in the tailpiece, but Nico was far more interested in the way the fiddle's strings perfectly crossed the ebony bridge as they ran up the fingerboard. When he first arrived at St. Elizabeths, he spent his first two weeks sitting in the exact same place, staring out the exact same window. Naturally, the doctors discouraged it – '*antisocial and escapist,*' they declared.

It only got worse when they examined Nico's view: on his right, a burned-out brick building with an army crest on it ('*too symbolic of his military past*'); on his left, the edges of the Anacostia River ('*don't reward him with a quality view*'); and in the far distance, at the very edge of the property, half a dozen fenced-in fields with hundreds of crumbling headstones from the Civil War to World War I, when army and navy patients were still buried on the property ('*death should never be a focal point*'). Yet when Nico mentioned to a nurse that the dogwood tree just outside his window reminded him of his childhood home in Wisconsin, where his mother played cello and the wind sent the tree's branches swaying to the music, the doctors not only backed off, they got someone to donate the fiddle with the four-leaf clover inlay. '*Positive memories were to be encouraged.*' Nico knew it was a sign. Just as God had written in the Book. As God had sent them. The Fiddlers Three.

Eight years later, Nico still lived in the same room, surrounded by the same small bed, the same nightstand, and the same painted dresser that held his Bible and red glass rosary beads.

But what Nico always kept to himself was that while he did study the dogwood, and it did remind him of early days with his mom, he was far more focused on the well-worn service road that ran just in front of it, up from the main gate, across the property, and around to the parking lot that led to the entrance of the John Howard Pavilion. The tree was surely a sign – Christ's cross was built from a dogwood – but the road in front of it . . . the road was the path of Nico's salvation. He knew it in his heart. He knew it in his soul. He knew it the very first day he saw the road, littered with weeds and grass that cracked and clawed through its beaten, asphalt hide. Every year, the ground buckled slightly as the weeds shoved a bit further. Like a monster, Nico thought. A monster within. Just like the monsters who killed his mother.

He didn't want to pull the trigger. Not at first. Not even when The Three reminded him of his father's sin.

But as he stared down at the proof – at the delivery log from the hospital . . .

'Ask your father,' Number Three said. 'He won't deny it.'

Rocking to himself as he stared out the window of the hospital, Nico could still hear the words. Still smell his dad's sweet cigar smoke. Still feel the sharp Wisconsin wind cracking his lungs as he hopped up the metal front steps of his dad's mobile home. He hadn't seen his father in almost six years. Before the army . . . before the discharge . . . before the shelter. Nico didn't even know how to find him. But The Three did. The Three helped him. The Three, God bless them, were bringing Nico home. To punish the monster. And set things right.

'Dad, she was supposed to die for *my* sins!' he'd shouted, tugging the door open and rushing inside. Nico could still hear the words. Still smell the cigar smoke. Still feel the ball of his finger tightening on the trigger as his father begged, pleaded, sobbed – *Please, Nico, you're my – Let me get you help.* But the only thing Nico saw was his mother's photograph – her wedding photo! – perfectly preserved beneath the glass top of the coffee table. So young and beautiful . . . all dressed in white . . . like an angel. His angel. His angel who was taken. Taken by the monsters. By the Beasts.

'Nico, on my life – on all that's holy – I'm innocent!'

'Nobody's innocent, Dad.'

The next thing Nico felt was his foot slipping across the peeling linoleum floor, which was soaked with . . . soaked with red. A dark red puddle. All that blood.

'Dad . . . ?' Nico whispered, flicks of blood freckled across his face.

His dad never answered.

'Don't doubt yourself, Nico,' Number Three told him. 'Check his ankle. You'll find their mark.'

And as Nico moved in – ignoring the bullet hole in his father's hand (to make him feel Jesus's pain) and the other bullet hole in his heart – he lifted his father's leg and pulled down his sock. There it was. Just as Number Three had said. The hidden mark. Hidden from his son. Hidden from his wife. A tiny tattoo.

The compass and a square – the most sacred of all Masonic symbols. Tools of the trade for an architect . . . tools to build their doorway . . . plus a *G* for the Great Architect of the Universe.

'To show he's of them,' Number Three explained.

Nico nodded, still reeling from the fact his father had kept it secret for so long. Yet now the monster was slain. But as Number Three pointed out, thanks to the Masons, there were more monsters fighting to get out. More Beasts. Still, by fighting now – by serving God – he could turn his mother's death into a blessing.

The Three called it *fatum*. Latin for *fate*. Nico's destiny.

Nico looked up as he heard the word. Fate. 'Yes . . . that's what she— Like the Book.'

Right there, Nico knew his mission – and why his mom was taken.

'Please . . . I need to— Let me help you slay the monsters,' Nico volunteered.

Number Three watched him carefully. He could've dumped Nico right there. Could've left him . . . abandoned him . . . chosen to continue the fight by himself. Instead, he said the one thing only a true man of God could.

'Son, let us pray.'

Number Three opened his arms, and Nico collapsed inside. He heard Number Three's sobs. Saw his tears. No longer just a stranger. Family. Like a father.

Fatum, Nico decided that day. His fate.

Over the next month, The Three revealed the full mission. Told him of the enemy and the strength on their side. From Voltaire to Napoleon to Winston Churchill, the Freemasons spent centuries cultivating the most powerful members of society. In the arts, they had Mozart, Beethoven, and Bach. In literature, Arthur Conan Doyle, Rudyard Kipling, and Oscar Wilde. In business, they grew with funding by Henry Ford, Frederick Maytag, and J. C. Penney.

In the United States, they built their power to new heights: From Benjamin Franklin to John Hancock, eight signers of the Declaration of Independence were Masons. Nine signers of the U.S. Constitution. Thirty-one generals in Washington's army. Five Supreme Court chief justices, from John Marshall to Earl Warren. Year by year, century by century, the Masons collected those with the greatest influence on society: Paul Revere, Benedict Arnold, Mark Twain, John Wayne, Roy Rogers, Cecil B. DeMille, Douglas Fairbanks, Clark Gable, even Harry Houdini. Was it any coincidence that Douglas MacArthur became General of the Army? Or that Joseph Smith founded an entire religion? Or that J. Edgar Hoover was given the FBI? Or even that Buzz Aldrin was on that first rocket to the moon? All of those landmarks. All of them by Masons. And that didn't even consider the sixteen times they took the White House: Presidents George Washington, James Monroe, Teddy Roosevelt, FDR, Truman, LBJ, Gerald Ford . . . and most important, The Three explained, President Leland F. Manning and the monster known as Ron Boyle.

One month after the day they met, The Three revealed Boyle's sin. Just like they did with Nico's father.

Still rocking to himself and strumming on the A-string, Nico heard the throat-clearing grunt of tires scraping uphill against the ice. A black SUV rumbled into view, its windshield wipers swatting snow aside like a bothersome fly. Nico continued to strum, well aware that black SUVs usually meant the Service. But as the car cut in front of the dogwood, Nico saw that the passenger seat was empty. Service never came alone.

Three and a half minutes, Nico told himself as he studied the second hand on his watch. By now, he had it timed perfectly. Three and a half was the average. For his doctors, for his nurses, even for his sister before she stopped coming to visit. She'd always need an extra thirty seconds to steel herself, but even on the worst days – on that dark Sunday when he tried to hurt himself – three and a half minutes was more than enough.

Nico glanced down again at the second hand on his watch. *One minute . . . two . . . three . . .* He closed his eyes, bobbed his head, and prayed. *Three and a half.* Nico opened his eyes and turned to the door of his ten-by-fifteen room.

The doorknob twisted slightly, and the orderly with the bloodshot eyes appeared in the doorway.

'Nico, you decent? You got a visitor,' the orderly called out.

Eight years watching. Eight years waiting. Eight years believing that the Book of Fate could never be denied.

Nico could feel the tears flood his eyes as a man with pale Irish features and midnight-black hair entered the room.

'Nice to see you, Nico,' The Roman said as he stepped inside. 'Been far too long.'

24

'Manning Presidential Library. How can I assist you?' the receptionist answers.

'I have some questions on presidential records,' I say, checking for the second time that the door to my office is closed. Rogo said I could use his office to make the call, but between lunch and all our chatting, I've already been gone too long.

'Let me transfer you to the archivist of the day,' the receptionist adds.

With a click, I'm on my way. And while I could just call the head of the entire library, like Rogo said, better to keep it low-key.

'Kara speaking. What can I help you with today?' a soft female voice asks.

'Hi, Kara. This is Wes over in the personal office. We're trying to get some of Ron Boyle's old files for a tribute book we're working on, so I was just wondering if you could help us pull some of those together?'

'I'm sorry, and your name again?'

'Wes Holloway. Don't worry . . . I'm on the staff list,' I say with a laugh. She doesn't laugh back.

'I'm sorry, Wes, but before we release any documents, we need you to fill out a FOIA request stating who it's for—'

'President Manning. He requested them personally,' I interrupt.

Every law has exceptions. Cops can run red lights. Doctors can illegally park during emergencies. And when your name is Leland Manning, you get any sheet of paper you want from the Leland Manning Presidential Library.

'J-Just tell us what you need. I'll start pulling it together,' she offers.

'Fantastic,' I say, flipping open the thick loose-leaf binder on my desk. The first page is labeled *Presidential Records and Historical Materials*. We call it the guide to the world's biggest diary.

For four years in the White House, every file, every e-mail, every Christmas card that was sent out was logged, copied, and saved. By the time we left Washington, it took five battle-sized military cargo planes to haul the forty million documents, 1.1 million photographs, twenty million printed e-mail messages, and forty thousand 'artifacts,' including four different Cowardly Lion telephones, two of which were handmade with the President's face on them. Still, the only way to find the needle is to jump into the haystack. And the only way to figure out what Boyle was up to is to pull open his desk drawers and see what's inside.

'Under White House Staff, let's start with all of Boyle's records as deputy chief,' I say, flipping to the first few pages of the records guide, 'and naturally, all of his own files, including correspondence to and from him.' I flip to the next tab in the notebook. 'And I'd also like to get his personnel records. Those would include any work complaints filed against him, correct?'

'It should,' the archivist says, now suspicious.

'Don't worry,' I laugh, hearing the change in her voice, 'that's just to vet him so we know for sure where all the skeletons are.'

'Yeah . . . of course . . . it's just – what do you need these for again?'

'A book the President's working on – about Boyle's years of service, from the White House to the shooting at the speedway—'

'If you want, we have the actual clip – y'know, with Boyle . . . and that young man who got hit in the face . . .'

When John Hinckley tried to kill Ronald Reagan, he hit the President, James Brady, Secret Service Agent Tim McCarthy, and police officer Thomas Delahanty. We all know James Brady. McCarthy and Delahanty became Trivial Pursuit answers. Just like me.

'So how fast do you think you can pull that together?' I ask.

She pants slightly into the phone. It's the closest thing she's got to a laugh. 'Let me just . . . fourteen, fifteen, sixteen . . . you're probably looking at something like eighteen linear feet – or about . . . let's see . . . 36,000 pages.'

'Thirty-six thousand pages,' I repeat, my own voice sinking. The haystack just got eighteen feet taller.

'If you tell me a little bit more what you're looking for, I probably can help you narrow your search a little better . . .'

'Actually, there're a couple of things we were trying to get as soon as possible. The President said there were some other researchers on the book who were working with the library. Is there a way to tell us what files they pulled so we don't overlap?'

'Sure, but . . . when it comes to other people's requests, we're not supposed to—'

'Kara . . . it is Kara, right?' I ask, stealing one straight from Manning. 'Kara, it's for the President . . .'

'I realize that, but the rules—'

'I appreciate the rules. I really do. But these are people working with the President. We're all on the same side, Kara,' I add, trying not to beg. 'And if I don't find this, then *I'm* the person who didn't get the President his list. Please tell me you know what that's like. I need this job, Kara – more than you'll ever realize.'

There's a long pause on the other line, but like any librarian, Kara's a pragmatist. I hear her typing in the background. 'What're their names?' she asks.

'Last name *Weiss*, first name *Eric*,' I say, once again starting with Boyle's old Houdini codename.

There's a loud click as she hits the *Enter* key. I check my door for the third time. All clear.

'We've got two different Eric Weisses. One did some research the first year we were open. The other made a request about a year and a half ago, though it looks like it was a book report kid who wanted to know the President's favorite movie . . .'

'*All the President's Men*,' we both say simultaneously.

She again laughs that panting laugh. 'I don't think that's your researcher,' she adds, finally warming up.

'What about the other Weiss?'

'As I said, he's from the first year we opened . . . mailing address in Valencia, Spain . . .'

'That's him!' I blurt, quickly catching myself.

'Certainly looks like it,' Kara says. 'He's got a few similar requests . . . some of Boyle's files . . . the President's schedule from the day of the shooting . . . The odd thing is, according to the notes here, he paid for copies – expensive too, almost six hundred dollars' worth – but when we sent them out, the package bounced back to us. According to the file, no one was listed at that address.'

Like a photo in a darkroom, the edges of the picture slowly harden and flower into view. The FBI said Boyle was spotted in Spain. If that was his first request from the library, and then he ran, maybe he was worried people knew that his name was . . . 'Try *Carl Stewart*,' I say, switching to the codename Boyle used in the Malaysian hotel.

'Carl Stewart,' Kara repeats, clicking away. 'Yep – here we go . . .'

'You have him?'

'How could we not? Almost two hundred requests over the past three years. He's requested over 12,000 pages . . .'

'Yeah, no . . . he's thorough,' I tell her, careful not to lose focus. 'And just to be sure we have the right one, what's the last address you have for him?'

'In London . . . it's care of the post office at 92A Balham High Road. And the zip is SW12 9AF.'

'That's the one,' I say, scribbling it down, even though I know it's the British equivalent of a P.O. box. And just as untraceable.

Before I can say another word, the door to my office swings open. 'He's in the closet,' Claudia announces, referring to the President. I was afraid of this. *Closet* is her code for the bathroom – Manning's last stop before we head out to an event. If he's true to form – and he always is – that's my two-minute warning.

'So would you like me to just send you a list of what else he requested?' the librarian asks through the receiver.

'Wes, you hear what I said?' Claudia adds.

I hold a finger up to our chief of staff. 'Yeah, if you can send me the list, that'd be perfect,' I tell the librarian. Claudia taps her watch, and I throw her a nod. 'And if I can ask you one last favor – that last document he received – when was that sent?'

'Let's see . . . says here the fifteenth, so about ten days ago,' the librarian replies.

I sit up straight, and the picture in the darkroom starts to take on brand-new details. Since the day the library opened, Boyle's been pulling documents and hunting through files. Ten days ago, he requested his final one – then suddenly came out of hiding. I don't know much, but it's pretty clear that finding that file is the only way out of the darkroom and into the light.

'Service are mobilizing,' Claudia says, glancing up the hallway and watching the agents gather at the front door of the office.

I stand up and stretch the phone cord to the chair that holds my suit jacket. Sliding my arm in, I stay with the librarian. 'How long would it take you to send me a copy of the last document he received?'

'Let's see, it went out last week, so it still might be in Shelly's . . . Hold on, let me check.' There's a short pause on the line.

I look over at Claudia. We don't have many rules, but one of the vital ones is to never keep the President waiting. 'Don't worry – I'm coming.'

She looks over her shoulder and down the hallway. 'I'm serious, Wes,' she threatens. 'Who you talking to anyway?'

'Library. Just trying to get the final list of the honchos who'll be there tonight.'

In our office, when the President gets lonely for his old life, we'll catch him calling his Formers: former British prime minister, former Canadian prime minister, even the former French president. But the help I need is far closer than that.

'Got it right here. It's just a one-pager,' the librarian interrupts. 'What's your fax number?'

Relaying the number, I fight my other arm into my sleeve. The President's and First Lady's metal heads jingle on my lapel pin. 'And you'll send it now?'

'Whenever you want . . . it's—'

'Now.'

I hang up the phone, grab my bag of tricks, and dart for the door. 'Just tell me when Manning's coming,' I say to Claudia as I squeeze past her and duck into the copy room directly across from my office.

'Wes, this isn't funny,' she says, clearly annoyed.

'It's coming through right now,' I lie, standing in front of our secure fax machine. Every day at six a.m., Manning's NIDs – the National Intelligence Daily – arrive by secure fax in the exact same spot. Sent out by the CIA, the NIDs contain briefs on an array of sensitive intelligence topics and are the last umbilical cord all Formers have with the White House. Manning races for it like catnip. But for me, what's being transmitted right now is far more potent.

'Wes, go to the door. I'll take care of the fax.'

'It'll just—'

'I said go to the door. Now.'

I turn around to face Claudia just as the fax machine hiccups to life. Her smoker's lips purse, and she looks angry – angrier than anyone should be over a silly little fax.

'It's okay,' I stutter. 'I'll get it.'

'Dammit, Wes—'

Before she can finish, my phone vibrates in my pocket. I pull it out as a simple distraction. 'Just gimme one sec,' I say to Claudia as I check caller ID. *Undisclosed caller.* There aren't many people who have this number.

'Wes here,' I answer.

'Don't react. Just smile and act like it's an old friend,' a grainy voice crackles through the receiver. I recognize him instantly.

Boyle.

25

'Nice room,' The Roman said, eyeing the mostly bare, sun-faded walls of Nico's home for the past eight years. Above the nightstand was a free Washington Redskins calendar from the local grocery store. Above the bed was a small crucifix. On the ceiling, a spiderweb of cracked plaster rounded out the sum total of the decor. 'Really nice,' The Roman added, remembering how much Nico thrived on positive reinforcement.

'It is nice,' Nico agreed, his eyes locked on the orderly as he left the room.

'And you've been well?' The Roman asked.

Keeping his arms wrapped around his violin and hugging it like a doll, Nico didn't answer. The way his ear was cocked, it was clear he was listening to the fading squeaks of the orderly's rubber soles against the linoleum.

'Nico—'

'Wait . . .' Nico interrupted, still listening.

The Roman stayed silent, unable to hear a thing. Of course, that was yet another reason why they'd picked Nico all those years ago. The average adult hears at a level of twenty-five decibels. According to his army reports, Nico was gifted with the ability to hear at ten decibels. His eyesight was even more uncanny, measured officially at 20/6.

Nico's army supervisors labeled it a gift. His doctors

labeled it a burden, suggesting that overwhelming auditory and visual stimuli caused his desensitization with reality. And The Roman . . . The Roman *knew* it was an opportunity.

'Tell me when we're clear,' The Roman whispered.

As the sound faded, Nico scratched his bulbous nose and studied The Roman carefully, his close chocolate eyes flicking back and forth, slowly picking apart his guest's hair, face, overcoat, shoes, even his leather briefcase. The Roman had forgotten how methodical he was.

'You forgot an umbrella,' Nico blurted.

The Roman patted down the back of his slightly damp hair. 'It's just a short walk from the parking lo—'

'You brought a gun,' Nico said, staring at The Roman's ankle holster as it peeked out from his pant leg.

'It's not loaded,' The Roman said, remembering that short answers were the best way to rein him in.

'That's not your name,' Nico again interrupted. He pointed at the visitor ID sticker on The Roman's lapel. 'I know that name.'

The Roman didn't even bother looking down. He used his badge to get past the guards, but for the ID, of course the name was fake. Only a fool would put his real name on a list that regularly got sent to his supervisors at the Service. Still, with all Nico's years here, with all the drugs the doctors pumped into him, he was sharp. Sniper training didn't dull easily. 'Names are fictions,' The Roman said. 'Especially the enemy's.'

Still holding tight to his fiddle, Nico could barely contain himself. 'You're of The Three.' From the excitement in his voice, it wasn't a question.

'Let's not—'

'Are you One or Two? I only spoke to Three. He was

my liaison – with me when my father – when he passed. He said the rest of you were too big, and that the President was one of—' Nico bit his lip, straining to restrain himself. 'Praise all! Did you see the cross on the brick chapel?'

The Roman nodded, remembering what they told Nico all those years ago. That he should look for the signs. That physical structures have always been sources of inexplicable power. The Druids and Stonehenge . . . the Egyptian pyramids . . . even Solomon's First and Second Temples in Jerusalem. The Freemasons spent centuries studying them all – each one an architectural marvel that's served as a doorway to a greater miracle. Centuries later, that knowledge was passed to Freemason James Hoban, who designed the White House, and Freemason Gutzon Borglum, who did Mount Rushmore. But as they also explained to Nico, some doors weren't meant to be opened.

'Praise all!' Nico repeated. 'He said when you came, redemption would—'

'Redemption will come,' The Roman promised. 'As the Book promises.'

For the first time, Nico was silent. He lowered the fiddle to the ground and bowed his head.

'That's it, my son,' The Roman said with a nod. 'Of course, before redemption, let's start with a little . . .' He reached over to the dresser and picked up the red glass rosary beads. '. . . confession.'

Dropping to his knees, Nico clasped his hands together and leaned on the side of his mattress like a child at bedtime.

The Roman wasn't surprised. He did the same thing when they found him in the shelter. And for almost two full days after he confronted his father. 'There'll be time for prayer later, Nico. Right now I just need you to tell me the truth about something.'

'I'm always truthful, sir.'

'I know you are, Nico.' The Roman sat on the opposite side of the bed and placed the rosary beads between them. The fading sun boomeranged through the prisms of red glass. Still on his knees, Nico studied it, mesmerized. From his briefcase, The Roman pulled out a black-and-white photo and tossed it between them on the bed. 'Now, tell me everything you know about Wes Holloway.'

26

'Hey, how's everything?' I sing into my cell phone as Claudia stares me down from the doorway of the copy room.

'You know who this is?' Boyle asks on the other line. His tone is sharp, each syllable chiseling like an ice pick. He's impatient. And clearly riled.

'Of course. Good to hear your voice, Eric.' I purposely use his old codename instead of *Carl Stewart*. He doesn't need to know I've figured that one out.

'You alone?' he asks as Claudia's lips purse even tighter and she lowers her chin with a burning glare.

'Sure, I've got Claudia right here—'

'Stay away from this, Wes. This isn't your fight. Y'hear me? It's not your fight.'

The line goes dead. Boyle's gone.

He hung up.

'No, that's great,' I say to the now-silent line. 'See you soon.' I'm not the world's greatest liar, but I'm still good enough to convince Claudia nothing's wrong.

'What's wrong?' she asks.

'That was . . . it was Manning. He said he'd be another few minutes . . .'

Her eyes narrow as she processes the news. Behind me, the fax machine grumbles to life. I jump at the sound, which hits me like a bullet.

'What?' she asks.

'No, it just . . . it startled me.' For almost a year after the shooting, every car that backfired, every loud door that slammed . . . even action scenes in movies . . . the loud noises echoed from Nico's attack. The doctors said it would fade over time. And it did. Until now.

Knowing that look on my face, Claudia pauses and softens, but as always, reverts to her one priority. 'You should still be out there,' she says.

'I will . . . just let me get this. Y'know how he likes knowing names,' I add, selling it as a benefit for Manning. That alone buys me a few more seconds.

By the time I spin back to the fax, the cover sheet is already through. So is half of the final page.

I grab the left-hand corner of the sheet as it churns out of the machine, then tilt my head, struggling to read it upside down. Top corner says *Washington Post*. From what I can tell, it's from the comics section of the paper. *Hagar the Horrible* . . . then *Beetle Bailey*. But as *Beetle Bailey* rolls out, there's something handwritten in the open space of the comic strip's second panel: boxy and clunky cursive lettering that looks like it was written on the dashboard of a moving car. It's almost unreadable to the untrained eye. Fortunately, my eyes've been trained for years. I'd know Manning's handwriting anywhere.

Gov. Roche . . . M. Heatson, I read to myself.

On the next line, it makes even less sense. *Host – Mary Angel.*

Roche is the former governor of New York, but Heatson or Mary Angel . . . nothing rings a bell.

As the rest of the fax shimmies from the machine, there's nothing but more comics. *Peanuts, Garfield,* and *Blondie.*

This was the final piece of Boyle's puzzle? I look back at the handwritten note. *Gov. Roche . . . M. Heatson . . . Mary Angel.* Doesn't even make sense. Three names with no information? I study it again, reading each letter. This is the last page Boyle found before coming out of hiding. Eight years dead, and *this* is what lured him back into his life? *Gov. Roche . . . M. Heatson . . . Host – Mary Angel.* Still means nothing.

'Wes, he's here,' Claudia calls out, disappearing up the hallway.

'Coming,' I say as the final lines of *Beetle Bailey* scroll out from the machine. As I spin around to take off, the cover sheet drops to the floor. Pausing to pick it up, I glance at the line that says *Number of Pages.* To my surprise, it says *3.*

The fax machine again hiccups, and a final sheet of paper crawls toward me. The librarian called it a one-pager. And it is one page . . . with two sides. Front and back.

I hunch down to the fax and try to read the document as each line of fresh ink is printed on the page. Like the comics page, it has the light gray tone of photocopied newsprint filled with more of the President's handwriting. But as I read it to myself, the picture in the darkroom feels overexposed, foggier than ever.

'Wes . . .' the President calls from the front door.

'On my way,' I say, picking up my travel bag, ripping the sheet from the fax, and darting into the hallway. I give it one last glance before shoving it into my jacket pocket. It doesn't make sense. What the hell could Boyle possibly be doing with *this*?

27

'He's the one I shot, isn't he?' Nico whispered, staring down at the recent photo of Wes. 'The innocent.'

'In every war, there are innocents,' The Roman said. 'But what I need to know is—'

'He's older . . .'

'It's been years, Nico. Of course, he's older.'

Nico pulled the picture close to him. 'I broke him, didn't I? He's broken now.'

'Excuse me?'

'In his eyes,' Nico replied, focusing even tighter on the photo. 'I've seen that look . . . in battle . . . kids in battle have that look.'

'I'm sure they do,' The Roman said, snatching the picture and fighting to keep Nico on track. 'But I need you to tell me if—'

'We relieve them from duty when they have that look,' Nico said, almost proudly. 'They lose sight of the cause.'

'Exactly. They lose sight of the cause. Let's focus on that.' Tapping Wes's picture, The Roman added, 'Remember what he said about you? At the hearing a few years back?'

Nico stayed silent.

'What'd he call you again? A savage?'

'A monster,' Nico growled.

The Roman shook his head, well aware of Wes's

description. But like any interrogation, the key was hiding the big questions. 'And that's the last you heard from him?' The Roman asked.

'He blames me. Refuses to see what I saved us from.'

The Roman watched Nico carefully, now convinced that Wes hadn't been in touch. Of course, that was only part of the reason for his visit. 'Speaking of which, do you think about Boyle?'

Nico looked up, his eyes angry for barely a second, then calm. The hatred disappeared almost instantly. Thanks to the doctors, he'd finally learned to bury it. 'Never,' Nico said.

'Not at all?'

'Never,' Nico repeated, his voice slow and measured. He'd spent eight years perfecting his answer.

'It's okay, Nico. You're safe now, so—'

'I don't think of him. I don't,' he insisted, still on his knees and staring straight at the fiery red of the rosaries. 'What happened to . . . him . . . he . . .' Swallowing hard, Nico reached for the beads, then stopped himself. 'He put me in here. He . . .'

'You can say his name, Nico.'

Nico shook his head, still eyeing the beads. 'Names are fictions. He . . . Masks for the devil.' Without warning, Nico's arm shot forward, snatching the rosary beads from the center of the bed. He pulled them to his chest, his thumb furiously climbing from bead to bead, counting to the rosary's small engraving of Mary.

'Nico, take it easy—'

'Only God is true.'

'I understand, but—'

'God is true!' he exploded, climbing the beads quicker than ever. Turning away, Nico rocked back and forth . . .

slowly, then faster. Gripping each bead, one by one. His shoulders sagged with each sway, and his body hunched lower and lower, practically curling into a ball at the side of the bed. He kept trying to speak, then abruptly cut himself off. The Roman had seen it before. The battle internal. Without warning, Nico looked back over his shoulder. The Roman didn't need 20/6 vision to spot the tears in his eyes.

'Are you here to redeem me?' Nico sobbed.

The Roman froze, assuming it was all about Boyle . . . and it was, but—

'Of course,' The Roman said as he moved to the other side of the bed. Putting a hand on Nico's shoulder, he picked up the violin from the floor. He'd read enough of Nico's file to know it was still his best transitional item. 'That's why I'm here,' he promised as Nico embraced the neck of the violin.

'For redemption?' Nico asked for the second time.

'For salvation.'

Nico eked out a smile, and the crimson beads sank to the floor. From the way Nico studied the violin with his half-closed eyes, The Roman knew he had a few minutes of calm. Better make it quick.

'In the name of The Three, I'm here for your cleansing . . . and to be sure that when it comes to Boyl – When it comes to the Beast, that his influence is no longer felt by your spirit.'

'Who increases our faith . . . Who strengthens our hope . . . Who perfects our love,' Nico began to pray.

'Then let us begin,' The Roman said. 'What is your last memory of him?'

'At the Revolt,' Nico began. 'His hand up in victory . . . preening for the masses with his white teeth glowing. Then the anger in his eyes when I pulled that trigger – he didn't know he'd been hit. He was angry . . . *enraged* as he gritted his teeth. That was his first reaction, even in death. Hatred and rage. Until he looked down and spotted his own blood.'

'And you saw him fall?'

'Two shots in the heart, one in the hand as they tore me down. Sliced his neck too. I heard him screaming as they clawed at me. Screaming for his life. Begging . . . even amid the roar . . . for himself. *Me . . . someone help* me . . . And then the screams stopped. And he laughed. I hear things. I could hear it. Through his own blood. Boyle was laughing.'

The Roman rolled his tongue against his teeth. No doubt, it was true. Laughing all the way to freedom. 'What about since?' he asked, choosing each word carefully. Regardless of the risk, he needed to know if Boyle had been here. 'Has he haunted you . . . recently?'

Nico stopped, looking up from the violin. 'Haunted?'

'In . . . in your dreams.'

'Never in my dreams. His threat was stopped when—'

'What about anywhere else, in visions or—?'

'Visions?'

'Not visions . . . y'know, like—'

'His power is that great?' Nico interrupted.

'No, but we—'

'To be able to do that . . . to call from beyond the ashes . . .'

'There's no such power,' The Roman insisted, again reaching for Nico's shoulder.

Scootching back on his rear, Nico pulled away from The Roman's grasp. His back slammed into the radiator and his violin again dropped to the floor. 'For the Beast to rise . . .'

'I never said that.'

'You didn't deny it!' Nico said, his eyes zipping back and forth in full panic. Clenching his fists, he swung his hands wildly, like he couldn't control his movements. A thick vein popped from his neck. 'But for him to be alive . . . the Great Tribulation lasts seven years – my time away – followed by resurrection of the dead . . .'

The Roman stepped back, frozen.

'You believe it too,' Nico said.

'That's not true.'

'I hear your voice. The quiver! I'm right, aren't I?'

'Nico—'

'He is! With resurrection . . . the Beast lives!'

'I never—'

'He lives! My God, my Lord, he *lives*!' Nico yelled, still on his knees as he turned toward the shatterproof window, screaming at the sky.

The Roman had been afraid it'd come to this. Reaching into his jacket pocket, he pulled out his cell phone, an old, thick model. With a shove of his thumb, he unlatched the back of the phone and unveiled a lead compartment holding a small syringe and a loose razor blade. His fake ID and Secret Service badge allowed him to bring in the gun that was tucked into his ankle holster, but syringes and razors? Not in a mental hospital.

'Nico, time to calm down,' he said as he slid the syringe between his pointer and middle fingers. The fentanyl would easily knock him out, but it'd take the razor to make it look like a suicide.

'Y-You attack me?' Nico asked as he turned around and saw the needle. His eyes grew dark and his nostrils flared. 'He sent you!' Nico shouted, pressed against the radiator and trapped in the corner. 'You're of them!'

'Nico, I'm with you,' The Roman soothed as he stepped closer. There was no pleasure in putting an animal down. 'This is just to calm you down,' he added, knowing he had no choice. Leaving a body would certainly bring questions, but it wouldn't be half as bad as letting Nico scream for the next month that The Three existed and that Boyle was still alive.

Nico's eyes narrowed, focusing on The Roman's gun in the ankle holster. As if he'd spotted an old friend.

'Don't think it, Nico. You can't—'

The door to the room whipped open, slamming into the wall. 'What's all the hollering abou—? What the hell you think you're doing?!' a deep voice asked.

The Roman glanced back just in time to see two orderlies burst inside. That was all Nico needed.

Like an uncoiled snake, Nico sprang toward The Roman's legs. His right hand gripped The Roman's kneecap, twisting it like a bottle cap. His left hand went straight for the gun in the ankle holster.

'Gaaaah!' The Roman howled, crumbling backward toward the floor. Even before the impact, Nico was tearing the gun from its holster.

'Nico, don't—' the orderly with the hoop earring threatened.

It was already too late. Like a virtuoso painter reunited with his long-lost brush, Nico grinned as the gun slid into his palm. Still on his knees, he bounced his hand slightly, letting the gun wobble in his grip. 'Built-in silencer . . . neither muzzle nor butt heavy,' he said to The Roman, who was still writhing on the floor. 'Beautiful work,' he added with a handsome squint as he smiled at the orderlies.

'Nico—!'

Four muffled shots hissed out. Both orderlies screamed. The first two shots pierced their hands. Just like he did with his father. And with Boyle. The stigmata. To show them Jesus's pain. Both slammed into the wall before they even realized the final two bullets were in their hearts.

Climbing to his feet, Nico didn't even watch as the orderlies wilted to the floor, their bodies leaving parallel red streaks down the white wall. Spinning around, he turned the gun toward The Roman, who was on his back, clutching something close to his chest. The shot would be quick and easy, but as Nico's finger hugged the trigger . . .

'Man of God!' The Roman shouted, holding up Nico's red glass rosary beads. They dangled down from his fist, swaying like a hypnotist's pocketwatch. 'You know it, Nico. Whatever else you think . . . Never kill a man of God.'

Nico paused, mesmerized by the rosary shimmering in the fading light. The beads continued to sway, matching pace with The Roman's quick breathing. A puddle of sweat gathered on The Roman's lip. Staring up from the floor, he could see straight into the barrel. Nico wouldn't make eye contact. Wouldn't even acknowledge he was there. Lost in the rosary beads, Nico searched for his answer, never moving the gun. His brow went from creased to calm to creased again, as if he were flipping a coin in his own head. And then the coin landed. Nico pulled the trigger.

The Roman shut his eyes as a single shot hissed out. The bullet pierced his empty left hand, straight through the center of his palm. Jesus's pain. Before he could even feel it, the blood puddled in his hand, rushing down his wrist toward his elbow.

'Where is he!?' Nico demanded.

'I-I'll kill you for that,' The Roman growled.

'Another lie.' Turning slightly to the right, Nico took

aim at The Roman's other hand. 'After everything you promised . . . to come to me now and protect him. What power does the Beast hold over you?'

'Nico, stop!'

Without hesitation, Nico pulled back the hammer of the gun. 'Answer my question: Where is he?'

'I-I have no i—'

'Please move the rosary,' Nico politely asked, motioning to the beads, which were down by The Roman's leg. As The Roman picked them up, Nico squeezed the trigger and a second silenced shot wisped through the air, burrowing through The Roman's foot. Both wounds burned like thick needles twisting through his skin. He gritted his teeth and held his breath, waiting for the initial sting to pass. All it did was get worse. 'Nnnnuhhh!' he shouted.

'Where. Is. Boyle?' Nico demanded.

'If . . . if I knew, do you really think I'd come here?'

Nico stood silent for a moment, processing the thought. 'But you've seen him?'

The Roman shook his head, still struggling against the pain. He could feel his foot swelling, filling his shoe.

'Has anyone else seen him?' Nico asked.

The Roman didn't answer. Nico watched him carefully, tilting his ear slightly toward him.

'Your breathing's starting to quicken. I hope you don't have a stroke,' Nico said.

The Roman looked away from the bed. Nico looked right at it.

On the covers, just by the edge, was the black-and-white photograph of Wes. 'Him?' Nico asked, reaching for the picture. 'Is that—? That's why you asked me about him, yes? The one I broke . . . he's the one who saw the Beast.'

'All he did was see hi—'

'But to communicate . . . to be in league with the Beast. Wes is corrupted now, isn't he? Polluted. That's why the ricochet—' Nico nodded quickly. 'Of course! That's why God sent the bullet his way. No coincidences. Fate. God's will. To strike Wes down. And what God began . . .' Nico's eyes narrowed at the photo. 'I will make him bleed again. I missed it before, but I see it now . . . in the Book. Bleeding Wes.'

Looking up from the photo, Nico raised his gun and pointed it at The Roman's head. From the window over the radiator, the panes in the glass cast the thick shadow of a cross directly onto The Roman's face.

'God's mercy,' Nico whispered, lowering his gun, turning his back to The Roman, and staring out the over-size shatterproof window. The gun's silencer was quiet, but security would be there soon. He didn't pause for a second. He'd had eight years to think about this moment. *Shatterproof.* Not bulletproof.

Two more shots snarled from the gun, piercing the bottom left and right corners of the glass, exploiting the foundation of the window.

Still on the floor, The Roman pulled off his tie to make a tourniquet for his foot. A tight fist eased the pain in his hand. The blood already filled his shoe, and his heartbeat felt like it was thumping up his arm and down his leg. A few feet away, he heard the thud of a bowling ball, then the crackling of glass. He looked up just in time to see Nico slamming his foot against the bullet hole on the bottom left of the window. True to its name, the glass wouldn't shatter, but it did give, popping like bubble wrap as the tiny shards fought to stay together in an almost bendable plastic sheet. Now he had an opening. Licking his lips, Nico put his foot against the glass and gripped the radiator for leverage. With another shove, a fist-sized hunk of the sea-green window broke off from the rest. He pushed again. And again. Almost there. There was a tiny tear and a kitten shriek as the window slowly peeled outward and upward like old wallpaper. Then a final thud and— Nothing.

The Roman looked up as a blast of cold air slapped him in the face.

Nico was already gone.

Crawling to the window, The Roman gripped the top of the radiator and pulled himself up. Two stories down, he spotted the small bluff of snow that had broken Nico's fall. Thinking about giving chase, he took another look at the height and felt the blood seeping through his own sock. *Not a chance*, he told himself. He could barely stand now.

Craning his neck out the window and following the footprints – out of the bluff, through the slush on the service road – he quickly spotted Nico: his sweatshirt creating a tiny brown spot plowing through the bright white layer of snow. Nico never looked back.

Within seconds, Nico's faded brown spot gained a speck of black as he raised the gun and pointed it downhill. From the angle of the window, The Roman couldn't see what Nico was aiming at. There was a guard at the gate, but that was over fifty yards a—

A whispered *psst* and a hiccup of smoke belched from the gun's barrel. Right there, Nico slowed his pace to a calm, almost relaxing walk. The Roman didn't need to see the body to know it was another direct hit.

Shoving the gun into the pouch of his sweatshirt, Nico looked like a man without a care in the world. Just strolling past the old army building, past the graveyards, past the leafless dogwood, and – as he faded from view – straight out the front gate.

Hobbling toward the door, The Roman grabbed the syringe and the razor blade from the floor.

'You guys okay?' a female voice asked through one of the orderlies' walkie-talkies.

The Roman leaned down and pulled it off the orderly's belt clip. 'Just fine,' he mumbled into the receiver.

Carrying it with him, he turned around and took a final survey of the room. It wasn't until that moment that he realized Nico had also taken the black-and-white photograph of Wes. Bleeding Wes.

28

'Right this way,' I say as I cup the elbow of the older woman with the beehive of blond hair and escort her and her husband toward President Manning and the First Lady, who're posed in front of a floral bouquet the size of a small car. Trapped in this small anteroom in the back of the Kravis Center for the Performing Arts, the President looks my way, never losing his grin. It's all the signal I need. He has no idea who they are.

I put it on a platter. 'Mr President, you remember the Talbots—'

'George . . . Leonor . . .' the First Lady jumps in, shaking hands and swapping air kisses. Thirty-four books, five unauthorized biographies, and two TV movies have argued she's the better politician in the family. All the proof is right here. 'And how's Lauren?' she asks, pulling off their daughter's name as well. That's when I'm impressed. The Talbots aren't longtime donors. They're NBFs – new best friends, which is what we call the rich groupies who glommed onto the Mannings *after* they'd left the White House. Old friends liked the power; new friends like the fame.

'We just think you're the greatest,' Mrs Talbot gushes, her eyes solely on the First Lady. It's never bothered Manning. Dr. First Lady has always been a part of their political package – and thanks to her science background, the better at analyzing poll numbers, which is why some say she was even more crushed than the President when they handed over their keys to the White House. Still, as someone who was with the President that day as he flew home to Florida, and placed his final call on Air Force One, and lingered on the line just long enough to say his final good-bye to the phone operator, I can't help but disagree. Manning went from having a steward who used to wear a pager just to bring him coffee, to lugging his own suitcases back to his garage. You can't give away all that power without some pain.

'What'm I, chopped herring all of a sudden?' Manning asks.

'What do you mean, *all of a sudden*?' the First Lady replies as they all cocktail-party laugh. It's the kind of joke that'll be repeated for the rest of the social season, turning the Talbots into minor wine and cheese stars, and simultaneously ensuring that Palm Beach society keeps coming to these thousand-dollar-a-plate charity shindigs.

'On three,' the photographer calls out as I squeeze the Talbots between the Mannings. 'One . . . two . . .'

The flashbulb pops, and I race back to the receiving line to palm the next donor's elbow. Manning's look is exactly the same.

'Mr President, you remember Liz Westbrook . . .'

In the White House, we called it the *push/pull*. I *pull* Mrs Westbrook toward the President, which *pushes* the Talbots out of the way, forcing them to stop gawking and say their good-byes. True to form, it works perfectly – until someone pushes back.

'You're trying the push/pull with me? I *invented* it!' a familiar voice calls out as the flashbulb pops. By the time

I spin back toward the line, Dreidel's already halfway to the President with a huge smile on his face.

Manning lights up like he's seeing his childhood pet. I know better than to get in the way of that. 'My boy!' Manning says, embracing Dreidel. I still get a handshake. Dreidel gets a hug.

'We wanted it to be a surprise,' I offer, shooting a look at Dreidel.

Behind him, the honcho line is no longer moving. Over the President's shoulder, the First Lady glares my way. I also know better than to get in the way of that.

'Sir . . . we should really . . .'

'I hope you're staying for the event,' Manning interrupts as he backs up toward his wife.

'Of course, sir,' Dreidel says.

'Mr President, you remember the Lindzons,' I say, pulling the next set of donors into place. Manning fake-smiles and shoots me a look. I promised him it was only fifty clicks tonight. He's clearly been counting. This is souvenir photo number 58. As I head back to the line, Dreidel's right there with me.

'How many clicks you over?' Dreidel asks.

'Eight,' I whisper. 'What happened to your fundraiser?'

'It was cocktails. We finished early, so I figured I'd come say hello. What happened with the gossip columnist?'

'All taken care of.'

A flashbulb pops, and I grab the elbow of the next honcho, an overweight woman in a red pants suit. Falling back into old form, Dreidel puts a hand on the shoulder of her husband and motions him forward.

'Mr President, you remember Stan Joseph,' I announce as we drop him off for click number 59. Whispering to Dreidel, I add, 'I also snagged Boyle's London address and his last request from the library.'

Dreidel picks up speed as another flashbulb explodes. He's half a step ahead. He thinks I don't notice. 'So what was on the final sheet?' he asks softly.

As I turn back to the honchos, there's only one person left in line. One click to go. But when I see who it is, my throat constricts.

'What?' Dreidel asks, reading my expression.

I stop right in front of our final honcho, a young redhead in a modest black suit. Dreidel goes to put a hand on her elbow to escort her forward. She brushes him off and puts a hand on his shoulder. 'Just the people I'm looking for,' she says proudly. 'Lisbeth Dodson – *Palm Beach Post*. You must be Dreidel.'

29

Mclean, Virginia

Limping up the icy driveway and holding his fist against his chest, The Roman eyed the front windows of the classic stucco Colonial with the *For Sale* sign in the front yard. Although the lights were off, it didn't slow him down. After hiding his wound – by slipping his bloody foot into one of Nico's old shoes – he flashed his badge to push his way out of the hospital and quickly made the call. He knew Benjamin was home.

Sure enough, as he reached the side of the house, he grabbed the cold metal handrail and hobbled down a short cement staircase. At the bottom, he reached a door with a faint glow of light peeking out from under it. A small sign above the doorbell said *Appointments Only*. The Roman didn't have an appointment. He had something far more valuable.

'Les?' he called out, barely able to stand. Leaning against the doorjamb, he couldn't feel his left hand, which was still in the same blood-soaked glove that helped him hide it at the hospital. His foot had gone dead almost an hour ago.

'Coming,' a muffled voice said from inside. As the pins and springs of the lock turned, the door opened, revealing a bushy-haired man with bifocals balanced on a plump nose. 'Okay, what'd you do this ti—? Oh, jeez, is that blood?'

'I-I need—' Before he could finish, The Roman collapsed, falling forward through the doorway. As always, Dr. Les Benjamin caught him. That's what brothers-in-law were for.

30

'Mr President, you remember Ms Dodson . . . columnist for the *Palm Beach Post*,' Wes said mid-handoff.

'Lisbeth,' she insisted, extending a handshake and hoping to keep things light. She glanced back to Wes, who was already pale white.

'Lisbeth, I would've gotten your name,' Manning promised. 'Even if I don't know the donors, only a fool doesn't remember the press.'

'I appreciate that, sir,' Lisbeth said, believing his every word, even as she told herself not to. *Could I be more pathetic?* she asked herself, fighting off a strange desire to curtsy. Sacred Rule #7: Presidents lie best. 'Nice to see you again, sir.'

'Is that Lisbeth?' the First Lady asked, knowing the answer as she moved in for her own cheek-to-cheek hug. 'Oh, you know I adore your column,' she gushed. 'Except that piece when you listed how much Lee was tipping local waitresses. That one almost had me take you off our invite list.'

'You actually did take me off,' Lisbeth pointed out.

'Only for two weeks. Life's too short to hold a grudge.'

Appreciating the honesty, Lisbeth couldn't help but smile. 'You're a smart woman, Dr. Manning.'

'Dear, we're the ones who're supposed to be currying favor with you – though I will say you can do better than silly little squibs about what people are tipping, which, let's just admit, is below you.' Slapping her husband on the arm, she added, 'Lee, give the girl a nice quote about cystic fibrosis research so she can do her job.'

'Actually,' Lisbeth began, 'I'm just here . . .'

'We should get you onstage, sir,' Wes interrupted.

'. . . to see your right-hand men,' Lisbeth added, pointing at Dreidel and Wes. 'I'm doing a piece on loyalty. Thought maybe I could grab their quotes and turn them into superstars.'

'Good – you *should*,' the President said, putting an arm around Dreidel. 'This one's running for Senate. And if I still had the keys . . . he's Vice President caliber.' The President paused, waiting for Lisbeth to write it down.

Pulling a notepad from her overstuffed black purse, Lisbeth took the cue and pretended to scribble. Over her shoulder, she could feel Wes seething.

'Don't worry,' Lisbeth said to Manning. 'I'll take it easy on them.'

'Mr President,' a throaty female voice called out as they all turned to the middle-aged woman in the designer suit and matching designer hairdo. As honorary chairperson for the Cystic Fibrosis Foundation, Myrna Opal tapped her diamond Chopard watch, determined to keep the program running on time. 'I think we're ready, sir.'

The instant the President took his first step toward the stage door, Wes fell in line right beside him. 'Wes, I'm fine.'

'I know, but it's . . .'

'. . . less than ten feet to the door. I'll make it. And Dreidel – I hope you're at my table later.'

He says the words while looking at Wes. In the White House, they used to follow etiquette and make sure the

President was always sitting next to whomever he needed to be near. For four years, he didn't pick his tablemates. These days, he no longer bothered with political favors. It was the only perk of losing the White House. The President could finally sit next to the people he liked.

'Just make sure you get these nice cystic fibrosis folks in tomorrow's column,' the First Lady added, motioning to Lisbeth.

'Yes, ma'am,' Lisbeth blurted, never taking her eyes off Wes. He'd been around the world's best politicians for almost a decade, but he still was a novice when it came to hiding his own emotions. Nose flaring . . . fists tight . . . whatever he was burying, it was eating him alive.

'This way, sir,' one of two Secret Service agents said, motioning the President and First Lady toward the stage door. Like mice behind the piper, the cystic fibrosis chairperson, and P.R. person, and fundraising person, and photographer, and remaining honchos all fell in line behind them, an instant entourage that sucked every straggler from the room.

As the door slammed behind them, the quiet was overwhelming. To Lisbeth's surprise, Wes wasn't the only one to stay put. Dreidel was right next to him, a warm grin on his face.

'Come . . . sit,' he offered, pointing to three empty seats at the cloth-covered round table that was used as a sign-in desk. Lisbeth obliged but wasn't fooled. Fear always brought out kindness. And if the hotshot state-senator-to-be was anxious, her B+ story just became an A–.

'So how'd the birthday party planning go?' she asked, pulling a seat up to the table.

'The what?' Dreidel asked.

'For Manning's birthday,' Wes insisted. 'Our meeting this morning . . .'

'Oh, it was great,' Dreidel insisted, repatting the part in his hair and readjusting his wire-rim glasses. 'I thought you meant my fundraiser.'

'Figure out where you're gonna have it?' she added.

'Still deciding,' Wes and Dreidel said simultaneously.

Lisbeth nodded. These guys were White House trained. They weren't falling for minor-league tricks. Better to go in soft. 'C'mon, didn't you hear what the First Lady said?' she asked. '*Adores the column.* I'm not here to drink your blood.'

'Then why'd you bring your cup?' Dreidel asked, pointing with his chin at her notepad.

'That's what's scaring you? What if I put it back in its holster?' she said, reaching under her seat and tucking the pad and pen back in her purse. Still bent over, she looked up, struggling to keep eye contact. 'That better?' she asked.

'I was joking,' Dreidel said, clearly playing nice. Without a doubt, it was his secret they were smuggling.

'Listen, fellas,' Lisbeth begged. 'Before you get all – Damn, sorry about this . . .' Reaching into the jacket pocket of her black suit, Lisbeth took out her cell phone and hit the *Receive* button. 'Hey, Vincent . . . Yeah, I just . . . Oh, you're kidding. Hold on, gimme a sec,' she said into the phone. Turning to Wes and Dreidel, she added, 'Sorry, I gotta take this . . . it'll just be a minute.' Before either of them could react, Lisbeth was out of her seat, speed-walking toward the main door. 'Just watch my purse!' she called back to Dreidel and Wes, shoving her shoulder into the door and crossing into the ornate chandeliered lobby of the Kravis Center. With a tight grip on her phone, she pressed it to her ear. But the only things she heard were the voices of the two young men she'd just left inside.

'You told her we were *party planning*?' Dreidel hissed.

'What'd you want me to say?' Wes shot back. 'That I was trying to save what was left of your marriage?'

Sacred Rule #8: If you really want to know what people think about you, leave the room and listen to what they say. Lisbeth learned this one the hard way on the Palm Beach party circuit, when a local socialite paid a parking valet $1,500 to eavesdrop on Lisbeth's conversation with a confidential source. A week later, Lisbeth saved the $1,500 and simply signed up for two separate cell phones. Today, cell phone A was in her purse, back with Wes and Dreidel. Cell phone B was pressed to her ear. When she put her notepad away, all it took was the press of a button for A to speed-dial B. One faked important call later, Sacred Rule #8 proved why it would forever be in the top ten.

'But if she finds out about Boyle . . .' Wes said on the other line.

'Easy, poppa – she's not finding out about Boyle,' Dreidel shot back. 'Though speaking of which, tell me what you found . . .'

Alone in the lobby, Lisbeth stopped short, almost falling out of her scuffed high heels. *Boyle?* She looked around, but no one was there. They were all inside, lost in the hum of *An Evening with President Leland F. Manning.* Lisbeth could hear his voice rumbling off the main stage. A rush of excitement flushed her freckled cheeks. Finally . . . after all these years . . . an honest-to-God A+.

31

'Ahhh!' The Roman roared as Benjamin used sterilized scissors to cut the dead gray skin from the edges of the wound in his palm. 'That *hurts*!'

'Good – that's a sign of no nerve damage,' Benjamin said dryly in the small basement office his ex-wife used to use for her electrolysis practice. The Roman sat on a modern leather sofa; Benjamin swiveled slightly on a stainless-steel rolling chair. 'Hold still,' he added. Pressing his thumb in The Roman's palm and his fingers on the back of The Roman's hand, Benjamin squeezed tightly on the wound. This time, The Roman was ready. He didn't scream at all.

'No bony tenderness or instability . . . though I still think you should have it X-rayed to be sure.'

'I'm fine.'

'Yeah, I could tell that by the way you passed out in the doorway. Just a picture of health.' Unbending a paper-clip, Benjamin twisted the metal until the two tips of the clip were almost touching, barely half a centimeter apart. 'Do me a favor and close your eyes.' As the Roman obliged, Benjamin lightly pressed the tips of the paperclip against the side of The Roman's thumb. 'How many points do you feel?'

'Two,' The Roman said.

'Good.' Finger by finger, Benjamin repeated the question, then wrapped The Roman's hand in fresh gauze.

Eventually working down to The Roman's bloodied foot, he tweezed pieces of sock and shards of shoelace from the wound and applied the same paperclip test to each toe. 'How many now?'

'One.'

'Good. Y'know, it's a miracle you didn't fracture any tarsal bones.'

'Yeah, God's on my side,' The Roman said, wiggling his fingers and tapping the gauze bandage on his palm. The blood was gone, but the pain was still there. Nico would pay for that one.

'Just keep it clean and elevated,' Benjamin said as he eventually wrapped The Roman's foot.

'So I'm okay to fly?'

'Fly? No . . . forget it. This is rest time. Understand? Take it easy for a few days.'

The Roman stayed silent, leaning down and carefully sliding his foot into the shoes Benjamin had brought from upstairs.

'Did you hear what I said?' Benjamin asked. 'This isn't the time to run around.'

'Just do me a favor and call in those prescriptions,' The Roman said, fighting the urge to limp as he headed for the door. 'I'll call you later.' Without looking back, he stepped outside and pulled his cell phone from his pocket.

Ten digits later, a female voice answered, 'Travel Office, how can I assist you?'

'I'm trying to make a reservation,' The Roman said, walking out into the darkness as a gust of Virginia chill tried to blow him sideways. 'I need the next flight you have for Palm Beach.'

32

'This?' Dreidel asks as he stares down at the unfolded fax. 'This's the last thing Boyle got from the library?'

'According to the archivist.'

'It doesn't even make sense,' Dreidel moans. 'I mean, a personnel file, I could understand . . . even an old targeting memo for some attack that went wrong . . . but a *crossword puzzle*?'

'That's what she sent: one sheet with some names on a stupid *Beetle Bailey* cartoon – and on the opposite side, a faded, mostly finished . . .'

'. . . crossword puzzle,' Dreidel repeats. He studies the crossword's handwritten answers. 'It's definitely Manning's writing.'

'And Albright's,' I say, referring to our former chief of staff. 'Remember? Albright started the puzzles . . .'

'. . . and Manning finished them.' Turning back to the crossword, he points to a jumble of doodles and random letters on the right side of the puzzle. *AMB . . . JABR . . . FRF . . . JAR . . .* 'What're these?'

'No idea. I checked the initials, but they're no one he knows. To be honest, it looks like gibberish.'

Dreidel nods, checking for himself. 'My mother does the same thing when she's working a puzzle. I think it's just work space – testing letters . . . trying different permutations.' Focusing back on the puzzle itself, he reads each answer one by one. 'What about the actual boxes? Anything interesting?'

'Just obscure words with lots of vowels. *Damp* . . . *aral* . . . *peewee*,' I read across the top, leaning over his shoulder.

'So the answers are right?'

'I've had a total of twelve seconds to look at it, much less solve it.'

'Definitely looks right,' Dreidel says, studying the finished puzzle. 'Though maybe this's what the FBI guy meant by *The Three*,' he adds. 'Maybe it's a number in the crossword.'

I shake my head. 'He said it was a group.'

'It could still be in the crossword.'

Eyeing the only 'three' in the puzzle, I point to the four-letter answer for 3 down. '*Merc*,' I say, reading from the puzzle.

'Short for *mercenary*,' Dreidel says, now excited. 'A mercenary who knew to leave Boyle alive.'

'Now you're reaching.'

'How can you say that? Maybe that's exactly what we're missing . . .'

'What, some hidden code that says, *At the end of the first term, fake Boyle's death and let him come back years later in Malaysia*? C'mon, be real. There's no secret message hidden in a *Washington Post* crossword puzzle.'

'So where does that leave us?' Dreidel asks.

'Stuck,' a female voice announces from the corner.

Spinning around, I almost swallow my tongue. Lisbeth enters quieter than a cat, her eyes searching the room to make sure we're alone. The girl's not dumb. She knows what happens if this gets out.

'This is a private conversation,' Dreidel insists.

'I can help you,' she offers. In her hand is a cell phone. I glance down at her purse and spot another. Son of a –

'Did you record us!? Is that why you left?' Dreidel explodes, already in lawyer mode as he hops out of his seat. 'It's illegal in Florida without consent!'

'I didn't record you . . .'

'Then you can't prove anything – without a record, it's all just—'

'*It could still be in the crossword . . . Merc . . . short for mercenary . . .*' she begins, staring down at her left palm. Her voice never speeds up, always a perfect, unsettling calm. '*A mercenary who knew to leave Boyle alive . . .*' She turns her palm counterclockwise as she reads. '*Now you're reaching.* I can keep going if you want. I haven't even gotten to my wrist yet.'

'You tricked us,' I say, frozen at the table.

She stops at the accusation. 'No, that's not— I was just trying to see why you were lying to me.'

'So you do that by lying to *us*?'

'That wasn't what I—' She cuts herself off and looks down, weighing the moment. This is harder than she thought. 'Listen, I'm . . . I'm sorry, okay? But I'm serious . . . I can work with you on this.'

'Work with us? No, no no!' Dreidel shouts.

'You don't understand . . .'

'Actually, I'm pretty damn fluent at this stuff – and the last thing I need right now is more time with you, listening to your bullshit! I have a *no comment* on all this, and anything you print, I'll not only deny, but I'll sue your ass back to whatever crappy high school newspaper taught you that damn phone trick in the first place!'

'Yeah, I'm sure a public lawsuit will really help your state election campaign,' Lisbeth says calmly.

'Don't you dare bring that into— *Dammit!*' Dreidel screams, spinning around and slamming both fists against the welcoming table.

Still standing in the doorway, Lisbeth should be wearing a smile so wide, there'd be canary feathers dangling from her lips. Instead, she rubs the back of her neck as her front teeth click anxiously. I wore that same look when I walked in on one of the many fights between the President and First Lady. It's like walking in on someone having sex. An initial thrill, followed instantly by the hollow dread that in a world of infinite possibilities, physical and temporal happenstance have conspired to place you at the regrettable, unreturnable moment that currently passes for your life.

Lisbeth takes a step back, bumping into the door. Then she takes a step forward. 'I really can help you,' she says.

'Whattya mean?' I ask, standing up.

'Wes, don't,' Dreidel moans. 'This is stupid. We already—'

'I can get you information,' Lisbeth continues. 'The newspaper . . . our contacts—'

'Contacts?' Dreidel asks. 'We have the President's Rolodex.'

'But you can't call them,' Lisbeth shoots back. 'And neither can Wes – not without tipping someone off.'

'That's not true,' Dreidel argues.

'Really? So no one'll raise an eyebrow when Manning's two former aides start dissecting his old assassination attempt? No one'll tattle to the President when you start sniffing around Boyle's old life?'

We're both speechless. Dreidel stops pacing. I brush some imaginary dirt from the table. If the President found out . . .

Lisbeth watches us carefully. Her freckles shift as her eyes narrow. She reads social cues for a living. 'You don't even trust Manning, do you?' she asks.

'You can't print that,' Dreidel threatens.

Lisbeth's mouth falls open, shocked by the answer. 'You're serious . . .'

It takes me a second to process what just happened. I look to Lisbeth, then back to Dreidel. I don't believe it. She was bluffing.

'Don't you dare print it,' Dreidel adds. 'We didn't say that.'

'I know . . . I'm not printing it . . . I just – you guys really punched the hornet's nest on this, didn't you?'

Dreidel's done answering questions. He storms at her, jabbing a finger at her face. 'You have no proof of anything! And the fact that—'

'Can you really help us?' I call out from the table.

Turning to me, she doesn't hesitate. 'Absolutely.'

'Wes, don't be stupid . . .'

'How?' I ask her.

Dreidel turns my way. 'Wait . . . you're actually *listening* to her?'

'By being the one person no one can ever trace back to you,' Lisbeth explains, stepping around Dreidel and heading toward me. 'You make a phone call, people'll know something's up. Same with Dreidel. But if I make it, I'm just a crackpot reporter sniffing for story and hoping to be the next Woodward and Bernstein.'

'So why help us?' I ask.

'To be the next Woodward and Bernstein.' Through her designer eyeglasses, she studies me with dark green eyes – and never once glances down at my cheek. 'I want the story,' she adds. 'When it's all over . . . when all the secrets are out, and the book deals are falling into place, I just want to be the one to write it up.'

'And if we tell you to go screw yourself?'

'I break it now, and the news vans start lining up outside your apartment, feeding your lives to the cable news grinder. Lying to all of America . . . a giant cover-up . . . They'll eat you like Cheerios. And even if you get the truth out there, your lives'll be like picked-over bones.'

'So that's it?' Dreidel asks, rushing back and tapping his knuckle on the table. 'You threaten us, and we're supposed to just comply? How do we know you won't break it tomorrow morning just to get the quick kill?'

'Because only a moron goes for the quick kill,' Lisbeth says as she sits on the edge of the table. 'You know how it works: I run this tomorrow and I'll get a nice pat on the head that'll last a total of twenty-four hours, at which point the *Times* and the *Washington Post* will grab my football, fly a dozen reporters down here, and dance it all the way to the end zone. At least my way, you're in control. You get your answers; I get my story. If you're innocent, you've got nothing to fear.'

I look up from my seat. At the edge of the table, Lisbeth's right leg swings slightly. She knows she's got a point.

'And we can trust you on that?' I ask. 'You'll stay quiet until it's over?'

Her leg stops swinging. 'Wes, the only reason you know Woodward and Bernstein is because they had the ending . . . not just the first hit. Only a fool wouldn't stick with you till we get all the answers.'

I've been burned by reporters. I don't like reporters. And I certainly don't like Lisbeth. But as I glance over at Dreidel, who's finally fallen silent, it's clear we're out of options. If we don't work with her, she'll take this whole shitstorm public and unleash it in a way that we'll never be able to take back. If we *do* work with her, at least we buy some time to figure out what's really going on. I give another look to Dreidel. From the way he pinches the bridge of his nose, we've already stepped on the land mine. The only question now is, how long until we hear the big—?

'Nobody move!' a deep voice yells as the door whips into the wall and half a dozen suit-and-tie Secret Service agents flood the room, guns drawn.

'Let's go!' a beefy agent with a thin yellow tie says as he grabs Dreidel by the shoulder and shoves him toward the door. 'Out. Now!'

'Get off me!'

'You too!' another says to Lisbeth as she follows right behind. 'Go!'

The rest of the agents swarm inside, but to my surprise, run right past me, fanning out in onion-peel formation as they circle through the room. This isn't an attack; it's a sweep.

The only thing that's odd is none of these guys look familiar. I know everyone on our detail. Maybe we got a bomb threat and they called in local—

'Both of you, *move!*' the yellow-tie agent barks at Dreidel and Lisbeth. I assume he doesn't see me – Lisbeth's still in front of me near the table, but as I shoot out of my seat and follow them toward the door, I feel a sharp tug on the back of my jacket.

'Hey, what're you—?'

'You're with me,' Yellow Tie insists, yanking me backward as my tie digs into my neck. With a hard shove to the left, he sends me stumbling toward the far corner of the room. We're moving so fast, I can barely keep my balance.

'Wes!' Lisbeth calls out.

'He's fine,' an agent with bad acne insists, grabbing her elbow and tugging her to the door. He says something else to her, but I can't hear it.

Looking back to me over her shoulder, Lisbeth is still off balance as she staggers toward the doorway's white rectangle of light. With one last wrench, she disappears. When the first agent grabbed her, she was pissed. But now . . . the last look I see before the door slams behind her . . . the way her eyes go wide . . . whatever the agent said to her, she's terrified.

'Let go – I'm a friendly!' I insist, fighting to get to my ID.

Yellow Tie doesn't care. 'Keep moving!' he tells me, practically holding me up by my collar. The last time the Service moved this fast was when Boyle was— No. I stop myself, refusing to replay it. Don't panic. Get the facts.

'Is Manning okay?' I ask.

'Just move!' he insists as we rush toward the corner of the room, where I spot a carpeted, almost hidden door.

'C'mon!' Yellow Tie says, undoing a latch and ramming me into the door to shove it open. Unlike the door that Lisbeth and Dreidel went through, this one doesn't dump us in the lobby. The ceiling rises up, and the concrete hallway is gray and narrow. Loose wires, grimy fire extinguishers, and some random white pipes are the only things on the walls. Maintenance corridor from the ammonia smell of it.

I try to break free, but we're moving too fast. 'If you don't tell me where the hell we're going, I'll personally make sure you're—'

'Here,' Yellow Tie says, stopping at the first door on my right. A red and white sign reads *Storage Only*. He reaches the door with his free hand, revealing a room that's bigger than my office. With one final shove, he lets go of my collar and flings me inside like the evening's trash.

My shoes slide against the floor as I fight for balance, but it's not until I spot two other sets of black shiny shoes that I realize I'm not alone.

'All yours,' Yellow Tie calls out as I hear the door slam behind me.

My skidding stops as my funny bone bangs into a metal utility rack. A hiccup of sawdust belches into the air.

'Busy day, huh?' the man in the U.S. Open hat says, arms folded across his chest. His partner scratches at the nick of skin missing from his ear. O'Shea and Micah. The FBI agents from this morning.

'What the hell's going on?' I demand.

'Nico Hadrian escaped from St. Elizabeths about an hour and a half ago. What we wanna know is, why was your name in the hospital's log as his last visitor?'

33

Richmond, Virginia

It was easy for Nico to get the jeans and the blue button-down shirt from the dryer in the Laundromat. Same with the Baltimore Orioles baseball cap he took from a dumpster. But once he made his way into Carmel's Irish Pub, it took a full nine minutes before an older black man, nursing whiskey and a runny nose, hobbled over to the restroom and left his faded army jacket sagging like a corpse on the seat of his bar-stool. Approaching the stool, Nico was calm. The Lord would always provide.

It was the same thought swirling through his head right now as he stood on the gravelly shoulder of I-95 and an eighteen-wheel truck ferociously blew by, kicking up a trail of tiny pebbles and chocolate-brown slush. Shielding his eyes, Nico squinted through the instant hurricane as the pull of wind sent him reeling to the right. One hand was pressed down on his head to keep his Orioles hat from blowing away, while the other gripped his cardboard sign that flapped like a kite in the truck's backdraft. As the truck disappeared and the wind died, the sign went limp, brushing against Nico's right leg. Calmly as ever, Nico raised his hand and put out his thumb.

He was already in Richmond, well out of the thirty-mile radius that the FBI and D.C. Police were currently combing near St. Elizabeths. The first driver took him up

South Capitol Street. The second helped him navigate I-295. And the third took him down I-95, all the way to Richmond.

Without question, Nico knew he couldn't afford to be standing out in the open for long. With the nightly news approaching, his picture would be everywhere. Still, there wasn't much he could do. From a statistical standpoint, the odds of a fourth driver picking him up in the next few minutes were already low. Anyone else would be panicking. Not Nico. As with anything in life, statistics meant nothing if you believed in fate.

Spotting the pair of owl-eyed headlights in the distance, he calmly stepped toward the road and once again held up his handmade sign with the big block letters: *Fellow Christian Looking for a Ride*.

A piercing screech knifed through the night as the driver of a beat-up flatbed hit his brakes, and all ten wheels clenched and skidded along the ice on the shoulder of the road. Even now, as the semi rumbled to a stop fifty yards to his right, Nico relished the belches, shrieks, and hisses of the outside world. He'd been locked away too long.

Tucking his sign under his armpit, he strolled to the side of the main cab just as the door to the passenger side flew open, and a faint light within the cab poured outward. 'God bless you for stopping,' Nico called out. In his pocket, he fingered the trigger of his gun. Just in case.

'Where you need to get at?' a man with a blond mustache and beard asked.

'Florida,' Nico replied, mentally replaying Revelation 13:1. *And I stood upon the sand of the sea, and saw a beast.* It was all coming together. Heed the Book. Finish God's will. Finish Wes, and in his blood, he'd find the Beast. 'Palm Beach, to be exact.'

'Sick of the cold, eh? Tallahassee good enough?'

Nico didn't say a word as he stared up at the olive wood rosary and silver cross that dangled from the man's rearview. 'That'd be perfect,' Nico said. Reaching for the grab handle, he tugged himself up into the main cab.

With a lurch and a few more belches from the transmission, the oversize flatbed grumbled back onto I-95.

'So you got family down in Florida?' the driver asked, shifting into gear.

'Naw . . .' Nico said, his eyes still on the wooden cross as it swayed like a child's swing. 'Just going to see an old friend.'

34

'What're you talking about?' I ask anxiously.

'Your name, Wes. It was on the—'

'When'd he break out?'

'That's the point. We think he had—'

'A-Are you looking for him? Is he gone, or— Are you sure he's gone?' A needle of bile stabs my stomach, making me want to bend over in pain. It took me seven months of therapy before I could hear Nico's name and not feel puddles of sweat fill my palms and soak my feet. It was another year and a half before I could sleep through the night without him jarring me awake as he lurked in the periphery of my dreams. Nico Hadrian didn't take my life. But he took the life I was living. And now . . . with this . . . with him out . . . he could easily take the rest. 'Doesn't he have guards?' I ask. 'How could they . . . how could this happen?'

O'Shea lets the questions bounce off his chest, never losing sight of his own investigation. 'Your name, Wes. It was on the hospital sign-in sheet,' he insists. 'According to their records, you were there.'

'Where? Washington? You saw me here on the beach this morning!'

'I saw you leave the Four Seasons at almost nine-thirty. According to the receptionist in your office, you didn't return to work until after three. That's a long time to be gone.'

'I was with my fr—my lawyer all morning. He'll tell you. Call him right now: Andrew Rogozinski.'

Micah laughs softly. 'And I assume the fact he's also your high school pal and current roommate means he'd never lie to protect you? You were gone for almost six hours, Wes. That's more than enough time to—'

'To what? To jump on my private jet, fly two and a half hours to Washington, go free Nico – who, oh yeah, once tried to *kill me* – and then fly back to work, hoping no one noticed I was gone? Yeah, that sounds like a genius plan. Go see the one guy I still have nightmares about, be dumb enough to use my real name on the sign-in sheet, and let him loose so he can hunt me down.'

'Who says he's hunting you?' O'Shea challenges.

'What're you talking about?'

'Enough with the idiot act, Wes. You know Nico's just a bullet. Even back then, someone else pulled the trigger.'

'Someone else? What does that—?'

'You speak to Boyle today?' O'Shea interrupts.

I try to bite my top lip, momentarily forgetting the nerve damage that makes it impossible.

'We're not here to hurt you, Wes. Just be honest with us: Are you chasing him or helping him?' Micah adds. He grabs a nearby mop, tossing its handle from one hand to the other, then back again, like the tick-tock of a metronome.

'You know I didn't free Nico,' I tell them.

'That wasn't the question.'

'And I haven't spoken to Boyle,' I shoot back.

'You're sure about that?' O'Shea asks.

'I just told you—'

'Did you speak to him or not? I'm asking you as an officer in an ongoing investigation.'

Micah's mop ticks back and forth. They're acting like they know the answer, but if they did, I'd be in handcuffs right now instead of trapped in a supply closet. I look them dead in the eyes. 'No.'

O'Shea shakes his head. 'At noon today, an unidentified male came into St. Elizabeths requesting a private visit with Nico by identifying himself as a member of the Secret Service, complete with a badge and picture ID, both of which you have access to. Now, I'm willing to accept that only a moron would use his own name, and I'm also willing to keep your name from the press – for no other reason than out of respect for your boss – but in a situation you claim to know nothing about, it's sorta fascinating that yours is the only name that keeps popping up outta the daisy patch.'

'What's your point?'

'My point is, when you're in Malaysia, Boyle's there . . . when your name's on a sign-in sheet in Washington, Nico escapes. This isn't exactly Morse code. You tracking the trend?'

'I didn't go to Washington!'

'And you didn't see a dead man in Malaysia. And you didn't get sent backstage by the President, who wanted you to pick up the message from Boyle, right? Or was that just something we invented to make ourselves feel better – y'know, kinda like your old door-locking and light-switch-on-and-off obsessions? Or better yet, the repetitive praying that—'

'Just because I saw a counselor—'

'*Counselor?* It was a shrink.'

'He was a critical incident specialist . . .'

'I looked it up, Wes. He was a clinical psychologist who had you medicated for the better part of a year. Alprazolam for the anxiety disorders, coupled with some heavy-duty olanzapine for all the compulsions. That's an antipsychotic. Plus his notes, which said that in a strange way, he thought you actually relished your scars – that you saw the pain as atonement for putting Boyle in that limo. Doesn't say much about the shape you were in.'

'The guy blew my friggin' face off!'

'Which is why you've got the best motive and the worst alibis – especially in Malaysia. Do me a favor – for the next few days, unless you're traveling with the President, stay put for a bit. At least until we figure out what's going on.'

'What, so now I'm under house arrest? You can't do that.'

'Wes, I've got a homicidal paranoid schizophrenic on the loose, who, two hours from now, will feel a brand-new tingling on the right side of his brain as the drugs that help manage his psychosis slowly wear off. He already shot two orderlies and a security guard – all three in their hearts and, like Boyle, with stigmata through their hands – and that's when he was *on* medication. So not only can I do whatever the hell I want, I'm telling you right now, if you try to take another little jaunt out of town, and I find out you have *any* involvement with this case – trying to contact Boyle, or Nico, or even the guy who was selling popcorn in the stands at the speedway that day – I will slap you with obstruction of justice charges and rip you apart faster than that nutbag ever did.'

'That is, unless you want to tell us what message Boyle was bringing the President in Malaysia,' Micah offers, the mop-handle metronome smacking into his left palm. 'C'mon, Wes – they were clearly trying to meet that night – and trying to maintain all the dirt they thought they'd covered up. You're with him every day now. All we want to know is when they're meeting again.'

Like before – like any FBI agents trying to make a name for themselves – all they really want is Manning, who no doubt had a major hand in helping Boyle hide and lie to the entire country. I rat on him, and they'll happily let me out of the mousetrap. The problem is, I don't even know what I'm ratting about. And even when I try scraping deeper . . . Back at the beach, they mentioned Boyle's ability to work people's weaknesses. Fine, so what were Manning's weaknesses? Something from their past? Or maybe that's where The Roman and The Three came in. Whatever the reason, I'm not finding it out unless I buy some time.

'Let me just . . . let me think about it for a bit, okay?' I ask.

O'Shea nods, knowing he's made his point.

I turn to leave the closet but stop short at the door. 'What about Nico? Any idea where he's heading?' I add, feeling my fingers start to shake. I shove them into my pants pockets before anyone notices.

O'Shea studies me carefully. This is the easiest moment for him to be a prick. He readjusts his U.S. Open baseball cap. 'D.C. Police found his clothes in a Laundromat about a mile away from St. Elizabeths. According to his doctors, Nico hasn't talked about Manning in years, but the Service is still adding double duty just to be safe.'

I nod but still don't take my hands out of my pockets. 'Thanks.'

Micah's about to give me some good cop, but O'Shea puts a hand on his chest, cutting him off. 'You're not alone, Wes,' O'Shea adds. 'Not unless you want to be.'

It's a perfect offer presented in the kindest way. But

that doesn't make it any less of a tactic. Tattling to the FBI . . . taking on Manning . . . all start a domino game that eventually sends me falling. From here on in, the only safe way out of this mess is finding the truth and wrapping myself in it. That's the only bulletproof vest that works.

In my pocket, my phone begins to vibrate. I pull it out and spot Lisbeth's name on the caller ID. Good-bye rock, hello hard place. 'It's my mother,' I tell O'Shea. 'I should go. She probably heard about Nico on the news.'

'Be careful what you say,' Micah calls out.

No doubt about that. Still, it's a simple choice. Going with the FBI means they'll ram me at Manning. But before I put the knife in Caesar's back, I need to make sure I have the right target. At least with Lisbeth, I'll buy that time to figure out what's really going on.

'Think about it, Wes. You're not alone,' O'Shea calls back as I duck out of the closet. Back in the hallway, I wait until the third ring just to make sure I'm out of earshot.

'Wes here,' I answer.

'Where are you?' Lisbeth asks. 'You okay? Did they tell you Nico—?'

'Just listen,' I interrupt. 'What you said earlier about finding stuff out for us . . . were you serious?'

There's a slight pause on the other line. 'More serious than a Pulitzer.'

'You sure? I mean, if you put yourself in this— You sure you're ready to put yourself in this?'

Now the silence lasts even longer. This isn't some fifty-word favor about the First Lady's new dress. However they did this – Boyle, Manning, the Secret Service – you don't pull this off without help from people at the highest levels of government and law enforcement. That's the fight she's picking. Even worse, when the word gets out, they'll be using all that power to make us look like lunatics who saw a ghost. And the worm in the apple is, with Boyle alive, Nico has the best reason of all to come back here and finish his original job.

At the end of the hallway, I ram my hip into the metal latch of the door, which opens to the empty lobby of the theater. A rumble of laughter echoes from the auditorium. The Secret Service may've swarmed the back rooms, but from the sound of it, the President's still killing onstage. On my right, a woman with white hair sells a four-dollar bottle of water to a man in a pin-striped suit. A set of two other Secret Service agents rushes through the lobby on a standard sweep. But what catches my eye is the slightly overweight redhead standing outside the theater, just beyond the tall plate-glass doors. Her back's to me, and as she paces slightly in the cottony moonlight and presses her phone to her ear, Lisbeth has no idea I'm there.

'This is why I became a reporter, Wes,' she says through the phone, her voice strong as ever. 'I've waited my whole life for this.'

'And that's a nice speech,' I tell her, still watching from behind. 'But you do know who you're messing with, right?'

She stops pacing and takes a seat on the edge of one of the half dozen concrete planters that serve as a barrier against any sort of vehicular attack on the Kravis Center. When Manning moved to town, they went up all over. But as Lisbeth scootches back, her body practically sags into it. She can barely keep her head up as her chin sinks down, kissing her neck. Her right hand still holds the phone, but her left slithers like a snake around her own waist, cradling herself. The concrete planters are built to withstand an impact from an almost five-thousand-pound pickup truck traveling over forty-five miles per hour. But that doesn't mean they offer any protection against the sickening recognition of your own self-doubt.

Lisbeth said she'd been waiting her whole life for this. I believe her. But as she looks out at the crush of Secret Service black sedans, their flashing red lights spraying crimson shadow puppets across the facade of the building, it's clear she's wondering if she has what it takes to make it happen. She sinks slightly as her arms cradle her waist even tighter. There's nothing more depressing than when aspirations get guillotined by limitations.

Standing alone in the lobby, I don't say a word. Eight years ago, Nico Hadrian served me my own limits on a public platter. So as I watch Lisbeth sink lower, I know exactly how she—

'I'm in,' she blurts.

'Lisbeth—'

'I'll do it . . . I'm in. Count me in,' she demands, her shoulders bolting upright. Hopping off the planter, she looks around. 'Where are you anyw—?' She cuts herself off as our eyes lock through the glass.

My instinct is to turn away. She comes marching toward me, already excited. Her red hair fans out behind her. 'Don't say no, Wes. I can help you. I really can.'

I don't even bother to argue.

35

St. Pauls, North Carolina

Nico told himself not to ask about the maps. Don't ask for them, don't talk about them, don't bring them up. But as he sat Indian-style in the cab of the flatbed truck . . . as the olive wood rosary beads swayed from the rearview mirror . . . he couldn't help but notice the frayed edge of paper peeking out from the closed glove compartment. Like the crosses he saw in every passing telephone pole and lamppost that lined the darkness of the highway, some things were better left unsaid.

Focusing his attention through the front windshield, he watched as the highway's bright yellow dividing lines were sucked one by one beneath the truck's tires.

'You don't have any maps, do you?' Nico asked.

In the driver's seat next to him, Edmund Waylon, a rail-thin man hunched like a parenthesis, gripped the wide steering wheel with his palms facing upward. 'Check the glove box,' Edmund said as he licked the salt of his sour cream and onion potato chips from the tips of his blond mustache.

Ignoring the scratch of Edmund's fingernails against the black rubber steering wheel, Nico popped open the glove box. Inside was a pack of tissues, four uncapped pens, a mini-flashlight, and – tucked between a thick manual for the truck and an uneven stack of napkins from fast-food restaurants – a dog-eared map.

Twisting it around as it tumbled open like a damaged accordion, Nico saw the word *Michigan* printed in the legend box. 'Any others?' he asked, clearly disappointed.

'Might be some more in the doghouse,' Edmund said, pointing to the plastic console between his seat and Nico's. 'So you were saying about your momma . . . she passed when you were little?'

'When I was ten.' Studying the truck's swaying rosary to bury the image, Nico leaned left in his seat and ran his hand down past the cup holders, to the mesh netting attached to the back of the console. Feeling the tickle of paper, he pulled at least a dozen different maps from the netting.

'Man, losing your momma at ten . . . that'll mess you up good. What about your daddy?' Edmund asked. 'He passed too?'

'Everyone but my sister,' Nico replied, flipping through the stack of maps. North Carolina, Massachusetts, Maine . . . It'd been almost twelve hours since he last had his medication. He never felt better in his life.

'Can't even imagine it,' Edmund said, eyes still on the road. 'My daddy's a sombitch – used to smack all of us . . . my sisters too . . . fist closed, knuckles right across the nose – but the day we have to put him in the ground . . . when a man loses his daddy, it cracks him in two.'

Nico didn't bother to answer. Georgia, Louisiana, Tennessee, Indiana . . .

'Whatcha looking for anyway?' Edmund asked with a quick lick of his mustache.

Don't tell him Washington, Nico insisted.

'Washington,' Nico said, shuffling the maps into a clean pile.

'Which – state or D.C.?'

Tell him state. *If he hears otherwise . . . if he sees the proof of the Masons' sin . . . and their nest . . . The last hour approaches. The Beast is already loosed – communicating, corrupting Wes.*

'State,' Nico said as he reached around the console, tucking the maps back into the mesh netting. 'Washington State.'

'Yeah, now you're outta my range. I'm all Northeast corridor and east of Mississippi.' Covering his mustache with his palm and hooking his nose in the groove between his thumb and pointer finger, Edmund slid his hand down, unsuccessfully trying to contain a long-overdue yawn. 'Sorry,' he apologized, violently shaking his head to stay awake.

Nico glanced at the football-shaped digital clock glued to the dashboard. It was almost two in the morning.

'Listen, if you still need one of them maps,' Edmund said, 'right as we pass I-20 in Florence, there's one of those Circle 'n Stations with the big magazine sections – they got maps, travel guides, I swear I might've even seen an atlas or two. If you want, we can make it our next stop.'

Nico asked the voices what they thought. They couldn't be more excited.

'Edmund, you're a fine Christian,' Nico said, staring out at a passing telephone pole. 'Your rewards will be bountiful in the end.'

36

As I pull into the parking lot at the back of my apartment building, I feel my phone vibrate and look down at caller ID. Crap. *New York Times*.

Surprised it took them this long, I push the *Send* button and brace myself. 'Wes here.'

'Hey, Wes – Caleb Cohen. From the *Times*,' he announces with the forced familiarity of every reporter. Caleb used to cover Manning during White House days, meaning he called every day. But these days, we're in the former-President rotation, which is barely a notch above second cousin once removed. Until right now.

'You have a statement on the escape yet?' Caleb asks.

'You know we never comment on Nico,' I tell him, following years of protocol. Last thing we need is to let some runaway quote rile up the mad dog.

'No, I don't mean from Manning,' Caleb interrupts. 'I mean from you. You're the one with the scars. Aren't you worried he's out there, ready to hit you with something harder than a ricochet?'

He says it to get a rise, hoping I'll blurt a quick response. That worked once, with *Newsweek*, right after the accident. I'm not twenty-three anymore.

'Nice talking to you, Caleb. And if you want to talk again, don't print a *no comment* from us either. Just say we couldn't be reached.'

I slam the phone shut, but as Caleb disappears, I'm swallowed by the haunting silence of the open-air parking lot, which is tucked just behind my apartment building. It's almost midnight on a Thursday. At least fifty cars surround me, but no one's in sight. Squeezing between two matching Hondas, I push the *Door Lock* button on my key ring just to hear the noise. It fades far too fast, leaving me alone with the reality of Caleb's question: If Nico's out there, what's preventing him from coming back to finish the job?

Glancing around the empty parking lot, I don't have an answer. But as I study the tall, slender shadows between the twelve-foot shrubs that surround the lot, I suddenly can't shake that awkward, stomach-piercing anxiety that I'm no longer alone. Ignoring the skeleton arms of overgrown branches, I scan the darkness between the tall shrubs, holding my breath to listen even closer. My only reward is the droning buzz of crickets who fight for dominance against the hum of the lot's overhead lampposts. Catching my breath, I take a few steps.

That's when I hear the tiny metal jingling. Like coins rattling in a pocket. Or someone hitting a chain-link fence. I turn around slightly, scanning between the branches and spotting the fence that surrounds the parking lot and runs behind the hedges.

Time to get inside. Spinning back toward the building, I speed-walk toward the yellow-striped awning that juts out over the back entrance. On my far left, the crickets fall silent. There's a rustling by the group of hedges that blocks the view to the pool area. Just the wind, I tell myself as I pick up my pace and move even faster toward the awning, which seems almost submerged in darkness.

Behind me, the rustling from the hedges gets louder. *Please, God, just let me—*

My phone vibrates in my hand as caller ID shows me a 334 prefix. *Washington Post.* Last year, Manning, like LBJ before him, had a secret actuarial done to see how long he'd live. The way things are going, I can't help but wonder the same about myself. And while I'm tempted to pick it up just to have some sort of audio witness, the last thing I need right now is another reminder that Nico's out there, waiting.

Shifting from speed walk to jog, I fumble through my shoulder bag and search for my house keys. I glance over my shoulder as the leaves continue to shake. Forget it. I go to full-fledged sprint. Under the awning, my feet slide against the blacktop. I ram the key into the lock and twist to the right. The metal door clicks open, and I slip inside, colliding with the shopping cart that people use to move their groceries. My knee slams into the corner of the cart, and I shove it out of the way, hobbling up the narrow beige hallway and into one of the lobby's waiting elevators.

Crashing against the brown Formica walls of the elevator, I jab the button for the fifth floor and smash the *Door Close* button like a punching bag. The elevator door's still open. In the hallway, a broken fluorescent light sizzles at half-power, adding a yellow, mucusy pallor to the floor and walls. I close my eyes for some quick calm, but as I open them, the world goes black-and-white, my own personal newsreel. In the distance, a woman screams in C minor as Boyle's ambulance doors bite shut. *No, that's not . . .* I blink again and I'm back. *There's no one screaming.* As the door eventually rumbles shut, I touch my ear as my hand shakes uncontrollably. *C'mon, Wes . . . hold it together . . .*

Pressing my back into the corner to keep myself upright,

I grit my teeth to slow my breathing. The elevator rises with a lurch, and I focus on the indicator lights. Second floor . . . third floor . . .

By the time I step out on the fifth floor, beads of sweat ski down across my rib cage. Leaving nothing to chance, I check the left side of the hallway before darting out and heading right.

I run for apartment 527, ram my key in the lock, and twist the knob as fast as I can. Inside, I flick on every light I can find . . . the entryway . . . the living room . . . the lamp on the end table . . . I even double back to do the hall closet. No . . . better to leave it off. I flick it on, then off. On, then off. On, then off. *Stop* . . . Stepping backward and crashing into the wall, I shut my eyes, lower my head, and whisper to myself. 'Thank you, God, for keeping my family safe . . .' *Stop* . . . 'For keeping me safe, and the President safe . . .' *Find a focal point*, I tell myself, hearing the counselor's voice in my head. '. . . for me and . . .' *Find a focal point.*

Pounding myself in the ear, I stumble around, almost tripping over the ottoman from my parents' old leather sectional sofa in the living room. *Find her.* Sprinting up the hallway that leads to the back half of the apartment, I run past the flea market picnic bench we put in our dining room, past Rogo's room with the stack of unread newspapers outside the door, past the hallway's life-size cutout of President Manning with a hand-drawn word balloon on his head that says *I don't remember how to drive, but I lovey that downwithtickets.com!* and eventually make a sharp right into my bedroom.

Tripping over a pile of dress shirts on the floor, I race for the square metal birdcage that sits atop my dresser. As the door slams into the wall, Lolo pulls back, wildly flapping her beige wings and bobbing her yellow head from side to side. Watching her reaction, I catch myself and quickly find my calm. Lolo does the same, lowering her wings and grinding her beak. Her head sways slowly as I catch my breath. Just seeing her, just the sight . . .

'Hi, Melissa – whattya doin'?' my cinnamon cockatiel asks. She's got a bright orange circle on each cheek and a pointy yellow crest on her head that curves forward like a feathery tidal wave. 'Melissa, whattya doin'?'

The joke's too old to make me laugh – Lolo's been calling me by her old owner's name for almost seven years – but the counselor was right. Focal points are good. Though familiar voices are even better.

'Crap away,' I tell Lolo, who for some reason was trained to poop on command.

True to form, three tiny runny droppings splatter through the bottom of the cage onto the waiting newsprint, which I quickly replace, along with fresh food and water.

The bird was my dad's idea. It was six months after the accident, when light switches and repetitive prayers were starting to overwhelm me. He'd heard the story from one of his students about a rape victim whose parents bought her a dog so she wouldn't feel alone when she came home every night. I rolled my eyes. And not just because I'm allergic to dogs.

Still, people never understand. It was never just the bird. It was the need. The need to be needed.

With a quick flick of the lock, I open the cage and offer my left pointer finger as a perch. Lolo hops on immediately, riding it up to her usual spot on my right shoulder. I turn my face toward her, and she tries to bite at my cheek, which means she wants to be scratched. I crouch down to my tan-carpeted floor and cross my legs into

Indian position as the stress of the day starts to wash away. Lolo nuzzles in close, her feathers tenderly tickling the grooves of my face. For all their vaunted eyesight, birds don't see scars.

Her talons loosen their grip on my shoulder, and she lowers her crest, slicking it back Elvis-style. Within a minute, she's already calmed down, and on most nights, that'd be enough to get me to do the same. But not tonight.

In my pocket, my cell phone vibrates. As I check caller ID, I also see that I got two new messages just during the ride in the elevator. Scrolling down, I see all the old numbers. Current call is *L.A. Times*. Messages are CNN and Fox News. My answering machine at home is no better. Nineteen new messages. Family, friends, and the few reporters smart enough to track my home address. They all want the same thing. A piece of the action . . . piece of the story . . . piece of me.

The front door to the apartment swings open down the hall. 'Wes, you still up?' Rogo calls out. His voice grows louder as he turns the corner. 'Your light's on, so if you're touching yourself, now's the time to stop!'

Lolo's talons dig deep into my shoulder. I know exactly how she feels. The last thing I need is another person reminding me about Nico and Manning and Boyle and every other time bomb ticking in my life. *How you doing? How you feeling? How you holding up?* Enough with the damn—

My bedroom door opens slowly. Rogo's been around long enough to know if he kicks it in, it'll send Lolo flapping.

I look up from the carpet, just waiting for the onslaught of questions.

Rogo scratches at his bald head and leans his meatball

physique against the door frame. 'So . . . uh, I rented *Purple Rain*,' he says, pulling the movie from the red knapsack he calls his briefcase. 'Figured we could . . . I don't know . . . order some pizza, maybe just hang – and then, of course, spend some time rewinding the part where Apollonia jumps naked into the river.'

I sit there for a moment, digesting the offer.

'Hi, Melissa – whattya doin'?' Lolo squawks.

'Shut up, bird. I ain't talking to you,' Rogo threatens.

A tiny smile lifts my left cheek. 'Apollonia gets naked? You sure?' I ask.

'Wes, when I was sixteen, I wanted my first car to be a purple motorcycle. Now, who's ready for some bad pizza and Prince doing that pouty thing with his lips? C'mon, Melissa, time to party like it's 1999!'

He runs back up the hallway before I can even say thank you.

37

Florence, South Carolina

Nico knew they'd have them.

'Maps?'

Nico asked, stepping into the gas station minimart and holding up the map of Michigan he took from Edmund's truck.

'Back left,' a ponytailed attendant with peach-fuzz side-burns said without looking up from the small TV he was watching behind the counter.

Before Nico could even take a step, a loud chime rang from where he crossed into the electric eye of the auto-mated doorbell. Wincing at the sound, he still wasn't used to being out in public. But the way his heart was jack-hammering with excitement, it didn't slow him down.

Counting three surveillance cameras – one by the atten-dant, two in the aisles – Nico hit the brakes and eased his pace to a walk as he headed for the spinner rack of maps in the back. It was no different from his old assignments: No need to rush. Don't look around. Disappear in the mundane.

He read most of the maps from halfway down the aisle. California, Colorado, Connecticut, Delaware . . .

It was a good sign. But not half as good as stepping in and seeing that the central spine of the spinner rack was made up of dozens of intersecting metal crosses. Exhaling with relief, Nico practically laughed out loud. Of course his map would be here. Just like with Wes. As in the Book, God's will was always clear.

Tucking his Michigan map under his armpit, he gave the spinner rack a confident whirl, going straight to the end. Sure enough. Second from the top. Right between Washington State and West Virginia. Washington, D.C.

Lightning bolts of adrenaline surged up Nico's legs. He covered his mouth as his eyes flooded with tears of joy. Even though he never doubted . . . to finally see it after being denied for so long. *The nest . . . the devil's nest . . . the M Men buried it so long ago. And now the proof was back.* 'Thank you, Father,' Nico whispered.

Without even hesitating, he pulled the D.C. map from its metal tower, replacing it with the Michigan map he'd brought from the truck. Fair trade.

Wiping his eyes with the heel of his palm, he took a moment to catch his breath. Slowly heading back for the door, he tipped his baseball cap at the attendant. 'Thanks for the help.'

As the ding-dong of the automated chime sounded, the attendant nodded without even looking up.

Outside, a deep gulp of the crisp South Carolina air chilled Nico's lungs, but it didn't come close to cooling the rising thrill bubbling inside his chest. Seeing Edmund pumping gas at the back of the flatbed, Nico darted for the front. As he ducked into the narrow gap between the front grille of Edmund's truck and the back bumper of the truck in front of them, Nico blinked a fresh set of tears from his eyes. For eight years at St. Elizabeths, it was the one thing he never spoke of. The one truth they'd never understand. Sure, they figured out the crosses through observation, and the whispering to himself that

he used to do in the early years. But this . . . like Number
Three taught . . . Some secrets weren't meant to be shared.
And when it came to the nest . . .

Open it! he insisted, nodding to himself.

Like a child sneaking a cookie from the jar, Nico kept
his shoulders pitched as he studied the front page of the
map. Closing his eyes, he took one last scan of the area:
the metal clicking of the truck's idle engines . . . the garden
hose hiss from the pumps . . . even the chalky scratch of
claws against concrete as a raccoon prowled toward the
dumpster around back.

'Thank you, Father,' Nico whispered, keeping his eyes
shut as he tugged the map open and let it unfold in front
of him. His head bobbed up and down sixteen times as
he mouthed his final prayer. *Amen.*

His eyes sprang open, staring straight at the familiar
blue and black grid of the D.C. streets. Orienting himself
on the wide-open patches of the Tidal Basin and National
Mall, he quickly found the marker for the Washington
Monument. From there, he traced a path up to Dupont
Circle, where—

'*D.C?*' Edmund asked, resting a hand on Nico's shoulder
and peeking over at the map. 'I thought you wanted Washington *State?*'

Refusing to turn around, Nico stood up straight as his
legs, arms, and whole body stiffened. If it weren't for his
sniper training, his hands would've been shaking. Still, he
felt the bad vein between his eyebrows. The vein that
swelled, pregnant and full, when they took away his
violin . . . when his father told him his mother was gone . . .
when The Three told him the truth.

Just to keep himself steady, he clenched his toes into
tiny fists that gripped the earth right through his shoes.

The vein still throbbed. Pulsating even faster. Picking up speed. *Father, please don't let it burst* . . . And then . . . as Nico clamped his lips shut and held his breath and focused everything he had on the web of veins swelling against his sinuses, it all went away.

Turning just his head, Nico slowly peered over his own shoulder at Edmund.

'Whoa . . . y'okay?' Edmund asked, stepping back slightly and pointing at Nico's face. 'Your nose . . . it's bleedin' like a bitch, bro.'

'I know,' Nico said, dropping the map as he reached out and palmed Edmund's shoulder. 'Blood of our savior.'

38

Reagan National Airport, Washington, D.C.

'And you're all set, Mr Benoit,' the airline attendant said at the boarding gate.

'Great,' The Roman replied, careful to keep his head tilted down to the left. He didn't have to hide. Or use the fake name. Indeed, the one benefit of Nico's escape was that it gave The Roman the perfect excuse to justify his trip down South. As deputy assistant director, that was his job. Still, he kept his head down. He knew where the cameras were hidden. No need to tell anyone he was coming.

After heading toward the plate-glass window behind the check-in desk and sitting at the far end of a long row of seats, The Roman dialed a number on his phone, ignored the chitchatting of his fellow passengers, and focused on the black, predawn sky.

'D-Do you have any idea what time it is?' a groggy voice begged, picking up the other line.

'Almost six,' The Roman replied, staring outside. It was still too early to see slivers of orange cracking through the horizon as prologue to the sun's arrival. But that didn't mean he had to sit in the dark.

'Did you get the new schedule yet?' The Roman asked.

'I told you last night, with Nico running around,

Manning's entire day is in flux . . . you of all people should know that.'

Staring at his own reflection in the glass, The Roman nodded. Behind him, an armed agent in a *Security* windbreaker weaved through the food court, scanning the crowd. Back by the metal detectors when he first came in, he'd counted three more agents doing the same – and that didn't include the dozen or so who operated in plainclothes to stay out of sight. The FBI wanted Nico back – and in their minds, the best way to get him was to cover every airport, train station, and travel hub. It was a good plan, following years of typical FBI procedure. But Nico was far from typical. And at this point, in all likelihood, far from here.

'What about Wes? When does he get his copy of the schedule?' The Roman asked.

'It's not like the White House anymore. No matter how close he is to Manning, he gets it same as the rest of us – first thing in the morning.'

'Well, when he does get it—'

'You'll have it,' his associate said. 'Though I still don't understand why. You already have the microphone f—'

'*Send it!*' The Roman roared. On his right, a few passengers turned to stare. Refusing to lose it, he shut the phone and calmly slipped it back into the pocket of his overcoat. It wasn't until he unclenched his fist that he saw a tiny dot of blood seeping through the gauze.

39

'A reporter?' Rogo asks in full Southern twang as we weave through morning traffic on Okeechobee Boulevard. 'You're sitting on the biggest political scandal since Boss Tweed started Teapot Dome, and you threw it in the lap of a reporter?'

'First, Boss Tweed had nothing to do with Teapot Dome. They were fifty years apart,' I tell him. 'Second, what happened to all that *Purple Rain* calmness from last night?'

'I was trying to make you feel better! But this . . . You threw it in the lap of a reporter?'

'We didn't have a choice, Rogo. She heard us talking.' Just below the glove compartment, his feet barely touch the Yosemite Sam floor mat with the words *Back Off!* in giant white letters. He bought the mat for me for my birthday a few years back as some sort of personal lesson. From the look on his face, he still thinks I need to learn it. 'If she wanted, she could've run the story today,' I add.

'And this is she? Below the Fold?' he asks, flipping open the newspaper and turning to Lisbeth's column in the Accent section. The headline reads *Still the One – Dr. First Lady Outshines All*. It opens with a fawning item about Mrs Manning's chartreuse Narciso Rodriguez suit as well as her gold eagle pin, which Lisbeth calls 'Americana elegance.' To her credit, she doesn't even go for the snarky mention of Nico's escape.

'See, she's making nice,' I point out.

'That's just so you don't notice that she's maneuvering you in front of the bull's-eye. Think for a sec.'

'Believe me, I know what Lisbeth wants.'

'Yet you're ignoring the fact she'll eventually stop writing about the First Lady's suit and instead be using *your* name to cut to the head of the class. Screw the gossip column, Wes – she'll have the whole front page to herself.'

'She can have it right now! Don't you understand? She heard it all last night: Boyle being alive, us not trusting Manning . . . but like me, she knows that if she goes public now, it'll bring a tidal wave of feces crashing down on all of us.'

'Actually, it'll just be crashing down on Manning and Boyle. Y'know, the people who, well, *actually caused this*!'

'Are you even listening, Rogo? Whatever happened that day, it was pulled off by some of the most powerful people around, including – according to these FBI guys – the former President of the United States, who's also been like a father to me for nearly a decade . . .'

'Here we go – always afraid to hurt Daddy.'

'I'm not afraid to hurt anyone – especially whoever the hell did this to me,' I say, pointing to my cheek. 'But your solution? You want me – before I even know what's going on – to shout everything from the rooftops and go stick a fistful of dynamite into the dam.'

'That's not what I said.'

'It *is* what you said. But if I unleash this, Rogo – if I go public – I can't take it back. And you know that the moment I open my mouth, these people – people who were powerful and connected enough to convince millions that their illusion was real – are going to aim all their resources and energy at making me look like the crackpot who swears he saw a dead man. So if the water's gonna be raging, and I'm wrecking every professional relationship in my entire life, I want to be absolutely sure before I blow it all up.'

'No doubt,' Rogo says calmly. 'Which is why if you go with the FBI—'

'I what? Save myself? I have nothing to offer the FBI. They already know Boyle's alive. They only want me so they can get Manning and light the dynamite themselves. At least my way, I'm the one holding the fuse, and we'll get some information, which is more than we got from your so-called law enforcement buddies.'

'They're trying their best. They're just . . .'

'. . . traffic cops. I understand. And I appreciate you trying. But between The Roman and The Three, we need some actual answers.'

'That doesn't mean you have to sacrifice yourself. Lisbeth's still gonna burn you in the end.'

Holding tight to the wheel, I pump the gas and speed through a yellow light. The car dips and bounces as we climb up Royal Park Bridge.

'Sixty-nine bucks for the ticket and three points on your license,' Rogo warns as the yellow light turns red just above us. 'Though I guess that's nothing compared to wrecking your life with an overanxious reporter.'

'Rogo, y'know why no one knew who Deep Throat was all those years? Because he controlled the story.'

'And that's your grand plan? Be Deep Throat?'

'No, the grand plan is to get all the facts, put my hands around Boyle's throat, and find out why the hell all this actually happened!' I don't motion to my face, but Rogo knows what I'm talking about. It's the one thing he won't argue.

the jingling of the two dangling presidential faces on the lapel pin that's attached to my navy suit jacket.

'Here's hoping you're right,' Rogo offers as he stares down at Yosemite Sam. 'Because, no offense, pal – but the last thing you need right now is another enemy.'

40

'What'd she write?' Micah asked, gripping the steering wheel and trying to read the newspaper in O'Shea's lap. Four cars ahead of them, Wes's Toyota chugged back and forth through traffic.

'Some fluffy mention about the First Lady's suit,' O'Shea said from the passenger seat, still scanning Lisbeth's column. 'Though she did manage to work in a Dreidel mention.'

'You think Wes told her what's going on?'

'No idea – though you saw the body language last night. All the hesitations . . . just barely looking her in the eyes. If he hasn't said anything, he's thinking about it.' Pointing ahead to the Toyota, O'Shea added, 'Not so close – pull back a hair.'

'But for him to go to the press,' Micah began, hitting the brakes and dropping back a few cars. 'He's safer with us.'

'Not in his eyes. Don't forget, the kid's been wrecked by the best, and he's somehow still standing. Deep down, he knows how the world works. Until he gets a better bargaining chip, in his mind, he's not safe with anyone.'

'See, that's why we should just offer him straight clemency. *Okay, Wes, next time you hear from Boyle, tell him Manning wants to meet with him and give him a time and place. Then call us and we'll take care of the rest.* I know you've got big eyes, O'Shea, but unless we finally put hands on Boyle—'

'I appreciate the concern, Micah – but trust me, we stick with Wes and we'll get our Boyle.'

'Not if Wes thinks we're gonna bite back. I'm telling you, forget the vague promises – put a deal on the table.'

'No need,' O'Shea said, knowing that Micah always went for the easy way out. 'Wes knows what we want. And after everything Boyle's so-called death put him through, he wants him more than any of us.'

'Not more than me,' Micah insisted. 'After what him and Manning pulled—'

'Get up there! He's running the red light!'

Micah punched the gas, but it was already too late. With a screech, the car in front of them came to an abrupt halt, forcing them to do the same. In the distance, Wes's Toyota climbed up the bridge and out of sight.

'I told you to—'

'Relax,' Micah said. 'He's just going to work. Losing him for two minutes isn't gonna kill anyone.'

41

Woodbine, Georgia

'. . . but that's the problem with hiding a treasure,' Nico said as the early morning sun punched through the damp Georgia clouds. 'You don't pick the right spot, some stranger's gonna come along and dig it up.'

But to say they hid it in a map . . .

'Dammit, Edmund, it's no different than hiding it in a crossword or a—' Cutting himself off, Nico gripped the steering wheel and turned toward his friend in the passenger seat. It was harder than he thought. Trusting people never came easy. But Nico understood the power of the Lord. The power that delivered Edmund to his side. From the rearview mirror, the wooden rosary swayed in a tight circle, like a marble in its last seconds before circling down an open drain. Edmund was sent for a reason. And Nico knew never to ignore the signs. Even if it meant exposing his own weaknesses. 'I'm not crazy,' Nico said, his voice soft and tender.

I never thought you were. By the way, you sure you're okay driving?

'I'm fine. But just know, if you wanna help, you need to understand that this battle didn't start eight years ago. It started in '91.'

1991?

'*1791*,' Nico said, watching Edmund's reaction. 'The

year they drew the battle lines . . . by drawing the city lines,' he explained, jabbing a finger against the map that was spread out across the wide dashboard between them.

City lines to what? Washington, D.C.?

'That's what they were designing – the layout for our nation's capital. President George Washington himself picked out a U.S. army major for the job: French-born architect Pierre Charles L'Enfant. And when you look at his early plans . . . it laid the groundwork for everything here today,' Nico said, pointing Edmund back toward the map.

So when this French guy designed the city—

'No!' Nico insisted. 'Unlock yourself from history's lies. L'Enfant is the one most often credited with the plans, but after being hired by President Washington, a known Freemason, there was one other man who helped sketch the details of the city. *That's* the man who marked the entryway. And used the skills of the Masons to build the devil's door.'

Is it someone I know, or some other French guy?

'Unlock yourself, Edmund. Ever hear of Thomas Jefferson?'

42

'ID, please,' the burly African-American security guard insists as I step through the glass doors and into the gray marble lobby of our building. Most mornings I pass with nothing more than a wave to Norma, the overweight Hispanic woman who's worked the morning shift for the past three years. Today, Norma's gone. A quick glance at the new guard's hand shows me the beige sleeve-microphone concealed in his fist. The patch on his shoulder reads *Flamingo Security Corp.* But I know Secret Service when I see it.

With Nico loose, no one's taking any chances.

It's no different when I step out of the elevator on the fourth floor. In addition to the regular suit-and-tie agent who stands guard by the flags in our welcoming area, there's an agent outside our bulletproof doors, and a third just outside the President's personal office at the end of the hallway. Still, none of it surprises me half as much as the familiar voice I hear a few doors down as I cut into my own office.

'You're sure it's okay?' the voice asks from our chief of staff's office.

'Absolutely,' Claudia promises as they step into the hall. 'In fact, if you didn't call – oh, I would've *killed* you. And so would *he*,' she says, referring to the President.

She stops short right in front of my door. 'Wes, guess

who's going to be working out of our office for the next week?' she asks, stepping inside and waving like a magician's assistant toward the door.

'H-Hey, pal,' Dreidel says as he enters my office, a thick file folder pressed against his hip.

I clap my hands, pretending to be amused. *What're you doing?* I ask with a glance.

'My firm asked if I could—'

'They didn't *ask*,' Claudia jumps in, already seizing control. 'They had a last-minute rescheduling on a deposition, and since he was down here, they *told* him to stay. But we can't let him scrounge in some hotel executive center, right? Not when we've got all this office space here.'

'It's just for a week,' Dreidel says, already reading my reaction.

'Wes, you okay?' Claudia asks. 'I figured with all this Nico mess, it'd be nice to have someone familiar to—' She cuts herself off, realizing what she's missed. 'Nico. Oh, how could I be so *stupid*? Wes, I'm so sorry . . . I didn't even think that you and Nico—' She steps back, tapping the tight bun in her hair as if she wants to bury herself under it. From there, the pity comes quickly. 'How're you holding up? If you need to go home—'

'I'm fine,' I insist.

'After all these years, it's just . . . I don't even think of you as—' She doesn't say the word, but I still hear it. *Disabled. Scarred.*

'A *victim*,' Dreidel clarifies as Claudia offers a thankful nod.

'Exactly. A victim,' she repeats, finding her footing. 'That's all I meant. Just that you . . . you're not a victim, Wes. Not now, not ever,' she insists as if that makes it so. Like any career politician, she doesn't let the apology linger.

'Meanwhile, Dreidel, let me show you the volunteer room in back – it's got a computer, a phone – you'll be set for the week. Wes, just so you know, I talked to the Service this morning, and they said they're not expecting any incidents, so unless we hear otherwise, schedule stays pretty much the same.'

'Pretty much?'

'They're keeping him home most of the day – y'know, just to be safe,' she says, hoping to soothe. The problem is, the last time Manning altered his schedule was when they thought he had rectal cancer a few years back. Life-or-death. 'So forget the PSA taping,' she quickly adds, heading for the door. 'Though he'll still need you for the Madame Tussaud thing at the house tonight.'

Before I can say a word, my phone rings on my desk.

'If it's press . . .' Claudia says.

I shoot her a look.

'Sorry,' she offers. 'I just, if you saw how many calls I got last night . . .'

'Believe me, I've been saying no all morning,' I tell her as she waves and leaves. I let the phone ring, waiting for Dreidel to trail behind her. He stays put.

'Claudia, I'll be there in a sec,' he calls out, standing next to me at my desk.

I stare at him in disbelief. 'What the hell're you doing here?' I whisper.

He looks back with the same disbelief. 'You kidding? I'm helping you.'

The phone rings again, and I glance down at caller ID, which is angled so Dreidel can't read it from his side of the desk. *Presidential Library.*

'Could be the archivist,' Dreidel says, leaning forward for a quick glance. 'Maybe she got Boyle's papers ready.'

The phone rings again.

'What, now you don't want the papers?' he adds.

I roll my eyes but can't ignore the logic. Grabbing the receiver, I answer, 'Wes here.'

Dreidel makes a beeline for the door, peeking out into the hallway to make sure we're alone.

'Heya there, Wes,' a soft voice says through the phone. 'Gerald Lang . . . from the curator's office? Wondering if you had a moment to talk about that presidential aide exhibit?'

As Dreidel cranes his neck into the hall, a sudden, fake smile lights up his face. Someone's there.

'Heeey!' he announces, motioning them into my office.

'Dreidel, *don't*!' I hiss, covering the phone. I don't need the circus to—

'Dreidel?' Lang asks on the line, clearly overhearing. 'I was just trying to reach him. He was Manning's aide in the White House, no?'

In front of me, Bev and Oren embrace Dreidel in a Mary Tyler Moore group hug. Bev squeezes him so tightly, her fake boobs practically crush the personalized Manning letter she's holding. The prodigal son's returned. But as I watch them celebrate, a hollow pain crawls through my stomach. Not out of jealousy. Or envy. I don't need them to ask me about Nico or how I'm holding up. I don't need more pity. But I do need to know why Dreidel, still in mid-hug, keeps glancing over his shoulder, studying me on the phone. His eyes are tired, the dark moons below them betraying his lack of sleep last night. Whatever kept him up, kept him up late.

'Wes, you there?' Lang asks on the other line.

'Yeah, no—I'm here,' I reply, crossing around to the seat side of the desk. 'Let me just . . . can I think about it for a bit? With all this Nico mess, we're just running a little crazy.'

Hanging up the phone, I look back at my friend. My friend who got me my job. And taught me everything I know. And visited me when . . . when only my parents and Rogo visited. I don't care what Rogo says. If Dreidel's here, it's for a good reason.

With a back pat for Oren and a cheek kiss for Bev, Dreidel sends them on their way and bounces back into my office. Curling one leg under my tush, I take a seat behind my desk and study the smile on his face. No doubt about it. He's here to help.

'So *no* on the archivist, huh?' he asks. 'What about Lisbeth? What time we seeing her?' When I don't answer immediately, he adds, 'Last night . . . I was there, Wes. You said you were meeting this morning.'

'We are, but—'

'Then let's not be stupid.' He heads for the door and slams it shut for privacy. 'Instead of rushing in like imbeciles, let's make sure we're ready for once.' Reading my reaction, he adds, 'What? You do want me to come, right?'

'No . . . of course,' I stutter, sinking slightly in my seat. 'Why wouldn't I want that?'

43

Kingsland, Georgia

THE Thomas Jefferson?

'A trinity – can't you see it?' Nico asked, both hands on the six o'clock position of the steering wheel. Motioning Edmund to the map on the dashboard between them, he added, 'Washington, Jefferson, L'Enfant. The original Three.'

The original three what?

'The Three, Edmund. From the earliest days, there have always been The Three. The Three who were born to destroy – and today, The Three who're here to save.'

So The Three are chasing The Three – sorta like a circle . . .

'Exactly! Exactly a circle,' Nico said, already excited as he reached up to the sun visor above his seat and pulled out a pen. 'That's how they picked the symbol!' Holding the steering wheel and leaning over toward the dashboard, Nico sketched furiously on the corner of the map.

A circle with a star?

'Five-pointed star, also known as a pentagram – the most widely used religious symbol in history – vital to every culture, from the Mayans to the Egyptians to the Chinese.'

And Washington and Jefferson somehow unearthed this?

No, no, no – pay attention – Washington was a Freemason . . . Jefferson was rumored to be one too. D'you really think they didn't know what they were doing? This wasn't something they unearthed. This was something they were *taught*. Five points on the star, right? In ancient Greece, five was the number of man. And the number of elements: fire, water, air, earth, and psyche. Even the church used to embrace the pentagram – just look at it – the five wounds of Jesus,' Nico said, giving a quick glance to the wood rosary on the rearview. 'But when the symbol is inverted – turned upside down – it becomes the opposite of that. A sign embraced by witches, by the occult, and by . . .

. . . *the Freemasons.*

'You see it, don't you? I knew you would, Edmund! They've been invoking the symbol for centuries – placing it on their buildings . . . above their archways . . . even *here*,' Nico said, jabbing down at the map, his pointer finger stabbing the most well known block of Pennsylvania Avenue.

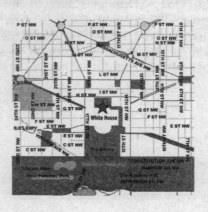

The White House?

'They tried it for centuries all over the world. Fortresses in Spain, castles in Ireland, even in the old stone churches in Chicago. But for the doorway to open, they needed more than just the right symbols and incantations . . .

. . . they needed power.

'Supreme power. That was the lesson of the pyramids and Solomon's Temples – centers of power – to this day, the Freemasons still call Solomon their first grand master! That's why they collected all of history's leaders! The access to power! I knew you'd see it! Praise be all!' Just watching Edmund's reaction, Nico could barely contain himself. 'I knew you'd see!'

But . . . how could no one in the White House notice there was a door with a pentagram on it?

'*Door?* Doors can be removed and replaced, Edmund. Even the White House has been burned and renovated. No, for this, the Masons marked something far more permanent . . .' Nico again turned to the map. 'Follow the landmarks,' he explained, already circling each point on the map. 'One – Dupont Circle . . . two – Logan Circle . . . three – Washington Circle . . . four – Mount Vernon Square . . . and five—' He lifted his pen and jabbed down at the final spot: '1600 Pennsylvania Avenue.'

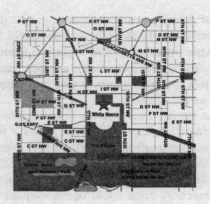

'The building *is* the door. Right in front of us for over two hundred years,' he added as he connected the dots. Just as The Three had done for him.

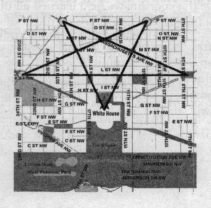

Oh, God.

'God had nothing to do with it, Edmund. Monsters,' Nico insisted. 'That's who we're fighting. To mark the territory, Jefferson even branded it with their own emblem.'

On the edge of the map, Nico again started to draw. To his own surprise, his eyes welled up with each scratch of his pen. It was the one symbol he'd never forget.

Nico, you okay there?

Nico nodded, grinding his teeth and refusing to look back down at the symbol – the compass and the square. *Remember the lessons. No tears. Just victory.* Locked on the road, he gave the coordinates he'd learned all those years ago. 'Start at the Capitol and run your finger down Pennsylvania Avenue, all the way to the White House,' Nico explained, feeling the pressure building in his skull. *Fight it. Fight the monster back.* 'Now do the same from the Capitol down Maryland Avenue – follow it all the way to the Jefferson Memorial – his own shrine! Now go to Union Station and draw a line down Louisiana Avenue, then on the south side of the Capitol, draw another down Washington Avenue. The lines will connect in front of the Capitol . . .'

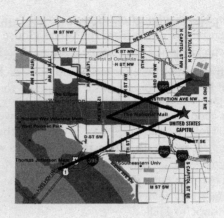

This time, Edmund was silent.

'The compass and the square. The most sacred Masonic symbol . . .'

. . . pointing right to the doorway of the White House . . . all that power in one place. Why would—? What're they doing, trying to take over the world?

'No,' Nico said coldly. 'They're trying to *destroy* it.' Already forgetting the pain in his skull, he added, 'Welcome, Edmund – welcome to the truth.'

I . . . I can't believe this.

'Those were my words . . . my thoughts too.'

But to get this done with no one knowing . . .

'They did it in plain view! On October 13, 1792, Maryland's Masonic Lodge number 9 laid the cornerstone of the White House in a ceremony filled with Freemason rituals. Look it up – it's true! The inscription on the brass plate of that cornerstone says it was laid on the twelfth, but every reputable history book in existence says it was laid on the *thirteenth*!'

Thirteen. The number of the Beast.

'Thirteen blocks north from the White House is where they built the House of the Temple, national headquarters of the Freemasons!'

Thirteen again!

'Now you understand their treachery. They've been waiting for centuries! Seven hundred years ago, we thought it was the Holy Roman Emperor – the one the church labeled the first enemy. But the Masons knew to wait. Wait for the signs. Wait for the true world power to emerge. Prepare. Then the end-times would come!'

So the door they were trying to open . . .

'. . . the door to Hell.'

Of course! They were trying to free the Creatures . . . begin the motions! Nico, do you have any idea what you're on to? Scripture predicts it! It begins when the Two Beasts arrive . . .

'. . . they come through hosts! First, a disciple – a man of sin . . .'

That's Boyle, right? The man of sin!

'Then the Leader – a man of power . . .'

Manning!

'Through him the Dark One – the true Beast – will arise, creating the most powerful kingdom of all!'

So the Beast they were trying to free . . .

'The Antichrist, Edmund. They want the Antichrist! If it weren't for The Three, he would've come! Tell me you see that! Without The Three, Manning's reelection was imminent! Supreme power in Manning! A man of sin in Boyle! Together, the keys to open the door!'

The original Three dedicated to birthing him – the final Three dedicated to destroying him! Alpha and Omega! Their destiny fulfilled!

'Yes, yes . . . destiny – their fate – just as in scripture!

"*Dear children . . . the antichrist is coming. He is now already in the world!*" Nico screamed as spit flew from his mouth and sprayed the inside windshield.

So the reason you shot Boyle instead of Manning . . .

'In a coliseum of his admirers? Surrounded by his supplicants? *Manning's influence was at its peak!* What if that were the catalyst for his awakening? No – like The Three said . . . better to go with Boyle, who was–was–was— *Don't you see?*' he yelled, pounding the steering wheel. 'Without Boyle, there'd be only *one* Beast! *One key instead of two! With only one, the door couldn't open!*' He kept looking to Edmund, then back to the road. His breathing was galloping, his whole body shaking. Being silent for so long . . . to finally let it out . . . he could barely catch his breath.

'Th-Th-The man of sin – like my father – has always been the sign! Have you not . . . have you not heard of Boyle's sin?' Nico shouted, gasping between breaths as a sudden flush of tears blurred the road in front of him. He hunched forward, gripping the wheel as a dry heave clenched his stomach. 'What he did to his own—? And then to my—?' He jabbed a finger at his eyes, digging away the tears. They rolled down his face, dangling like raindrops from his jaw. *Don't fight it,* he told himself. *Be thankful to get it out . . . Heed the Book . . . Thank you, Mother . . . Thank you . . .*

'D-D'ya understand?' he pleaded with Edmund, his voice cracking with the Wisconsin accent he'd buried years ago. 'People know nothing, Edmund. Teacher and student. Master and supplicant. Manning and Boyle,' he repeated, sinking forward on the steering wheel. 'Like father and son. That's why I was chosen. Why my mother was taken. To test me . . . to stop my father . . . to close the devil's door. To keep the door shut and the Great Darkness from coming.'

In the passenger seat next to him, Edmund didn't say a word.

'P-Please, Edmund . . . please tell me you understand . . .'

Once again, Edmund was silent. As silent as he'd been for the past five hours when they pulled out of the gas station in South Carolina.

With his seat belt in a diagonal bear hug across his chest, Edmund slumped slightly to the right, his shoulder pressed against the passenger door. His arms dangled at his side, his left wrist bent in his lap.

As the flatbed truck rumbled onto the overpass that ran across St. Marys River, a bump of uneven concrete sent Edmund's head sagging to the right, his forehead thumping lightly into the glass of the passenger window. With each new seam in the asphalt, the flatbed hiccupped. With each hiccup, Edmund's head thumped over and over against the glass.

'I knew you would, Edmund,' Nico said excitedly. 'Thank you. Thank you for believing . . .'

Thump . . . thump . . . thump. Like a hammer to a stubborn nail, Edmund's head banged the glass. The baritone drumbeat was ruthlessly unavoidable. Nico didn't notice. Just like he didn't notice the slurpy sound of Edmund's bloody fingers sticking and unsticking from the truck's vinyl seats. Or the dried waterfall of blood that'd poured down Edmund's chest from where Nico slit his throat with his car keys.

'I know, but I'm just glad you understand,' Nico said, catching his breath and wiping the last of the tears from his eyes. With one final thump, the truck cleared the St.

Marys River overpass and officially crossed the state line of Georgia. On the right, they blew past a faded orange and green highway sign. *Welcome to Florida—The Sunshine State.*

44

An hour and a half later, I pull up to the curb in front of
First of America Bank, which houses Rogo's offices on
the second floor. As my car bucks to a stop, Rogo trudges
slowly out the building's front door, heading for the front
passenger door. He's still pissed I'm meeting with Lisbeth.
But not half as pissed as seeing Dreidel sitting in his seat.

'How's the world of traffic tickets?' Dreidel calls out as
he rolls down the window.

'Same as Chicago politics,' Rogo replies, shooting me
a look as he opens the door for the backseat. 'Completely
corrupt.'

It was no better the first time they met, years ago. Both
lawyers, both opinionated, both too stubborn to see
anything but the other's flaws.

For the rest of the ride, Rogo sulks in the back as we
blow by the past-their-prime mom-and-pop shops that
line South Dixie Highway. Every once in a while, he peers
out the back to make sure we're not being followed. I use
my side mirror for the same.

'There . . .' Dreidel points as if I haven't been here a
dozen times. Hitting the brakes, I make a sharp right into
the front lot of our destination: the wide, off-white office
building that takes up most of the block. Just in front of
the building is a small plaza with a statue of a turtle
dressed in a black suit and sunglasses, comically playing

an electric keyboard. It's supposed to be funny. None of us laugh.

'Park underneath,' Rogo says, pointing to the two-story concrete parking garage that connects to the building. 'The fewer people who see us, the better.' He glares at me in the rearview. It doesn't take a genius to get the point. It's bad enough I brought us here. It's even worse that I brought Dreidel.

Still, Dreidel doesn't seem to notice Rogo's tantrum. Staring out the window, he's far too focused on the huge brown sign that's partially blocked by the building's faux-cement pillars: *Palm Beach Post*.

'You sure this is smart?' Dreidel asks as the sun disappears, and we wind our way up to the second level of the already dark garage.

'You got a better place?' I challenge.

And that's the point. No matter where we go, it's a cakewalk for anyone to listen in. But here, in the heart of it . . . I don't care how powerful they are – Manning, the FBI, even the Service – none of them can afford to fist-fight with the press.

'What's the backup plan for when she screws us?' Rogo asks as we head through the front door of the building and across the lobby's salmon and black marble floor. It's his last-ditch effort to turn us around. Dreidel nods to show he agrees, but he still doesn't slow down. Like me, he's got a personal stake. And based on what I saw in his hotel room, he doesn't want to give Lisbeth another excuse to put his name in bold.

'Cell phones and pagers,' a tan guard with silver hair announces as we approach the metal detector and X-ray. I put my shoulder bag on the belt, along with my phone.

But as I step through the X-ray, a loud beep echoes through the tall marble canyon.

Feeling myself up, I check for a pen or a—

'Your pin,' the guard blurts, pointing to my lapel.

Rolling my eyes and stepping back through the X-ray, I fight my way out of my suit jacket and lay it across the conveyor.

'You should just throw the pin away,' Dreidel says, following right behind me. 'Those creepy shrunken heads bobbling like that—'

'Hey, fellas,' the security guard interrupts, his head cocked sideways as he studies the video monitor for the X-ray. He taps the screen and makes a face. 'Think you might wanna take a glance at this . . .'

45

'Ladies and gentlemen, welcome to Palm Beach International Airport,' the flight attendant announced through the plane's intercom. 'Please remain seated with your seat belts fastened until the aircraft comes to a complete stop and the captain turns off the seat belt sign.'

Flicking the metal clasp, The Roman undid his seat belt, reached under the seat in front of him, and pulled out a thick aluminum photographer's briefcase with the Secret Service logo on it. He flexed his thumbs, triggering the clasps that opened the case. From inside, tucked into a gray foam protective shell, he pulled out a small receiver that reminded him of the old transistor radios his grandfather used to collect. Unwrapping a black wire from around the receiver, he inserted the earpiece in his right ear and flicked the *On* switch on the side of the receiver.

'. . . *pin away,*' Dreidel said, his voice far more muffled than before. '*Those creepy shrunken heads bobbling like that—*'

Checking the reception on the square electronic screen, The Roman saw four out of five digital bars. It was no different than a cell phone with a souped-up military battery.

'*Hey, fellas,*' a new voice interrupted. '*Think you might wanna take a glance at this . . .* '

The Roman put a finger in his free ear and turned a dial to raise the volume. All he got was silence.

Up above, a loud chime sounded in the plane as a metal symphony of unfastened seat belts filled the cabin. Sitting perfectly still, The Roman turned up the volume even higher. Still nothing. For a moment, there was some mumbling, but nothing audible.

'*What floor?*' Rogo asked, coming through loud and clear.

'*Second,*' Wes replied.

'*Just do me a favor,*' Rogo added. '*When dealing with Lisbeth, let's try to be smart about this, okay?*'

Closing his suitcase and following his fellow passengers into the aisle, The Roman nodded to himself. Them being smart was exactly what he planned.

46

'Gotta give the boy credit,' Micah offered, circling through the parking lot as Wes, Rogo, and Dreidel disappeared inside the *Palm Beach Post* building.

'Who, Wes?' O'Shea asked, watching from the passenger seat of their government-rented Chevy. 'Why, because he's running for help?'

'See, that's where you're underestimating. I don't think he's running. Once he steps inside that building, he's zipping himself in a force field he knows we won't pierce.'

'Either that or he's running out of options.'

'Maybe,' Micah said, holding the steering wheel and facing his longtime partner. 'But when I was trailing him yesterday morning, every single person he ran into was staring at his face. The valet, the doorman, the guests he passed in the lobby . . . if he can handle that on a daily basis, he can take more punches than you think.'

'And that's supposed to impress me?'

'I'm just saying, the immovable object is just as deadly as our unstoppable force.'

'Yeah, but the unstoppable force is still the one people're afraid of. And until we catch Boyle's ass, that's the one I'd rather be.'

'. . . because it's served us so well thus far,' Micah said.

'You're missing the point. Even if Boyle knows we're searching . . .'

'. . . which he does. He's known for years.'

'But what he *doesn't* know is that Wes has suddenly become the best carrot on our stick. Turn—in there,' O'Shea added, pointing to the entrance to the two-story parking garage.

Rounding the turn and weaving up to the second level, it didn't take long for them to pull up to Wes's rusted black Toyota. As soon as he saw it, Micah hit the brakes.

'Just pull in back there,' O'Shea said, motioning to an open parking spot diagonally across from the Toyota.

Tapping the gas, Micah eased into the spot. Through the back window, the view of Wes's car was perfect.

'We got the carrot,' O'Shea said. 'When you hold tight to that, the horse'll always follow.'

47

Crowding around the small TV monitor of the X-ray, we all stand frozen as the guard points to the screen. The rectangular outline of my lapel pin glows dark gray. Just below it, the two sculpted heads dangle like matching gray tears. But what's far more interesting are the tiny metal pieces – they almost look like shards of shattered glass – glowing bright white at the center of the rectangle.

We're all squinting, struggling to make them out, until the guard hits a button on his keyboard and pulls in on the picture. On-screen, the pieces – a coiled antenna, a miniature microchip, and an even smaller hearing-aid battery – bloom into view.

As always, Rogo's mouth opens first. 'Sonofa—'

I pinch his elbow and shoot him a look.

'That's just . . . that's my voice recorder – all digital – y'know, to save good ideas,' I whisper, trying to sound like I have a sore throat. 'Cool, huh?'

'They make 'em even tinier than those little cassettes,' Rogo adds, quickly catching on.

'Here, try it,' I bluff to the guard as the conveyor returns my jacket. Folding it over my arm and shoving it toward him, I hold out the lapel to give him a closer look. He waves me off, satisfied by the offer.

Quickly heading for the elevators, we paint on fake smiles as if everything's perfect. The way Dreidel's eyes are dancing back and forth, he's in full panic. I don't blame him. Whoever's listening knows about what he was doing in that hotel room. But now's not the time. I glance back at the guard, who's still watching us, then down at the metal White House, which is presumably still broadcasting.

Just wait, I say to Dreidel with nothing but an open palm aimed in his direction. His eyes dance even faster. As we step into the waiting elevator, he bites at his manicured thumbnail, unable to contain himself. But just as he's about to whisper a response, Rogo grabs him by the biceps.

'What floor?' Rogo asks, leaning in and motioning upward with his chin. In the corner of the elevator, a security camera stares down at us.

'Second,' I reply as casually as possible.

'Just do me a favor,' Rogo adds. 'When dealing with Lisbeth, let's try to be smart about this, okay?'

No one says another word until the door pings open on the second floor. I make two quick lefts, following the gray carpet down the main hallway. Along the left wall are the closed glass doors and private offices of the paper's top editors. We go straight for the cubicles in back.

'This is stupid,' Dreidel whispers as my hand covers the lapel pin. 'We should get out of here. Just dump the jacket and abort.'

For once, Rogo agrees. 'Take it as a sign, Wes. For all we know, she's only gonna make it worse.'

'You don't know that,' I whisper.

'Hey,' Lisbeth calls out, popping her head over the cubicle just as we approach. She reads our reactions instantly. 'What's wr—?'

I put a finger to my lips and cut her off. Holding up my jacket, I point to the lapel pin and mouth the word *bug*. 'Thanks again for having us over,' I add as she pantomimes and points to her own ear.

They can hear us? she asks.

I nod and drape the jacket across the back of her chair.

'Sorry about the air-conditioning,' she adds, already one step ahead of us as she grabs a thick file folder from her desk. 'If you want, just leave your jackets here . . .' Before we can react, she's out of the cubicle and darting up the hallway, her red hair bouncing and her arms swaying at her sides. The way the sleeves of her crisp white shirt are rolled up to her elbows, I can see the pale freckles that dot most of her forearm. Trailing behind her, Rogo sees them too, but he doesn't say a word. He either hates her or loves her. As always with him, it's hard to tell which.

'I'm Rogo,' he says, extending a hand and racing to catch up to her.

'In here,' she says, ignoring him and pulling open the door to a sunny conference room with three glass walls, each of them with open vertical blinds. Lisbeth circles the room and, one by one, tugs on the pull cords, snapping the blinds shut. She does the same with the blinds on the plate-glass window that looks out over the front parking lot. Within three seconds, sunlight's replaced by the quiet drone of fluorescents.

'You sure no one can hear us?'

'Editorial board meets here every morning to decide whose lives they're ripping apart each day. Rumor is, they sweep it for bugs at least once a week.'

Unlike Dreidel or Rogo, or even myself, Lisbeth's not

the least bit thrown or intimidated. We've been out of fighting shape since the day we left the White House. She picks public battles every day. And she's clearly good at it.

'So who gave you the pin?' Lisbeth asks as we take seats around the large oval conference table.

'Claudia,' I stutter, referring to our chief of staff as I accidentally back my chair into the black Formica credenza that runs against the back wall. 'It goes to whoever's late . . .'

'You think she's the one that put the mike in there?' Dreidel asks.

'I-I have no idea,' I say, replaying yesterday's meeting in my head. Oren . . . Bev . . . even B.B. 'It could've been anyone. All they needed was access to it.'

'Who was wearing it last?' Lisbeth asks.

'I don't know . . . Bev maybe? Oren never wears it. Maybe B.B.? But by the end of the week, people sometimes just leave it on their desk. I mean, I wouldn't have noticed if someone went into my office and pulled it off my jacket . . .'

'But to squeeze a wireless mike into something so small,' Dreidel says. 'Doesn't that seem a little high-tech for – no offense, Wes – but for the scrubs on the White House B-team?'

'What's your point?' I ask, ignoring the snobbery.

'Maybe they had help,' Dreidel says.

'From who? The Service?'

'Or the FBI,' Rogo suggests.

'Or from someone who's good at collecting secrets,' Lisbeth adds, a bit too enthusiastically. The way her fingertips flick at the edge of her file folder, she's clearly got something to say.

'You got someone who fits the bill?' Dreidel asks skeptically.

'You tell me,' she says, flipping open her file folder. 'Who wants to hear the real story behind The Roman?'

48

Mostly, it was like the hum of an escalator or the churn of an airport conveyor belt. Soothing at first, then maddening in repetition.

For The Roman, it'd been almost half an hour since he'd heard Wes's scratchy voice echo through the wiretap. If he was lucky, it wouldn't be much longer. But as he picked up his rental car, fought through the airport traffic, and eventually made his way down Southern Boulevard, the wiretap hummed with nothing but emptiness. Every once in a while, as two people passed by Lisbeth's cubicle, he'd pick up the distant buzz of a conversation. Then back to the hum.

Gripping the steering wheel as his white rental car scaled up the Southern Boulevard Bridge, he tried to calm himself with the aquamarine views of the Intracoastal Waterway. As usual, it did the trick, reminding him of the last time he was here: during Manning's final year, casting in Lake Okeechobee, and reeling in nothing smaller than nine-pounders. No question, the bass were bigger in Florida – back in D.C., a six-pounder was considered huge – but that didn't make them any easier to catch. Not unless you were willing to have some patience.

With a glance at his silver briefcase that sat wide-open on the passenger seat, The Roman double-checked the wiretap's signal strength and readjusted his earpiece. After a sharp left on Ocean Boulevard, it wasn't long before he saw the top of the squat, glass office building peeking above the green leaves of the banyan trees that were relocated there to shield it from public view. As he turned left into the main driveway, he knew they'd have security. What he didn't know was that they'd also have two police cars, two unmarked Chevys, and an ambulance right outside the building's entrance. They were definitely starting to panic.

The Roman banked into a nearby parking spot, shut his briefcase, and pulled the earpiece from his ear. Wes was smarter than they'd bargained for. He wouldn't be hearing Wes's voice anytime soon. But that was why he made the trip in the first place. Having patience was fine for catching fish. But the way things were going, some problems required an approach that was more hands-on.

From the bottom of the briefcase, The Roman pulled his 9mm SIG revolver, cocked it once, then slid it into the leather holster inside his black suit jacket. Slamming his car door with a thunderclap, he marched straight for the front entrance of the building.

'Sir, I'll need to see some ID,' an officer in a sheriff's uniform called out with a hint of North Florida twang.

The Roman stopped, arcing his head sideways. Touching the tip of his tongue to the dip in his top lip, he reached into his jacket . . .

'Hands where I can—!'

'Easy there,' The Roman replied as he pulled out a black eelskin wallet. 'We're all on the same side.' Flipping open the wallet, he revealed a photo ID and a gold badge with a familiar five-pronged star. 'Deputy Assistant Director Egen,' The Roman said. 'Secret Service.'

'Damn, man, why didn't you just say so?' the sheriff

asked with a laugh as he refastened the strap for his gun. 'I almost put a few in ya.'

'No need for that,' The Roman said, studying his own wavy reflection as he approached the front glass doors. 'Especially on such a beautiful day.'

Inside, he approached the sign-in desk and eyed the sculpted bronze bust in the corner of the lobby. He didn't need to read the engraved plaque below it to identify the rest.

Welcome to the offices of Leland F. Manning. Former President of the United States.

49

'The Roman's a hero,' Lisbeth begins, reading from the narrow reporter's pad that she pulls out of her folder. 'Or a self-serving narc, depending on your political affiliation.'

'Republican vs. Democrat?' Dreidel asks.

'Worse,' Lisbeth clarifies. 'Reasonable people vs. ruthless lunatics.'

'I don't understand,' I tell her.

'The Roman's a C.I. – confidential informant. Last year, the CIA paid him $70,000 for a tip about the whereabouts of two Iranian men trying to build a chemical bomb in Weybridge, just outside of London. Two years ago, they paid him $120,000 to help them track an al-Zarqawi group supposedly smuggling VX gas through Syria. But the real heyday was almost a decade ago, when they paid him regularly – $150,000 a pop – for tips about nearly every terrorist activity hatching inside Sudan. Those were his specialties. Arms sales . . . terrorist whereabouts . . . weapons collection. He knew what the real U.S. currency was.'

'I'm not sure I follow,' Rogo says.

'Money, soldiers, weapons . . . all the old measuring sticks for winning a war are gone,' Lisbeth adds. 'In today's world, the most important thing the military needs – and rarely has – is good, solid, reliable intel. Information is king. And it's the one thing The Roman somehow always had the inside track on.'

'Says *who*?' Dreidel asks skeptically. After all his time in the Oval, he knows that a story's only as good as the research behind it.

'One of our old reporters who used to cover the CIA for the *L.A. Times*,' Lisbeth shoots back. 'Or is that not a prestigious enough paper for you?'

'Wait, so The Roman's on *our* side?' I ask.

Lisbeth shakes her head. 'Informants don't take sides – they just dance for the highest bidder.'

'So he's a good informant?' I ask.

'*Good* would be the guy who ratted out those Asian terrorists who were targeting Philadelphia a few years back. The Roman's great.'

'How great?' Rogo asks.

Lisbeth flips to a new sheet of her notepad. 'Great enough to ask for a six-million-dollar payout for a single tip. Though apparently, he didn't get it. CIA eventually said no.'

'That's a lot of money,' Rogo says, leaning in and reading off her notepad.

'And that's the point,' Lisbeth agrees. 'The average payout for an informant is small: $10,000 or so. Maybe they'll give you $25,000 to $50,000 if you're really helpful . . . then up to $500,000 if you're giving them specific info about an actual terrorist cell. But six million? Let's put it this way: You better be close enough to know bin Laden's taste in toothpaste. So for The Roman to even demand that kind of cash . . .'

'He must've been sitting on an elephant-sized secret,' I say, completing the thought.

'Maybe he tipped them about Boyle being shot,' Rogo adds.

'Or whatever it was that led up to it,' Lisbeth says.

'Apparently, the request was about a year before the shooting.'

'But you said the CIA didn't pay it,' Dreidel counters.

'They wanted to. But they apparently couldn't clear it with the higher-ups,' Lisbeth explains.

'Higher-ups?' I ask. 'How higher up?'

Dreidel knows where I'm going. 'What, you think Manning denied The Roman's pot of gold?'

'I have no idea,' I tell him.

'But it makes sense,' Rogo interrupts. ''Cause if someone got in the way of *me* getting a six-million-dollar payday, I'd be grabbing my daddy's shotgun to take a few potshots.'

Lisbeth stares him down. 'You go to those action movies on opening night, don't you?'

'Can we please stay on track?' I beg, then ask her, 'Did your reporter friend say anything else about what the six-million-dollar tip was about?'

'No one knows. He was actually more fascinated with how The Roman kept pulling rabbits out of his hat year after year. Apparently, he'd just appear out of nowhere, drop a bombshell about a terrorist cell in Sudan or a group of captured hostages, then disappear until the next emergency.'

'Like Superman,' Rogo says.

'Yeah, except Superman doesn't charge you a few hundred grand before he saves your life. Make no mistake, The Roman's heartless. If the CIA didn't meet his price, he was just as happy to walk away and let a hostage get his head sawed off. That's why he got the big cash. He didn't care. And apparently still doesn't.'

'Is he still based in Sudan?' I ask.

'No one knows. Some say he might be in the States. Others wonder if he's getting fed directly from inside.'

'Y'mean like he's got someone in the CIA?' Rogo asks.

'Or FBI. Or NSA. Or even the Service. They all gather intelligence.'

'It happens all the time,' Dreidel agrees. 'Some midlevel agent gets tired of his midlevel salary and one day decides that instead of typing up a report about Criminal X, he'll pass it along to a so-called informant, who then sells it right back and splits the reward with him.'

'Or he makes up a fake identity – maybe calls himself something ridiculous like *The Roman* – and then just sells it back to himself. Now he's getting a huge payday for what he'd otherwise do in the course of his job,' I say.

'Either way, The Roman's supposedly dug in so deep, his handlers had to design this whole ridiculous communication system just to get in touch with him. Y'know, like reading every fifth letter in some classified ad . . .'

'Or mixing up the letters in a crossword,' Dreidel mutters, suddenly sitting up straight. Turning to me, he adds, 'Let me see the puzzle . . .'

From my pants pocket, I pull out the fax of the crossword and flatten it with my palm on the conference table. Dreidel and I lean in from one side. Rogo and Lisbeth lean in from the other. Although they both heard the story last night, this is the first time Rogo and Lisbeth have seen it.

Studying the puzzle, they focus on the filled-in boxes, but don't see anything beyond a bunch of crossword answers and some random doodling in the margins.

'What about those names on the other sheet?' Lisbeth asks, pulling out the page below the crossword and revealing the first page of the fax, with the *Beetle Bailey* and *Blondie* comic strips. Just above Beetle Bailey's head,

Rogo goes back to reading Lisbeth's column, which ends with a quick mention of Dreidel stopping by. *Old Friends Still Visit*, according to the subhead. It's Lisbeth's way of reminding us that she could've easily gone with the mention of Dreidel's and my breakfast.

'Dreidel was there last night?' Rogo asks. 'I thought he had a fundraiser.'

'He did. Then he came over to see Manning.'

Rogo scratches at his bald head, first on the side, then back behind his ear. I know that scratch. He's silent as the car reaches the peak of the bridge. Three, two, one . . .

'You don't think that's odd?' he asks.

'What, that Dreidel likes to suck up to Manning?'

'No, that on the day after you spot Boyle, Dreidel happens to be in Palm Beach, and happens to get you in trouble with the press, and just *happens* to be raising money in Florida for a congressional race that only matters to people in *Illinois*. That doesn't smell a little stinky feet to you?'

I shake my head as we leave the metal droning of the bridge and glide onto the perfectly paved Royal Palm Way. On both sides of the street, tucked between the towering, immaculate palm trees, are the private banks and investment firms that juggle some of the biggest accounts in the city. 'You know how fundraising works,' I tell Rogo. 'Palm Beach was, is, and will always be the capital of Manningland. If Dreidel wants to cash in on his old connections, here's where he has to come to kiss the rings.'

Rogo scratches again at his head. He's tempted to argue, but after seeing the shape I was in last night, he knows he can only push so far. Lost in the silence, he taps a knuckle against the passenger window to the tune of 'Hail to the Chief.' The only other sound in the car comes from in the President's handwriting, are the words *Gov. Roche . . . M. Heatson . . . Host – Mary Angel.*

'I looked those up last night,' I say. 'The puzzle's dated February 25, right at the beginning of the administration. That night, Governor Tom Roche introduced the President at a literacy event in New York. In his opening remarks, Manning thanked the main organizer, Michael Heatson, and his host for the event, a woman named Mary Angel.'

'So those names were just a crib sheet?' Lisbeth asks.

'He does it all the time,' Dreidel says.

'*All* the time,' I agree. 'I'll hand him a speech, and as he's up on the dais, he'll jot some quick notes to himself adding a few more people to thank – some big donor he sees in the front row . . . an old friend whose name he just remembered . . . This one just happens to be on the back of a crossword.'

'I'm just amazed they save his old puzzles,' Lisbeth says.

'That's the thing. They don't,' I tell her. 'And believe me, we used to save *everything*: scribbled notes on a Post-it . . . an added line for a speech that he jotted on a cocktail napkin. All of that's work product. Crosswords aren't, which is why they're one of the few things we were allowed to throw away.'

'So why'd this one get saved?' Lisbeth asks.

'Because *this* is part of a speech,' Dreidel replies, slapping his hand against Beetle Bailey's face. *Gov. Roche . . . M. Heatson . . . Host – Mary Angel.* 'Once he wrote those, it was like locking the whole damn document in amber. We had to save it.'

'So for eight years, Boyle's out there, requesting thousands of documents, looking for whatever he's looking for,' Lisbeth says. 'And one week ago, he got these pages and suddenly comes out of hiding.' She sits up straight, sliding her leg under her rear end. I can hear the speed in her voice. She knows it's in here.

'Lemme see the puzzle again,' she says.

Like before, all four of us crowd around it, picking it apart.

'Who's the other handwriting besides Manning's?' Lisbeth asks, pointing to the meticulous, squat scribbles.

'Albright's, our old chief of staff,' Dreidel answers.

'He died a few years ago, right?'

'Yeah – though so did Boyle,' I say, leaning forward so hard, the conference table digs into my stomach.

Lisbeth's still scanning the puzzle. 'From what I can tell, all the answers seem right.'

'What about this stuff over here?' Rogo asks, tapping at the doodles and random lettering on the right side of the puzzle.

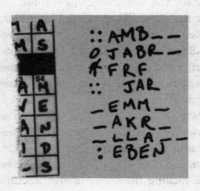

'The first word's *amble* . . . see 7 across?' I ask. 'The spaces are for the *L* and the *E*. Dreidel said his mom does the same thing when she does puzzles.'

'Sorta scribbles out different permutations to see what fits,' Dreidel explains.

'My dad used to do the same,' Lisbeth agrees.

Rogo nods to himself but won't take his eyes off it.

'Maybe the answer's in the crossword clues,' Lisbeth suggests.

'What, like The Roman had an in with the puzzle-maker?' Dreidel asks, shaking his head.

'And that's more insane than it being hidden in the answers?'

'What was the name of that guy from the White House with the chipmunk cheeks?' Rogo interrupts, his eyes still on the puzzle.

'Rosenman,' Dreidel and I say simultaneously.

'And your old national security guy?' Rogo asks.

'Carl Moss,' Dreidel and I say again in perfect sync.

I stay with Rogo. Whenever he's this quiet, the pot's about to boil. 'You see something?' I ask.

Looking up slightly, Rogo smiles his wide butcher's dog smile.

'What? Say it already,' Dreidel demands.

Rogo grips the edge of the crossword and flicks it like a Frisbee across the table. 'From the looks of it, the names of all your staffers are hidden right there.'

50

In the lobby, The Roman didn't hesitate to sign in. Even made small talk about crummy assignments with the agent behind the desk. At the elevators, he rang the call button without worrying about his fingerprints. Same when the elevator doors opened and he hit the button for the fourth floor.

It was exactly why they got organized. The key to any war was information. And as they learned with the cross-word puzzle all those years ago, the best information always came from having someone on the inside.

A loud ping flicked the air as the elevator doors slid open.

'ID, please,' a suit-and-tie agent announced before The Roman could even step out into the beige-carpeted hallway.

'Egen,' The Roman replied, once again flashing his ID and badge.

'Yes . . . of course . . . sorry, sir,' the agent said, stepping back as he read the title on The Roman's ID.

With a wave, The Roman motioned for him to calm down.

'So if you don't mind me asking, what's the mood at headquarters?' the agent asked.

'Take a guess.'

'Director's pretty pissed, huh?'

'He's just mad he'll be spending the next six months

on the damage control circuit. Ain't nothing worse than a daily diet of cable talk shows and congressional hearings explaining why Nico Hadrian wandered out of his hospital room.'

'Those congressmen sure like having their faces on TV, don't they?'

'Doesn't everyone?' The Roman asked, eyeing the surveillance camera and heading toward the black bullet-proof doors of the President's office.

'Pop the locks, Paulie,' the suit-and-tie agent called out to another agent sitting just inside the Secret Service offices on the right-hand side of the hallway.

On the left, there was a muted thunk as the magnetic lock unlatched. 'Thank you, son,' The Roman said. He tugged the door open without ever looking back.

'Hell-o,' a Hispanic receptionist with a high-pitched voice sang as the heavy door slammed behind The Roman. 'How can I help you today?'

Crossing the presidential seal in the carpet, The Roman scanned the left-hand wall for the agent who usually stood guard by the American flag. The agent wasn't there, which meant neither was the President. The only other good news was the yellow Post-it note on the side of the receptionist's computer monitor. In swirling, cursive writing were the words *Dreidel – Ext. 6/Back office*.

'Dreidel's not in, is he?' The Roman asked.

'No, he's out with Wes,' the receptionist replied. 'And you are . . . ?'

The Roman again flashed his ID and badge. 'Actually, I'm here to see Ms Lapin . . .'

'Sure . . . of course,' the receptionist said, pointing to The Roman's left. 'You want me to call her or—'

'No need,' The Roman insisted, calmly marching down the hallway. 'She's already expecting me.'

On the right-hand side of the hall, The Roman breezed past nearly a dozen glass frames filled with ribboned Medals of Honor from every major country. Poland's Great Cross of the Order, Qatar's Collar of Independence, even the U.K.'s Order of the Bath. The Roman didn't even glance at them, already focused on the open door on his left.

Across the hallway, he peeked into the office with the *Chief of Staff* nameplate attached to it. The lights were off, the desk empty. Claudia was already at lunch. Good. The fewer people around, the better.

Cutting left, he stepped into the well-lit office that smelled like fresh popcorn and stale vanilla mint candle. From his angle looking down at her desk, he had a perfect view of the tight red V-neck sweater that fought against her decade-old breast implants.

Before she could even react, The Roman gripped the spine of the door, slowly closing it behind himself.

'Nice to see you, Bev,' he said as it slapped shut. 'Florida looks good on you.'

51

'Right here,' Rogo says, pointing to the column of scribbles on the right side of the puzzle. 'In the work space . . .'

I recheck the vertical column of doodles and

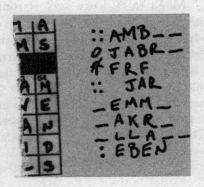

'AMB? JABR? FRF?' Dreidel asks. 'Those aren't any initials I know.'

'Don't go left to right. Go up and down . . .' With his pen, Rogo makes a circle from top to bottom.

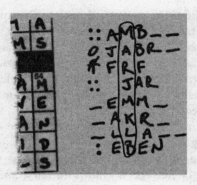

'M, A, R, J, M, K, L, B,' Rogo says, starting me off. 'Fill it in: Manning, Albright, Rosenman . . .'

'Jeffer,' I add.

'Who's Jeffer?' Lisbeth interrupts.

'Me,' Dreidel says.

'Moss, Kutz, Lemonick,' I add, hitting the rest. 'And B . . .'

'For Boyle,' Rogo says proudly. 'Eight people, all with major Oval Office access.'

Lisbeth nods, still studying the crossword. 'But why would the President keep a list with his top staffers' names on it?'

We all look to Dreidel. 'I've never seen it in my life,' he says with a laugh. But from the shake in his voice, it's the one time he's not thrilled to be included on an exclusive list.

Already impatient, Rogo hops from his seat, walking toward the head of the table. 'Manning wrote down eight people's names, then camouflaged it with doodles so no one would notice they were there. Not to play Nancy Drew, but what do they all have in common?'

Lisbeth slides the crossword back to the middle of the conference table. I look down at the list of names. Lemonick was White House counsel, Rosenman was press secretary, Carl Moss was national security adviser. Combined with Manning, Albright, and Boyle, they were the biggest names we had – the knights of our own round table. 'It's clearly a power list.'

'Except for Dreidel,' Rogo points out. 'No offense,' he adds, turning Dreidel's way.

'Were you all working on something at that time?' Lisbeth asks. 'When was it again, February during the first year?'

'We weren't even there a month,' Dreidel points out. But as he sees the seniority of the people on the list, I can already hear the change in his voice. 'Maybe it's who he wanted at the morning sessions – for the PDB.' Reading the confusion of Lisbeth's and Rogo's faces, he explains, 'Every morning at six a.m., an armed courier comes from CIA headquarters to the White House with a legal briefcase handcuffed to his wrist. Inside is the President's Daily Brief – the summary report of the most highly classified news that's happening around the world. Troop movements in North Korea . . . spy networks in Albania . . . whatever the President needs to know, he gets at his first meeting of the day, along with a few select others.'

'Yeah, but everyone knew who was invited to those meetings,' I point out.

'They knew *eventually*,' Dreidel says. 'But during those first weeks, you think Rosenman and Lemonick didn't try to elbow their way inside?'

'I don't know,' Lisbeth says, staring at the list with a small crease between her eyebrows. 'If you're just cutting names, why be so secretive?'

'People're only secretive when there's a reason,' Dreidel says. 'And it seems pretty clear they didn't want anyone else seeing what they were writing.'

'Okay, fine – so what're the things you could write about your top dozen or so staffers that you wouldn't want anyone else to see?' Lisbeth asks. 'You don't like the person . . . you don't want them there . . . you're afraid of them . . .'

'There you go – blackmail's juicy,' Rogo says. 'Maybe one of them had a secret . . .'

'Or *knew* a secret,' Dreidel says.

'You mean about the President?' I ask.

'About anyone,' Lisbeth agrees.

'I don't know,' I say. 'The level of people you're talking about . . . that's the group you're not supposed to worry about keeping their mouths shut.'

'Unless one of them gets you worried that they *can't* keep their mouth shut,' Dreidel blurts.

'You mean like a *trust* list?' Lisbeth asks.

'I guess . . . sure,' Dreidel replies. 'That's what *I'd* want to know if I had a new staff.' For the first time, he's stopped biting his manicured hand.

'I'm not sure I follow,' I say.

'Think about what was actually going on those first few weeks we were in the White House. That bus bomb in France and all the internal arguing over whether Manning's response took it seriously enough. Then we had all those slap-fights about redecorating the Oval . . .'

'Those I remember,' Lisbeth says. 'There was that piece in *Newsweek* about the red-striped carpet . . . what'd they say the First Lady called it again?'

'Fruit-stripe gum,' Dreidel says dryly. 'The bombing and the bad carpet – those were nonsense stories about internal arguments. *Uh-oh, captain can't steer his new ship* . . . But the only reason those things got out was because some loudmouthed staffer decided to take it out.'

Lisbeth nods, knowing this one all too well. 'So what Manning was really worried about back then . . .'

'. . . was finding out who was leaking all our internal baggage,' Dreidel says. 'When you have that many new staffers flushed with that much new power, there's always someone who wants to rush off and brag to their friends. Or the press. Or their friends who happen to be press. And until you can plug the leaks, those stories take away from your entire agenda.'

'Okay,' I say. 'Which means when this list was made, Manning was hunting for staffers who were leaking to the press?'

'Not just staffers,' Dreidel adds. 'Those stories were from conversations happening at *senior staff* levels. That's why Manning was so nuts back then. It's one thing when some intern leaks that the President's wearing unmatched socks. It's another to open up the *Washington Post* and read a verbatim blow-by-blow on the front page from a meeting with your five most trustworthy lieutenants.'

'If that's the case, then why include himself on the list?' Rogo asks as we all glance back at the crossword.

'Maybe it's a list of who was at a particular meeting – Manning, Albright, Boyle, etc. – then they were just trying to narrow who let a particular piece of info out,' I say.

'That would explain why *I'm* there,' Dreidel adds. 'Though maybe it wasn't just leaking to the press.'

'Who else is there?' Lisbeth asks.

'Think back to what you said about The Roman and the six-million-dollar prize they wouldn't approve. Those top informant payments are in the PDB too.'

I nod, remembering the old meetings. 'It's not a bad call. Whoever was leaking the info could've leaked it to The Roman, telling him who was responsible for denying his payout.'

'And you think that's why Boyle got shot?' Lisbeth asks. 'Because Boyle was the one who said no to The Roman's payday?'

'I'd believe that,' Rogo says. 'Six million bucks is a lot of money.'

'No question,' Dreidel says. 'But it seems pretty clear that if you want to know who on the list couldn't be trusted, it's the guy who, until recently, we thought was dead. Y'know, the one the FBI is chasing . . . rhymes with *Doyle* . . .'

'That's why I had the Presidential Library pull Boyle's files,' I say. 'They've got everything: his schedules, what issues he was working on, even his official personnel file with his FBI background check. We'll have every single sheet of paper that was ever in Boyle's desk, or written about him.'

'That's fine – so two of us can go to the library,' Lisbeth says. 'But it still doesn't tell us why a secret list Manning made during the first year of the administration has anything to do with Boyle being shot three years later.'

'Maybe Boyle was mad at the President for not trusting him,' Rogo says.

'No,' Dreidel says. 'According to Wes's FBI guys, whatever Boyle and Manning were up to, they were in it together.'

'Which has to be true,' I point out. 'The ambulance . . . having the blood type ready . . . how else could Boyle possibly pull that off without help from Manning and the Service?'

'So what're you saying? That they didn't trust someone *else* on the list?' Lisbeth asks, her eyes already on Dreidel.

I shake my head. 'All I'm saying is President Manning and Albright spent one of their very first days in office building a hidden list with the names of eight people that shared daily access to some of the best-kept secrets in the entire world. More important, by keeping that list on a crossword puzzle, they figured out a way to create the impossible: a presidential document – potentially containing Manning's innermost thoughts – that wouldn't be inspected, cataloged, studied, or seen by anyone else around him.'

'Unless, of course, you absentmindedly jot a few notes to yourself on the back,' Rogo says.

'The point is, the list still needs narrowing,' I say. 'And as far as I can tell, besides the President, the only people on here who were at the speedway that day were Boyle and Albright – and Albright's dead.'

'You sure those were the only two?' Lisbeth asks.

'Whattya mean?'

'Have you ever looked at any of the archival footage from that day? Maybe take a peek to see if everything you think you remember matches up with reality?'

I shake my head. A week after the shooting, when I was still in the hospital, I caught a clip of the footage while flipping through channels. It took three nurses to calm me down that night. 'I haven't seen the footage for a bit,' I tell her.

'Yeah, I figured this isn't exactly your favorite home movie. But if you really want to know what happened, you have to start at the scene of the crime.' Before I can react, she reaches into her file folder and pulls out a black videocassette. 'Lucky for you, I've got connections at the local TV stations.'

As she pops out of her seat and heads for the black Formica credenza with the VCR/TV combo, my throat tightens and my hands flood with sweat.

I can already tell this is a bad idea.

52

'What about Claudia?' The Roman asked calmly, strolling over to Bev's window and staring down at the agents, sheriff, and ambulance crew crowded into the rotary at the front of the building.

'You told me not to – that it was an internal investigation,' Bev said as she watched The Roman from her desk and anxiously picked at an open bag of microwave popcorn.

'And Oren?'

'I just told you—'

'Tell me again!' The Roman insisted, turning from the window, his pale skin and black hair practically glowing in the noon sunlight.

Bev stayed silent, her hand frozen in the popcorn.

The Roman knew he'd scared her, but he wasn't about to apologize. Not until he had what he wanted.

'You said not to tell anyone – I didn't tell anyone,' Bev finally offered. 'Not B.B., not the President . . . no one.' Fidgeting with the tips of her dyed-black hair, she added, 'Though I still don't get how any of this helps Wes.'

The Roman turned back to the window, taking a moment to choose his words. Bev had known Wes since his first days in the White House. Like any protective parent, she wasn't turning on her kid unless it was for his own good. 'What helps Wes is finding out just who he ran into that night in Malaysia,' The Roman explained. 'If what he said in the report is right – that it was just some drunk looking for the bathroom – then there's nothing to worry about.'

'But to have me put a microphone in his pin . . . to hide it from everyone on staff . . . Why can't you just tell me who you think approached him?'

'Bev, I told you from the start, this is part of a long-term inquiry that we believe – and hope – Wes accidentally stumbled onto. Trust me, we want to protect him as much as you do, which is why—'

'Does it have to do with Nico? Is that why he escaped?'

'This has nothing to do with Nico,' The Roman insisted.

'I just thought . . . with your hand . . .' she said, motioning to the white gauze wrapped around his palm.

The Roman knew that was the risk coming to the office. But with the wiretap silent, and Boyle still unaccounted for . . . some things had to be done face-to-face.

Sitting on the edge of Bev's desk, The Roman cupped her hand between his palms. 'Bev, I know you don't know me. And I know it's odd to suddenly get a call from an agent about an investigation you know nothing about, but I swear to you, this has nothing to do with Nico. Understand? *Nothing*. Everything I've asked of you . . . it's only in the interests of national security and for Wes's benefit,' he added, his pale blue eyes locked on hers. 'Now I appreciate how you look out for him . . . we all know the pity you took . . .'

'It's not pity. He's a sweet kid . . .'

'. . . who should've left this job years ago, but didn't because he's terrified of stepping out of the thoughtful but crippling security blanket you've all tucked him into. Think about it, Bev. If you really care that much about

him, *this* is the moment he needs you. So, is there anyone
else out there we might've overlooked? Old White House
contacts? Current in-house contacts? Anyone you can
think of that he might turn to if he's in trouble?'

Rolling backward on the wheels of her desk chair, Bev
was silent at the onslaught of questions. For a moment,
her eyes stayed with The Roman's pale blues. But the
more he pushed, the more she glanced around. At her
keyboard. At her leather blotter. Even at the blurry 5×9
perched under her computer monitor, from her office
birthday party a few years back. In the photo, the entire
staff was in mid-laugh as the President blew out the candles
on Bev's birthday cake. It was the kind of photo that never
existed in the White House, but decorated nearly every
office here: slightly off-center, slightly funny, and slightly
out of focus. Not a professional photo taken by a White
House photographer. A family photo – taken by one of
their own.

'Sorry,' Bev said, pulling her hand away and glancing
down at The Roman's gauze pad. 'There's no one else I
can think of.'

53

'—*ies and gentlemen, the President of the United States!*' the announcer bellows through the P.A. system as the tape begins to roll, and the shiny black Cadillac One lumbers out onto the racetrack.

From the wide angle – showing half the motorcade in profile – I'm guessing it's from a camera up in the stadium's press box.

'There's the ambulance with Boyle's blood,' Dreidel points out, running around the conference table so he can get closer to the TV. He stops right next to Lisbeth, who's just to the left of the screen. On my far right, Rogo's back at the head of the oval table. But instead of moving toward the screen, he circles back. Toward me.

He doesn't have to say a word. He juts his chin slightly to the left and lowers his eyebrows. *You okay?*

Tightening my jaw, I nod confidently. Rogo's been my friend since before I could drive. He knows the truth.

'Lisbeth,' he calls out. 'Maybe we should . . .'

'Leave it – I'm fine,' I insist.

As the limo leaves the final turn and heads toward the finish line, the camera pulls out to reveal the entire motorcade, which is now headed straight at us. I used to call it a funeral procession. I had no idea.

On-screen, the camera slowly pulls in on Cadillac One. I swear, I can smell the leather seats of the car, the oily whiff of Manning's daily shoeshine, and the sweet tinge of gasoline from pit road.

'Okay, here we go,' Lisbeth says.

The video jump-cuts to a brand-new camera angle from the infield of the track – we're now at eye level. On the passenger side, the Secret Service detail leader gets out of the limo and races to open the back door. Two other agents swoop into place, blocking any clear shot from the crowd. My feet ball up as my toes try to dig through the soles of my shoes. I know what's coming. But just as the door opens, the picture freezes and pauses.

'Slow motion?' Dreidel asks.

'It's the only way to get a good look at who's in the background,' Lisbeth explains, gripping the edge of the top left corner of the TV. Dreidel crosses over and does the same on the right corner. Both lean in. They don't want to miss a thing.

On the other side of the conference table, I twist in my seat. In slow motion, two more Secret Service agents slowly creep into the background near the open door that faces the crowd.

'And these are all guys you know?' Lisbeth asks, making a big circle around the five suit-and-tie agents on-screen.

'Geoff, Judd, Greg, Allan, and . . .' Dreidel pauses on the last one.

'Eddie,' I call out, never taking my eyes off the screen.

'It'll be done in a sec,' Dreidel promises as if that's supposed to make me feel better. He turns back toward the TV just in time to see five fingertips peek out like tiny pink worms above the roofline of the limo. My toes dig even deeper, practically burrowing through my shoes. I close my eyes for a second and swear I can smell popcorn and stale beer.

'Here he comes,' Dreidel whispers as Manning slowly leaves the limo, one hand already up in a frozen, celebratory wave. Behind him, with her own hand raised, the First Lady does the same.

'Now watch the President here,' Lisbeth says as each frame clicks by, and he slowly turns toward the camera for the first time.

On-screen, Manning's grin is so wide, his top gums are showing. Same with the First Lady, who holds his hand. They're definitely enjoying the crowd.

'Doesn't exactly look like a man who knows shots are about to be fired, does he?' Lisbeth asks as Manning continues to wave, his black windbreaker bubbling up like a helium balloon.

'I'm telling you, he didn't know it was coming,' Dreidel agrees. 'I mean, I don't care what they were prepared for, or how much of Boyle's blood they had in the ambulance, there's no way Manning, the Service, or anyone else is going to risk a head shot.'

'You're still assuming they were aiming for Manning,' Lisbeth says as Albright appears on-screen, rising at a turtle's pace from the limo. 'I think Nico hit exactly who he wanted to hit. Just look at his escape from the hospital last night. Both orderlies shot through the heart and the palm of their right hand. Sound like anyone you know?'

On TV, at the center of a bushy mess of gray hair, a tiny bald spot rises above the limo's roofline like the morning sun. Here comes Boyle.

'Now *he's* the one who's anxious,' Lisbeth says, tapping his face on the monitor.

'He was always miserable, though. Even on day one,' Dreidel replies.

I swallow hard as Boyle's profile glows on-screen. The

olive skin's the same, but his thin, pointy nose is far sharper than the stubby nose job I saw him with two days ago. His jowls are longer now too. Even plastic surgery can't stop the aging process.

'See, he's not even looking around,' Dreidel adds as Boyle follows behind the President. 'They've both got no idea what's coming.'

'There you are,' Dreidel says, tapping the far right-hand corner of the screen, where you can barely see me in profile. As I leave the limo, the camera pans left – away from me – as it tries to stay with the President. But since I'm only a few steps behind, there's a tiny shot of me gawking in the background.

'Man, you were a *baby*,' Lisbeth says.

The video flickers, and my head turns like a creaky robot toward the camera. It's the first time we all get a clear look. In my right hand, my middle and ring fingers quickly knead at the heel of my palm. My eyes well up just seeing it. My face . . . God, it's been so long – but there it is . . . the real me.

On-screen, President Manning's hand rises to meet the NASCAR CEO and his now-famous wife. The First Lady adjusts her sapphire necklace, her lips spread in an eternal *hello*. Albright sticks his hands in his pockets. Boyle straightens his tie. And I chase behind them all, frozen midstep with my bag of tricks dangling from my shoulder and a sharp, cocky squint in my eyes.

I know what happens next.

Pop, pop, pop.

On TV, the camera angle jerks upward in a blur, panning past the fans in the stands as the cameraman ducks at the shots. The screen is quickly filled with the blue sky. But to me, it's already fading to black and white. A boy in a

Dolphins T-shirt screams for his mom. Boyle falls to the ground, facedown in his own vomit. And a bee sting rips through my cheek. My head whips back at just the thought of it.

The camera jerks again, sliding back down to earth, past the blur of fans running and shouting and stampeding from the stands. On the left side of the screen, Cadillac One rumbles and takes off. The President and First Lady are already inside. Already safe.

As the car leaves, the camera whizzes back and forth, searching the aftermath and sifting through the ballet of slow-motion chaos: Secret Service agents with their mouths frozen open in mid-yell . . . bystanders darting in every direction . . . and on the top right of the screen, just as the limo pulls away, a pale, skinny kid crashing to the ground, twisting in pain like a worm along the concrete, his hand gripping his face.

The tears tumble down my cheeks. My fingers press so tight into the heel of my palm, I feel my own pulse. I tell myself to look away . . . to get up and turn on the lights . . . but I can't move.

On-screen, two suit-and-tie agents carry Boyle off the battlefield and to the ambulance. Since their backs are to us, it's impossible to make them out. But in the swirl of dust behind the limo, I'm still lying on my back, pressing my face so hard, I look like I'm pinning the back of my head to the asphalt. And while it's all in full color on TV, I still see it in black and white. A flashbulb goes supernova. My fingertips scratch against the sharpened metal in my face. Boyle's ambulance doors slam shut.

'Wes, you with us?' Rogo whispers.

Why won't they stop slamming shut—?

'Wes . . .' Rogo continues to whisper. He says it again,

and I realize it's not a whisper. His voice is loud. Like he's yelling.

Something clenches my right shoulder, shaking.

'Wes!' Rogo shouts as I blink back to reality and find his meaty paw holding my shirt.

'No, no . . . yeah . . . I'm fine,' I insist, pulling my shoulder free of his grip. It's not until I look around the conference room that I realize the videotape is no longer running. In the corner, Lisbeth flicks on the lights, looking back to see what's going on.

'He's fine,' Rogo insists, trying to block her view. 'He's just . . . just give him a second, okay?'

Heading back from the light switch, Lisbeth still continues to stare, but if she sees what's going on, she's kind enough to keep it to herself.

'So that basically accomplished a big fat nothing, huh?' Dreidel asks, still clearly annoyed we're even here. 'I mean, except for giving Wes a few brand-new nightmares to deal with.'

'That's not true,' Lisbeth says, heading back to the opposite side of the table. Instead of sitting next to Dreidel, she decides to stand. 'We got to see the agents that carried Boyle off.'

'Which means nothing since we can't see their faces – not to mention the fact that since the Service clearly helped, I personally don't think it's safe asking any of their agents for help.'

'We would've gotten more if the camera weren't swirling like my mom taking home movies,' Lisbeth points out.

'Yeah, that cameraman was a real jerk-off for ducking down and trying to protect his life like that,' Dreidel shoots back.

'Dreidel,' I interrupt.

'Don't *Dreidel* me, Wes.'

'How 'bout if *I* Dreidel you?' Rogo threatens.

'How 'bout you sit back down and let the boy fight his own fight for once?' Dreidel pushes back. 'Wes, no offense, but this was stupid. Except for getting inside juice for when Drudge-ette here writes her best-selling tell-all, there's not a single good reason to come here. She could've just sent us the info we needed.'

'I was trying to help,' Lisbeth insists.

'This was helping? We've got a thousand unanswered questions, half a dozen absurd theories, and you wanna spend the day watching the one video that Congress, the public, and every conspiracy junkie in the world has combed through and *still* didn't find anything suspicious? It didn't even give us a good shot of Nico to see if there's anything else we might've been missing.'

I shake my head. 'That's not—'

'He's right,' Lisbeth admits from just behind Dreidel, who has to spin around to see her. She's got her back to us as she stands in front of the big plate-glass window. 'We *didn't* get any good shots.' Turning back to us with that same crooked little smile from when she was picking fights with us last night, she adds, 'Fortunately, I know exactly how to change that.'

54

'Y'know there *is* a back entrance,' Micah pointed out, tucked into a *Compacts Only* parking spot and checking his rearview mirror for the third time in the last minute. Diagonally behind them in the parking garage, Wes's empty Toyota hadn't moved. 'I can take a quick look and—'

'No need,' O'Shea said from the passenger seat, his elbow perched on the edge of the car's open window as he worked the morning's crossword. 'This is Florida – he's not going anywhere without his car.'

'Unless he takes someone else's. Remember that woman in Syria?'

'Syria was different. We needed her to run.'

'Why? So you had a good excuse to bring her in?'

'She would've killed you, Micah. You know that.'

'I was luring her in.'

'That's your interpretation,' O'Shea shot back. 'But if you try anything as hotheaded as Syria, I promise you right now, *I'll* be the one putting the gun to *your* head.' Refusing to look up from the crossword, O'Shea pointed over his own shoulder with the back of his pen. 'See that junk shop Subaru diagonally down at the bottom there . . . with the Grateful Dead stickers? We saw it last night. That's Lisbeth's. The one up here is Wes's. Rogo's is still in the shop. No one's going anywhere.'

Unconvinced, Micah checked his rearview for the

fourth time, then glanced over at O'Shea's elbow resting in the open window. 'You should close that up,' he said, motioning to the window. 'In case he comes . . .'

'Micah, it's seventy-two degrees here. In December. You know how cold it was in France? Let me enjoy the damn warmth.'

'But Wes could—'

'It's under control.'

'Yeah, just like this,' Micah said, jabbing a finger at the photo of Nico on the front page of the newspaper that wilted across the armrest between them.

'What, you still think that was The Roman?' O'Shea asked.

'How could it not be? Boyle gets spotted . . . Nico gets out . . . hell of a coincidence, don't you think?'

O'Shea nodded, finally looking up from the crossword. 'But if he used Wes's name to get in . . .'

'I'm just glad you got it purged from the official report. If that went out, the whole world would've swarmed Wes's front steps, and we'd've lost our best—'

'*Tsssttt!*' O'Shea hissed, cutting Micah off. Behind them, a familiar voice echoed off the walls of the garage.

'—e should still call the office,' Wes said as Dreidel followed him up the concrete incline.

'Why, just to panic them?' Dreidel asked.

Studying their respective side mirrors, O'Shea and Micah watched the scene unfold diagonally behind them. From their spot in the garage, they had a perfect view of the passenger side of Wes's Toyota. And it didn't take anything more than that to notice Rogo was missing.

'Where's the fat kid?' Micah whispered.

'Hitting on the girl?' O'Shea guessed.

Just as Wes stepped around to the driver's-side door

and opened the locks, his car keys slipped from his hand. Spinning to catch them, he twisted toward Micah and O'Shea, who didn't flinch. From their angle in the garage, they were near impossible to spot.

There was a loud clink as the keys hit the pavement. For a fraction of a second, O'Shea saw Wes's glance turn toward him. O'Shea still didn't move. No way was Wes that good.

'What's wrong?' Dreidel called out to his friend.

O'Shea stared in his passenger-side mirror and stood his ground. Next to him, watching his own rearview, Micah did the same. They'd been at this too long to panic.

'You hear something?' Wes asked.

'Don't get paranoid,' Dreidel warned.

In the edge of his mirror, O'Shea could see the outline of the back of Wes's head as he turned to his Toyota, picked his keys up off the ground, and slid into the car.

'No, you're right,' Wes replied.

Within seconds, the Toyota's engine grumbled to life and its wheels screeched against the concrete.

Following years of training, Micah waited before going for the ignition. At least until they heard the metallic thunk of Wes's Toyota cresting over the speed bump just outside the garage.

By the time Micah and O'Shea reached the speed bump, Wes's Toyota was pulling into traffic, making a sharp left back onto South Dixie.

'Any idea where he's headed?'

'I'm guessing his office . . .'

'Guess again,' O'Shea said as the Toyota made another sharp left at the first traffic light – in the opposite direction of Manning's office.

Carefully staying at least three cars back, Micah pulled

his own quick left just as the Toyota blew past a sign for I-95. 'He's driving fast.'

'Maybe headed for the highway,' O'Shea guessed as the Toyota took off, shrinking in the distance. Calm as ever, Micah stayed tucked behind two minivans and a white Honda, never losing focus on the two heads in the front seat of Wes's car.

Sure enough, a minute later, the Toyota veered left, following signs for I-95 South and hugging to the curve of the on-ramp at Belvedere Road. But as they merged onto the highway, Micah and O'Shea were surprised to see that Wes wasn't picking up speed. He was slowing down.

'He's at fifty-five exactly,' Micah said, checking the speedometer. 'Think he's trying to flush us out?'

Pointing to the nearest exit sign, O'Shea said, 'Maybe he's just headed home.'

'Strike one,' Micah said as the Toyota merged into the middle lane of the highway. 'Okeechobee's the other way.'

'What about the airport?'

'Strike two,' Micah said as Wes's car chugged past the runways at Southern Boulevard. 'Wanna go for a third?'

Falling silent, O'Shea reached outside his window and readjusted his side mirror.

'You got something?'

'Unclear,' O'Shea replied, studying the cars behind him. 'Just don't let him get too far.'

Tucked behind a car carrier filled with SUVs, O'Shea and Micah spent the next twenty minutes trailing Wes's Toyota as it continued south on 95, past Lake Worth, and Lantana, and Boynton Beach, and Delray . . . cruising past each city, but never going more than sixty miles an hour, never weaving through traffic, never leaving the middle lane. Through the unwashed back window, with cars zipping past them on both sides, Wes and Dreidel sat perfectly still, never panicking or checking over their shoulders. It was almost as if they weren't in a rush. Or didn't have a place to—

'Pull up,' O'Shea blurted.

'What're you—?'

'Let's go – get up there,' he insisted, patting the dashboard and pointing through the windshield. '*Now.*'

Micah punched the gas, and O'Shea's head snapped back, his sandy-blond hair bumping for a half second against the headrest. As their car slid out from behind the car carrier, it didn't take Micah long to weave across traffic and pull right behind Wes.

For the first time since he got on the highway, Wes merged into the far left lane, speeding up just enough to keep pace with a convertible Mercedes on their right.

With another punch of the gas, Micah tugged the wheel to the left, plowing the car into the poorly paved emergency lane on the inside shoulder of the road. Pebbles, trash, and shards of shattered glass spun under the tires, swirling in the car's wake. Careful to keep the driver's side from scraping against the concrete divider, Micah had no trouble catching up to Wes's Toyota, which was still barely doing sixty.

As they pulled neck and neck, Wes's window slowly rolled down.

'Careful driving in that lane – it's *illegal*!' Rogo shouted from the driver's seat, tapping his thumbs against the steering wheel as the two cars whipped down the highway. The only other occupant was Dreidel, who refused to make eye contact.

'Son of a—'

Ramming the brakes at a sign marked *Emergency Vehicles Only*, Micah cranked the steering wheel toward the open patch of grass on his left, skidding into a U-turn and heading back the way they came.

At this rate, Wes already had at least an hour head start.

55

Flat on my back underneath a silver Audi, I press my chin to my chest and stare out between the back tires and sagging muffler into the silence of the *Palm Beach Post*'s parking garage. It's been nearly fifteen minutes since Rogo and Dreidel pulled out in my Toyota. And nearly fourteen minutes since O'Shea and Micah's blue Chevy slinked down the incline of the garage and trailed Rogo out to the street.

Based on the mic in my lapel pin, we knew we were dealing with pros. Dreidel said it was the FBI. We needed to see if he was right.

When Dreidel and I first came down to my car, I pulled out my keys and popped the locks. But it wasn't until I gripped the door handle that I spotted his shadow underneath. Below the car, Rogo stuck his head out like a mechanic and pumped his eyebrows.

'You owe me a new suit,' he'd whispered from a puddle of grease.

All he needed was ten minutes of lead time to crawl on his stomach underneath the cars.

'You're lucky I fit,' he'd said.

Looking up at the grease- and dirt-caked axle directly above me, he was right about that. Just like he was right that if we pulled it off fast enough, no one would notice.

I had to step back to give him some room, but from

there, Rogo was a pro. I pulled open the car door just as he rolled out from underneath. Dropping my keys covered most of the sound. Even I started to get excited. Climbing to his knees, Rogo held up his fingers to count. *One . . . two . . .*

In one quick motion, I ducked down to pick up my keys just as Rogo popped up in my place and slid into my car.

'No, you're right,' I'd called out from the ground to complete the illusion. With a quick roll, I went under the car next to mine, which is where I've been ever since. Houdini would've been proud.

Staring out between the back tires, I turn on my side, and my elbow slides through the grease. By now, Rogo should have O'Shea and Micah halfway to Boca Raton. Still, I'm not sure what's worse. The fact that they were watching, or the fact we got rid of them. With Nico still out there . . . At least with the FBI around, I was safe.

As I'm about to roll out, there's a faint creak on my left. Hushed . . . like corduroy rubbing together. Craning my neck and peering out from under the car, I search the pocked concrete floor of the garage. The sound's long gone. But something else takes its place.

I know it from years of people's stares. It's even worse in public places – at a movie or in the supermarket – when they're trying to pretend they don't care. There's no scientific term to explain it. But I feel it every day. At this point, I've probably honed it. That haunting tug at the back of your skull . . . the nearly telepathic scream that demands you turn around. That indescribable feeling when you know you're being watched.

A single set of footsteps echoes through the garage, followed by the mild roar of another engine.

Right on time.

Tires churn and brakes squeal as the car flies in reverse up the ramp, backing halfway into my Toyota's now-empty parking spot. Rolling out from my hiding place, I'm face-to-face with a full row of Grateful Dead bumper stickers, which lurch to a stop barely an inch from my forehead.

'Hey, magic man – David Copperfield called . . . wants to know if you can still sub for him next Thursday?' Lisbeth says, leaning out the driver's-side window.

Most people would laugh, which is the only reason I force a grin. She doesn't buy it for a second. Fake smiles are a gossip columnist's bread and butter. Climbing to my feet, I brush the dirt from my clothes.

'If it makes you feel better, Wes, all the hiding and rolling under cars? That was the scary part.'

She waits for some plucky response like I'm some lantern-jawed action-movie hero. 'That's not even true,' I tell her.

Shaking her head, she studies me carefully. 'Is it actually against the law to try and cheer you up?'

Again, she waits for a smile. Again, I don't give it.

'Just get in the car, Wes. The only way we're pulling this off is if we move fast.'

She's right about that. Hopping in the passenger seat, I slam the door as Lisbeth tosses me a silver cell phone with a little ladybug sticker on it.

'I traded with a friend who writes for the gardening section,' she explains. 'Now we're untraceable.'

Refusing to celebrate, I flip open the phone and punch in the number.

'It's a beautiful day in President Manning's office. How can I help you?' the receptionist answers.

'Jana, it's Wes. Can you put me through to Oren?'

'Hiya, Wes. Of course – transferring you to Oren right now.' There's a soft click, two chirps, and then . . .

'This is Oren,' my officemate answers.

'How we looking?'

'They're getting it set up right now,' he replies. He's even faster than I thought. 'All you have to do is go pick it up.'

I nod to Lisbeth. She rams the gas. And away we go.

56

'Got everything you need?' the secretary asked The Roman as he left Bev's office and trudged across the presidential seal carpet in the main reception area.

'Apparently so,' The Roman replied, hiding his bandaged hand from view. 'Though I—'

The receptionist's phone rang on her desk. 'Oop – excuse me,' she said, putting on her headset. 'It's a beautiful day in President Manning's office. How can I help you?'

The Roman headed for the door.

The receptionist waved good-bye, never taking her attention away from the caller on her headset. 'Hiya, Wes. Of course – transferring you to Oren right now . . .'

The Roman stopped midstep, the toe of his left foot digging into the head of the eagle on the presidential seal. A thin grin returned to his face as he pivoted around.

Tapping a few buttons on her phone, the receptionist sent the call on its way and looked up at her guest. 'I'm sorry . . . you were saying?'

'Just that I need some directions,' The Roman replied, pointing left, then right. 'Which way is Oren's office again?'

'Second on your right. See it?' the receptionist called out.

The Roman nodded. 'You're an angel.'

He paused outside the office and waited for the click

of Oren hanging up his phone. With a sharp rap of knuckles against the door, he stepped inside and flashed his badge. 'Oren, right? Agent Roland Egen. United States Secret Service.'

'Everything okay?' Oren asked, already halfway out of his chair.

The Roman shrugged. 'You have a few minutes to chat?'

57

Standing outside the Mediterranean cypress plank doors set into an arched coral stone entryway, I ring the pearl doorbell and offer a smile for the security camera that stares down at us.

'Who's calling?' a delicate female voice asks through the intercom, even though she just buzzed us in three minutes ago when we first pulled up to the twenty-foot-tall hedges and wrought-iron gate that protect the estate.

'Mrs Sant, it's Wes Holloway,' I say into the intercom. 'From President Manning's office.'

With a click, the front door opens by remote control. Ten feet away, a young woman with perfectly arched eyebrows, sheer lip gloss, and flowing blond hair straight out of a shampoo commercial strolls toward us through the anteroom. She's wearing a peach cashmere sweater with a low enough V-neck to reveal why she's a trophy wife. And like the best trophies in town, she has breasts that are perfect and real, just like the diamond bracelet that engulfs most of her wrist.

Anxious to be out of sight, I go to step inside. Lisbeth tugs on the back of my button-down, keeping me in place. Protocol says I'm supposed to wait to be invited in. And with money this big, protocol rules.

'So nice to see you again,' Mrs Sant says in an Australian accent, even though we've never met. Like most Palm Beach wives, she knows better than to take a chance.

Finally reaching the doorway, she studies my face, then glances over my shoulder at Lisbeth's beat-up car. Again, perfect Palm Beach. Judgment first, niceties later.

'I take it the President's not with you,' she adds, still staring at our car. It's not until she's done with me that she even notices Lisbeth.

'No, he's actually meeting us in—'

'Ms Dodson?' she asks excitedly, grabbing Lisbeth's hand as if she were proposing marriage. 'I met you that night at the Alsops – oh, I'm sorry,' she adds, patting her own chest. 'Cammie Sant – my husband's Victor,' she explains as if that's all the introduction she needs. 'Oh, what a treat! I read you every day! Come in, come in . . .'

I don't know why I'm surprised. When you cover society, part of the job is having society suck up. But instead of reveling in the moment, Lisbeth shrinks from it, consciously slowing down so she's a full step behind me as we enter the anteroom.

'Oh, and that mention you did of Rose DuVall . . . *good* for you. We all knew it was her husband who dragged the kids to court.'

Next to me, Lisbeth looks away, fighting to avoid eye contact. At first, I thought it was modesty. But the way her face falls . . . the way she anxiously scratches at the freckles on her neck . . . I know shame when I see it. Especially when it comes from not meeting your own personal expectations.

'Oh, and please ignore the mess,' Cammie adds, leading us through the sumptuous Mediterranean-style living room and pointing to the white billowy painter's cloths that're draped over every piece of artwork on the walls. 'The jury's coming tomorrow.'

Two years ago, the previous owners of Cammie's spectacular fourteen-bedroom, twenty-thousand-square-foot home were brutally gunned down by their only son. With the parents dead, the house was sold to Cammie and her husband, an heir to the Tylenol fortune, who, according to the stories, were so desperate to make a splash in the P.B. social scene, they swooped in and bought it for twenty-seven million even before they wiped the chalk marks off the wide, cypress plank floors.

'The sheets were Victor's idea,' Cammie explains. 'You know, with the jury set to walk through the old crime scene, we just thought . . . when it comes to the collection . . . we don't need everyone knowing how many Francis Bacons we have.' She raises her eyebrows at us.

I nod, staring at the stark white sheets. Traveling with the President, I've been to plenty of billionaires' homes with a Rembrandt or Monet or Warhol on the wall. Some'll even have two or three. But here . . . as we pass from the living room, through the library, through the blood-red billiard room in back, I count at least thirty covered pictures.

'Of course. Of course, you'd want to be discreet,' Lisbeth says, finally looking up.

Stopping short at the double French doors that lead out back, Cammie spins around at the word *discreet*. A lesser clubwoman would take it as a threat. It's not. And Cammie's not *lesser* at anything. Tugging on the bottom of her peach sweater, she smooths it over her flat stomach and smiles to herself. It's every hostess's dream: being owed a favor by the local gossip queen.

'Listen, I have some errands to run – what a pleasure

meeting you,' Cammie adds, happily excusing herself. 'Tommaso's out back. He'll take perfect care of you.'

With a flick of the antique brass doorknob, the French doors swing open, leading us out across a stone path that takes us past the saltwater pool, through an expansive formal garden, and into a fruit orchard filled with the sweet smells of grapefruits, tangerines, and Persian limes.

'Am I shallow for hating her perfect, yoga-trainered ass?' Lisbeth asks as we pass one of the lime trees. 'Or should I just be content in despising her for the mere fact that I now owe her one?'

'If you wanna get technical, we actually owe her *two*,' I say, pointing to our destination.

Beyond the orchard, beyond the stone amphitheater, even beyond the football-field-sized patch of meticulously mowed grass that runs down toward the water, sits a pristine, 160-foot, three-deck, black-and-cream-colored mega-yacht that towers over every other boat floating behind it on the calm currents of Lake Worth. *The Pequod*, it says in fine gold script along the transom at the stern. It's not until we're right alongside it that I even appreciate how big the yacht is – from front to back, it's gotta be three eighteen-wheelers parked end-to-end.

'You sure it's fast enough?' Lisbeth asks, craning her neck back and shielding her eyes from the sun.

She's not talking about the boat. As fast as we need to move, we don't have time for a pleasure cruise. Nor can we afford to risk heading to the local airport and getting tracked by our IDs and airline tickets. I take two steps back to get a clearer view of our target. It sits on the rear sundeck with its three still blades arched slightly downward.

A car would take over four hours. A seaplane would

take an hour and forty minutes. But a French-built, twin-engine helicopter with no boarding, taxi, or wait time since it's parked on a yacht? We'll be there in an hour, easy. Plenty of time to get what we need and be back at Manning's house tonight.

'She's gorgeous, no?' a man calls out in a heavy Spanish accent. Sticking his head over the railing, Tommaso stares down at us from the edge of the deck. 'The President is joining us, yes?'

'No,' I say, still craning my neck up. 'He's meeting us there.'

Tommaso shrugs it off without a care. In a pilot's navy blazer and a blue-and-white-striped shirt, he's dressed as staff, which means he's used to spoiled honchos changing their minds at the last minute. 'Come, let us go,' he adds, motioning palms-up to a metal staircase that leads up to the main deck. Within seconds, we're aboard.

That's why I called Oren in the first place. When we went to Saudi Arabia, Oren found a sheik who was happy to loan the President his jet. When we flew to North Carolina for vacation, he found an heir of the Kentucky Fried Chicken family to do the same. It's not snobbery. It's Oren's job. As director of travel, he's there to collect the name of every person who says the phrase that's uttered most often to every former U.S. President: *Let me know if you ever need anything.*

On most trips, the President just needs privacy. Today, I need the same.

Naturally, Oren was hesitant. But when I told him that I was having trouble breathing . . . that Nico's escape . . . just seeing his face on the news . . . and the pains in my chest . . . *Please, Oren, you know I never ask. I just need to get away . . . as fast as possible . . .*

Forget the presidency – the most powerful cards to play are pity and guilt. One phone call later, recent donors and NBFs Victor and Cammie Sant were honored, just honored, to offer up their personal helicopter for the President and his staff. No questions asked, no flight plan to file, no possible way to be traced.

'Welcome to the *Pequod*,' Tommaso says as we reach the top of the metal stairs and climb on board the yacht. Across the sundeck-turned-landing-pad, he twists a latch and opens the door to the matching black and cream helicopter. 'Ready to ride the white whale?'

'Palm Beach Tower, thees copter two-seven-niner-five-Juliett lifting off,' Tommaso says into his radio.

'Seven-niner-five,' a radio voice calmly crackles back. 'Depart at your own risk.'

Lisbeth looks to me as she hears the words through the intercom, then raps her knuckles against the Plexiglas divider that separates our cabin – with its four leather club chairs – from the two seats up by the pilot. '*At our own risk?*' she calls to Tommaso, flipping a switch on the intercom.

'Is fine, miss. Regulation,' he explains as he pushes a button to start the first engine.

Behind us, just above our heads on the back of the helicopter, an exhaust pipe clears its throat, hacking itself awake. I jump at the sound, which rings louder than a gunshot.

A few seconds later, Tommaso hits another button, starting engine two. A second exhaust pipe explodes with a sputter. I jump again, searching over my shoulder, even though I know no one's there. My eyes blink over and over and over.

'Take a breath,' Lisbeth says, reaching over from her seat and grabbing my wrist. The whole helicopter starts vibrating as the blades begin to spin. *Vrrrrrrr . . . rrr . . . rrr . . .* like a race car whipping around the track.

'Just pretend it's Marine One,' she adds, referring to the helicopter I used to ride at the White House.

I turn to the wide window on my right and hold my breath. It doesn't help. A tidal wave of nausea pirouettes through my stomach.

Vrrrrrr . . . rrr . . . rrr . . . the blades pick up speed. Leaning closer to the window, I press my forehead against the glass. The blades whip so fast, they disappear above us.

'Wes, I swear to you, there's no one out there. We're in good shape.'

She thinks I'm staring at the lush grounds that lead back to the Sants' Mediterranean mansion. Or that I'm scanning every tree, shrub, and Greek Revival statue looking to see if we were followed. But as the helicopter pitches forward and lifts off the landing pad, the only thing I see in the window is my own reflection.

'And you wanted to sit inside all day,' Lisbeth reminds me, hoping to reassure as we climb straight up into the blue sky and the Sants' yacht shrinks below us. 'Bye-bye, rich people with perfect lives who make me feel inadequate and fat – we're off to endanger ourselves!'

Staying silent, I keep my forehead pressed to the window. At the sandy tip of the Palm Beach inlet, where Lake Worth flows into the Atlantic Ocean, the glowing blue-green water expands to the horizon, its colors more mesmerizing than a peacock's tail. It barely registers.

'C'mon, Wes – you've earned a smile,' Lisbeth adds, her voice still racing. 'We've got a lead on The Roman, some hints into the crossword, Rogo and Dreidel are on their way to dig up the scoop on Boyle, and we, in a mad stroke of your own genius, are now flying on a three-million-dollar whirlybird to the one person who was in the absolute best position to show us what happened that day. I'm not saying you should order the confetti and schedule the victory parade, but you definitely can't just sit there and sulk.'

With my head still pressed against the glass, I shut my eyes and replay the video. She'll never understand.

'Listen, I know it was hard watching that tape . . .'

I press even harder.

'. . . and just to see yourself without the scars . . .' Unlike most, she doesn't shrink from the issue. I can feel her looking – not staring – right at me. The helicopter banks into position, heading south down the golden coastline, then quickly cutting right and heading inland, southwest over the carpeted green waves of the country club golf course. At five hundred feet, we're about as high as a plane coming in for a landing. Golf carts scurry like tiny white ants across the grass, while the course's sand traps dot the landscape like dozens of round beige kiddie pools. Within minutes, the beachfront homes and breathtaking yachts of Palm Beach give way to the mossy, mosquito-filled brown marshes of the Everglades. It changes so damn quickly.

'I'm just saying,' she adds, 'whatever you've been through . . . it's still the same you.'

Staring out the window, I watch as the tall strands of sawgrass peek out and sway in the Everglades' shallow brown waters. 'It's not about my face,' I blurt.

Ignoring my reflection and pulling back slightly, I use the polish of the window to stare over my shoulder. Behind me, Lisbeth doesn't move, still watching me carefully, with no hesitation as she studies my face.

'You saw the tape,' I add. 'The way I stepped out of that limo . . . waving to the crowd . . . the swaggering sway in my shoulders . . .'

'You're better off. You looked like Dreidel.'

'See, but that's the point. When I see that tape . . . when I see the old me . . . I don't just miss my face. What I miss – what I *mourn* – is my old life. *That's* what they took from me, Lisbeth. You can see it on the tape: A twenty-three-year-old cocky kid strutting like only a twenty-three-year-old cocky kid can. Back then, when I imagined my future, from the White House to – I was rocketing so high, I couldn't even pick the next coordinate. The whole damn world was possible. I mean, that's the promise, right? I run and run and run this race – and then, in one stupid day, with one stupid ricochet . . .' My chin starts to quiver, but after all these years, I know exactly how to grit my teeth to bury it. '. . . I find out I'm never getting any further th-th-than . . . than halfway there.' The quivering's gone. It's not much of a victory. 'That's my life. Halfway there.'

In the reflection of the window, Lisbeth tucks a red curl behind her ear. 'You got further than halfway, Wes.'

'Why, because I fetch the President's Diet Coke and know which of his friends he hates? Rogo said it for years, but I wouldn't listen. It was supposed to be a stepping-stone. Somehow it became a destination. Can you possibly fathom how pathetic you have to be to let that happen?'

'Probably as pathetic as settling for a local gossip job, even though the real dream was to challenge the world with risky, investigative news items.'

For the first time since we've taken off, I turn away

from the window and stare at Lisbeth. 'That's different,' I tell her.

'It's *not*,' she shoots back. 'You saw my office – all those letters on the walls of my cubicle . . .'

'The ones to your dad.'

'Not *to* him. *About* him. Those letters are proof, Wes. They're proof that you can use this job to change someone's life for the better. They're proof that there's a power in reporting. And what do I do with that power? I spend every day trying to find twenty inches' worth of local divorces, country club backstabbing, and all-around nail-biters, like who got stuck at the crappy table at Morton's? When I took this job, I promised myself it was for a year or two, until I could properly feed my cats. That was seven years ago, Wes,' she says, more serious than ever. 'And y'know what the worst part is?'

'That you gave up your dream?'

She shakes her head. 'That I can leave at any time.'

As I study her, she scratches at the freckles on her cheek.

'It's still different,' I insist, turning back to the window. 'My goal is to walk down the street and not be noticeable. You're at least the same person you always were.'

She shifts in her seat as the leather crunches below her. 'My dad used to say that God puts cracks in everything. That's how the light gets in.'

'Yeah, well, your dad stole that from an old Leonard Cohen song.'

'Doesn't make it any less true.'

Through the window, I stare down at the river of grass, its muted green and brown strands braided across the water like a head of wet hair. About a hundred feet down, a small flock of white birds glides through the sky.

'Those herons?' Lisbeth asks, staring out her own window.

'Egrets,' I reply. 'Beaks are blacker and pointier.'

Staring downward, I think of my own bird, Lolo, and how much she'd enjoy the view. Then I remind myself that she can't fly. Not while her wings are clipped.

For the second time, I turn away from the window and look over my shoulder at Lisbeth. She's got caramel freckles along her neck. 'You really that miserable with your job?' I ask her.

'Last month, I didn't go to my ten-year high school reunion because the little bio of me in the program listed me as "gossip queen." I know it's so seventh grade, but I just . . . I couldn't show my face there.'

'Imagine that,' I tease, turning my head so she gets a good look at my scars.

'Oh, jeez, Wes, you know I didn't—'

'I know,' I tell her, flashing the best full smile I can offer. As always, the right half of my mouth doesn't move. But for once, as the left half rises toward the roof of the helicopter, it actually seems like enough.

58

'What about phone records?' O'Shea asked, sitting in the passenger seat as Micah steered through the lunch-hour traffic that clogged I-95.

'Goose egg,' Paul Kessiminan replied through O'Shea's phone in a fat Chicago sausage accent. As a student of applied mathematics and a dropout from the U.S. Naval Academy, Paul wasn't a scholar. As a senior associate in the FBI's Investigative Technology Division, he was a genius. And rarely wrong. 'Kid hasn't made a cell call since late last night.'

'Credit cards?'

'I ran it all – cards, ATM withdrawals, airline reservations, even his Blockbuster card. Whoever he is, this Wes's no schmuck. Kid's quieter than a caterpillar.'

'Then track the phone itself,' O'Shea said into his cell as their Chevy came to a short stop just shy of a black pickup. Tapping the dashboard with his fist, he pointed to the far left shoulder of the road, pantomiming for Micah to keep moving. 'He should be pinging off some nearby cell tower as we speak.'

'Really? I'd totally forgotten how GPS and, indeed, my entire job worked,' Paul said.

O'Shea didn't laugh. 'Don't fuck with me on this, Paul.'

'Hey, hey . . . easy with the mouth. You didn't say it was that important.'

'It's that important. Now is he pinging or not?'

'He *should* be,' Paul began as O'Shea heard the clicking of computer keys through the phone. 'But if his phone's issued by Manning's office – which according to this it is – they cloak all their GPS so our former Presidents can get some privacy.'

'So you can't track it?'

'Of course, we can track it. You really think we let these guys run around without protection? The annoying part is, I'm not getting anything traceable.'

'Why? He's got his phone off?'

'Even if it's off, GPS should still be transmitting,' Paul explained as Micah cut back into traffic, finding an opening in the center lane. 'Which means he's in the air, under-ground, or otherwise out of range.'

'He's in the air,' O'Shea said to Micah, pointing to the exit ramp for Palm Beach Airport. 'Get off here!'

Without even hesitating, Micah swerved the blue Chevy across two lanes of traffic, ramming toward the exit. Angry car horns faded behind them. 'Maybe Wes is using someone else's phone,' Micah said, his eyes locked on the road. 'Ask him to trace Dreidel's calls.'

'Paul, do me a favor and run those other three names – the two guys and the girl,' O'Shea said as they curved along the off-ramp. 'Call you back in a minute.'

'What're you doing?' Micah asked as O'Shea ended the call. 'We need that info *now.*'

'Which is why I'm getting it,' O'Shea said, his thumb pounding at a brand-new phone number. 'If Wes isn't using credit cards or his own ID, he's not getting on a plane without some heavyweight help.'

'It's a beautiful day in President Manning's office,' the receptionist said through the phone. 'How can I help you?'

'Hi there, this is Agent O'Shea calling from the FBI. We're doing some work on the current Nico investigation. Can I speak to the person in charge of the President's transportation? We need to make sure he's aware of all the recent precautions we and the Service have put in place.'

'Of course,' the receptionist replied. 'Let me transfer you to Oren.'

There was a quick click followed by two sharp chirps.

'This is Oren.'

'Oren, Agent O'Shea calling from—'

'Wow, I'm getting popular – two in one day,' Oren interrupted.

'Pardon?'

'You're calling from the Service, right? Just spoke to your buddy – left here a minute ago.'

'Absolutely,' O'Shea said without even a stutter. 'So you already spoke to Agent . . .'

'Egen . . . Roland Egen? I say that right?'

'He's the one,' O'Shea replied, squeezing his phone in his fist. 'Pale skin and black hair, right?'

Micah turned at the description, his jaw almost hitting the steering wheel. 'Wait, is he—?'

O'Shea put up his hand, cutting Micah off. 'So you gave him the quick update on Wes?'

'Of course. Though all I had was his flight to Key West,' Oren explained. 'We really appreciate you looking out for him, though. I mean, he's always been a little more, y'know, *jumpy* since the accident, but with Nico suddenly on the loose, I could hear it in his voice – he sounded pretty torn apart.'

'Who could blame him?' O'Shea asked, anxious to get off. 'Oren, you've been a lifesaver. Thanks for all the help.'

As O'Shea shut his phone, Micah could read the look on his partner's face.

'Motherf—'

'Please tell me The Roman was just standing in his office,' Micah demanded.

'*Enough,*' O'Shea said. 'Either we just hit the lottery or we jumped face-first on an even bigger land mine.'

Nodding in agreement, Micah punched the gas and pointed with his eyebrows at a billboard offering daily charter flights to Key West. O'Shea was already dialing.

'Hi, I'd like to rent one of your seaplanes,' he said into the phone. 'Think you can have it ready in the next five minutes?'

59

'You sure he didn't call?' Dreidel asked from the passenger seat as the car idled in the stranglehold of traffic that regularly gripped Miami's US-1. 'Do me a favor and just check your phone.'

Tapping his thumbs against the steering wheel, Rogo didn't bother checking his phone. 'He didn't call.'

'But if something happened . . . if he didn't get to Key West—'

'Wes is smart – he knows they'll trace it if we call. If there was a problem, we'd know.'

'Unless there was a problem and we *didn't* know,' Dreidel insisted. 'Dammit, why didn't we get his info: the name of the helicopter guy . . . where they're flying from . . . we don't even have the address he's at in Key – ' Before Dreidel could finish, his own phone vibrated in his pocket. Ripping it out, he anxiously flipped the phone open, checking caller ID. Rogo glanced across the seat just in time to see the 202 prefix. Washington, D.C.

'Hello?' Dreidel answered. His jaw quickly slid off-center. 'Listen, I'm in the middle of something. Can we talk about it later? . . . Yeah, I will . . . *I will* . . . Bye.' Turning to Rogo as he closed the phone, Dreidel added, 'My wife.'

'With a Washington phone number?' Rogo asked, his thumbs no longer tapping. 'I thought you lived in Chicago.'

'My old cell. We kept the number from D.C.,' Dreidel explained.

Speeding up, then slowing back to a full halt, the car stood motionless in traffic. Rogo didn't say a word.

'What, you think I'm lying?' Dreidel blurted.

'I didn't say anything. Enough with the witch trials.'

Shifting in his seat, Dreidel looked over his own shoulder and checked the lane next to them. 'You're clear on the right.'

Clenching the steering wheel, Rogo didn't make a move.

'Rogo, you hear what I—?'

'Traffic's bad enough. Don't tell me how to drive.'

In the middle lane, the car inched past the cause of the slowdown: a tow truck with yellow sirens loading up a tan Cadillac on the left side of the road.

'I'm not an imbecile, Rogo. I know what you think of me.'

'Dreidel . . .'

'I see it in your face . . . and how, when we split up, how quick you were to keep me from going with Wes. Don't tell me I'm wrong. Instead, let me paint this picture as best I can: I'd never do anything to hurt him. *Never.*'

'I'm sure you wouldn't,' Rogo said.

'I'm not saying I'm the best husband, okay? But I'm still a damn good friend. Don't forget, I'm the one who got Wes the job in the first place.'

'That fact hasn't been lost on me.'

'Oh, so now that's my fault too?' Dreidel asked. 'This was my master plot to somehow put him in my old job so a once-in-a-lifetime ricochet could hit him in the face?'

'That's not what I said.'

'Then be clear for once instead of your lovable facade that treats Wes like some fragile, overprotected china doll.

I know why you do it, Rogo – I know plenty of under-achievers who love to be needed.'

'Just like I know plenty of overachievers who love aban-doning people the instant they don't need those people anymore. Enough rewriting history. I was there with him the week they took the bandages off . . . and when that *Times* reporter used the front page to describe his face as *ruined* . . . and when Wes finally decided to look at himself only to say he wished he was the dead one instead of Boyle. But that's the thing, Dreidel – for eight years, Wes *has* been the dead one. You and the rest of your White House crew may have gone on to your own TV shows and newspaper columns, but Wes was the one who never got to move on to his new life. Now that that chance is here, I'm not letting anyone rip it away from him.'

'That's a wonderful speech, Rogo, but do me a favor: If you don't trust me, have the balls to say it and just let me out right here.'

'If I didn't trust you, Dreidel, I would've left you in Palm Beach.'

'That's not even true,' Dreidel challenged. 'You brought me here because you wanted to see Boyle's files, and you know I'm the only one who can get you in.'

With a flick of his blinker, Rogo turned into the far right lane. Looking over at the passenger seat, he was silent.

Dreidel nodded to himself, biting at the skin on the inside of his bottom lip. 'Fuck you too, Rogo.'

Tapping his thumbs on the steering wheel, Rogo made a sharp right on Stanford Drive and headed toward a guard gate and lawn that served as the main entrance to the campus. On their right, a forest-green and gold metal sign bolted into a concrete wall read:

WELCOME TO THE UNIVERSITY OF MIAMI
HOME OF THE LELAND F. MANNING
PRESIDENTIAL LIBRARY

Neither said another word to each other until they were inside.

60

Jacksonville, Florida

Nico, maybe we should stop.

'There's no need.'

But if you don't rest—

'I've been resting for eight years, Edmund. This is the calling,' Nico said, sitting so far forward in the driver's seat, his chest nuzzled the steering wheel of the giant flatbed. Just behind him in his seat was the balled-up army jacket he'd stolen from the Irish Pub. With Florida's noon sun burning overhead, winter seemed long gone. He didn't need the jacket. Or Edmund's blood, which soaked the front of it.

You're telling me you're not tired?

Nico glanced over at Edmund's lifeless body drooping in the seat next to him. His friend knew him all too well.

You've been driving nearly ten hours, Nico. It's okay to take a break – in fact, it's necessary, son. Especially if we plan on staying out of sight.

Nico knew what he was getting at. 'So you still think—?'

Nico, I don't care how cautious a driver you are – you take a forty-ton flatbed through the dainty streets of downtown Palm Beach, someone's gonna bat an eye.

Staring at the wooden rosary beads swaying from the rearview, Nico knew Edmund was right. They'd been lucky so far, but if a cop pulled them over . . . if they were taken into custody . . . No, after all this, the cause was too great. And when they were this close . . . to Wes . . . to Boyle . . . to completing God's will and delivering the redemption for his mother . . . No, this was no time for risk.

'Tell me what you think is best,' he said, looking to Edmund.

Hard as it is to say, we need to dump the truck and get something that's a bit less noticeable in traffic.

'That's fine, but how do we do that?'

How do we do anything, Nico? As the truck hit a divot in the road, Edmund's head jerked up and back, crashing into the headrest and revealing the bubbling black and red gash across his neck. *You look outside your window and search for the opportunity.*

Following Edmund's gaze through the front windshield, Nico searched the blacktop of highway, eventually spotting what his friend was staring at in the distance. The moment he saw it, a broad smile lifted his cheeks.

'You think we should—?'

Of course, we should, Nico. Heed the Book. Why else would God put them there?

Nodding to himself, Nico hit the brakes, and the truck rumbled and shuddered, eventually screeching to a stop right behind a maroon Pontiac on the shoulder of the highway. On the passenger side of the car, a woman with cropped black hair watched as her tank-topped boyfriend fought to change the flat tire on their car.

'You guys need some help?' Nico asked as he hopped out of the cab.

'You from Triple A?' the woman asked.

'No. It just looked like you needed an assist, so we thought we'd pitch in.'

'I actually think I'm done,' the boyfriend said, tightening the last lug nut.

'Wow, a real Good Samaritan,' the woman teased.

'Funny,' Nico replied, stepping into the woman's personal space. 'Though I much prefer the term *guardian angel*.'

The woman stepped back. But not nearly fast enough.

61

Key West, Florida

'Here you go,' the cabdriver says as his bright pink Key West cab jerks to a stop. He's got thick white sunblock caked all over his nose, and a ratty *Shrek* beach blanket with the words *Can I Get a Whoop Whoop* draped over the back of his seat. 'Three twenty-seven William Street.'

'You kidding? We barely went three blocks,' Lisbeth barks from our seats in the back. 'Why didn't you just tell us we could walk?'

'You got in the cab,' the driver says, not the least bit riled as he turns up the dial on the *Paul & Young Ron* radio show. Standard Key West – everything's sunny. 'That'll be two bucks,' he adds, poking a button on the meter.

'I shouldn't pay you a single—'

'Thanks for the ride,' I interrupt, tossing three bucks into the front seat. When our helicopter touched down on another private yacht in Key West's Historic Seaport, we decided that the rest of the trip should be low-key and untraceable. The driver studies my face in his rearview mirror, and I realize we're already well off course. Fortunately, we've still got a few tricks left.

Kicking the door open and hopping outside, we watch as the cab disappears up the lush but narrow residential street. We're standing in front of a modest two-story conch cottage at 327 William, but as the cab turns the corner at the end of the block, we cross the street and trace the house numbers to our actual destination: the pale peach cottage with the white shutters and gingerbread trim at 324.

Grabbing the wooden railing that leans slightly when you put weight on it, Lisbeth bounds up the weather-beaten front porch like she's racing home for lemonade. But before she reaches the front door, her phone rings. Or rather, her colleague's phone rings, since they switched back at the paper. 'Lemme just check this,' Lisbeth says as she pulls the phone from her purse. She told her friend to only call if it was life-or-death. I look over her shoulder as we both check caller ID. The number is Lisbeth's work line. Here comes death.

'Eve?' Lisbeth answers.

'Oh, thank God,' her colleague from the gardening section says, loud enough that it's easy to hear. 'Hold on, I'm patching her in right now.'

'Huh – patching *who* in?'

'Your phone call. I know you said not to pick up, but when I saw who it was . . . I mean, how'm I gonna say no to Lenore Manning?'

'Wait . . . *what?* The First Lady?'

'She asked for you – says she wants to talk to you about your column this morning.'

I nod, telling her it's okay, and with a click, Eve announces, 'Dr. Manning, you're on with Lisbeth.'

'Hi, there,' the First Lady opens, always first out of the gate.

'H-Hi, Dr. Manning.'

'Oh, dear – you sound busy,' the First Lady says, reading it perfectly as always. 'Listen, I don't mean to waste your time – I just wanted to thank you for the generous mention for cystic fibrosis. You're a darling for that.'

Lisbeth is speechless as she hears the words. But for Lenore Manning, it's standard fare. She used to do the same thing in the White House – anytime a mention ran, good or bad, she'd call or send a thank-you note to the reporter. It's not out of kindness. It's a trick used by nearly every President. Once a reporter knows there's a person on the other end, it's twice as hard for them to tear you down.

'No, happy to help,' Lisbeth says, meaning every word.

'Ask her if Manning went into the office,' I whisper in Lisbeth's ear.

'Ma'am, can I also—?'

'Let me let you run,' the First Lady says, sidestepping with such grace, Lisbeth barely realizes she hasn't even gotten the question out. With a click, Dr. Manning is gone.

Lisbeth turns my way and shuts her phone. 'Wow, she doesn't miss an opportunity, huh?'

'She's just happy you called her an icon.'

'She actually cares abou—?'

'Let me tell you something: On days like today, when the wires are filled with Nico's escape, and old clips are running from the Manning administration, she misses it more than anyone.'

Lisbeth races back across the sun-faded porch, where a hand-painted wooden crab on the front door pinches a sign that says *Crabby on more than just Mondays*. She tugs on the screen door and reaches for the doorbell.

'*It's open!*' a throaty, cigarette-stained voice calls from inside, awakening a flush of old memories.

I reach over Lisbeth's shoulder and give the door a shove. Inside, the bitter acidic smell of chemicals drills through my sinuses.

'Sorry, been airing out the darkroom,' a short, over-weight man with a spotty gray beard and a matching head of brushed-back thinning gray hair announces. Wiping his hands with a baby wipe, he rolls up the sleeves of his creased shirt and steps a bit too close to Lisbeth. That's the problem with White House photographers – always overstepping their limits.

'You're not Wes,' he says to Lisbeth with no hint of irony.

'You must be Kenny,' she says, shaking his hand and taking half a step back. 'Lisbeth. From the President's library.'

He doesn't even notice. He's far too focused on me as I step inside. Never taking his eyes off his subject.

'The Boy King,' he says, whipping out my old nick-name.

'Popeye the Photographer Man,' I say, whipping his right back. He taps his pointer finger against the crow's-feet of his left eye. After years of looking through a lens with his right eye, Kenny's left is always closed a hair more.

'C'mere, Bluto, gimme a kiss,' he teases, embracing me with the kind of hug you get from an old camp friend – a deep-tissue squeeze that brings with it a flush of memo-ries. 'You look fantastic,' he says, believing every word.

During trips on Air Force One, Kenny ran the press pool's poker game in back. As I step inside, he's already searching for my tells.

'Still can't leave it behind, can you?' he asks, tracing my glance to the *New York Times* on his painted Arts and Crafts–style kitchen table. On the front page, there's a huge picture of current President Ted Hartson standing at a podium, his hands resting just below the microphone.

'Who took that? Kahan?' I ask.

'Arms resting flat . . . no motion . . . no reaction shot . . . of course, it's Kahan. President might as well be a corpse.'

In the world of podiums and White House photographers, the only real action shot comes when the President moves. A hand gesture. Raised eyebrows. That's when the firing squad of cameras pulls its triggers. Miss that and you miss the shot.

Kenny rarely missed the shot. Especially when it mattered. But after thirty-five years of running city to city and country to country, it became clear that even if it's not a young man's game, it's not an old one's either. Kenny never took it personally. Even the best horses get put out to pasture.

'So how're the twilight years?' I joke, even though he's barely pushing sixty.

Cocking his Popeye eye, he motions us into his living room, which is clearly more of a welcome area for his studio. Centered around a pine cocktail table surrounded by four Mission-style armchairs, the room is covered almost to the ceiling with dozens of black-and-white photographs, all displayed in sleek white matting and museum-quality black frames. As I step toward them, I'm surprised to see that while most of the photos are in the candid journalistic style that White House photographers are famous for, the shots themselves are of young brides throwing bouquets, and well-clad grooms being fed mouthfuls of cake.

'You're doing *weddings*?' I ask.

'Six Presidents, forty-two kings, countless ambassadors . . . and Miriam Mendelsohn's bridal party, complete with a reunion shot of her Pi Phi pledge class,' Kenny says, all excitement and no shame.

'You're serious?'

'Don't laugh, Wes – I work two days a month, then get to go sailing all week. All I gotta do is make 'em look like the Kennedys.'

'They're really beautiful,' Lisbeth says, examining the photos.

'They should be,' Kenny says, straightening one of the frames. 'I pour my heart into them. I mean, life doesn't just peak in the White House, right?'

I nod instinctively. So does Lisbeth, who reaches out and straightens another frame. Just over her shoulder, on a nearby end table, I spot one of Kenny's most famous photos of Manning: a crisp black-and-white shot of the President in the White House kitchen, fixing his tie in the reflection of a shining silver water pitcher just before his first state dinner. Turning back to the wall of brides, I find a blond beauty queen looking over her own shoulder and admiring her French braid in the mirror. The new shot's just as good. Maybe even better.

'So how's the Kingfish?' Kenny adds, referring to Manning. 'Still mad at me for taking the shot?'

'He's not mad at you, Popeye.'

'Really? You tell him you were coming here?'

'You crazy?' I ask. 'You have any idea how mad he is at you?'

Kenny laughs, well aware of his social standing in the Manning house. 'Some laws are immutable,' he says, pulling a thick three-ring binder off the end table with Manning's picture. 'White used cars sell best . . . strip clubs only shut down if there's a fire . . . and President Leland Manning will never forgive the man who gave him *this* . . .' Flipping open the three-ring binder, Kenny reveals a plastic-encased, pristine copy of the most famous presidential photo since

Truman held up the *Dewey Defeats Truman* headline: the black-and-white Cowardly Lion shot – Manning in mid-scream at the shooting, tugged down in the pile as the CEO's wife became his human shield.

'God, I remember seeing this on the front page the next day,' Lisbeth says, sitting in one of the armchairs as he lowers the binder onto her lap. 'This's . . . it's history . . .'

'What paper?' Kenny asks.

'*Palm Beach Post*,' Lisbeth replies, looking up.

'Yep, that was me. Another few thousand dollars I'll never see.'

Reading the incomprehension on Lisbeth's face, I explain, 'Since Kenny was working for the AP at the time, they made all the money from the reprint sales.'

'Hundreds of newspapers and forty-nine magazine covers – all for bubkes,' Kenny says. 'Meanwhile, that college kid NASCAR hired to take some shots for their Web site? He was freelance, lucky schmuck. Made $800,000 – *eight hundred thousand* – and he *missed the shot!*'

'Yeah, but who's the one who got the Pulitzer for the full sequence?' I point out.

'Pulitzer? That was a pity vote,' Kenny interrupts. 'I didn't squeeze the shutter in a hail of gunfire. I panicked at the noise and accidentally hit the button. Manning's only in three of the frames.' Turning back to Lisbeth, he adds, 'It happened so fast, if you looked away and then looked back, you missed it.'

'Doesn't look like you missed anything,' Lisbeth says as she turns past the first page of the book and stares down at the double-page spread of contact sheets filled with sixty or so tiny black-and-white shots, each one barely bigger than a postage stamp.

'If you keep flipping, there should be six more – eight

rolls total, including reaction shots,' Kenny says. 'I've got most of them blown to 8×10, but you said the library was looking for some new angles, so . . .' From his pocket, he pulls out a photographer's loupe – a small, round magnifier to see the details of the photos – and hands it to Lisbeth.

For a half second, she forgets that she introduced herself as library staff. 'No . . . no, that's great,' she says. 'With the ten-year anniversary of the shooting coming up, we just want an exhibit that does more than reprint the same old stuff.'

'Sure, that makes perfect sense,' Kenny says dryly, his Popeye eye narrowing as he calmly stares me down. 'With two years to go, it's much smarter for you to come all the way to Key West than to have me make a few copies and mail them to you at the library.'

Lisbeth freezes. So do I. The Popeye eye is barely a sliver.

'No bullshit, Wes. This for you or for *him*?' Kenny asks. He says *him* in that tone that people reserve for God. The same tone we all used during our days in the White House.

'Me,' I say, feeling my throat go dry.

He doesn't respond.

'I swear, Kenny. On my mom.'

Still nothing.

'Kenny, please—'

'Listen, that's my phone,' Kenny interrupts, even though the house is dead silent. 'Lemme go grab this call. I'll be upstairs if you need me. Understand?'

I nod, holding my breath. Kenny pats me on my scars like a godfather, then disappears up the staircase, never looking back. It's not until I hear his upstairs bedroom door close that I finally exhale.

Lisbeth pops open the notebook's binder rings with a metallic thunk. 'You take the loupe – I'll take the 8×10s,' she says, unlatching the first eight sheets and sliding them my way.

Kneeling over the cocktail table, I put the loupe over the first photo and lean in like a jeweler studying a diamond.

The first shot is a close-up on the limo just as we pulled into the pits of the racetrack. Unlike the video at Lisbeth's office, the background here is crisp and clear. But the camera's so close up on the car, all I see are the backs of a few NASCAR drivers' heads and the first row of people sitting in the stands.

One picture down . . . 287 to go . . .

62

'We're looking for Kara Lipof,' Rogo said, stepping into the messy room that was as wide and long as two side-by-side bowling lanes.

'Two to the right,' a male archivist with a phone number written on his hand said as he pointed his thumb two desks away.

Housing all eight archivists in a shared space with nothing but a metal bookshelf to separate each desk from the one next to it, the room was littered with paper on every desk, shelf, chair, computer monitor, mini-fridge, and window ledge. Fortunately for Rogo, the paper didn't cover the plastic nameplate on the front of Kara's desk.

'Kara?' Rogo asked warmly, always preferring to charm.

From behind her desk, a woman in her early thirties with auburn hair and a trendy floral-print blouse looked up from her computer screen. 'Can I help you?'

'I hope so,' Rogo replied, adding a smile. 'I'm Wes Holloway – from the personal office. I spoke to you yesterday about Ron Boyle's files.' Before she could register any difference in Wes's and Rogo's voices, Rogo added the one thing guaranteed to get her attention. 'The President wanted to know if you'd pulled them together yet.'

'Yes . . . of course,' Kara said, fidgeting with the piles

on her desk. 'It's just . . . I'm sorry, I didn't realize you were coming to pick them up.'

'You said there were 36,000 pages to copy,' Rogo added, keeping the smile as he repeated the details Wes gave him. 'We figured if we came down here and flipped through them first, we'd save you on the Kinko's bills.'

Kara laughed. So did Dreidel, just for effect.

'You have no idea how much you're saving my life right now,' Rogo added. 'Thanks to you, I'll actually live to my twenty-third birthday. Okay . . . twenty-fifth. Twenty-ninth, tops.'

'Don't go turning me into a saint just yet,' Kara said, pulling out a thin manila folder. 'Faxing you a crossword was one thing – but if you want access to Boyle's full file, I need an official FOIA request, plus authorization that – '

'See, that's the tickle,' Dreidel interrupted, putting a hand on Rogo's shoulder and trying to get him to step aside. Rogo didn't budge. 'If the President makes an official request, people take notice. They start thinking something's happened. That there must be news with Boyle's case. Next thing we know, Boyle's family wants to know what the government's hiding. We say *nothing*, they say *everything*, and that's how conspiracies are born. So how about saving all of us the migraines and instead treating this as an *unofficial* request? As for authorization, I'm happy to sign for it.'

'I'm sorry . . . do I know—?'

'Gavin Jeffer,' Dreidel replied before she could even finish the question. 'Y'know . . . from *here* . . .'

Pointing a finger down toward her desk, Dreidel stabbed a piece of library letterhead just next to where his name appeared along the left margin.

To this day, it was Dreidel's greatest get. In order to build the Manning Library, a separate foundation was set up with a board of directors that included the President's closest friends, biggest donors, and most loyal staff. The select group included Manning's daughters, his former secretary of state, the former CEO of General Motors, and – to almost everyone's surprise – Dreidel. It took surgically precise phone calls and begging in all the right places, but those were always Dreidel's specialties.

'So the files?' he said to the archivist.

Kara looked to Rogo, then back to Dreidel. The way she flicked her thumb against the edge of the manila folder, she was clearly still on the bubble.

'Kara, if you want, call the President's office,' Dreidel added. 'You know Claudia's number.'

'That's not what I—'

'It's not like we're talking about NSC staff,' Dreidel said, continuing to pound away as he referred to the National Security Council. 'Boyle's domestic.'

'And dead,' Rogo said, bouncing on his feet to keep the mood upbeat. 'C'mon, what's the worst that happens? He suddenly comes back to life?'

For the second time, Kara laughed. For the second time, Dreidel pretended to.

'And you'll sign off on it?' she asked Dreidel.

'Gimme the form and I'm your man. And if it makes you feel better, I'll have President Manning write you a thank-you note personally.'

Shaking her head, she stood from her desk. 'This better not get me fi—'

Rogo's phone rang in his pocket. 'Sorry,' he said, fishing it from his pants and flipping it open. Caller ID said *PB Sher. Off.* Palm Beach Sheriff's Office.

'I'll catch up in a second,' he said to Dreidel and Kara as they headed for the door. Turning to the phone, he answered, 'This is Rogo.'

'Hey, fatty, we missed you in court today,' a man teased with a high voice and unforgivable New York accent. Rogo knew it instantly. Deputy Terry Mechaber. Palm Beach County's number one writer of illegal U-turn tickets . . . and Rogo's oldest friend in law enforcement.

'Yeah, receptionist was sick, so I had to stay back and kiss my own butt this morning,' Rogo replied.

'That's funny, because I just spoke to your receptionist. Sounded like her lips were just fine – especially when she said you'd been gone since this morning.'

For a moment, Rogo was quiet. 'Listen, Terry—'

'I don't wanna know, I don't wanna hear, I don't wanna read about it in tomorrow's paper,' Terry said. 'And based on this fight you're picking, I don't even wanna see the bad TV movie with the scene of me passing this along to you.'

'Wh-What're you—?'

'The Three . . . y'know, the guys you asked me to run through the databases here . . .'

'Wait, you found something?'

'Yeah, here in the Florida DMV, we have records of all the international bad guys. No, I passed it to my partner's sister's brother-in-law, who's been spending the last few years doing some high-tech computer job I still don't understand for DOD.'

'Dee-oh-dee?'

'Department of Defense,' Terry replied, his voice slow and serious. 'And when he ran *The Three* through there, well, remember the time when that eighteen-wheeler hauling all that rebar triple-flipped on I-95, sending metal javelins through the air and impaling nearly everyone in the ten nearest cars behind it?'

'Yeah . . .'

'It's worse than that.'

63

'Welcome to Key West,' the pilot called out, brushing his wispy blond hair back on his head.

Following him out of the seaplane door and down the scaffolding to the white pontoon floats that gave the orange and red plane its buoyancy, O'Shea and Micah barely waited for the plane to be tied to the dock.

'How long you gonna be?' the pilot asked.

'Not long,' O'Shea said, careful to time his jump just right. Waiting for the seaport's light waves to sink, then swell, he hopped from the edge of the pontoon float and landed square on the dock. 'Just make sure—'

'Don't stress so much,' the pilot called back. 'I know every dockmaster working this place. Soon as I tie us up, I'll take care of it – no one'll ever know we were here.'

'We should call Wes's office again,' Micah said, only a few steps behind. 'Maybe he checked in.'

'He didn't check in.'

Tracing the maze of wooden planks past dozens of sailboats and charter boats that swayed against the docks, O'Shea didn't stop until he reached the end of William Street. As Micah skidded to a stop next to him, the sound of acoustic folk rock drifted in from the bar on their far right. O'Shea narrowed his eyes, searching through the crowds of tourists clogging the shops along the docks.

From the side streets, a steady stream of cars and cabs circled the block, replenishing the tourist supply.

'What're you—?'

'All the cabs are pink,' O'Shea blurted. '*Taxi!*'

On their right, a bright pink cab shrieked and stopped. Opening the back door, O'Shea slid inside. 'You have radios in these cars?'

The skinny African-American cabbie glanced over his shoulder at O'Shea's dark blue suit, then over at Micah, whose tie dangled downward as he leaned in through the open door. 'Let me guess – lost your wallet in a pink cab.'

'Actually, I lost my friend.' O'Shea laughed, playing nice. 'He's pretty unforgettable, though – huge mess of scars on the side of his face. Plus the redhead he's running around with. So whattya say,' he added, lowering a twenty-dollar bill onto the armrest of the front seat. 'Think you can help me track him down?'

The cabbie grinned. 'Damn, man, why didn't you just say so in the first place?'

One quick description later, a slow, easy voice squawked through the radio's receiver. 'Yeah, I seen 'em, Rogers. Kid with the scars . . . Dropped 'em twenty minutes ago. Three twenty-seven William Street.'

'That far from here?' O'Shea asked as the cabbie looked at him in the rearview.

'You can walk if you want.'

Micah hopped inside, tugging the door shut.

'We'll drive,' O'Shea said as he tossed another twenty onto the armrest. 'Fast as you can.'

'Like your life depended on it,' Micah added.

64

With my knees digging into the carpet, my chest pinned against the coffee table, and the weight of my face pressed against the photographer's loupe, I study a black-and-white profile shot of the President and First Lady as they leave Cadillac One, their chins up toward the astonished crowd. Like the best White House photos, the moment is flush with the pomp of the presidency mixed with the humanity of the players involved.

Manning has his hand on the small of his wife's back, gently edging her out of the limo and into his world. As she leaves the car, one foot already on the pavement of the racetrack, she's in mid-blink, frozen awkwardly between the private quiet of the limo and the public roar of the crowd. For support, the First Lady holds the hand that the President's extended to her. But even in that moment – her holding him, his fingertips on the curve of her back – whatever tenderness exists between husband and wife is swallowed by the fact that instead of looking at each other, both smile up to the fans in the stands.

'These are unreal,' Lisbeth says, flipping through the notebook of 8×10s in her lap.

I glance over to see what she's looking at. She's about ten seconds ahead of my sequence, moments after the last shot was fired and Manning was pulled down by the swarm of drivers, guests, and Secret Service agents. In her photo, people in the stands scream and scurry in every direction, their hair spiked as they run.

In mine, they're enraptured and calm, completely immobile on the edge of their seats. In Lisbeth's, I hear the screams. In mine, I hear the thrill of their first true look at the President and his wife. *There he is . . . There he is . . . There they are . . .*

Ten seconds apart. Ten seconds to change everyth – No. It didn't change everything. It changed me.

An electronic ring interrupts the thought as I quickly trace the noise to the cell phone we borrowed from Lisbeth's coworker at the paper. Pulling it from my inside jacket pocket, I see *Pres. Manning Library* on caller ID. At least he's smart enough not to call from his—

'They're all in it together,' he insists before I can even say hello. 'That's how they pulled it off.'

'What're you—?'

'It's just like we said, Wes – you can't do this without help.'

'Slow down . . . who're you talking about?'

'The Three – that's what Boyle called them. But they're not what you—'

'Who'd you get this from? Dreidel or someone else?'

'My—'

'Does Dreidel even know?'

'Will you shut the hell up and let me tell you!?' Rogo shouts through the phone. I turn to see if Lisbeth hears, but she's too lost in the 8×10s.

Catching his breath in the silence, Rogo starts at a whisper. Wherever he is, he's definitely not alone. 'They started as a myth, Wes. Like some old law enforcement ghost story. You've heard it for years: politicians bitching and moaning that all our law enforcement groups don't work well together – that the FBI won't share information with the CIA, who won't share with the Secret Service. The result leaves half the agencies complaining that they're in the dark. But there are some who argue – not publicly, of course – that the lack of coordination isn't such a bad thing. The more adversarial they are, the more each agency is a check on the other. If the CIA does something corrupt, the FBI is there to call them on it. But if they all got together and ganged up against us . . . well, y'know what kinda power's in those numbers?'

'Wait, so now you're trying to tell me that someone's convinced *thousands* of our country's top, most trusted agents to suddenly switch sides?'

'Not thousands,' Rogo says, his voice still a whisper. 'Just three.'

Climbing from my knees, I sit back on the couch. Next to me, Lisbeth's carefully studying one of the photos.

'Hey . . . uh . . . Wes,' she says, pointing to a photo.

I give her the *one minute* sign with my pointer finger and stay focused on the phone.

'Three members,' Rogo adds. 'One from the FBI, one from the CIA, one from the Secret Service. Alone, they can only do limited damage. Together, fully aware of all the tricks, including how to sidestep three of our most powerful agencies? They can pull down the whole damn sky.'

'Wes, I think you should look at this,' Lisbeth says.

Once again, I put up the *one minute* sign.

'Apparently, it was the great urban myth of law enforcement – until eight years ago, when the first internal investigation was opened,' Rogo says. 'My guy said there's some sky-level memo from Boyle to the President, warning him to look into it.'

'So Manning and Boyle were chasing The Three?'

'Or The Three were chasing them – for all we know, they were fighting over the same corrupt pie,' Rogo replies.

'And you think three guys could really keep their jobs and stay hidden that long?'

'You kidding? Robert Hanssen spent twenty years selling secrets from within the FBI before anyone took notice. The Three are pros within their agencies. And the way they're backing each other up, they're doing triple damage. Oh, and just to crap on your day a little more: The last – and only – known sighting for one of these guys was that beautiful little terrorist hot spot known as Sudan.'

'Sudan? As in, the one country The Roman specializes in?'

'Wes, I'm serious,' Lisbeth says, popping open the rings of the notebook.

'Just one sec,' I tell her. 'No jokes, Rogo,' I say into the phone. 'You think The Roman gets info from The Three?'

'Or *gives* info *to* The Three. Hell, for all we know, The Roman's *part of* The Three, though I guess it could be anyone in the Service.'

Next to me, Lisbeth pulls the photo from the notebook, then holds it almost to her nose to check it up close.

'You mean that he's CIA or FBI?' I ask Rogo.

'No, he's Secret Service,' Rogo says a bit too confidently. I know that tone.

'Rogo, don't play games. Say what you're saying.'

'Wes, just take a second to look at this,' Lisbeth says, now annoyed I'm ignoring her.

'It was actually Dreidel's brainstorm,' Rogo says. 'Once he heard *FBI*, he asked my guy if he could look up your favorite investigators, Agents O'Shea and Micah.

According to his records, O'Shea started with the Bureau in July of 1986. Same exact year as Micah.'

'So what's the problem?'

'Wes . . .' Lisbeth pleads.

'The problem,' Rogo says, refusing to slow down, 'is that Micah doesn't work for the Bureau. As near as we can tell, he works as a case officer. For the CIA.'

'Just look!' Lisbeth adds, shoving the photo into my lap.

My lungs crater, like someone's shot an arrow into my chest. It only gets worse as I look down at the photograph. In my lap is a black-and-white reaction shot taken a few minutes after the shooting. Unlike the others, this one faces the infield of the raceway, where NASCAR drivers, mechanics, and their staff embrace, hug, sob, and retell the story that just unfolded in front of them. Most look shell-shocked. A few look angry. And one – all alone in the far right corner of the photo, glancing over his shoulder as he walks away – looks oddly curious.

At first, he blends right in because of his racing jump-suit. But there's no mistaking the finely combed hair and the small nick missing from the top of his ear. Eight years ago, I was shot in the face, Boyle was supposedly killed, and the Manning presidency was decimated. Micah was there to witness it all.

'That's him, right?' Lisbeth asks. 'That's Micah . . .'

The Secret Service is in charge of presidential protection. The FBI handled the investigation of Nico. 'What the hell was the CIA doing there that day?' I blurt.

'CIA?' Lisbeth asks.

'Wes, don't answer her!' Rogo calls out through the phone.

'What're you talking about?'

'Think for a second,' he tells me. 'You've always been alone when O'Shea and Micah corner you, right? So if Lisbeth never met Micah before, how the hell can she pick him out of a photograph?'

I look over at Lisbeth, who's still next to me on the couch. 'What's wrong?' she asks, reaching for the picture. She pulls it out of my hands before I can react.

'Lemme call you right back,' I say to Rogo as I hang up the phone.

65

'Sorry I couldn't be more help,' an elderly black woman with a beaded bracelet said as she walked O'Shea to the door of her modest conch cottage at 327 William Street. 'Though I do hope you find him.'

'I'm sure we will,' O'Shea replied, stepping back outside and tucking his badge back into his jacket pocket. 'Thanks for letting us look around, though.'

A few steps behind him, Micah held his phone to his ear, trying hard not to look frustrated. He didn't say a word until the woman shut the door behind them.

'Told you the kid's sharp,' The Roman said through Micah's phone.

'That's real helpful,' Micah shot back. 'Almost as helpful as showing up in Florida and heading into Manning's office without telling anyone.'

'You know the rules,' The Roman said calmly. 'No contact unless—'

'You telling me this isn't a fucking emergency?' Micah exploded. 'We got Wes sniffing everywhere, no bead on Boyle, and you're waltzing into the one place that has the very best chance of asking what the hell're you doing here in the first place? When'd you plan on filling us in – before or after they start staring at you and report you back to headquarters?'

Just as he did before, The Roman stayed calm. 'I *did*

call you, Micah. That's why we're talking. And if it makes
you feel better, no one's reporting me anywhere. I'm here
because it's my job, which is more than I can say about
you and the half dozen people you've held yourself out
to as an FBI agent. The Agency teach you to be that dumb,
or were you just panicking that O'Shea would turn on
you if you didn't stay close to him?'

'I told headquarters my father was sick. O'Shea said
he had his niece's graduation. You think we didn't clear
ourselves for being back here?'

'And that makes you think you can hold hands in public
like that? Using your real names, no less? O'Shea I understand – just in case Wes calls the Bureau to check him
out. But *you*!? Have you forgotten how we got this far in
the first place?'

'Actually, I haven't forgotten any of it,' Micah shot back.
'Which is why, when I first started smelling the flames
from the *Towering Inferno*, I called O'Shea instead of you.
So don't *you* forget, pinhead – in the FBI, O'Shea's a Legal
Attaché, meaning he coordinates resources for foreign
investigations. That means he's authorized – hell, he's
encouraged – to pair up with Agency folks like me. That's
his job! So no offense, but as long as it's my ass on the
clothesline, I plan on being front and center for saving it!'

For a moment, The Roman was silent. 'No contact,' he
finally said. '*Ever.*'

Micah turned to O'Shea, who mouthed the words *Hang
up.* After almost ten years together, they both knew it
wasn't worth the argument. When The Roman wanted
something, he always went after it himself. It was the same
for all of them. Personal drive was what brought them
together all those years ago at War College. It was no coincidence that each was invited to attend one of the army's

prestigious leadership conferences, where top military officials and representatives from the State Department, CIA,
FBI, DIA, Customs, and Secret Service spend two weeks
studying national defense and military interactions. It was
there that they were lectured on military tactics. There
that they learned strategic leadership. And there that each
realized how much they'd given to their government – and
how little the government had given back. That's where
The Three was born.

No doubt, personal drive made them successful over
time. It helped them maneuver through the system, main-
taining their jobs to this day without any of their colleagues
being the wiser. Yet personal drive, they also knew, would
someday be their undoing. Boyle called them The Three,
but even on their best days, they were always looking out
for number one.

'Just find Wes – he's still the only one Boyle's contacted,
which means Boyle'll reach out again,' The Roman added.
'And even with the fake address Wes gave, you should still
be able t—'

With a click, Micah hung up the phone. 'Guy's unreal,'
he bitched to O'Shea. 'First, he snakes in without telling
us, now he wants to play quarterback.'

'He's just nervous,' O'Shea said. 'And personally, I don't
blame him.'

'But to let Nico out—'

'By accident . . .'

'You believe him on that?'

'Micah, Roman's a scumbag, but he's not a moron. He
knows Nico can *Hindenburg* at any moment, which is why
he needed to see if Boyle had been in touch. But let me
tell you right now, if we don't find Wes – and Boyle –
quickly, I'm done. No joke. It's enough.'

'Can you please stop with the ultimatums?'

'It's not an ultimatum,' O'Shea insisted. 'Just being here – snooping this close and giving this kid every reason to look us up – you have any idea what we're risking?'

'We're being smart.'

'No, being smart is walking away now, and being thankful we made some cash and lasted this long.'

'Not when there's so much more cash to be made. The Roman said next month in India, there's a—'

'Of course, it's India. And eight months ago, it was Argentina, and eight years ago, it was Daytona. It's enough, Micah. Yes, we added some feathers to the nest egg, but the giant pot of gold? It's never coming.'

'You're wrong.'

'I'm right.'

'You're *wrong*!' Micah insisted, his finely combed hair flying out of place.

O'Shea stopped at the curb, knowing better than to keep arguing. It didn't matter anyway – he'd made his decision the moment he got the call yesterday: If they could wrap this up quickly, fantastic. If not, well, that's why he saved his money and bought that bungalow in Rio. Eyeing Micah, he knew that if it all cratered and it came down to finger-pointing, he had no problem breaking a few fingers.

'Everything okay?' Micah asked.

O'Shea nodded from the curb, both of them studying each house on the lush, narrow street. O'Shea checked windows and doors, searching for shadows and suddenly closed curtains. Micah checked front porches and pathways, searching for footprints in the light layer of sand that regularly blew across the Key West sidewalks. Neither found a thing. Until . . .

'There,' O'Shea said, marching diagonally across the street and heading straight for the peach cottage with the white shutters and gingerbread trim.

'Where?' Micah asked, still searching for himself.

'The car.'

A few steps behind O'Shea, Micah studied the old red Mustang parked in the driveway at 324 William Street. Florida license plate. Registration stickers up to date. Nothing out of the ordinary. Except for the ratty, weather-worn Washington Redskins bumper sticker on the back left bumper.

'Go Skins,' Micah whispered, barely able to contain his grin. Picking up speed, he followed his partner up the steps to the front door with the hand-painted wooden crab sign hanging on it.

'One sec,' Micah added as he reached into his suit jacket and flicked off the safety on his gun. Signaling to O'Shea with a nod, he took a half-step back, just in case they'd have to knock down the door.

With a jab of his finger, O'Shea rang the doorbell and checked on his own gun. 'Coming,' a voice called from inside.

Micah checked the street behind them. No one in sight.

The doorknob twisted with a creak, and the door flew open.

'Hey there,' O'Shea announced, purposely not pulling his FBI badge. 'We're friends of Wes Holloway and just wanted to check in and make sure he's okay.'

'Oh, he's great,' Kenny said, purposely blocking the doorway, even though the only thing to see was his empty kitchen and living room. 'But I'm sorry to say he's long gone.'

Craning his neck to look over Kenny's shoulder, Micah

ignored the kitchen and living room and instead focused on the far back wall of the house, where a painted screen door led out to the backyard.

'Yeah, we thought that might be the case,' O'Shea said. 'But even so, you mind if we come inside and just ask a few questions?'

66

'So you've been down to the stacks before?' Kara asked as the elevator doors slid open, revealing a concrete hallway with narrow windows on either side and all the charm of a prison.

'Absolutely,' Rogo replied, keeping his voice peppy and his head down as they passed the first of two security cameras attached to the wall. Two steps in front of him, next to Kara, Dreidel fidgeted with his tie and did the same.

When a President builds his library, it's his chance to rewrite history. In LBJ's library, there's an exhaustive exhibit on why the U.S. *had* to go to Vietnam. In Manning's, the only mention of the Cowardly Lion was down in the stacks.

'We really appreciate you pulling everything so fast,' Dreidel said.

'That's our job,' Kara replied as they approached a steel-reinforced door that was nearly as thick as a bank vault. 'I just hope you guys aren't claustrophobic . . .'

'No – in fact, we hate the sunlight,' Rogo said. 'Darn vitamin D *pisses* me off!'

Glancing over her shoulder, Kara offered another panting laugh. This time, Dreidel didn't join in. 'Just point us to the files and we'll be gone before you know it,' he said.

Kara punched in a five-digit code just above the doorknob. 'You asked for it,' she said as the thick metal door swung open, and the sweet smell of an old bookstore wafted through the air. In front of them, in a room as big as a basketball court, was row after row of gray metal storage shelves. But instead of being filled with books, they were stacked with thousands of square and rectangular acid-free storage boxes. On their far right, well past the shelves, a metal cage ran from floor to ceiling, separating them from another set of about ten metal shelves: secure storage for national security files. Just in front of the cage, a lanky Hispanic man with reading glasses sat in front of one of two computer terminals.

'If you have any problems, ask Freddy,' Kara explained, motioning to one of the library's four research room attendants.

Freddy waved to Rogo and Dreidel. Rogo and Dreidel waved back. But the way Kara eyed Freddy, and Freddy eyed Dreidel . . . Even Rogo took the hint. Kara may've been nice enough to let them in the stacks, but there's no way she was dumb enough to leave them unsupervised in the heart of the archives.

'So our stuff . . .' Dreidel asked.

'. . . is right here,' Kara said, pointing to the end of one of the metal stacks, where a small worktable was buried under at least forty boxes. 'These small ones have already been processed through FOIA,' she explained, waving her open palm at the dozen or so narrow, vertical boxes that looked like they each held a phone book. 'And these FRCs . . . these're the ones from closed storage,' she added, pointing to the thirty or so square boxes that were each about the size of a milk crate.

'And this is everything Boyle had?' Rogo asked.

'If you went back in time and pulled open his desk drawers in the White House, here's what you would've found – his files, his memos, his printed-out e-mails – plus you asked for his personnel file and those 12,000 pages that were requested by your other researcher . . .'

'Carl Stewart,' Rogo said, remembering Wes's instructions as Kara handed him the list of every file Boyle requested under his fake name.

'You already have the crossword, right?' Kara asked.

'Right here,' Rogo said, patting the breast pocket of his shirt.

'Kara, we can't thank you enough,' Dreidel added, anxious to send her on her way.

Taking the cue, Kara headed for the door. Never forgetting her role as protector of the archives, though, she called out, 'Freddy, thanks for supervising.'

As Kara turned the corner and disappeared, Dreidel shot a smile at the attendant, then quickly turned back to Rogo. 'How 'bout you take Boyle's desk drawers, and I'll start hunting through the list of his requests.'

'I got a better idea,' Rogo challenged. 'You take the drawers, and *I'll* go through the requests.'

For a moment, Dreidel was silent. 'Fine,' he said, flipping open the nearest box. Behind him, Rogo did the same.

As Rogo pulled out the first file, he licked his fingers and turned to the first page. 'Okay, Boyle, you sneaky son of a bitch – time to see what you were searching for.'

67

Melbourne, Florida

'No, not her,' Nico said, glancing out the front windshield of his maroon Pontiac Grand Prix as a petite Peruvian woman sipped her coffee and headed toward her own car.

Why? What's wrong with her?

Nico looked shaken. 'She looks like my nurse. Pick someone else.'

What about him?

Nico didn't even turn toward Edmund's selection. From their corner spot in the Waffle House parking lot, he was still watching the woman who looked so amazingly like his night nurse. It'd been nearly a full day since he thought about the hospital. The doctors were wrong. So were the lawyers. All wrong. Out on his own – even without his meds – he felt just fine. Better even. More clear. Crackling crystal clear.

Nico, focus. What about him?

Following Edmund's glance, Nico studied the bearded man with teeny eyes and obvious hair plugs.

'I can't. No. I can't. He was in my dream last night.'

Fine, then her – the mom with the two boys . . .

'The short child has to pee – look how he grabs himself. She won't stop. I think the older boy wants M&M's. You can read his lips. *M . . . and . . . M's . . .*'

Nico, don't get loopy on me.

Sitting up straight, he pushed Edmund's imagined hand from his shoulder. 'I'm not – I'm good. I just need to—' Cutting himself off, he locked on a plump, middle-aged waitress with beautiful brown eyes coming out of the restaurant for a cigarette break. On the strap of her purse was an *Ask Me About Avon* button.

'There. Her. She knows rejection,' Nico announced, diving for the door handle and leaping out of the Pontiac. 'Hurry!' he called to Edmund as he crossed the parking lot and approached the waitress.

'Can I borrow your phone?' Nico asked, slowing down just as he reached the woman. 'It's an emergency. My – I have to call my mother.'

Seeing Nico's handsome squint, the waitress didn't even hesitate. 'Of course,' she replied, her chubby hand lowering like a skill-crane into her fake-leather purse.

Tell her you won't be long.

'I won't be long,' Nico said.

'Take as much time as you want, hon – I get a thousand minutes every month, God praise my divorce lawyer.'

Flipping the phone open, Nico turned his back to the waitress and dialed a simple three-digit number. There was a chime on the other line.

'Welcome to local 411. What city and state?' a female operator asked.

'Wes Holloway,' Nico said as he lowered his voice.

'*City* and *state*,' the operator repeated, clearly annoyed.

'Palm Beach. Florida.'

There was a short pause. 'Sir? I've got a Wes Holloway in *West* Palm Beach. Please hold for the—'

'Not the number,' Nico said. 'The address.'

Once again, there was a short pause. 'Eight three eight five Okeechobee Boulevard, apartment 527. And you sure you don't want the phone number – y'know, just in case?'

'No number,' Nico said, giving a quick thumbs-up to Edmund. 'No, no. No. This is a surprise.'

68

'What, now you don't believe me?' Lisbeth calls out.

'Just c'mon . . . let's go,' I say, cutting between two tourists and running past the ice cream store on our way to the docks. She wasn't happy when I asked her how she knew what Micah looked like, but it's tough to argue with her answer.

'Wes, when we were at the newspaper, they drove right past me in the garage,' she insists. 'I was hiding right by the entrance – your idea, remember? – waiting for them to leave so I could pick you up. Any of this sounding familiar?'

If I were Rogo, I'd ask her how she knew which was Micah and which was O'Shea.

'I believe you,' I tell her as I leap down two short steps and my feet slap against the wood of the docks. Over the past two days, I could've easily described Micah and O'Shea. More important, with everything we've been through, everything she's seen . . . After eight years of dealing with political schemers, I'm fluent in bullshit. Far as I can tell, Lisbeth doesn't speak a word of it.

'Wes, if I wanted to burn you—'

'I know – I just had to ask, okay?'

'But if you—'

'Lisbeth, I swear – we're fine,' I call out, weaving through the maze of docks, back toward the yacht that holds our helicopter. 'I swear to you. If we weren't, you wouldn't be holding the picture.'

As she runs behind me, the photo we swiped from Kenny flaps in the wind. It's the only proof we have that Micah was there that day – and the main reason we darted out Kenny's back door. For the past two days, O'Shea and Micah have played relatively nice in the vain hope that I'd help them get Boyle and Manning. But if they find out we know the truth . . . that one of them is actually CIA . . . that he was there at the racetrack and potentially part of The Three . . . I glance over my shoulder at Lisbeth, who's glancing over her shoulder at the mostly empty docks. Whoever they were shooting at that day, Micah and O'Shea weren't afraid to send bullets at the most powerful men in the world. I don't even want to think how fast they'd make us disappear.

'You think they're close?' Lisbeth asks, her voice shaking.

Right now it's the only question that matters. To answer it, I slam the brakes, stopping short right in front of a small wooden hut no bigger than a phone booth. 'Keep going,' I say to Lisbeth, waving her along. 'Tell Tommaso to get our ride ready. We need to leave now!'

She slows down, already worried I'm ditching her. 'Then why're you—?'

'Just looking for our *friends*,' I insist, shooting her a look as a man in a blue button-down and a wide-brimmed straw hat steps out of the hut. As dockmaster, he assigns all the boats to their different slips. Which means he sees every person coming and going. Lisbeth takes the hint and keeps running.

'Signing in or heading out?' the man asks, angling his hat back to reveal a mess of muddy tobacco chew in his mouth.

'Actually, was wondering if you happened to see some buddies of mine – probably just came in on a seaplane or helicopter from Palm Beach.'

'Sorry, we don't log departure cities,' he says quickly.

'What about in the last hour? Anybody new fly in?'

'Naw, we been pretty quiet all morning.'

'You're sure?'

The dockmaster studies me, checking out my shirt, my slacks, even my shoes. He grins slightly and two dimples dot his cheeks.

'Positive, Dapper Dan. Nobody's flown in 'cept the billionaires in back,' he says, motioning to our black and cream helicopter at the far end of the docks.

Nodding a thank-you, I dart back toward the yacht and breathe the smallest sigh of relief. At least for now, no one knows we're here – and as long as we have that . . . as long as they don't know what we found . . . we've finally got the advantage.

'Tommaso, you ready?' I call out to the back deck of the yacht.

'Waiting for you, sir,' he calls back with a thumbs-up sign.

'Where's Lisbeth?'

He points to the glass cabin right next to him. Lisbeth's inside with her back to the glass. I don't blame her. Better to be out of sight than be spotted.

Scrambling up the metal steps two at a time, I leap for the door on the main deck and shove it open. 'Good news,' I say. 'I think we're sa—'

Lisbeth spins around, her hands fighting to stuff what looks like a small cell phone into her purse.

'This for you or for him?' Kenny's voice echoes from the device.

'*Me. I swear—*' my own voice says. She hits a button and the playback stops with the loud pop of a . . . *tape recorder.*

My mouth gapes open, and my chest caves in.

Lisbeth looks at me, her wide eyes already shoveling up the apology.

'Wes, before you say anything,' she pleads, stuffing the recorder into her bag.

'You were recording us?'

'It's not how y—'

'How long were you doing it?'

'It's not for attribution – just to keep my notes strai—'

'That's not the question.'

'Listen, Wes – you . . . you knew I'd be writing the story. That was our deal.'

'How *long?*'

'You told me it was our deal.'

'Dammit, Lisbeth! *How fucking long?*'

She watches me carefully, then turns away to avoid the conflict. With her back to me, she stares out at the drumming waves of the Gulf of Mexico. 'Since you walked in this morning,' she eventually whispers.

'Including the helicopter ride here?'

She freezes, finally realizing what I'm getting at. Every reporter has a line they promise themselves they'll never cross. From the look on her face as she turns back to me, Lisbeth just skipped, hurdled, and jumped over it. 'I never would've used that stuff, Wes.'

My legs buckle, barely able to hold my weight.

'You know that's true, right?' she asks, reaching out for my shoulder.

As I pull away, an adrenaline surge crackles under my skin. I grit my teeth so tightly, I swear I have feeling in my lip again instead of just phantom pain. 'Gimme the recorder,' I growl.

She doesn't move.

'*Gimme the damn recorder!*'

Fumbling as she pulls it from her purse, she offers a look that says, *You don't have to do this.* But I'm done believing. I snatch the recorder from her hand and stride back to the deck.

'Wes, I know you don't believe this, but I never meant to hur—'

'Don't say it!' I snap, whipping back to face her and jamming a finger at her face. 'You knew what you were doing! You *knew* it!'

Shoving my way outside and plowing toward the stern of the yacht, I cross over to the far railing, chuck the tape recorder into the water, and pivot back toward the helicopter.

'Everything okay?' Tommaso asks as he holds the helicopter door open and ushers us inside.

'Perfect,' I snap. 'Just get us the hell out of here.'

69

Sitting cross-legged on the linoleum floor and surrounded by piles of stacked-up acid-free archival boxes, Rogo flipped through his fourth file folder in the past fifteen minutes. 'What's *I&W*?'

'I&W for what?' Dreidel asked, hunched forward on a wooden chair and reading through one of Boyle's files.

'Doesn't say. Just *I&W* with lots of dates next to – wait, here's one: *I&W for Berlin.*'

'*Indicators and Warnings.* Or as General Bakos used to put it: all the trash talk and warning signs that our intelligence picks up about specific threats,' Dreidel explained. 'Why? Is that what—?' He looked over at the attendant and kept his voice to a whisper. 'Is that what Boyle was requesting? All the different I&Ws?'

'Is that bad?'

'Not bad – just – indicators and warnings are the kinds of things you usually find in the PDB.'

'President's Daily Brief. That's the report you were talking about before, with the CIA guy and the handcuffed briefcase?'

'And the place where The Roman's payouts were decided,' Dreidel added. 'Don't forget, a year before the shooting, The Roman was denied a major sum of money for some hot tip in Sudan, which also, since they clearly were never stupid enough to be seen in the same place together, tells us which one of them used Sudan as their last — and only — known location.'

'I'm not sure I follow.'

'The Three — The Roman, Micah, O'Shea — are from the Service, the CIA, and FBI. When they link brains, think of all the information they have access to.'

'I understand how they work . . . but to do all that — to set it all up — no offense, but . . . just for a six-million-dollar payout?'

'What makes you think they were only doing it once? For all we know, if the payment went through, they would've come back every few months — and if they upped each payment, six million becomes ten million becomes an easy seventy to eighty million dollars by the time they're done. Not a bad annual salary for preying on America's fears.'

'So you think they—?'

'Don't just focus on the *they* — think of who else had access to that same info. I mean, nothing happens in a vacuum. To even ask for that first six-million-dollar payment, they clearly had to've known something big was about to happen. But what if they weren't the only ones?'

'So you think someone else knew?' Rogo asked.

'All this time, we've been assuming that The Three and Boyle were enemies. But what if they were *competitors*? What if that's why The Three's multimillion-dollar payday got turned down — because the White House already had a similar tip — a similar indicator and warning — from someone else?'

'I got ya — so while The Three or The Roman or what-ever they call themselves kept bringing the White House their best hot tips, Boyle — or someone else in that meeting

– was trying to prove he was a bigshot by leaking those very same tips to the press.'

'And in the process, making The Roman's so-called scoops look like day-old newspapers.'

'Which takes us back to the crossword – if it really was a trust list – if Manning and his chief of staff used the puzzle to try and figure out who was leaking to the press, maybe that's who Boyle was looking for,' Rogo said. 'The only thing I don't get is, why would Manning and his chief pass notes in secret code when they could just wait a few hours and discuss the matter in private?'

'Private? In a building where they once had secret tapes recording all conversations in the Oval?'

'Is that true? They still do those recordings?'

'Don't you see? That's the point, Rogo. In that world, everybody's listening. So if you plan on saying something bad about one of your top lieutenants, you better be sure not to say it out loud.'

'Even so, how's that get us any closer to figuring out who Manning was singling out in the puzzle?'

'You tell me. What's it say in the files?' Dreidel asked. 'Any other names mentioned in there?'

Rogo glanced around at the thirty-eight boxes and 21,500 sheets of paper, hundreds of schedules, and thousands of briefings they still had to go through. 'You really think we can get through all this before the library closes?'

'Have a little faith,' Dreidel said, fingering through a set of files. His eyes lit up and a sly grin spread across his face. 'For all we know, the smoking gun is right in front of us.'

'What? You got something?'

'Only Boyle's personnel file,' Dreidel said as he plucked

the inch-thick file from its box. 'Which means we're about to find out what the President *really* thought of his old buddy Ron Boyle.'

70

'Listen, I'm kinda busy,' Kenny said as he closed the door on O'Shea and Micah. 'Maybe you can come back another—'

O'Shea jammed his foot in the doorway, forcing it open. From his pocket, he pulled his FBI badge and slid it through the opening toward Kenny's nose. '*Now* is actually a better time for us,' O'Shea insisted. He wasn't surprised by Kenny's reaction. After family, old friends were the hardest to crack.

Kenny's Popeye eye glared at Micah, then back to O'Shea's badge. 'Wes is a good kid,' he insisted.

'No one said he wasn't,' O'Shea replied as he and Micah stepped inside. O'Shea quickly scanned the kitchen. It didn't matter that Wes was gone. What mattered was what he saw while he was here.

'So you from Key West?' Micah asked as he made eye contact with his partner. Micah stayed in the kitchen. O'Shea took the living room.

'No one's from Key West,' Kenny shot back, already riled.

'Then where do you know Wes from?' O'Shea asked as he approached the wall of black-and-white wedding photos.

'D'you mind telling me what this is about?' Kenny asked.

'These are beautiful,' O'Shea replied, stepping toward a shot of a short-haired bride playfully biting the ear of her groom. 'You take these?'

'I did, but—'

'Did you work at the White House with Wes?' Micah interrupted, keeping him off balance.

'Kinda,' Kenny replied. 'I was there as a—'

'Photographer,' O'Shea blurted as he scooped up the framed photo of President Manning checking his reflection in the White House water pitcher. 'I remember this one. You're a hotshot, aren't you, Mr – I'm sorry, I forgot your name.'

'I never gave it to you,' Kenny said.

'Well, why don't we fix that?' O'Shea demanded, laying the silver frame flat down on its back. 'I'm Agent O'Shea and you're . . .'

'Kenny. Kenny Quinn.'

'Wait . . . Kenny Quinn?' Micah asked. 'How do I know that name?'

'You don't,' Kenny said. 'Not unless you're a photo editor or working the White House press pool.'

'Actually, I spent some time in D.C.,' Micah said, leaving the kitchen and heading toward Kenny in the living room.

Just behind Kenny, O'Shea eyed the closed three-ring binder on the cocktail table.

'You're the guy who won the award, didn't you?' Micah asked, working hard to hold Kenny's attention.

'The Pulitzer,' Kenny replied dryly.

'So you were there that day?' Micah asked.

'At the racetrack? There were plenty of us there.'

'But you're the one who took the photo, right? The Cowardly Lion photo?'

'I'm sorry,' Kenny said, turning back toward O'Shea,

'but until you tell me what you're looking for, I don't think I shou—'

A hushed hiss carved through the air, and a dark red bullet hole singed Kenny's skin as it pierced his forehead. As Kenny crumpled lifelessly to the floor, Micah stared at O'Shea, who had his gun in one hand and the open three-ring binder in the other.

'You *nuts*!?' Micah exploded.

'They IDed you, Micah.'

'What're you talking about? There's no way!'

'Really? Then what the hell is *this*?' O'Shea shouted, tapping his gun against an empty Mylar protective sleeve in the binder.

'There could've been anything in—'

'Not the sleeve – *underneath*!' O'Shea said as he flipped aside the empty sheet to reveal a clear view of the photo on the next page. 'You're telling me that's not you?' he asked, pointing to the enormous crowd shot where, when you looked closely enough, Micah was tucked away, glancing to the side.

'It's . . . it's not possible – we bought every photo out there . . . went through every tape . . .'

'Well obviously, there were a few more Kenny decided to keep in his collection! Don't you get it, Micah? Wes knows! He's got the thread of the sweater – and when he starts pulling, *you're* gonna be the first one they look at!'

'Big deal, so they ask me a few questions. You know I'll never say anything. But *this* . . . y'know what kinda avalanche you just started?'

'Don't worry,' O'Shea said calmly. 'If I set the bodies right, it'll just look like a botched robbery.'

'*Bodies?*' Micah asked, confused. 'What're you talking about? You've got more than one?'

O'Shea raised his gun and pointed it straight at his partner's chest.

Following years of training, Micah spun to his right, then leaped like a cheetah at O'Shea. The way Micah's pointer and middle fingers were curled – like claws – it was clear he was aiming for O'Shea's eyes.

O'Shea was impressed. No doubt, Micah was fast. But no one was that fast.

As O'Shea tugged the trigger, his fair blond hair glowed in the afternoon Key West sun. 'Sorry, Micah.'

There was a soft *ssstt*. Then a grunt.

And The Three became The Two.

71

'Don't tell me you lost him. Don't say those words.'

'I didn't *lose* him,' Lisbeth told her editor, clutching her cell phone as she walked in through the front door of the building. 'I let him go.'

'Did I tell you not to tell me that? Do I speak and you not hear?' Vincent asked. 'What's Sacred Rule #1?'

'Always keep 'em talking.'

'Fine, then Sacred Rule #26½: Don't let Wes out of your damn sight!'

'You weren't there, Vincent – you didn't see how upset he was. For fifty minutes – the entire flight back – the only thing he said to me was—' Lisbeth went silent.

'Lisbeth, you there?' Vincent asked. 'I can't hear you.'

'*Exactly!*' she replied, waving to security and heading for the elevators. 'Fifty minutes of dead silence! The guy wouldn't look at me, wouldn't talk to me, wouldn't even curse me out. And believe me, I gave him every opportunity. He just stared out the window, pretending I wasn't there. And when he dropped me off, he wouldn't even say good-bye.'

'Okay, so you hurt his feelings.'

'See, but that's the thing – I didn't just hurt his feelings. He's been at this too long to feel burned by a reporter, but the pain on his face . . . I hurt *him*.'

'Spare me the sentimental, Lisbeth – you were doing your job. Oh, wait, you actually weren't. If you were, the moment he dropped you off, you would've turned around and followed him.'

'In what? He has my car.'

'He *stole* your car?'

Lisbeth paused. 'No.'

Vincent paused even longer. 'Oh, jeez – you *gave* it to him? You gave him your car?' Vincent shouted. 'Sacred Rule #27: Don't go soft! Rule 28: Don't fall in love with a dreamer. And 29: Don't let sad disfigured boys pluck your heartstrings and send you sailing on a guilt trip just because they're sad and disfigured!'

'You don't even know him.'

'Just because someone's in a wheelchair doesn't mean they won't roll over your toes. You know what this story means, Lisbeth – especially for you.'

'And you.'

'And *you*,' he said as Lisbeth stepped into the waiting elevator and hit the button for the second floor. 'You know the job: You have to piss on people to be read. So please make my month and at least tell me you were smart enough to get it on tape.'

As the doors slid shut and the elevator started to rise, Lisbeth leaned against the brass railing, her head tilting back against the Formica wall. Letting the day's events wash over her, she lifted her head and lightly tapped it back against the wall. *Tap, tap, tap.* Over and over against the wall.

'C'mon, you *did* get it on tape, right?' Vincent asked.

Opening her purse, Lisbeth pulled out the miniature cassette tape that held the last part of their conversations. Sure, she'd handed Wes the recorder, but it didn't take much for her to palm the cassette while he was ranting. Of course, now – no, not just now. Even as she was doing it – so damn instinctively – another part of her brain was watching in disbelief. Every reporter needs instinct. But not when it overwhelms ideals.

'Last time, Lisbeth – yes tape or no tape?'

The elevator pinged on the second floor, and Lisbeth stared at her open palm, rubbing her thumb against the tiny cassette. 'Sorry, Vincent,' she said, tucking it back in her purse. 'I tried to stop him, but Wes tossed it overboard.'

'Overboard. Really?'

'Really.'

As she left the elevator and followed the hallway around to the left, there was a long pause on the line. Even longer than the one before.

'Where are you right now?' Vincent asked coldly.

'Right behind you,' Lisbeth said into her phone.

Through an open door up the gray-carpeted hallway, Vincent stopped pacing in his office and spun around to face her. Still holding the phone to his ear, he licked his salt-and-pepper mustache. 'It's four o'clock. I need tomorrow's column. Now.'

'You'll have it, but . . . the way things were left with Wes, I still think we should take another day before we push a story that's—'

'Do what you want, Lisbeth. You always do anyway.'

With a swing of his arm, Vincent slammed his door shut, unleashing a thunderclap that echoed in front of her and through her cell phone. As her fellow employees turned to stare, Lisbeth trudged to her cubicle just across the hall. Collapsing in her seat, she flicked on her computer, where a nearly empty three-column grid filled the screen. On the corner of her desk, a crumpled sheet of paper held all the vital info about young Alexander John's recent victory in the ultra-competitive world of high school art. This late in the day, there was no escaping the inevitable.

Flattening the crumpled paper with the heel of her hand, she reread the details and instinctively punched in the code for her voice mail.

'You have seven new messages,' the robotic female voice announced through her speakerphone. The first five were from local maître d's hoping to get some free press for their restaurants by ratting out who was eating lunch with whom. The sixth was a follow-up call on Alexander John's art award. And the last . . .

'Hi . . . er . . . this message is for Lisbeth,' a soft female voice began. 'My name's . . .'

The woman paused, causing Lisbeth to sit up straight. The best tips always came from people who didn't want to identify themselves.

'My name's . . . Violet,' she finally said.

Fake name, Lisbeth decided. *Even better.*

'I just . . . I was reading your column today, and when I saw *his* name, my stomach just . . . it's not right, okay? I know he's powerful . . .'

Lisbeth mentally ran through every mention in today's column. *The First Lady . . . Manning . . . does she mean Manning?*

'. . . it's just not right, okay? Not after what he did.' She's careful how she puts the knife in. She knows to punch, but not too hard. 'Anyway, if you can give me a call . . .'

Furiously scribbling the number, Lisbeth flipped open her cell phone and immediately started dialing. Her ears flushed red as it rang.

C'mon . . . pick up, pick up, pick up, pick—

'Hello?' a woman answered.

'Hi, this is Lisbeth Dodson from Below the Fold – I'm looking for Violet.'

There was a second or two of dead silence. Lisbeth just waited. New sources always needed an extra moment to decide.

'Hiya, honey – hold on one second,' the woman said. In the background, Lisbeth heard a bell chime and the sudden wisp of wind buzzing the phone. Whatever store Violet was in, she just left for privacy. Which meant she was willing to talk.

'This isn't . . . you're not recording this, right?' Violet finally asked.

Lisbeth glanced at the digital recorder that always sat on her desk. But she didn't reach for it. 'No recordings.'

'And you won't give my name out? Because if my husband . . .'

'We're off the record. No one'll ever know who you are. I promise you that.'

Once again, the line was drowned in silence. Lisbeth knew better than to push.

'I just want you to know, I'm no snitch,' Violet said, her voice cracking. Based on Violet's inflection and speed, Lisbeth wrote *mid-30s?* in her notepad. 'Understand, okay? I don't want this. He just . . . seeing his name in print again . . . and so happy . . . people don't realize – there's a whole 'nother side of him . . . and what he did that night . . .'

'What night?' Lisbeth asked. 'What was the date?'

'I don't think he's a bad person – I really don't – but when he gets angry . . . he just . . . he gets angry with the best of 'em. And when he's *real* angry . . . You know how men get, right?'

'Of course,' Lisbeth agreed. 'Now, why don't you just tell me what happened that night.'

72

'I don't wanna talk about it,' I insist.

'She was recording the whole time?' Rogo asks, still in shock as his voice crackles through the cell phone.

'Rogo, can we please not—?'

'Maybe it's not how it looked. I mean, she gave you her car *and* her phone, right? Maybe you misread it.'

'I heard my voice on the tape! How else could that possibly be read!?' I shout, squeezing my fist around the steering wheel and jamming even harder on the gas. As I blow past the thick twisting banyan trees that shield both sides of County Road from the sun, I hear the shift in Rogo's voice. At first, he was surprised. Now he's just hurt, with a dab of confused. When it comes to judging someone's character, he's usually a master.

'I told you she'd burn us – didn't I call it?' Dreidel hisses in the background. His voice is barely a whisper, which means someone's there with them.

'Did she say why?' Rogo adds. 'I mean, I know Lisbeth's a reporter, but—'

'Enough already, okay? How many times do I need to say it? I don't wanna talk about it!'

'Where are you now anyway?' Rogo asks.

'No offense, but I shouldn't say. Y'know, just in case someone's listening.'

'Wes, you're full of manure – where the hell are you?' Rogo insists.

'On US-1.'

'You're lying – that was too fast.'

'I'm *not* lying.'

'Too fast again. C'mon, Pinocchio – I know the little stutter and stammer when you're fibbing. Just tell me where you are.'

'You have to understand, Rogo, he—'

'He? *He?* The royal *He*,' he moaned, more angry than ever. 'Son of Betsy Ross, Wes! You're going to see Manning?'

'He's expecting me. Schedule says I have to be there at four.'

'Schedule? The man's been lying to you for eight years about the single greatest tragedy in your life. Doesn't that—?' He lowers his voice, forcing himself to calm down. 'Doesn't that let you say F-you to the schedule for once?'

'He's going to Manning?' Dreidel asks in the background.

'Rogo, you don't understand—'

'I *do* understand. Lisbeth made you sad . . . The Three got you scared . . . and as always, you're running for your favorite presidential pacifier.'

'Actually, I'm trying to do the one thing we should've done the first moment I saw Boyle alive: go to the source and find out what the hell actually happened that day.'

Rogo's silent, which tells me he's seething. 'Wes, let me ask you something,' he finally says. 'That first night you saw Boyle, why didn't you go to Manning and tell him the truth? Because you were in shock? Because it seemed that Boyle was somehow invited to that hotel by his old best friend? Or because deep in the pit of your chest, no matter how much you've rationalized it over the years, you know that before he's a father, a mentor, or even a husband, Leland F. Manning is a politician – one of the world's greatest politicians – and for that alone, he's fully capable of lying to your face for eight years without you ever knowing it.'

'But that's what you're missing, Rogo – what if he didn't lie? What if he's just as clueless as we are? I mean, if O'Shea and Micah and whoever this Roman guy is – if they're the ones who sent Nico to shoot Boyle – maybe Manning and Boyle aren't the villains in all this.'

'What, so now they're victims?'

'Why not?'

'Please, he's the—' Catching himself and knowing I won't listen if he yells, Rogo adds, 'If Boyle and Manning were complete angels – if they had nothing to hide and were only doing good – why didn't they just take Boyle to the hospital and let the authorities investigate? C'mon, Wes, these two guys lied to the entire world – and the only reason people lie is because they have something to hide. Now, I'm not saying I have all the pieces, but just by the lie alone, there's no way Manning and Boyle are just helpless victims.'

'That still doesn't mean they're the enemy.'

'And you really believe that?'

'What I *believe* is that Ron Boyle's alive. That The Three, with all their connections, helped Nico sneak into the race-track that day. That O'Shea, Micah, and this Roman, as members of The Three, clearly have some grudge against Boyle. And for that reason, they're now doing anything in their power to find out where he is. As for how Manning fits into this, I've got no idea.'

'Then why race to him like a battered wife back to her abuser?'

'What're my other choices, Rogo? Go to the FBI, where O'Shea works? Or the Service, where The Roman is? Or better yet, I can go to the local authorities and tell them I saw dead man walking. Ten minutes after that happens, you think O'Shea and his little posse won't show up with their federal badges, take me into private custody, and put a bullet in the back of my head claiming I was trying to escape?'

'That's not even—'

'It *is* true and you *know* it's true, Rogo! These guys went after one of the most powerful men in the White House at a stadium filled with 200,000 people. You think they won't slice my neck open on some deserted road in Palm Beach?'

'Tell him not to mention my name to Manning,' Dreidel calls out in the background.

'Dreidel wants you to—'

'I heard him,' I interrupt, twisting the steering wheel into a sharp left on Via Las Brisas. As I curve around a well-manicured divider, the street narrows, and the privacy hedges rise, stretching as tall as twenty feet and blocking my view of all the multimillion-dollar homes hidden behind them. 'Rogo, I know you don't agree, but for the past two days, the only reason I stayed away from Manning is because O'Shea and Micah convinced me to. D'you understand? The man's been by my side for eight years, and the only reason I doubted him is because they – *two strangers with badges* – told me to. No offense, but after all our time together, Manning deserves better than that.'

'That's fine, Wes, but let's be clear about one thing:

Manning hasn't been *by your side* for eight years. You've been by his.'

I shake my head and pull up to the last house on my right. For security reasons, they don't allow parking in the driveway, so I head for the shoulder of the grassy divider and park directly behind a navy-blue rental car that's already there. His guests are early – which means, as I hop out and rush across the street, I'm officially late.

Even before I stop at the ten-foot-high, double-planked wooden fence, the intercom that's hidden in the shrubs crackles. 'Can I help you?' a deep voice asks.

'Hey there, Ray,' I call out to the agent on duty. 'It's Wes.'

'You don't have to do this,' Rogo pleads through my phone.

He's never been more wrong. This is exactly what I need to do. Not for Manning. For me. I need to know.

A metallic thunk unlocks the wooden gate, which slowly yawns open.

'Wes, at least just wait until we get through Boyle's personnel file,' Rogo begs.

'You've been searching for four hours already – it's enough. I'll call you when I'm done.'

'Don't be so stubborn.'

'Good-bye, Rogo,' I say, hanging up the phone. It's so easy for someone outside the ring to tell a fighter how to fight his fight. But this is *my* fight. I just never realized it.

As I walk up the driveway, there's no house number on the front door, and no mailbox to identify the occupants. But the four suit-and-tie Secret Service agents standing outside the garage are quite a giveaway. With

Nico on the loose, they kept Manning at home. Fortunately, as I lift my chin and stare up at the pale blue British Colonial, I know where the former President lives.

73

'And how'd you meet him again?' Lisbeth asked, holding her cell phone with one hand and taking notes with the other.

'Mutual friend,' Violet replied, her voice already shaking. 'It was years ago. At that point on the job, it was personal introductions only.'

'Introductions?'

'You have to understand, with a man like him, you don't just walk up and swing your tail. In this town – with all the money . . . with everything these guys have to lose – the only thing they care about is discretion, okay? That's why they sent him to me.'

'Of course,' Lisbeth said as she scribbled the word *Hooker* in her notepad. 'So you were . . .'

'I was twenty, is what I was,' Violet said with a verbal shove. She didn't like being judged. 'But lucky me, I could keep a secret. That's why I got the work. And with him . . . our first two appointments, I didn't even say his name. That alone guaranteed he'd invite me back. Gladiators need to conquer, right?' she asked, her laughter soft and hollow.

Lisbeth didn't laugh back. There was no pleasure in someone else's pain.

'I know what you're thinking,' Violet added, 'but it was nice in the beginning. He was, honestly . . . he was tender

– always asking if I was okay . . . he knew my mother was sick, so he'd ask about her. I know, I know – he's a politician, but I was twenty and he was . . .' Her voice trailed off.

Lisbeth didn't say anything. But as the silence wore on . . . 'Violet, are you—?'

'It sounds so damn stupid, but I was just thrilled he liked me,' she blurted, clearly trying to stifle a sob. From the sound of it, the flush of emotion surprised even her. 'I'm sorry – let me just . . . I'm sorry . . .'

'You have no reason to be sorry.'

'I know – I just . . . it mattered that he liked me . . . that he kept coming back,' she explained, sniffling it all back in. 'I wouldn't see him for a while, then the phone would ring, and I'd be jumping up and down, like I'd been asked to the prom. And that's how it was until . . . until he left one night and I didn't hear from him for almost three months. I was . . . to be honest, at first, I was worried. Maybe I did something wrong. Or he was mad. And then, when I heard he was in town, I did the one thing I never should've done – the dumbest thing I could possibly do, against every rule,' Violet explained, her voice barely a whisper. 'I called him.'

Right then Lisbeth stopped writing.

'He was at my place in ten minutes,' Violet said, another sob clogging her throat. 'Wh-When I opened the door, he stepped inside without a word . . . made sure he was out of view . . . and then he just – I swear to you, he never did it before . . .'

'Violet, it's okay to—'

'I didn't even see the first punch coming,' she said as the tears flooded forward. 'He just kept screaming at me, "How dare you! How *dare* you!" I tried fighting back – I did . . . I'm . . . I've never been weak – but he grabbed the back of my hair and he . . . he sent me straight for . . . there was a mirror above my dresser.'

Staring at her own rounded reflection in her computer screen, Lisbeth didn't move.

'I could see him behind me in the mirror . . . just as I hit it . . . I could see him behind me . . . his face . . . the red in his eyes. It was like he pulled off a mask and let out . . . like he freed something underneath,' Violet cried. 'And – and – and when he was gone . . . when the door slammed and the blood was pouring from my nose, I still – I know it's – can you believe I still missed him?' she asked, weeping uncontrollably. 'I-I mean, could I possibly be more pathetic than that?'

Lisbeth shook her head to herself, trying hard to stay focused. 'Violet, I know this is hard for you – I know what it takes to tell the story – but I just need – Before we do anything, I need to ask: Do you have any way of proving this . . . anything at all . . . videotapes, physical proof . . . ?'

'You don't believe me,' she insisted.

'No, no, no . . . it's just, look who you're fighting with here. Without a way of verifying—'

'I have proof,' Violet said, clearly annoyed as she caught her breath. 'I've got it right here. If you don't believe me, come get it.'

'I will, I'll come right now. Lemme just . . . hold on one second . . .' Pressing her cell phone to her chest and hopping out of her seat, Lisbeth grabbed the uncrumpled art award notes, darted out of her cubicle, and ducked into a blond reporter's cubicle directly across the hall. 'Eve, can I borrow your car?' Lisbeth asked.

'First my phone – which I still haven't gotten back – now my car—'

'*Eve!*'

Eve studied her friend, reading her expression. 'This's the one, isn't it?'

'Column's on my computer. Here's the last item,' Lisbeth said, tossing her the art award notes. 'Can you—?'

'On it,' Eve said as Lisbeth said thank you, took off up the hallway, and pressed her cell to her ear. 'Violet, I'm on my way,' she said, doing her best to keep her talking. Sacred Rule #9: Never let go of the big fish. 'So . . . how long were you two actually together?'

'A year and two months,' Violet replied, still sounding angry. 'Right before the shooting.'

Lisbeth stopped running. 'Wait, this was when he was still in the White House?'

'Of course. Every President goes home for vacation. Besides, he couldn't pull this off in Washington. But down here . . . I'd get the phone call and he could—'

'Violet, no bullshitting anymore – you're trying to tell me that despite all the security – despite dozens of Secret Service agents – you were sleeping with and got beat up by the President of the United States *while he was still in office?*'

'President?' Violet asked. 'You think I was sleeping with Manning? No, no, no . . . the other mention – about running for Senate . . .'

'You mean—'

'The little animal who mauled me. I was talking about Dreidel.'

74

'Think he'll go through with it?' Dreidel asked, readjusting his wire-rim glasses as he read from Boyle's personnel file.

'Who, Wes? Hard to say,' Rogo replied, still sitting on the floor and flipping through the documents in Boyle's requests. 'He was talking a tough game, but you know how he gets with Manning.'

'You've obviously never been on the receiving end of Manning.' Looking down at the file, Dreidel added, 'Y'know Boyle spoke Hebrew and Arabic?'

'Says who?'

'Says here: Hebrew, Arabic, and American Sign Language. Apparently, his sister was deaf. That's why they moved to Jersey – had one of the early schools for the hearing impaired. God, I remember filling this out,' he added, reading from Boyle's National Security Questionnaire. 'According to this, he won a Westinghouse prize when he was in high school – plus a Marshall Scholarship at Oxford. Guy was scary smart, especially when it came t— Hold on,' Dreidel said. '*Have you been over 180 days delinquent on any debts? Yes. If yes, explain below . . .*' Flipping to the next page, Dreidel read the single-spaced page that was stapled to the application. '*. . . to a total debt of $230,000 . . .*'

'Two hundred and thirty *thousand*? What'd he buy? Italy?'

'I don't think he bought anything,' Dreidel said. 'From what it says here, it was his *father's* debt. Apparently, Boyle volunteered to take it over so his dad wouldn't have to declare bankruptcy.'

'Boy loves his daddy.'

'Actually, hates his daddy. But loves his mom,' Dreidel said, reading even further. 'If Dad declared bankruptcy and the creditors swooped in, Mom would've been kicked out of the family restaurant that she'd worked in and run since Boyle was a kid.'

'Nice work by Dad – put the family business at risk, boot your wife out on the street, and stick your kid with all the leftover debt.'

'Wait, that's the good part,' Dreidel said, turning to the last few pages of the application. Here: *Is there anything in your personal life that could be used by someone to embarrass the President or the White House? Please provide full details.*' Flipping the page and revealing another single-spaced typed document, Dreidel shook his head, remembering the stories that Boyle had disclosed early in the campaign. Even at the beginning, Manning stood by his friend. 'Most of this we know: Dad was first arrested before Boyle was born. Then arrested again when Boyle was six, then again when he was thirteen – the last time for assault and battery on the owner of a Chinese laundry in Staten Island. Then he actually wound up staying out of trouble until just after Boyle left for college. That's when the FBI picked him up for selling fake insurance policies in a New Brunswick nursing home. The list keeps going . . . importing stolen scooters, check kiting for a few thousand bucks, but somehow, barely serving any time.'

'It's a Freudian field day, isn't it? Dad breaking all the

rules with the con man shtick, while Boyle throws himself into the preciseness of accounting. What was that *Time* story when Dad got arrested for shoplifting? Black eye . . .'

'. . . on the *White* House. Yeah, clever. That's almost as good as that political cartoon where they had him robbing Toys for Tots.'

'I still can't—' Rogo cut himself off, shaking his head. 'All this time, we're hunting for Boyle like he's the great white evil, but when you hear all the details: miserable childhood, deaf sister, working-class Italian mom . . . and yet he still manages to claw his way out and make his way to the White House . . .'

'Oh, please, Rogo – don't tell me you're feeling bad for him.'

'. . . and then his dad lies, cheats, steals, and on top of it all, leaves Boyle holding the bill. I mean, just think about it – how does a father do that to his own son?'

'Same way Boyle did it to his own wife and daughter when he disappeared from their lives and turned them into mourners. People are scumbags, Rogo – especially when they're desperate.'

'Yeah, but that's the thing. If Boyle were really that bad, why'd they even let him work in the White House? Isn't that the purpose of all these forms – to screen people like him out?'

'In theory, that's the goal, but it's not like it was some uncovered secret. Everyone knew his dad was trash. He used to talk about it – use it for sympathy in the press. It only became a problem when we won. But when your best friend is President of the United States, oh, what a surprise, the FBI can be convinced to make exceptions.

In fact, let me show you how they . . . here . . .' Dreidel said, once again thumbing through the folder. 'Okay, *here*,' he added, unclipping a sheet of stationery-sized paper as Rogo took a seat on the edge of the desk and started flipping through the rest of the file.

'Boyle had codeword clearance. Before they dole that out, they need to know what side you're on. FBI . . . Secret Service . . . they all take a look. Then Manning gets to see the results . . .' On the small sheet of paper was a list of typed letters lined up in a single column, each one with a check mark next to it:

BKD ✓

MH ✓

WEX ✓

ED ✓

REF ✓

AC

PRL ✓

FB ✓

PUB ✓

'Is that the same as *this*?' Rogo asked as he turned a page in the file and revealed a near-identical sheet.

'Exactly – that's the same report.'

'So why's Boyle have two?'

'One's from when he started, the other's probably from when they renewed his clearance. It's the same. *BKD* is background – your general background check. *MH* is your military history. *WEX* is work experience . . .'

'So this is all the dirt on Boyle?' Rogo asked, staring down at the sparsely covered page.

'No, *this* is the dirt – everything below *here*,' Dreidel said, pointing to the underlined letters *AC* halfway down the page.

'*AC?*'

'Areas of concern.'

'And all these letters below it: *PRL* . . . *FB* . . . *PUB* . . .'

'*PRL* is Boyle's personal history, which I'll wager refers to all the crap with his father. *FB* is his financial background; thanks again, Dad. And *PUB* . . .' Dreidel paused a moment, reading from his sheet as Rogo followed on his own copy. '*PUB* is the public perception issues if Boyle's background gets out, which in this case, it already was.'

'What about *PI?*' Rogo asked.

'Whattya mean?'

'*PI*,' Rogo repeated, turning his sheet toward Dreidel. 'Isn't your last one *PI?*'

Dreidel looked at his own sheet, which ended with *PUB*, then turned toward Rogo's, squinting to read the letters with the handwritten message next to them:

PI – *note May 27*

Dreidel's face went white.

'What?' Rogo asked. 'What's it mean?'

'What's the date on yours say?'

Reading from the top corner of the sheet, Rogo could barely get the words out. 'June 16th,' he said. 'Right before the shooting.'

'Mine's January 6th – days before we moved into the White House.'

'I don't understand, though. What's *PI*?'

'Paternity issues,' Dreidel said. 'According to this, just before he was shot, Boyle had a kid no one knew about.'

75

'What'd you *do*?' The Roman asked, his voice squawking through the scrambled satellite phone.

'It's fine. Problem solved,' O'Shea replied, keeping the phone close and staring out the small oval window of the chartered seaplane.

'What does that mean? Let me speak to Micah!'

'Yeah, well . . . that's a little harder than it used to be,' O'Shea said as the plane dropped down, approaching the aquamarine waves of Lake Worth. From the current height – barely a few hundred feet above the water – the back-yards of the Palm Beach mansions whizzed by in a blur.

'O'Shea, don't tell me— What'd you do to him?'

'Don't lecture me, okay? I didn't have a choice.'

'You *killed* him?'

O'Shea stared out the window as the plane sank down to just a few feet above the waves. 'Be smart. He's covert in Directorate of Operations. He shouldn't be working on U.S. soil. And for some reason, he's caught standing on the track at the speedway? Once Wes IDed him, they would've brought him right in.'

'That doesn't mean he'd talk!'

'You think so? You think if they offered him a deal and said they'd go easy on him, every one of Micah's fingers wouldn't've pointed our way?'

'He's still CIA!' The Roman shouted through the phone.

'You have any idea what kinda fire that starts? You just lit the damn volcano!'

'You think I enjoyed it? I've known Micah since War College. He was at my niece's communion.'

'Well, I guess there goes his invite for her sweet sixteen!'

With a final jolt, the plane dropped down for its landing. The instant the floats hit the water, the plane bounced and wobbled, slowing down until it was cruising with the current.

'*Enough,*' O'Shea warned as the floating plane chugged toward the floating dock of the Rybovich Spencer boatyard. 'It was hard enough as it is.'

'Really? Then maybe you should've thought twice before you decided to put a bullet in him! You know how hard it's gonna be to find another person inside the Agency?'

'*You're* lecturing *me* about forethought? Have you forgotten why we're even stamping around in all this manure? It's the same jackass thing you did with our so-called six-million-dollar payment for *Blackbird*. You rush in, stick your finger in all the electrical sockets, then get mad at me when I have to deal with the cleanup.'

'Don't even— *Blackbird* was a mutual decision!' The Roman exploded. 'We voted on that!'

'No, *you* voted. You're the one who put the number that high. Then when they decided they weren't paying it, you came crying that we needed an assist from the inside.'

'Okay, so now you didn't want that six mil?'

'What I didn't want was to have to ask for that kinda cash *twice*. We spent nearly a decade building up your damn Roman identity – all those tips we snatched and passed your way so it looked like you had some big, great informant out there – hell, they still think The Roman's a real person who feeds the government info – all for the goal of going in for that one huge multimillion-dollar hit. One time! One ask! That's all it was supposed to be – until you got the dollar signs in your eyes and thought we could do it on a regular basis.'

'We *could've* done it on a regular basis – fifty, sixty, seventy million, easy. You *know* you agreed.'

'Then you should've listened to us and never approached Boyle first,' O'Shea said, his voice calmer than ever. 'And unlike last time, I'm done letting a loose end come back to bite us in the ass. As long as Wes is out there with that photo, we've both got targets on our chests.'

'What, so now you're putting Wes on your hit list as well? I thought you agreed he was just bait.'

Without a word, O'Shea watched as the seaplane angled past half a dozen pristine yachts and nosed up to the floating dock.

'Check out that sailboat in front of us,' the pilot announced as he pulled off his headphones and entered the back of the plane. 'That's Jimmy Buffett's day sailer. You see the name of it? *Chill.*'

O'Shea nodded as the pilot opened the hatch, stepped outside, and tossed the grab line to the dock.

'O'Shea, before you get stupid, think about next month,' The Roman said through the phone. 'If this thing comes through in India . . .'

'Are you even listening? There is no next month! There's no India! Or Prague! Or Liberia! Or Lusaka! We brought our resources together – we created the perfect virtual informant – and we made some cash. But now I'm done, pal. D'you understand? The pot of gold – the seventy million – it's bullshit. I'm over.'

'But if you—'

'I don't care,' O'Shea said, heading for the door and stepping out to the edge of the plane's floats. A short hop took him onto the dock, where he waved a thank-you to the pilot and followed the path toward the buildings of the boatyard.

'O'Shea, don't be such a mule,' The Roman continued. 'If you touch Wes now—'

'Are you listening? I. Don't. Care. I don't care that he's bait. I don't care that he's our best bet for getting Boyle. I don't even care that Nico might get to him first. That kid knows my name, he knows what I look like, and worst of all—'

There was a soft beep on O'Shea's phone. He stopped midstep, halfway up the dock. Caller ID said *Unavailable*. On this line, there was only one person that could be.

'O'Shea, listen to me,' The Roman threatened.

'Sorry, signal's bad here. I'll call you later.' With a click, he switched over to the other line. 'This is O'Shea.'

'And this is your conscience – stop having sex with men at truck stops. Go to a bar – it's easier,' Paul Kessiminan said, laughing, in his fat Chicago accent.

O'Shea didn't even bother responding to the joke. Tech guys – especially those in the Bureau's Investigative Technology Division – always thought they were funnier than they were. 'Please tell me you got a hit on Wes's phone,' O'Shea said.

'Nope. But after taking your advice and watching his friends, I did get a hit on the fat kid's.'

'Rogo's?'

'For the past few hours, it's quiet as death. Then ping, incoming call from a number registered to an Eve Goldstein.'

'Who's Eve Goldstein?'

'Which is why I looked her up. Y'know how many Eve Goldsteins there are in Palm Beach County? Seven. One owns a Judaica store, one's a school principal, two retirees—'

'Paulie!'

'. . . and one who writes the gardening section for the *Palm Beach Post*.'

'They switched phones.'

'Ooooh, you're good. You should get a job with the FBI.'

'So Wes is still with Lisbeth?'

'I don't think so. I just called the newsroom. She's apparently on another line. I think she gave Wes her friend's phone and ditched his on the plane or something. Telling you – boy's smart,' Paul said. 'Lucky for you, I'm smarter.'

'But you traced the new phone to his current location?'

'It's an old model, so there's no GPS. But I *can* get you to the closest cell tower. Cell site 626A. On County Road, just a few blocks south of Via Las Brisas.'

At the center of the long dock, O'Shea froze. 'Las Brisas? You think he went to—?'

'Only one way to find out, Tonto. Be careful, though. With Nico out there, headquarters just opened their own investigation.'

Nodding to himself, O'Shea reached into his inside jacket pocket and pulled out a black ostrich-skin wallet and matching CIA badge. As he flipped it open, he took one last look at the picture in Micah's driver's license. From the messy brown hairstyle and the crooked bottom teeth, the photo had to be almost a decade old. Before the teeth were fixed. Before the hair got meticulously slicked back. Before they were making real money.

O'Shea didn't like lifting his old friend's wallet, but he knew it'd buy him at least a day in IDing the body. Though right now, as he readjusted his shoulder holster and rechecked his gun, all he needed was an hour or so to wrap things up and leave this life behind.

They'd created an alter ego for Egen as The Roman. Certainly, O'Shea could create something new for himself.

'How fast you think you can get there?' Paul asked through the phone.

Grinning to himself, O'Shea tossed Micah's IDs from the dock into the water. They floated for half a second, then sank out of sight. 'At this rate? I'll be in and out lickety-split.'

76

'Try calling him again,' Dreidel said as he spun the acid-free archival box around and checked the dates on its typed spine: *Boyle, Ron – Domestic Policy Council – October 15– December 31.*

'Just did,' Rogo said, working his way through his own stack and checking the last few boxes in the pile. 'You know how Wes gets on the job – he won't pick up if he's with Manning.'

'You should still try him agai—'

'And tell him what? That it looks like Boyle had a kid? That there's some note referencing May 27th? Until we get some details, it doesn't even help us.'

'It helps us to keep Wes informed – especially where he is right now. He should know that Manning knew.'

'And you're sure about that?' Rogo asked. 'Manning knew about Boyle's kid?'

'It's his best friend – and it's in the file,' Dreidel said. His voice cracked slightly as he looked up from the last few boxes. 'Manning definitely knew.'

Rogo watched Dreidel carefully, sensing the change in his tone. 'You're doubting him, aren't you, Dreidel? For the first time, you're realizing there might be a crack in the Manning mask.'

'Let's just keep looking, okay?' Dreidel asked as he tilted the final two milk-crate-sized boxes and scanned the dates.

One was labeled *Memoranda – January 1–March 31*. The other was *Congressional AIDS Hearing – June 17–June 19*. 'Damn,' he whispered, shoving them aside.

'Nothing here either,' Rogo said, closing the last box and climbing up from his knees. 'Okay, so grand total – how many boxes do we have that include the May 27 date?'

'Just these,' Dreidel said, pointing to the four archival boxes that they'd set up on the worktable. 'Plus you pulled the schedule, right?'

'Not that it helps,' Rogo replied as he waved Manning's official schedule from May 27. 'According to this, the President was with his wife and daughter at their cabin in North Carolina. At noon, he went biking. Then lunch and some fishing on the lake. Nothing but relaxing the whole day.'

'Who was staffing him?' Dreidel asked, well aware that the President never traveled without at least some work.

'Albright . . .'

'No surprise – he took his chief of staff everywhere.'

'. . . and Lemonick.'

'Odd, but not out of the ordinary.'

'And then those same names you said were from the Travel Office – Westman, McCarthy, Lindelof—'

'But not Boyle?'

'Not according to this,' Rogo said, flipping through the rest of the schedule.

'Okay, so on May 27th, barely two months before the shooting, Manning was in North Carolina and Boyle was presumably in D.C. So the real question is, what was Boyle doing while the cat was away?'

'And you think the answer's in one of these?' Rogo asked, circling the tops of the four boxes with his hand.

'Those're the ones that have date ranges that include May 27th,' Dreidel said. 'I'm telling you,' he added as he flipped off the top of the first box, 'I've got a good feeling. The answer's in here.'

'There's no *way* it's in here!' Rogo moaned forty-five minutes later.

'Maybe we should go through them again.'

'We already went through them twice. I picked through every sheet of paper, every file, every stupid little Post-it note. Look at these paper cuts!' he said, extending his pointer and middle fingers in a peace sign.

'*Voice down!*' Dreidel hissed, motioning to the attendant by the computers.

Rogo glanced over at Freddy, who offered a warm smile and a wave. Turning back to Dreidel, he added, 'Okay, so now what?'

'Not much choice,' Dreidel said as he scanned the remaining thirty-eight boxes that were stacked like tiny pyramids across the floor. 'Maybe they filed it out of order. Flip through each box – pull out anything that has the date May 27th on it.'

'That's over 20,000 pages.'

'And the sooner we start, the sooner we'll know the full story,' Dreidel said, tugging a brand-new box up to the worktable.

'I don't know,' Rogo said as he gripped the handholds of a beaten old box and heaved it up toward the desk. As it landed back-to-back with Dreidel's box, a puff of dust swirled like a sandstorm. 'Part of me worries we're sifting through the wrong haystack.'

77

Port St. Lucie, Florida

Edmund had been dead for nearly twelve hours. During hour one, as Nico strapped him into the passenger seat of the truck, thick frothy blood bubbles multiplied at the wound in Edmund's neck. Nico barely noticed, too excited about telling his friend about Thomas Jefferson and the original Three.

By hour four, Edmund's body had stiffened. His arms stopped flopping. His head, bent awkwardly back and to the right, no longer bobbed with each bump. Instead of a rag doll, Edmund was a frozen mannequin. Rigor mortis had settled in. Nico still didn't notice.

By hour ten, the cab of the truck began to take its own beating. On the seats . . . the floor mat . . . across the vinyl interior of the passenger-side door, the blood began to decompose, turning each stain a darker, richer red, tiny speckles of liquid rubies.

But even when they left all that behind – when they abandoned the truck and used Edmund's wool blanket to switch to the clean maroon Pontiac – there was no escaping the smell. And it wasn't from the body. That would take days to decompose, even in the Florida heat. The true foul horror came from what was inside, as Edmund's lack of muscle control caused everything from feces to flatulence to leak out, soaking his clothes, his pants, all the way through to the once-parchment-colored cloth seat and the dusty blanket that covered Edmund from the neck down.

In the driver's seat next to him, Nico couldn't have been happier. Up ahead, despite rush hour, traffic looked clear. On his right, out west, the sun was a perfect orange circle as it began its slow bow from the sky. And most important, as they blew past another green highway sign, they were even closer than Nico expected.

PALM BEACH   48 MILES

Less than an hour and we're there.

Barely able to contain himself, Nico smiled and took a deep breath of the car's outhouse reek.

He didn't smell a thing. He couldn't. Not when life was this sweet.

Quickly picking up speed, Nico reached for the wipers as a late-day sun-shower sent a few speckles against the Pontiac's front windshield. But before he could flick the wipers on, he thought twice and left them off. The rain was light. Just a drizzle. Enough to cleanse.

Maybe you should—

'Yeah, I was just thinking the same thing,' Nico said, nodding to himself. With the push of a button on the dash, he opened the sunroof of the car, held his stolen Orioles baseball cap, and tilted his head back to stare up at the gray sky.

'Hold the wheel,' he told Edmund as he clamped his eyes shut.

At eighty miles an hour, Nico let go of the steering wheel. The Pontiac veered slightly to the right, cutting off a woman in a silver Honda.

Saying a prayer to himself, Nico kept his head back. The wind from outside lashed against the brim, blowing his baseball cap from his head. Needles of rain tap-danced against his forehead and face. The baptism had begun. Wes's home address was clutched in his hand. Salvation – for Nico and his mom – was less than an hour away.

78

Lisbeth thought the neighborhood would be a dump. But as she drove west on Palm Beach Lakes Boulevard and followed Violet's directions – past the Home Depot and Best Buy and Olive Garden, then a right on Village Boulevard – it was clear she didn't need to lock the car doors. Indeed, as she pulled up to the guard gate for *Misty Lake – A Townhome Community*, the only thing she had to do was lower her window.

'Hi, I'm visiting unit 326,' Lisbeth explained to the guard, remembering Violet's instructions to not use her name. Of course, it was silly. Lisbeth already had her address – who cared about her name?

'ID, please,' the guard said.

As she handed over her driver's license, Lisbeth added, 'I'm sorry, I think it's unit 326 – I'm looking for . . .'

'The Schopfs – Debbie and Josh,' the guard replied, handing her a guest parking pass for the dashboard.

Lisbeth nodded. 'That's them.' Waiting until the security gate closed behind her to scribble the name *Debbie Schopf* in her notepad, she followed the signs and never-ending speed bumps past row after row of identical pink townhomes, eventually pulling into the guest spot just outside the narrow two-story house with blinking holiday lights dangling from above the door and an inflatable snowman in the thriving green garden. Christmas in Florida at unit 326.

Heading up the front path, Lisbeth tucked her notepad into her purse and out of sight. Violet was already nervous on the phone. No reason to add to—

'Lisbeth?' a female voice called out as the door of the townhouse swung open.

Lisbeth looked up at eye level, which put her directly at Violet's dark brown neck. It wasn't until she craned her neck up that Lisbeth saw the full picture of the stunning 5'10' African-American woman standing in the doorway. Wearing faded jeans and a white V-neck T-shirt, Violet almost seemed to be trying to dress like a mom. But even standard suburban uniforms couldn't mask the beauty underneath.

'You . . . uh . . . you wanna come in?' Violet asked, her voice shaky as she lowered her head and looked away.

Lisbeth assumed she was being shy. Probably embarrassed. But as she got closer – walking past Violet and entering the house – she got her first good look at Violet's left eyebrow, which appeared to be cut in two by a tiny white scar that sliced through her dark, otherwise perfect skin.

'That from— He do that?' Lisbeth asked, even though she knew the answer.

Violet looked up, her shoulders arching like a cornered cat – then just as quickly, her posture leveled as she regained her calm. For Lisbeth, it was like glancing too late at a just-missed lightning bolt. Two seconds ago, rage detonated in Violet's eyes, then disappeared in an eyeblink. Still, like the lost lightning bolt, the afterimage was too strong. Lisbeth couldn't miss it. And in that moment, she saw the brash, confident, and swaggering self-assured woman that the young twenty-six-year-old Violet used to be. And who she'd never be again.

'I don't want my picture in the paper. Or my name,' Violet whispered, tugging her bangs over the fleshy white scar.

'I'd never do that,' Lisbeth promised, already kicking herself for pushing too fast. From the plastic pink tea set scattered along the floor and the baby doll stroller in the entryway, Violet had a great deal to lose. No way Lisbeth was getting the story without a softer touch.

'Adorable,' Lisbeth said, heading up the main hallway and admiring a framed family photo of a little white girl running through a sprinkler, her mouth open with her tongue licking the water.

Violet barely responded.

Lisbeth turned. Every parent likes to talk about their kids.

Halfway up the main hallway, Lisbeth scanned the rest of the family photos along the wall. The girl in the sprinkler. Pictured again with a redheaded woman at the beach. And again with the redhead at a pumpkin patch.

As Lisbeth scanned all the photos, she noticed that every shot had white people in it. Indeed, not one – not a single one – had anyone who was black.

Lisbeth underestimated her. Violet – or whatever her name was – wasn't some dumb novice.

'This isn't your house, is it?' Lisbeth asked.

Violet stopped in the small, cluttered kitchen. A child-size plastic Cinderella table sat next to a full-size faux-wood one. Half a dozen photos cluttered the refrigerator door. Again, everyone was white.

'And your name's not Debbie Schopf, is it?' Lisbeth added.

'Leave Debbie out of this—'

'Violet, if she's your friend . . .'

'She's just doing me a favor.'

'Violet . . .'

'Please don't drag her in— Oh, God,' Violet said, shielding her eyes with her hand. It was the first time Lisbeth got a look at the thin gold wedding band on Violet's ring finger. The one detail Lisbeth believed.

'Listen,' Lisbeth said, touching Violet's shoulder. 'You listening? I'm not here to catch you or trap you or drag your friends in. I swear. I just need to know if what you said about Dreidel—'

'I didn't make it up.'

'No one thinks you did.'

'You just said my name wouldn't be used. You told me that.'

'And I stand by it, Violet,' Lisbeth said, knowing the fake name put her at ease. 'No one knows I'm here. Not my editor, not my colleagues, nobody. But let's remember: You invited me here for a reason. What Dreidel did to you . . . when he raised his hand—'

'He didn't raise his hand! He put his fist in my face, then gashed me with the mirror!' Violet erupted, her fear quickly smothered by rage. 'That bastard hurt me so bad I had to tell my mother I was in a car accident! She believed it too – after I kicked my headlight in to prove it! But when I saw him in the paper . . . If he thinks I'm just gonna keep it all quiet while he holds himself out there as State Senator Boy Scout . . . Oh, no, no, *no!*'

'I hear you, Violet – I do. But you need to understand, I can't do anything, I can't even help you, until I verify it. Now you said you had proof. Are they photos or—?'

'Photos? Even when he's dumb, Dreidel's not that

stupid.' Leaving the kitchen, Violet headed into the family
room, where beige vertical blinds kept the last bits of sun
from peeking through the sliding glass doors. Taking a
moment to calm down, she put her five fingertips against
the center of her chest.

'Y'okay?' Lisbeth asked.

'Yeah, just – just hating the past a little, know what I
mean?'

'You kidding? I even hate the present.'

It was an easy joke, but exactly what Violet needed to
catch her breath. 'When we first – y'know, when we started,'
she said, kneeling down and fishing under the L-shaped
flower-print sofa, 'I wasn't even allowed to ask him about
work. But these White House boys . . . they're no different
than the money boys in Palm Beach or Miami or
anywhere . . . all egomaniacs love to talk about themselves,'
she added as she tugged a small pile of paperwork from
under the sofa. Bound by a thick rubber band, it looked
like a stack of catalogs and mail. As Violet whipped off
the rubber band, the pile fanned out across the cream-
colored Formica coffee table.

'*President Manning's Remarks for APEC Summit*. Signed
program from the Moroccan king's funeral . . .' Skimming
through the pile, Violet rattled them off one by one. 'Look
at this – personal business card of the owner of the Miami
Dolphins with his direct dial and cell numbers handwritten
on the back, along with a note that says *Mr President, Let's
play golf*. Asshole.'

'I don't understand. Dreidel left this stuff here?'

'Left it? He gave it to me. *Proudly* gave it to me. I
don't know, it was his pathetic way of proving he was
actually by the President's side. Every time he visited, I'd
get another piece from the presidential junk drawer:

Manning's handwritten lunch orders, scorecards from when he played bridge, military coins, crossword puzzles, luggage tags – '

'What'd you say?'

'Luggage tags?'

'Crossword puzzles,' Lisbeth repeated as she sat next to Violet on the couch and leaned toward the pile on the coffee table.

'Oh, I definitely got one,' Violet replied, digging through the stack. 'Manning was a nut at those. Dreidel said he could do a full puzzle while chatting on the phone with – Ah, here we go,' she added, pulling an old folded-up newspaper from the stack.

When Violet handed it over, Lisbeth's arms, legs, and whole body went cold as she finally got a look at the puzzle . . . and the President's handwritten answers . . . and the jumble of initials scribbled in the left-hand margin.

Her hands were shaking. She read it, then reread it to be sure. *I don't believe it. How could we be so—?*

'What?' Violet asked, clearly confused. 'What's wrong?'

'Nothing . . . just— I can reach you at this number, yes?' As Violet nodded, Lisbeth copied the phone number that was handwritten on the base of the phone. Standing from her seat, she continued to clutch the crossword in her hand. 'Listen, can I make a copy of this? I'll bring it right back as soon as I'm done.'

'Sure, but – I don't get it. What'd you find, Dreidel's handwriting?'

'No,' Lisbeth said, sprinting for the door, flipping open her cell phone, and already dialing Wes's number. 'Something far better than that.'

79

Silent for almost twenty-five minutes, Rogo was hunched over the archival box in his lap as his fingertips walked through each page of the open file. 'Who d'ya think the mom is?' he finally asked as the sun faded through the nearby window.

'Of Boyle's kid?' Dreidel replied, picking through his own box. 'I've got no idea.'

'You think it was someone big?'

'Define *big*.'

'I don't know – he could've been sleeping with anyone: a senior staffer . . . some intern . . . the First Lady—'

'First Lady? You joking? You think we wouldn't notice if Mrs Manning – *while in the White House* – started vomiting, gaining weight, and suddenly seeing a doctor – not to mention if she showed up one day with a kid that looked like Boyle?'

'Maybe she didn't have the kid. It could've been—'

'"Paternity issue" means the kid was born,' Dreidel insisted, crossing to the other side of the table and picking up a new box. 'It would've said *ABT* if they thought there was an abortion. And even if that weren't the case – the First Lady? Please . . . when it came time to leave the White House, she was more upset than the President himself. No way she'd put any of that at risk for some dumb fling with Boyle.'

'I'm just saying, it could've been anyone,' Rogo said, nearly halfway through the file box as he reached a thick brown accordion folder that held two framed photos. Pulling out the silver frame in front, he squinted down at the family shot of Boyle with his wife and daughter.

Posed in front of a waterfall, Boyle and his wife playfully hugged their sixteen-year-old daughter, Lydia, who, at the center of the photograph, was in mid-scream/mid-laugh as the ice-cold waterfall soaked her back. Laughing right along with her, Boyle had his mouth wide open, and despite his thick mustache, it was clear that Lydia had her father's smile. A huge, toothy grin. Rogo couldn't take his eyes off it. Just one big happy—

'It's just a photo,' Dreidel interrupted.

'Wha?' Rogo asked, looking over his shoulder.

Behind him, Dreidel stared down at the framed shot of the Boyles at the waterfall. 'That's it – just a photo,' he warned. 'Believe me, even though they're smiling, doesn't mean they're happy.'

Rogo looked down at the photo, then back to Dreidel, whose lips were pressed together. Rogo knew that look. He saw it every day on his speeding ticket clients. We all know our own sins.

'So the mom from Boyle's paternity problem . . .' Rogo began.

'. . . could be anyone,' Dreidel agreed, happy to be back on track. 'Though knowing Boyle, I bet it's someone we've never even heard of.'

'What makes you say that?' Rogo asked.

'I don't know – it's just . . . when we were in the White House, that's the way Boyle was. As Manning's oldest friend, he was never really part of the staff. He was more – he was *here*,' Dreidel said, holding his left hand palm-down at eye level. 'And he thought the rest of us were *here*,' he added, slapping his right palm against the worktable.

'That's the benefit of being First Friend.'

'But that's the thing – I know he kinda got sainthood when he was shot, but from where I was standing on the inside, Boyle spent plenty of days in the doghouse.'

'Maybe that's when Manning found out about the kid.'

For the second time, Dreidel was silent.

Rogo didn't say a word. Unloading the second picture from his own box, he propped open the back leg of the black matte picture frame and stood it up on the worktable. Inside was a close-up photo of Boyle and his wife, the apples of their cheeks pressed together as they smiled for the camera. From the bushiness of his mustache and the thickness of his hairline, the photo was an old one. Two people in love.

'What else you got in there besides photos?' Dreidel asked, turning the box slightly and reading the word *Misc.* on the main label.

'Mostly desk stuff,' Rogo said as he emptied the box, pulling out a hardcover book about the history of genocide, a softcover about the legacy of the Irish, and a rubber-banded preview copy of a highly critical book called *The Manning Myth*.

'I remember when that came out,' Dreidel said. 'Pompous ass never even called us to fact-check.'

'I just can't believe they keep all this crap,' Rogo said as he pulled out a decade-old parking pass for the Kennedy Center.

'To you, it's crap – to the library, it's history.'

'Let me tell you something – even to the library, this crap is crap,' Rogo said, unloading a small stack of taxi receipts, a scrap of paper with handwritten directions to the Arena Stage, a blank RSVP card to someone's wedding, a finger-paint drawing with the words *Uncle Ron* neatly printed on top, and a small spiral notebook with the Washington Redskins football logo on the front.

'Whoa, whoa, whoa – what're you doing?' Dreidel interrupted.

'What, *this*?' Rogo asked, pointing to the finger-paint drawing.

'*That,*' Dreidel insisted as he grabbed the spiral notebook with the football logo.

'I don't get it – whattya need a football schedule for?'

'This isn't a schedule.' Opening the book, Dreidel turned it toward Rogo, revealing a daily calendar for the first week of January. 'It's Boyle's datebook.'

Rogo's eyebrows rose as he palmed the top of his buzzed head. 'So we can see all his meetings . . .'

'Exactly,' Dreidel said, already skimming through it. 'Meetings, dinners, everything – and most particularly what he was up to on the night of May 27th.'

80

'Mr President?' I call out as I open the front door.

No one answers.

'Sir, it's Wes – are you there?' I ask again, even though I know the answer. If he weren't here, the Secret Service wouldn't be outside. But after all our years together, I'm always careful to know my place. It's one thing to walk into his office. It's quite another to step into his home.

'Back here,' a man's voice calls out, ricocheting down the long center hallway that leads to the living room. I pause a moment, unable to place the voice – polished, with a hint of British accent – but quickly step inside and shut the door. It was hard enough making the decision to come here. Even if he's got guests, I'm not turning back now.

Still trying to identify the voice, I head for the hallway and steal a glance at the poster-sized, framed black-and-white photograph that sits above the antique credenza and the vase of fresh flowers on my right. The photo is Manning's favorite: a panoramic view of his desk in the Oval Office, taken by a photographer who literally put the camera in the President's chair and hit the shutter.

The result is an exact re-creation of Manning's old view from behind the most powerful desk in the world: the family photos of his wife, the pen left for him by the previous President, a personal note written by his son, a small gold plaque with the John Lennon quote 'A working class hero is something to be,' and a shot of Manning sitting with his mom on the day he arrived at the White House – his first official meeting in the Oval. On the left of the desk, Manning's phone looms as large as a shoebox, the camera so close you can read the five typed names on his speed dial: *Lenore* (his wife), *Arlen* (the V.P.), *Carl* (national security adviser), *Warren* (chief of staff), and *Wes*. Me.

With the push of a button, we'd all come running. Eight years later, I haven't changed. Until now.

Plowing through the hallway, I head into the formal living room, where, at the center of the Tibetan rug, Manning is standing on a small stool while a fair-skinned man with messy blond hair that barely covers his large forehead flits around him like a tailor working on his suit.

'Please, Mr President, I just need you still,' he pleads in what I now realize is a genteel South African accent.

Just behind Big Forehead, a twenty-something female photographer with short spiky hair lowers her chin and a flashbulb explodes.

It's not until I see that Forehead is holding measuring calipers – which look like a ruler with an adjustable wrench on the end of it – that I even realize what's going on. The photographer snaps another picture of Manning. On the sofa, a square box that can easily be mistaken for a Chinese checkers set holds a dozen rows of glass eyeballs, each one a different shade of Manning gray. Manning himself stands perfectly still and the calipers *klik-klik* around his wrist, a digital readout giving Forehead another measurement. Madame Tussauds Wax Museum prides itself on accuracy. Even for celebrities no longer in the public eye.

'Whattya think – they're darker now, right?' a petite African-American woman says as she holds out two gunmetal-gray eyeballs that stare directly at me. The odd part is, even held out in the air, they look eerily like Manning's. 'These were from our original White House figure – hand-done, of course – but I feel like he's gone deeper gray in the past few years.'

'Yeah . . . sure,' I stutter, already looking at my watch. 'Listen, do you know how long this is going t—?'

'Relax, Wes,' Manning interrupts with the last kind of laugh I want to hear. The only time he's this excited is during the annual meeting where the board of his library gets together. With his old staff reunited, he once again feels like he's holding the power. It lasts four hours at most. Then he goes back to being yet another former President whose two-car motorcade still has to stop at the red lights. Today, the Tussauds folks bring with them the attention of the glory days. Manning's not letting it go. 'The schedule's clear,' he tells me. 'Where else you got to be?'

'Nowhere, sir. But now that – with Nico out there—'

'Now you sound like Claudia.' But as he turns and takes his first actual look at me, he cuts himself off. I may know how to read him perfectly, but he knows how to read me even better – especially when it comes to Nico. 'Wes,' he says, not even needing words.

I'm fine, I reply with nothing more than a nod. He knows it's a lie, but he also knows why. If I'm having this discussion, it's not going to be in front of an audience. Determined to get things moving, I head for Forehead, who seems to be the one in charge.

'Declan Reese – from Madame Tussauds. Thanks for having us back,' Forehead says, saluting me with the calipers and extending a handshake. 'We try to never call on our portraits twice, but the popularity of President Manning's figure—'

'They just think I'm getting old and want to make sure they get my wattle right,' Manning says, playfully swatting his own jowls.

All the Tussauds people laugh. Especially because it's true.

'No problem,' I say, never forgetting the job. 'Just remember—'

'Thirty minutes,' Declan promises as another flashbulb explodes. 'Don't worry – I did Rudy Giuliani in twenty-seven minutes, and we still got his cracked lips and the bright redness of his knuckles.'

As the eyeball woman readies a bite plate for a tooth impression, Declan pulls me aside and cups my elbow. 'We were also wondering if we could possibly get a new piece of clothing. Something to reflect the more casual post-presidency,' he whispers just loud enough so Manning can hear. 'Bush's and Clinton's offices sent us some golf shirts.'

'Sorry . . . we don't really do that kind of—'

'What'd Bush and Clinton send? Golf shirts?' Manning calls out, never wanting to be left out. Every day, we turn down dozens of endorsements, from *Got Milk?* ads, to presidential chess sets, to autograph deals, to a ten-million-dollar role for a two-day cameo in a movie. But when his fellow Formers are involved, Manning can't help himself. 'Wes, do me a favor and go grab them one of my blue blazers. We give 'em a golf shirt, they'll dress us like the Three Stooges.'

As the room again laughs, I sneak a look at Declan, who knows exactly what he's doing. He got Woody Allen's prescription glasses – he can swindle the clothes off a former President.

'Thank you, good sir,' Declan adds in his spit-shined accent as I head back through the hallway and toward the stairs. Usually, I'd fight – but the sooner they're out of here, the sooner I can find out what's going on with Boyle.

Focusing on just that, I clutch the banister, already role-playing the moment in my head. When it comes to giving Manning bad news, the best way is to just put it out there. *Sir, I think I saw Boyle the other night in Malaysia.* I know Manning's tells – how he grins when he's mad or raises his chin when he's feigning surprise. Just seeing his reaction'll give me all I need to know.

At the top of the stairs, my phone vibrates in my pocket. Caller ID says it's Lisbeth. I shut the phone, refusing to answer. My bullshit quota for the day is filled. The last thing I need is another fake apology.

More annoyed than ever, I quickly plow down the second-floor hallway that's lined with two American flags: one that flew over the White House on Manning's first day in office, the other that flew the day he left. By the time I approach the bedroom on my left, I'm already rethinking my Manning strategy. Maybe I shouldn't just blurt it. He's always better with a soft touch. *Sir, I know this'll sound odd . . . Sir, I'm not sure how to say this . . . Sir, am I really as big a puss as I think I am?* Knowing the answer, I shove open the bedroom door and—

'Daaah . . . !' the First Lady yelps, jumping back in her seat at the antique writing desk in the corner of the room. She spins to face me so fast, her reading glasses fly from her face, and even though she's fully dressed in a light blue blouse and white slacks, I cover my eyes, immediately backtracking.

'Forgive me, ma'am. Didn't realize you were—'

'I-It's okay,' she says, her right hand patting the air to reassure me. I'm waiting for her to rip me apart. Instead, she's caught so off guard, it doesn't come. Her face is flushed as her eyes blink over and over, searching for calm. 'Just . . . you just surprised me is all.'

Still mid-apology, I reach down for her glasses and stumble forward to hand them back. It's not until I'm right in front of her that I see her left hand tucking something under the cushion of her seat.

'Thank you, Wes,' she says, reaching for the glasses without looking up.

Spinning back on my heel, I make a beeline for the door – but not before taking one last glance over my shoulder. Dr. Lenore Manning has been through two presidential elections, three battles for governor, two natural childbirths, and four years of never-ending attacks against her, her husband, her children, her family, and nearly every close friend, including a *Vanity Fair* cover story with the homeliest picture ever taken of her, over the headline *The Doctor First Lady Is* In: *Why Pretty Is Out – and Brains Are All the Rage*. At this point, even the worst attacks roll off her. So when I see her glance back at me – when our eyes lock and I spot the bloodshot redness that she quickly tries to hide with a smile and another thank-you . . . Right there, my legs lock. She can blink all she wants. I know tears when I see them.

As I stumble back to the door, the awkwardness is overwhelming. *Go . . . move . . . disappear.* This isn't where I'm supposed to be. Without even thinking, I rush into the hallway and head back toward the stairs. Anything to get out of there. My brain's racing full speed, still struggling to process. *It's not even . . . In all my years with them . . . What's so god-awful, it could possibly make her cry?* Searching for the answer, I stop at the top of the stairs and glance back over my shoulder. On my right is the flag from the day we left the White Hou— No. We didn't *leave* the White House. We were thrown out. Thrown out for Manning's reaction that day at the speedway. Thrown out after Boyle was shot. Thrown out after Boyle *died* in that ambulance.

I watched the funeral on TV from my hospital bed. Naturally, they kept cutting away to the President's and First Lady's reactions. Hidden by her wide-brimmed black hat, she kept her head steady, trying to hold it in – but as Boyle's daughter started to speak . . . The camera caught it for half a second, never even realizing what was happening. The First Lady wiped her nose, then sat up straighter than ever. With that, it was done. It was still the only time I'd seen the First Lady cry.

Until just now.

Still looking over my shoulder, I stare up the hallway at the open door of the bedroom. No doubt, I should go downstairs. This isn't my business. There are infinite reasons she could be crying. But right now, two days after seeing Boyle's brown and light blue eyes . . . a day after Nico escaping from St. Elizabeths . . . plus whatever the First Lady was hiding under her seat . . . I hate myself for even thinking it. They should fire me for even thinking it. But with everything that's swirling, to just walk away now – to give up, to pretend it's not there, to walk downstairs without finding out why one of the most powerful women in the world is suddenly devastated . . . No. I can't. I need to know.

Pivoting back toward the bedroom, I take a silent step across the handwoven gold carpet that runs up the hall.

I hear a soft sniffle from her direction. Not crying. A strong, final sniff that buries everything back down. Clenching my fists and holding my breath, I take two more tiptoed steps. For eight years, I've fought to protect their privacy. Now I'm the one invading it. But if there's something she knows . . . something about what happened . . . I keep my pace, almost at the door. But instead of heading to the bedroom on my left, I crane my neck, check to make sure the First Lady can't see me, and duck into the open door of the bathroom that's diagonally across the hall on my right.

With the sun fading outside, the bathroom's dark. As I duck behind the door, my heart's pounding so fast, I feel it in the sides of my temples. To be safe, I shut the door halfway and peek out from the thin vertical gap between the door spine and the frame. Across the hall, in her bedroom, the First Lady's back is to me as she sits at her writer's desk. From the angle I'm at, I only see the right half of her body – like she's split vertically in two – but it's the only half I need, especially as she reaches under her seat cushion and pulls out whatever it was she hid.

Pressing my nose into the opening, I squint hard trying to see what it is. A photograph? A memo? I don't have a chance. Her back blocks everything. But as she holds the item, lowering her head to examine it, there's no mistaking the sudden droop in her posture. Her shoulders sag. Her right arm begins to tremble. She reaches up, as if she's pinching the bridge of her nose – but as another sniffle cuts through the air, followed by an almost inaudible whimper – I realize she's not pinching her nose. She's wiping her eyes. And once again cryi—

Just as quickly, her posture stiffens and shoulders rise. Like before, she buries the moment, a final sniffle patting the last bits of dirt on the grave of whatever previous emotion she momentarily let through. Even in solitude, even as her arm continues to tremble, the President's wife refuses to suffer weakness.

Moving like she's in a rush, she promptly folds up the memo or photo or whatever it is, and stuffs it between the back pages of what looks like a paperback on her desk. I almost forgot. Manning isn't the only one the Madame Tussauds folks are here to see. With a final deep breath, the First Lady smooths out her skirt, dabs her eyes, and lifts her chin. Public mask back in place.

As she turns to leave the bedroom, she stares across the hallway, at the dark space where I am, pausing for half a second. I shrink back from the sliver of doorway, and she keeps moving, looking away just as quickly. No, no way. She didn't see a thing. Hidden by the darkness, I watch as she plows toward me, cutting to my left as she reaches the hallway. Within seconds, her footsteps sound against the wooden stairs, fading with each step. I don't even take a breath until I hear her footsteps disappear into the carpet at the bottom. Even then, I still count to ten, just to be safe. A swell of nausea already has me reeling. What the hell am I doing?

Trying to shake it, I flush the toilet, run the faucet, and step out of the bathroom as if everything's normal. A quick scan of the hallway tells me no one's there. 'Dr. Manning?' I say softly. No answer. I'm all alone.

Through the open door of the Mannings' bedroom, the antique writer's desk is less than ten feet away. In all our years together, I've never once betrayed their trust. I tell myself that again as I stare at the book on her desk. It's just sitting there. With the answer inside.

If I were Rogo, I'd do it. If I were Dreidel, I'd do it.

If I were Lisbeth, I'd have done it two minutes ago. But I'm me. And therein lies the *real* problem. I know myself. I know my limitations. And I know if I go in there, it's an action I can never take back. The old me would've never even considered it. But I don't think I'm that man anymore.

Tightening my fists, I take four steps into the bedroom and up to the desk. The black book is thick with gold embossing on the cover. *Holy Bible*. I don't know why I'm surprised.

As I pick up the Bible and thumb through it from back to front, the folded-up sheet practically leaps out. I unfold it so fast, it almost rips. I thought it was a photograph or some kind of official memo. It's not. It's a letter. Handwritten on plain, unmarked stationery. The handwriting is unfamiliar but precise – perfect tiny block letters undistinguished by any style or idiosyncrasy. Like it was written by someone who's spent years perfecting ways to go unnoticed.

To be sure, I flip the sheet over to the signature on the back. Like the rest, the letters are simple, almost commonplace. The tip of the *R* drags longer than the rest. *Ron.* Ron Boyle.

Dear Lenore, I read as I flip it back, my brain hurtling so fast, all I can do is skim. *Please forgive me . . . never meant to mislead you . . . I just thought, for everyone's good . . . for all my sins . . . to finally protect those I hurt . . . My punishment, Lenore. My atonement. Please understand, they said it could be anyone – that it could've been you . . . And after there was no payment for Blackbird, when I found what he . . .*

He? Who's he? I wonder, still skimming. *And Blackbird? Is that what they called the six-million-dollar—?*

'Hey!' a female voice calls out behind me.

My lungs collapse and my body freezes. I'm already off balance as I spin back to face her.

The First Lady stands in the doorway, her leaf-green eyes on fire. 'What the hell do you think you're doing?'

81

'You gotta be kidding me.'

'It's bad?' Rogo asked, leaning in and reading over Dreidel's shoulder.

On the worktable in front of them, Boyle's datebook was opened to the week of May 22. In the square labeled *Monday, May 23* was the handwritten note *Manning in NY.* On Wednesday the twenty-fifth was the note *Elliot in the Morning interview.* And on Thursday the twenty-sixth was the note *Senator Okum fundraiser – Wash. Hilton – 7 p.m.* But what caught Rogo's eye was the box for May 27, which was blacked out with a thick marker:

'They crossed it out?' Rogo asked.

'That's the library's job – read through all the files and figure out what can be released to the public.'

'I understand *how.* I just mean . . . Hold on—' he said, cutting himself off and reaching down to touch the right-hand page of the calendar. Even before he rubbed it with his fingers, Rogo could see it was made from a thinner and brighter paper stock than the off-white sheets that filled the rest of the datebook. 'This isn't even the original, is it?'

'Photocopy – that's how redactions are done,' Dreidel explained. 'They can't ruin the original, so they make a second copy, black that out, and staple it back in the original's place.'

'Okay, fine – so how do we get the original?'

'Actually, they usually— Here, lemme see,' Dreidel said, reaching for the datebook and flipping back to the front inside cover. Sure enough, folded up and stapled to the first page was another photocopied sheet of paper. As Dreidel unfolded it, Rogo read the words *Withdrawal Sheet* across the top.

'Anytime they redact something, they have to document it,' Dreidel said as they both read from the sheet.

DOCUMENT TYPE	SUBJECT/TITLE	DATE	RESTRICTION
1. calendar	Boyle schedule 1p., partial	5/27	B6
1. calendar	Boyle schedule 1p., partial	6/3	B6

'What's B6?' Rogo asked.

Squinting to read the tiny font, Dreidel skimmed through the list of restrictions at the bottom of the withdrawal sheet.

'B1 is when it's classified . . . B2 is when an agency forbids it . . .'

'And B6?'

'Release would constitute a clearly unwarranted invasion of personal privacy,' Dreidel read from the sheet.

'So this is some secret from Manning's personal life?'

'Or his own,' Dreidel clarified. 'The meetings and the schedules may be work product of the White House, but if Boyle writes something . . . I don't know, like his ATM PIN code or his Social Security number . . . that clearly has nothing to do with the presidency and therefore gets the black pen as well.'

Rogo flipped the book back to the May 27 redaction.

'Looks like a few more letters than a PIN code.'

'Or a Social Security number,' Dreidel agreed.

'Maybe we can go back to the archivist, and you can pull rank on her again until she shows us the original.'

'You kidding? After everything we've said, she's already suspicious enough.'

'Can we find it ourselves? Is it in there?' Rogo asked, pointing to the metal cage in the far corner of the room where at least another ten sets of shelves were piled to the ceiling with archival boxes.

'Right – we'll just randomly search through an additional five million documents – right after we sidestep the guy who's watching us, and figure out how to break open the bombproof lock that guards all the other national security files. Look at that thing – it's like the *Die Hard* vault.'

Rogo turned around to check the cage. Even from across the room, the thickness of the battered steel lock was unmistakable. 'So that's it? We just give up?'

Lowering his chin and shooting Rogo a look, Dreidel grabbed the datebook and stuffed it underneath the worktable. 'Do I look like Wes to you?' he asked as he stared over Rogo's shoulder.

Following Dreidel's gaze, Rogo again turned around as he traced it to Freddy the attendant, who was still clicking away at the bank of computers.

'Guys, you ready to wrap up?' Freddy asked. 'It's almost five o'clock.'

'Ten more minutes – tops,' Dreidel promised. Outside, through the tall plate-glass windows that overlooked the shiny bronze statue of Manning, the December sun sank early in the sky. No doubt, it was getting late. Hunching down in his seat and blocking himself from Freddy's view, he whispered to Rogo, 'Move an inch to your left.'

'What're you—?'

'Nothing,' Dreidel said calmly, his hands still out of sight as he held the datebook under the worktable. 'And I'm certainly not defacing government property by tearing out a sheet of paper from this historically treasured calendar.' As a small smirk spread up Dreidel's cheeks, Rogo heard a quiet *kk, kk, kk* below the table – like the last few pimples of bubble-wrap popping . . . or a page being tugged from the teeth of a half dozen staples.

With a final tear, Dreidel freed the last piece, then folded up the May 27 calendar page and tucked it into his jacket pocket. 'I'm telling you, it's not here!' he called out, raising his voice as he brought the datebook back up to the worktable. 'Hey, Freddy, can you take a look at this? I think there's a page missing from one of the files.'

Hopping out of his seat, Dreidel held the datebook out to Freddy and pointed to the withdrawal sheet. 'See, it says here that there's a redaction on the entry for May 27th, but when you flip here,' he explained, turning back to the May calendar pages, 'it just picks up with the beginning of June.'

Freddy flipped back to the withdrawal page, then back to June. 'Yeah . . . no . . . the page is definitely missing. Can this hold till tomorrow? We're about to close and—'

'Trust me, we're on deadline too,' Dreidel said, glancing at his watch. 'Listen, can you do us a favor and just pull the original? If we don't bring this to Manning tonight, he'll have our testicles. Really. He'll reach down and take them away.'

'Listen, I'd love to help you guys, but if it's redacted—'

'Freddy, when I left Palm Beach this morning, the President said he wanted a full copy of this datebook for the memorial piece he's doing for Boyle's family,' Dreidel pleaded. 'Now we're talking about a nearly ten-year-old file for a man who's been dead for that entire time. If there's something embarrassing in that entry – if it says, *I hate the President* or *I'm a terrorist spy* or anything that truly affects national security – don't show it to us. But if it's just some dumb little detail nobody cares about like his sister's birthday, you'd really be saving us.'

Scratching his finger in the dimple of his chin, Freddy glanced down at the datebook, then up at Dreidel and Rogo.

'Just take a peek,' Rogo begged. 'If it's anything embarrassing, put it back on the shelf.'

Standing there, Freddy pointed them back to their file-covered worktable. 'Just give me the folder numbers on the box. I'll see what I can do . . .'

'Freddy,' Rogo began, his voice racing down the runway, 'when I get married, brother, you're my bridesmaid!'

'Folder OA16209,' Dreidel called out from the front of the archival box.

Fifteen minutes later, in the far corner of the room, the metal door to the cage opened, and Freddy walked out with a single sheet of paper in his hand.

'Here you go,' Freddy said as he handed it to Dreidel. 'Though I think you would've been better off getting his sister's birthday.'

82

'I-I-I was just—'

'Rummaging through my desk!' the First Lady explodes. 'That I can see for myself! You – you – after all our time together – to violate that trust!'

'Ma'am, please don't—'

'Don't bullshit me, Wes! I know what I saw. I see it right now! But this isn't your *business*!' she growls, ripping Boyle's letter from my hand.

I step back, my body shaking. Forget firing me; for a moment, I'm actually terrified she might hit me. But as she blurts the last part – *This isn't your business!* – something swells and erupts in my stomach. Blood flushes my cheeks, and I can't help but shake my head. 'That's not true,' I whisper, my eyes locked on her.

Right there, she pounces. 'Ex*cuse* me?'

I stay silent, still amazed the words came from my lips.

'*What'd* you just say?' she challenges.

'It's – that's not true,' I repeat, searching her face. 'I was at the speedway too – it *is* my business.'

Her eyes narrow. I stare out the window over her shoulder. Like all the windows in this house, it's bullet-proof and doesn't open. But right now she looks like she's ready to toss me through one. Waving the Boyle letter, she asks, 'Who put you up to this?'

'*What?*'

'Was it a reporter? Did they pay you to write this?'

'Ma'am, you really think I'd—?'

'Or is it just some sick practical joke to test my reaction? I've got a great idea,' she says in mock impersonation. 'Let's revisit the worst moment in Dr. Manning's life, then see if we can rip apart her reality until she finally snaps.'

'Ma'am, this isn't a joke—'

'Or better yet, let's have her husband's aide sneak into her bedroom . . .'

'Ma'am . . .'

'. . . take it from her desk . . .'

'Dr. Manning, I saw him.'

'. . . and that way, she'll start panicking, wondering if it was even real to begin with.'

'I saw Boyle. In Malaysia. He's alive.'

She freezes, the tips of her fingers touching her lips. Her head shakes slowly. Then faster. *No – no. Oh, no, no.*

'It was him, ma'am. I saw him.'

Her head continues to shake as her fingers move from her lips, to her chin, to her own shoulder. Curling forward and gripping her shoulder, she practically shrinks into a ball. 'How could he—? How could they both—? Oh, God . . .' She looks back up at me, and her eyes well with tears so fast, there's no time to blink them away. Earlier, I thought they were tears of guilt – that she might be hiding something. But to see her now – the frightened anguish that contorts her face, the shock that keeps her head shaking in denial – these tears are born in pain.

'Dr. Manning, I'm sure this . . . I know it seems impossible—'

'That's not – God! – it's not like I'm naive,' she insists. 'I'm *not* naive. I mean, I-I-I knew he'd keep things from me – not to deceive – that's just what he has to do. That's the job of being President.'

As she stumbles through the words, I realize she's no longer talking about Boyle. She's talking about her husband.

'There are secrets he *has* to keep, Wes. Troop positions . . . surveillance capabilities . . . those are the secrets we *need*,' she says. 'But something like this . . . good Lord, I was at Ron's funeral. I read a psalm!'

'Ma'am, what're you—?'

'I went to his house and cried with his wife and daughter! I was on my knees praying for his peaceful rest!' she shouts, her sadness shifting to rage. 'And now to find out it was all a sham . . . some weak-minded escape for his own cowardice . . .' The tears again flood forward and she sways off balance. 'Oh, Lord, if what Ron says . . . if it's true . . .' Stumbling toward me, she grabs the corner of the low Empire dresser on my left, barely able to stay on her feet.

'Ma'am!'

She holds up a hand to keep me back. Her eyes flit around the room. At first, I assume she's mid-panic-attack. But the way she keeps looking . . . from the side table on the left of the bed, to Manning's side table on the right, to the writer's desk, back to the Empire dresser . . . each is covered with picture frames – all shapes and sizes – all with photos of Manning. 'H-How could he . . . how could they do that?' she asks, looking at me for the answer.

All I can offer is a shell-shocked stare. I can't feel my arms. Everything's numb. Is she saying that Manning knew abou—?

'Did Boyle say anything when you saw him? Did he offer any explanation?'

'I just . . . I walked in on him,' I explain, barely hearing my own words. 'He took off before I even realized what was happening.'

The First Lady's hand starts shaking again. She's like me in Malaysia. Thanks to the letter, she's finally hearing that her dead friend is actually alive. And from what Boyle wrote, for some reason he blames himself, saying he did it to protect his family. Overwhelmed by the moment, Dr. Manning takes a seat on the hand-painted American flag chest at the foot of the bed and stares down at Boyle's handwritten letter. 'I just can't—'

'He called me yesterday and told me to stay away,' I add for no good reason. 'That it wasn't my fight.' I feel a flush of rage. 'But it *is* my fight.'

She looks at me absently as if she'd forgotten I was there. Her jaw tightens, and she presses her hand against her lap until it stops shaking. It's bad enough she's so emotionally distraught. It's even worse that it's happening in front of me. Within an eyeblink, her chin and posture stiffen, and her political instincts, honed by years of keeping private matters private, kick in. 'He's right,' she blurts.

'What're you talking about?'

'Listen to Boyle,' she says. Then, as an afterthought, 'Please.'

'But, ma'am—'

'Forget you ever saw him, forget he ever called you.' As her voice cracks, I realize I was wrong. This isn't about her being emotionally exposed. It's about her being protective. And not just of her husband. Of me too. 'Wes, if you walk away now, at least they won't know that you—'

'They already know. They know I saw him . . .'

'*They?* Who's *they?*' she asks, cocking an anxious eyebrow.

'The Three,' I insist.

She looks up as I say the words, and I spot the recognition in her eyes. They were messing with her friend too – of course, she knows the details. But that doesn't mean she wants to drag me into the rest of it.

'I know who they are,' I tell her.

'I don't think you do, Wes.'

'How can you—?' I cut myself off as adrenaline buries the nauseous undertow I'm feeling. I've let her protect me for eight years. It's enough. 'I know The Three were fighting with the President and Boyle. I know *Blackbird*, whatever it was, was worth a quick six-million-dollar payout for The Roman, who apparently was one of the government's top informants. I know that the payout was rejected by the President in one of the national security briefings. And I know that losing that kind of cash – and whatever else they would've made after it – had to've enraged them. The only thing I can't figure out is, where'd Boyle fit in, and what'd he do that had The Three angry enough to pull the trigger?'

I expect her to be relieved to have someone with her, but she looks more frightened than ever, which quickly reminds me that this letter is as much of a shock to her as spotting Boyle was to me. And even with me digging up her worst family secrets, regardless of what Boyle or her husband did, she doesn't want to see me hurt by it.

'How did you learn about The Three?' she asks.

I hesitate at first. 'Friend of a friend who works for DOD.'

'And who told you they were fighting with the President?'

'That part I guessed on.'

Panicking, she studies me, weighing the permutations. She knows I'm not her enemy. But that doesn't mean she's letting me be her friend. Still, I'm definitely close. Too close to just send me on my way.

'I can help you,' I tell her.

She shakes her head, unconvinced.

'Ma'am, they know I saw Boyle. If you're trying to keep me safe, it's already too late. Just tell me what Boyle did and—'

'It's not what Boyle *did*,' she whispers. 'It's what he *didn't* do.' She catches herself, already regretting it.

'Didn't do to *who*? To the President?'

'*No!*' But that's all she tosses my way. Looking down, she curls back into a ball.

'Then to who? To you? To Albright? Just tell me who it was.'

She's dead silent.

'Dr. Manning, please, you've known me eight years. Have I ever done anything that would hurt you?'

She continues to stare down, and I can't say I blame her. She's the former First Lady of the United States. She's not sharing her fears with some young aide. I don't care. I need to know.

'So that's it? I'm supposed to just walk away?'

Still no answer. No doubt, she's hoping I'll be my usual self and shrink from the conflict. Two days ago, I would've. Not today.

'That's fine,' I tell her as I head for the door. 'You have every right to keep it to yourself, but you need to understand this: When I leave here, I'm not giving up. That bullet hit *my* face. And until I find out what really happened that day, I'm going to keep searching, keep digging, keep asking questions of every single person that was—'

'Don't you see? It was an offer.'

I turn, but I'm not surprised. Whatever Boyle did, if

she tells me the truth, at least she has a chance of containing it. And for someone who already has third-degree burns from the glare of the public spotlight, containment is all.

'An offer for what?' I ask, well aware of the box she lives in. If there's something she needs to keep hidden, she can't risk letting me walk out of here armed with embarrassing questions.

But she's still hesitating.

'I'm sorry you don't trust me,' I say, heading for the door.

'You said it yourself, Wes. As an informant, The Roman started bringing in tips.'

'But The Roman was actually a Secret Service agent, right?'

'That's what they think *now*. But no one knew that back then. In those days, the agencies were just happy to get The Roman's tips. Especially after Iraq, a correct, well-corroborated tip about a hidden training camp in Sudan? You saw how the war on terror works – indicators and warnings are all we have. Amazingly for The Roman, if he brought an assassination tip to the Secret Service, when the Service would go verify it with other agencies, the FBI would confirm it, as would the CIA. If he brought a tip to the FBI, it'd get authenticated by the CIA and the Service – and that verification is exactly what he needed for them to pay him as a source.'

'So under the guise of The Roman, The Three would bring the tips into their separate agencies, then just corroborate them amongst themselves . . .'

'. . . making it look like everyone – FBI, CIA, and the Service – were all in agreement. Sad to say, it happens all the time – last year in the State Department, someone made up a tip. The difference is, in most cases, they get caught because it doesn't match what the other agencies are saying. But here . . . well, if they hadn't gotten so greedy, it might've been a simple way to supplement their midlevel government salaries.'

'But they got greedy?'

'Everyone's greedy,' the First Lady says as years of buried anger rise again to the surface. 'They knew the system. They knew that small tips about some hidden training camp would only net them fifty thousand or so. And they also knew that the only way to get the big money they were after was to lie low and save their energy for those onetime shock-and-awe tips: The Golden Gate Bridge is being targeted . . . that shoe warehouse in Pakistan is really a chemical factory. Once everyone's convinced that The Roman's last nine tips were right, they'll pay anything for the jumbo-sized tenth – even if it never happens. And when the FBI and CIA and Service all corroborate it and agree the threat is real? That's how the informant who brought it in gets his multimillion-dollar payday.'

'So what was their problem?' I ask, trying to sound strong. Adrenaline only lasts so long. With each new detail of our old lives, the nauseous undertow floods back.

'The problem was, FBI and CIA case officers can only approve payouts of $200,000. To get into the multimillion range that would put The Three in retirement, the payday had to be approved by the White House.'

'And that's what *Blackbird* was, right? They were starting to cash out with their first big tip, but it got shot down by the President.'

She nods, and eyes me, impressed. 'That's when they realized they needed someone on the inside. Boyle was warned about it back then – that they might try approaching him, especially because of his background . . .'

'Wait, whoa, whoa – so The Three—'

'Stop calling them that. Don't you see? None of this happened because of The Three. It happened because they got smart and reached out for a new member. The Three was done. This is about The Four.'

83

'You sure that's right?' Rogo asked, reading from the original May 27 entry in Boyle's datebook. He held it up to the redacted photocopy just to make sure it was a perfect fit. Underneath the

were the handwritten words

Dr. Eng 2678 Griffin Rd. Ft. L.

'That's the big secret they were hiding from the masses?' Rogo added. 'That Boyle had a doctor's appointment?'

'It *is* personal information,' Freddy pointed out, slowly approaching them as Rogo tucked the original into a nearby file.

'Makes complete sense.' Dreidel agreed. 'In every White House, half the staff lines up to see a shrink.'

Standing at the edge of one of the long research stacks, Rogo turned to his friend, who was sitting on the corner of a nearby desk. 'Who says he's a shrink?' Rogo challenged.

'Wha?'

'Dr. Eng. What makes you think he's a shrink?'

'I don't know, I just assumed he—'

'Listen, guys, I'd love to spend the rest of the night

debating the merits of Eng's particular practice,' Freddy interrupted, 'but this is still a government building, and like any government building, when the little hand reaches the five—'

'Can you just run one more quick search?' Rogo asked, pointing to the library computers.

'I'm trying to be helpful. Really. But c'mon – the library's closed.'

'Just one more search.'

'It's already—'

'Just put in the words *Dr. Eng*,' Rogo pleaded. 'Please – it'll take less than thirty seconds. It's just typing two words – *Dr.* and *Eng* – into the bat-computer. You do that and we'll be gone so fast, you'll be home in time for the early early news.'

Freddy stared at Rogo. 'One last search and that's it.'

A few keystrokes later, as Freddy hunched over the keyboard, the answer popped on-screen.

No other records found.

'And you—?'

'I checked everything: the WHORM file, staff and office collections, e-mail, even the few odd bits of microfiche from the old national security stuff,' Freddy said, well past annoyed. 'The library's now officially closed,' he added, standing from his seat and pointing to the door. 'So unless you'd like to be introduced to our well-trained security staff, I suggest you have a nice day.'

Walking swiftly through the brick and concrete courtyard in front of the library, Rogo was a full five feet in front of Dreidel as they headed toward the car. 'A business. Yes, in Fort Lauderdale,' Rogo said into his cell phone.

'I'm looking for the number of a Dr. Eng. E-N-G.'

'I have a Dr. *Brian* Eng on Griffin Road,' the operator said.

'Two six seven eight, exactly,' Rogo said, reading the address off the sheet of paper they had copied it to. 'And does it say what kind of doctor he is?'

'I'm sorry, sir – we don't list occupations. Please hold for that number.'

Within seconds, a mechanized female voice announced, 'At the customer's request, the number is nonpublished and is not listed in our records.'

'Are you friggin' – What kinda doctor keeps an unlisted phone number?' As he turned back to Dreidel, he added, 'Anything on the Web?'

Staring down at the tiny screen on his phone, Dreidel fidgeted with the buttons like a grandparent with a remote control. 'I know I'm set up for Internet access – I just can't figure out how to—'

'Then whattya been doing for the past five minutes? Give it here,' Rogo snapped, snatching the phone from his hand. With a few clicks and shifts, Rogo entered the name *Dr. Brian Eng* and hit *Enter*. For almost a full two minutes, he scrolled and clicked but didn't say a word.

'Anything?' Dreidel asked as they weaved around cars in the parking lot.

'Unreal,' Rogo moaned, still clicking buttons on the phone. 'Not only is his number unlisted – the guy's somehow managed to stay out of every major search engine. Google . . . Yahoo! . . . you name it – put in *Dr. Brian Eng* and nothing comes up – it's ridiculous! If I put in the words *Jewish Smurfs*, I get a page full of hits, but *Dr. Brian Eng* gives me goose egg?' Approaching the driver's side of the Toyota, Rogo slapped the phone shut and tossed it across the roof of the car to Dreidel. 'Which leads us right back to, what kinda doctor keeps himself so hidden, he's almost impossible to find?'

'I don't know . . . a mob doctor?' Dreidel guessed.

'Or an abortion doctor,' Rogo countered.

'What about a plastic surgeon – y'know, for the really rich who don't want people to know?'

'Actually, that's not a bad call. Wes said it looked like Boyle changed some of his features. Maybe the May 27th appointment was his first office consult.'

Sliding into the passenger seat, Dreidel glanced down at his watch. Outside, it was already starting to get dark. 'We can swing by when they open tomorrow morning.'

'You kidding?' Rogo said as he started the car. 'We should go right now.'

'He's probably closed.'

'Still, if the building's open, I bet the directory in the lobby'll at least tell us what kind of practice he has.'

'But to trek all the way to Fort Lauderdale . . .'

Halfway out of the parking spot, Rogo jammed the brakes and shifted the car back into *park*. Turning to his right, he glared at Dreidel, who was still staring out the front windshield.

'What?' Dreidel asked.

'Why don't you want me driving to this doctor right now?'

'What're you talking about? I'm just trying to save us time.'

Rogo lowered his chin. 'Good,' he said, jerking the car back into gear. 'Next stop, Dr. Brian Eng.'

84

'Wait, you're telling me Boyle—'

'They invited him in,' the First Lady explains, her voice shaking with each word. 'Why be three horsemen when you can be more effective as four?'

'And Boyle said yes?'

'We didn't know . . .' She pauses, wondering whether to tell me the rest. But she knows I'll run out and ask the questions myself if she doesn't. 'We didn't think so,' she says.

'I don't understand,' I say, my chest in knots.

'You think they gave Ron a choice? The Three had access to the same FBI files we did. They knew his weakness – the child he thought none of us knew about . . .'

'Child? He had a—?'

'I told Lee that would come back to rip us. I *told* him,' she insists, more angry than ever. 'I said it on the campaign – you could tell even back then. When you have a scab like that, someone's bound to come pick at it.'

I nod, knowing better than to slow her down. 'But for Boyle to actually join them—'

'That's not what I said. I said they *approached* him. But The Three didn't understand – with Ron . . . even with his child . . . with all the self-destructive messes he'd made . . . he'd never turn on us. Never. No matter the cost,' she says, looking up. I get the point. She expects the same from me.

'Dr. Manning, I'm sorry – but the way you said it . . . You knew all this back then?'

'Wes, you were there with us. You know what was at stake. With someone like Ron . . . that kind of pressure point to exploit . . . you really think the FBI doesn't keep an extra eye on him?'

She stabs me with a look that almost knocks me to the ground. 'Hold on . . . you're saying the FBI was watching Boyle? While we were in office?'

'They were trying to keep him safe, Wes. And even then, Lee fought them watching on every front – called Barry and Carl personally,' she says, referring to our old FBI director and national security adviser. 'Two days later, they found the deposit. Eleven thousand dollars in a bank account with Ron's daughter's name on it. Can you imagine? Using his *daughter's* name! They said that was probably The Three's opening offer. Take the money they slipped into his account, or they'd wreck his life and tell his wife about the child he was hiding on the side.'

As she says the words, I'm the one who needs to lean on the dresser to stand. 'But in . . . in the briefing book . . . I never saw anything about that.'

'Every file wasn't for you, Wes.'

'Still, if The Three were that close, couldn't you call—?'

'You think we weren't pulling up the floorboards? At that point, we didn't even have a name for who we were chasing. We knew they had someone from FBI because they'd clearly accessed Ron's files. Then when they transferred the money into Ron's bank account – Secret Service does financial crime – they said the way the money was sent, they were using techniques from inside. And blackmail? That's CIA bread and butter. We alerted every agency with an acronym and started telling them to look within!'

'I know . . . I just—' I catch myself, always careful to know my place. 'Maybe I'm missing something, ma'am, but if you knew Boyle was being pressured into joining The Three, why didn't you just warn *him* – or at least tell him that you knew he was being blackmailed?'

Looking down at the handwritten letter, Lenore Manning doesn't say a word.

'What?' I ask. 'He *was* being blackmailed, right?'

She sits on the hand-painted chest, still silent.

'Is there something I'm not—?'

'We needed to see what he would do,' she finally says, her voice softer than ever.

A sharp chill seizes my spine. 'You were testing him.'

'You have to understand, when The Roman got that close – to penetrate our circle like that – it wasn't about Boyle anymore – we were trying to catch The Three.' Her voice trembles – she's been holding this in for so long – she's practically pleading for forgiveness. 'It was the FBI's request. If the myth was real, if a group of dirty agents were truly in contact, this was their chance to catch them all.'

I nod like it makes sense. Ron Boyle was their oldest and dearest friend, but when The Three forced his head toward the mousetrap, the Mannings – the President and First Lady of the United States – still waited to see if he'd take the cheese.

'I know what you're thinking, Wes, but I swear to you, I was trying to protect Ron. I told them that: Give him time to resign. Make sure to look out for—' She swallows hard, shaking her head over and over and over. I've seen the First Lady angry, upset, sad, offended, enraged, distressed, anxious, worried, and even – when she came out of hip replacement surgery a few years back – in pain.

But I've never seen her like this. Not even when we left the White House. Catching herself, she presses her chin against her chest to stop her head from shaking. The way she turns away from me, she hopes I don't notice. But as always, in this job, I see it all. 'They were supposed to look out for him,' she whispers, lost in her own broken promise. 'They . . . they swore he'd be safe.'

'And Boyle never told you The Three approached him?'

'I was waiting for it . . . praying for him to take us aside. Every day, we'd get a report on whether he'd accepted their offer. *No response*, they kept saying. I knew Ron was fighting it. I knew it,' she insists as she hugs her own shoulder, curling even tighter. 'But they told us to keep waiting . . . just to be sure. And then when he was shot . . .' She stares down at the floor as a surprise sob and a decade of guilt seize her throat. 'I thought we'd buried him.'

As I stare across at the handwritten letter in her lap, the mental puzzle pieces slide into place. 'So all this time, the real reason Boyle was shot wasn't because he crossed The Three, it was because he refused to *join* them?'

She looks back, cocking her head. Her voice is still barely a whisper. 'You don't even know who you're fighting, do you?'

'What're you—?'

'Have you even read this?' she asks, slapping the letter against my chest. 'On the day he was shot, Ron hadn't given The Three a decision yet!' There's a shift in her tone. Her eyes widen. Her mouth hangs open. At first, I think she's angry, but she's not. She's afraid.

'Dr. Manning, are you okay?'

'Wes, you should go. This isn't . . . I can't—'

'You can't what? I don't underst—'

'Please, Wes, just go!' she pleads, but I'm already staring

back at the letter. My brain's racing so fast, I can't read it. But what she said – on the day of the shooting, if Boyle hadn't given The Three a decision yet . . . for all they knew, he still could've gone to join them.

My forehead crinkles, struggling to process. But if that was the case . . . 'Then why kill him?' I ask.

'Wes, before you jump to conclusions—'

'Unless they knew Ron was having second thoughts . . .'

'Did you hear what I said? You can't—'

'. . . or maybe they thought they'd revealed too much . . . or . . . or they realized he was under surveillance . . .'

'Wes, why aren't you listening to me!?' she shouts, trying to pull the letter from my hands.

'Or maybe they found someone better to fill the fourth spot,' I blurt, tugging the letter back.

The First Lady lets go, and the page hits my chest with a thunderclap. My whole body feels a thousand pounds heavier, weighed down by the kind of numbing, all-consuming dread that comes with bad news at a doctor's office. 'Is that what happened?' I demand.

Her answer comes far too slowly. 'No.'

My mouth goes dry. My tongue feels like a wad of damp newspaper.

'That's not . . . Ron didn't . . .' the First Lady says. 'Maybe Ron's wrong . . .'

'Boyle was deputy chief of staff. There aren't that many people who're better at getting the—'

'You don't understand. He's a good man . . . he must've been tricked,' she continues, practically rambling.

'Ma'am . . .'

'He never would've done it on purpose . . .'

'Ma'am, please—'

'. . . even if they promised four more years—'

'Can you please calm down!' I insist. 'Who could they possibly get that's bigger than Boyle?'

Still hunched forward on the trunk at the foot of her bed, the First Lady lifts her chin, staring straight at me. Like the President, like everyone in our office, she doesn't look at my scars. She hasn't for years. Until right now.

The question echoes over and over through my brain. They were looking for a fourth. Who would be the biggest fourth of all?

I glance down at the letter that's still in my hands. On the bottom of the page, the meticulous handwritten note reads:

> *But I never thought they'd be able to get him.*

Blood drains from my face. That's what she realized. That's why she asked me to leave. She'd never turn on – '*Him?*' I ask. 'You can't mean—?'

'Wes, everything okay up there?' President Lee Manning shouts from the base of the stairs. 'We're still waiting for that sport coat!'

I turn to the First Lady. The President's footsteps hammer up the stairway.

85

The First Lady starts to say something, but it's like she's talking underwater. Teetering backward, I crash into the desk with all the Manning photos, which wobble and shake. Like me. To do that to me— The room whirls, and my life swirls into the kaleidoscope. All these years . . . to lie to my— God, how could he—? There's no time for an answer. From the footsteps outside the bedroom, it's clear the President is almost at the top of the stairs. If he sees me with her—

'Wes?' he calls out.

'Coming, sir!' I yell as I rush to his closet, tug a navy sport coat off its hanger, and shoot one last look at the First Lady, who's still frozen on the hand-painted trunk. Her eyebrows lift, her cheeks seem almost hollow. She doesn't say a word, but the cry for help is deafening.

'He'd never – he wouldn't do that – not on purpose,' she whispers as I drop Boyle's note back in her lap. Nodding repeatedly, she's already convincing herself. 'In fact, maybe . . . maybe he was tricked. Maybe he got approached by The Roman and he didn't realize who he was talking to. He would look like a real agent, right? So–so–so maybe they got worried that Ron was taking so long, and they tried a more manipulative route that went straight to the top branch of the tree. And then . . . he could've thought he was actually *helping* the Service. Maybe – maybe he didn't even realize what he'd done.'

I nod. Maybe she's right. Maybe it wasn't intentional. Maybe it was Manning's greatest, most horrible mistake that he prayed would somehow go away. The problem is, I can still picture the President on his last walk across the South Lawn, clutching the First Lady's hand and refusing to look back as they headed for Marine One. Back then, the leaks from our own staff said she was more devastated than he was. But I was there. I saw how tightly he was squeezing her fingers.

The President's footsteps are nearly at the top of the stairs.

I wobble toward the door, burst into the hallway, and make a sharp right, almost ramming into the President's chest.

'H-Here you go, sir,' I say as I skid to a halt, my arm outstretched with his navy blazer.

He takes another step toward me. I stand my ground, making sure he doesn't go any farther.

For a moment, Manning's eyes narrow, his famous grays flattening into matching icy slivers. But just as quickly, a broad, warm smile lifts his cheeks and reveals a hint of yellow on his teeth. 'By the way, have you seen the wigs yet?' he asks, referring to the Madame Tussauds folks downstairs. 'They brought the one from when we left office. I'm telling you, Wes, it's grayer than I am now. I think I'm getting younger.'

I force a laugh and head for the stairs before he gets a good look at me.

'What's wrong?' he asks, barely a step behind.

'No . . . nothing,' I say, motioning with the navy sport coat and feeling a flush of hot blood rushing through my neck. 'I just wanted to be sure I didn't give away one of your good jackets.'

'I appreciate your looking out for the wax me,' he teases, putting a hand on my shoulder. That's the move. Hand on shoulder for instant intimacy and guaranteed trust. I've seen him use it on prime ministers, senators, congressmen, even on his own son. Now he's using it on me.

Halfway down the stairs, I pick up my pace. He stays right with me. Even if working with The Roman was his mistake, to lie to my face every single— Is that why he kept me here? Penance for his own guilt?

In my pocket, my phone starts vibrating. I pull it out and check the phone's tiny screen. Text message:

> *wes, it's lisbeth. pick up.*
> *i solved puzzle.*

A second later, the phone vibrates in my hand. 'Excuse me one second, sir,' I say to the President. 'It's Claudia, who— Hello?' I say, answering the phone.

'You need to get out of there,' Lisbeth says.

'Hey, Claudia. I did? Okay, hold on one sec.' Nearing the bottom step, I keep Lisbeth on hold and turn back to Manning, feeling like my body's on fire. 'She says I left my house keys in her office. I'm sorry, sir, but if it's okay, I may just run back there and—'

'Relax, Wes, I'm a big boy,' he says with a laugh, his shoulder grasp turning into a quick, forceful back pat that almost knocks me off the bottom step. 'Go do what you have to. I've handled one or two problems bigger than this.'

Handing him his sport coat, I laugh right back and head for the front door. I can feel the President's eyes burning into the back of my head.

'By the way, Wes, do me a favor and let the Service know where you're going too,' he says loud enough so the agents outside can hear. 'Just in case they need to get in touch.'

'Of course, sir,' I say as I jog down the front steps.

'You alone yet?' Lisbeth asks through the phone.

The moment the door slams behind me, the two suit-and-tie agents who're standing outside the garage look up.

'Everything okay?' the shorter agent, Stevie, asks.

'Don't look suspicious,' Lisbeth says through the phone. 'Tell him you forgot your keys.'

'Yeah, no . . . I forgot my keys,' I say, speed-walking to the tall wooden privacy gate at the end of the driveway and pretending that everything I've built my life on isn't now coming apart. My breathing starts to gallop. I've known Stevie for almost three years. He doesn't care whether I check in or not. But as I reach the gate and wait for it to slide open, to my surprise, it doesn't move.

'So where you headed to, Wes?' Stevie calls out.

'Wes, listen to me,' Lisbeth pleads. 'Thanks to your low-life friend Dreidel, I found another puzzle. Are you listening?'

I turn back to the two men, who're still standing in front of the closed garage and the matching Chevy Suburbans parked a few feet away. Stevie's hand disappears into his pants pocket. It's not until that moment that I realize that on the night I first saw Boyle, Stevie was driving the lead car in Malaysia. 'Wes,' he says coldly. 'I asked you a—'

'Just back to the office,' I blurt. Spinning clumsily to the gate, I stare at the double-plank wooden slats that keep people from looking in. I grip the phone to stop my hand from shaking. The sun's about to set in the purple-orange sky. Behind me, there's a metallic click. My heart leaps.

'See you soon,' Stevie calls out. There's a loud *rrrrrr*

as the wooden gate rolls to the right, sliding open just enough for me to squeeze through.

'I'm out,' I whisper to Lisbeth.

'Fine – then pay attention. Do you have the old puzzle on you?'

Staggering across the street to the car, I don't answer. All I see is Manning's grin and his yellow Chiclet teeth—

'Wes! Did you hear what I said!?' she shouts. 'Take out the original one!'

Nodding even though she can't see me, I reach into my pocket and hastily unfold the original crossword.

'See the handwritten initials down the center?' she asks. 'M, A, R, J . . .'

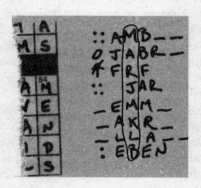

'Manning, Albright, Rosenman, Jeffer . . . what about them?'

'He's got the same list on the new puzzle. Same initials down the middle. Same order. Same everything.'

'Okay, so? Now there're two lists of top senior staff,' I say, stopping just outside the car. I have to lean against the door to keep standing.

'No. Pay attention, Wes. Same *everything*. Including those scribbles down the side.'

'What're you talking about?'

'On the left – before each set of initials: the four dots in a square, the little oval, the cross with a slash through it . . .'

I look at each one: **::** , *O* , **⚤** . 'The chicken scratch?'

'That's the thing, Wes,' she says, deadly serious. 'I don't think it's chicken scratch. Unless he's got some majorly smart chickens.'

86

'But those doodles,' I say as I study Manning's scribbles on the side of the crossword.

'Are you listening?' Lisbeth shouts through the phone. 'That's what they wanted it to look like – random doodles and extra letters that make the hidden initials disappear. But if you look at this new crossword, the exact same scribbled images are in the *exact same order*. There's nothing random about it, Wes! The four dots . . . the small oval – Manning was using them as some sort of message.'

'Why would—?'

'You said it yourself: Every politician needs allies – and every President needs to figure out who he can trust. Maybe this is how Manning ranked those closest to him. Y'know, like a report card.'

Nodding at the logic, I glance again at the list, mentally adding the real names.

⦂	Manning
0	Albright
⚲	Rosenman
⦂	Dreidel
——	Moss

—— Kutz

—— Lemonick

⫶ Boyle

'And no offense,' Lisbeth adds, 'but your boy Dreidel? He's a piece of shit. Real shit, Wes – as in beating-up-prostitutes-and-ramming-their-faces-into-mirrors kind of shit.'

As she relays Violet's story, I can still picture the woman in the bathrobe peeking out from Dreidel's hotel room. Still, to go from that to smashing faces . . . 'You sure you can trust this Violet woman?' I ask.

'Look at the list,' Lisbeth says. 'That *is* Manning's handwriting, right?' When I don't answer, she adds, 'Wes, c'mon! Is that Manning's handwriting or not?'

'It's his,' I say as my breathing again quickens.

'Exactly. So if he's the one filling in this report card, then the grade he gives himself – those four dots – you think in his own personal ranking, he's giving himself an A or a big, steaming F?'

'An A?' I say tentatively, staring at the ⫶⫶ .

'Absolutely an A. He's the cipher. In fact, I'll wager those four dots are a sparkling A+. Now look who else was lucky enough to get the exact same ranking.'

I look down at the list. It's the first time I realize Manning and Dreidel are both ranked with four dots.

'Red rover, red rover, we call Dreidel right over,' Lisbeth says through the phone.

'Lisbeth, that doesn't prove anything. So what if he trusted Dreidel more than any of the others?'

'Unless he trusted Dreidel to do what none of the others would.'

'Wait, so now Dreidel's a legbreaker?'

'You were there, Wes. You're telling me the President never had any personal issues that needed dealing with?'

'Of course, but those usually went to—' I cut myself off.

'What? Those were the problems that went to Boyle?'

'Yeah, they . . . they were supposed to. But what if that's the point? What if they *used* to go to Boyle . . .'

'. . . and suddenly they stopped?'

'And suddenly they started going to Dreidel,' I say with a nod. 'No one would even know the President made the switch unless . . .'

'. . . unless they happened to find their ranking on the list,' Lisbeth agrees, her voice now racing. 'So when Boyle found this, when he saw that Dreidel and Manning were ranked together . . .'

'. . . he could see the real ranking of the totem pole.'

An hour ago, I would've told Lisbeth she's crazy – that there's no way the President and Dreidel were scheming together. But now . . . I replay the last ten minutes in my head. What the First Lady said . . . what Boyle accused the President of . . . and what Lisbeth's already confirming . . . if even half of it's true . . . I inhale a warm burst of muggy air, then grit my teeth to slow my breathing. But it won't slow down. My chest rises and falls. My neck, my face – I'm soaked.

Up the block, on the corner of County Road, there's a white car with its blinker on, waiting to turn toward me.

'Get the hell out of there,' Lisbeth says.

'I'm leaving right now.'

Ripping the door open, I hop into the car and frantically claw through my pocket for my keys. I came here to confess . . . to get help from the biggest and the best.

But now – with the President as The Fourth, and Dreidel feeding us directly to the Lion . . . I ram the key at the ignition, but the way my hand's shaking, the key bounces off the steering column. I try again. *Dammit, why won't it—?* I take another stab, and the tip of the key scratches across the metal column, pinching my fingertip. The pain's sharp, like being jabbed with a needle. But as my eyes swell with tears, I know it's not from the pain. Or at least not this pain.

A sob rises like a bubble in my throat. I again clench my teeth, but it won't go down. *No, don't do this . . . not now,* I beg as I press my forehead as hard as I can against the steering wheel. But as I picture the President – all these years – I didn't just learn his shoe size and pillow preference. I know what he thinks: who annoys him, who he trusts, who he hates, even who he thinks is still using him. I know his goals, and what he's afraid of, and what he dreams about, and what he hopes . . . what I hoped . . . The bubble in my throat bursts and my body begins to shake with silent, heaving sobs. After eight years . . . every single day . . . *Oh, God – how could I not know this man?*

'Wes, you there?' Lisbeth asks through the phone.

Still breathing heavily and fighting for calm, I swallow hard, sit up straight, and finally shove the key into the ignition. 'One sec,' I whisper into the phone. Punching the gas, I feel the wheels gnaw through the grassy divider, eventually catching and whipping me forward. As I wipe the last tears from my eyes, I notice a Chinese restaurant menu tucked underneath my windshield wiper. Steering with one hand and lowering the window with the other, I flick on the wipers, reach outside, and nab the menu just as the wiper blade slings it across the glass. But as I toss the menu into the passenger seat, I spot familiar handwriting running across the back page of the menu, just below the coupons. I jam my foot against the brake, and the car skids to a halt a full twenty feet shy of the stop sign at the end of the block.

'You okay?' Lisbeth asks.

'Hold on . . .'

I dive for the menu. The handwriting's unmistakable. Perfect tiny block letters.

> *Wes, turn around. Make sure you're alone.*
> *(Sorry for the melodrama)*

Whipping around in my seat, I check through the back window and sniff away the rest of the tears. The gate to the Mannings' house is shut. The sidewalks are empty. And the grassy divider that splits the narrow street holds only the quiet navy-blue rental car of the Madame Tussauds folks.

'Did you find something?' Lisbeth asks.

Struggling to read the rest of the note, I can barely keep my hands from shaking.

> *You need to know what else he did. 7 p.m. at—*

My eyes go wide when I see the location. Like before, it's signed with a simple flourish. The tip of the *R* drags longer than the rest. *Ron.*

There's a flush of sweet-sour wetness across the left half of my tongue. I touch my lip and spot the bright red liquid on my fingertips. Blood. I was biting my lip so hard, I didn't even feel myself break the skin.

'What is it, Wes? What's there?' Lisbeth asks, now frantic.

I'm about to tell her, but I catch myself, remembering what she's done.

'Wes, what's wrong?'

'I'm fine,' I say as I reread the note. 'Just nervous.'

There's a pause on the line. She's been lied to by the best. I'm not even in the top ten. 'Okay, what're you not saying?' she asks.

'Nothing, I just—'

'Wes, if this is about the tape, I'm sorry. And if I could take it back—'

'Can we not talk about this?'

'I'm just trying to apologize. The last thing I wanted was to hurt you.'

'You didn't hurt me, Lisbeth. You just treated me like a story.'

For the second time, she's silent. It's cutting her deeper than I thought. 'Wes, you're right: This *is* a story. It's a big story. But there's one thing I need you to understand: That doesn't mean it's *only* a story to me.'

'And that's it?' I ask. 'You make the pretty speech, the musical score swells, and now I'm supposed to trust you again?'

'Of course not – if I were you, I wouldn't trust *anyone*. But that doesn't mean you don't need help. Or friends. And just FYI, if I were trying to burn you, when I got the new crossword . . . when I got the Violet and Dreidel story . . . I would've called my editor instead of you.'

I think on that for a moment. Just like I think about our first ride in the helicopter.

'And remember that trade where you promised that you'd give me the story?' she asks. 'Forget it. I'm off. I don't even want it anymore.'

'You're serious about that?'

'Wes, for the past ten minutes, my notepad has been in my purse.'

I believe Lisbeth. I think she's telling the truth. And

I'm convinced she's trying to do the right thing. But after today . . . after Manning . . . after Dreidel . . . after damn near everyone . . . the only person I can really put my faith in is myself.

'What about your visit to the Mannings?' she adds. 'They say anything I can help you with?'

I stare down at Boyle's handwritten note and the signature with his long-tipped *R*.

'No – just the usual,' I reply, rereading the message for myself.

You need to know what else he did. 7 p.m.

87

'What about your visit to the Mannings?' Lisbeth said into her phone as she walked briskly through the rain just outside the townhouse where she met Violet. 'They say anything I can help you with?'

Wes paused barely half a second. For Lisbeth, it was more than enough. If he wanted to lie, he would've already made up some story. A pause like this . . . whatever he's debating, it's tearing at him. And to her own surprise, the more she saw what he'd been through – and was still going through – the more it tore at her as well. Sacred Rule #10, she told herself: Get attached to the story, not the people in it.

'No – just the usual,' Wes finally offered. He added a quick good-bye to sidestep the awkwardness. It didn't.

Lisbeth couldn't blame him. By bringing that tape recorder, she'd shaken his trust. Yet as she slid behind the steering wheel of her car and started dialing a new number, it was clear she wasn't going to just sit still and let him hold her at a distance.

'*Palm Beach Post*,' a female voice answered on the other line. 'This is Eve.'

'Eve, it's Lisbeth. Are you—?'

'Don't worry, the column's all done.'

'Forget the column.'

'Even got the dumb art award in.'

'*Eve!*'

There was a pause on the other line. 'Please tell me you didn't wreck my car.'

'Can you please listen?' Lisbeth pleaded as she stared down at the crossword puzzle Violet had given her and spread it across the steering wheel. 'Remember that old guy from comics – y'know, with the creepy glasses and the moon-chin—'

'Kassal? The guy who designed our crossword puzzles?'

'Yeah, that's the – wait, whattya mean *designed*? Don't tell me he's dead.'

'Lisbeth, this newspaper's so cheap, they shrunk the font size on our headlines to save money on ink. You really think they'd pay an extra employee, extra benefits, extra health insurance, when they can get a syndicated daily crossword for thirty bucks?' Eve pointed out. 'They fired him two years ago. But lucky you, I happen to be staring at an employee directory from *three* years ago.'

'You really haven't cleaned your desk in that long?'

'You want the number or not?'

Ten digits later, Lisbeth watched a light rain skate down her windshield. Her foot anxiously tapped the floor mat as she waited for someone to pick up. 'Be home, be home, be home . . .'

'Hiya,' an older man with a horse voice and a creaky Midwest accent answered.

'Hi, I'm looking for Mr Kassal,' Lisbeth explained.

'Martin to you. And you are . . .'

'Lisbeth Dodson – we used to work together at the *Palm Beach Post* – and I promise you, sir, this'll be the strangest question you get all d—'

'Up the pace, sweetie. I got pancakes cooking for dinner, and it'll kill me to see 'em burn.'

'Yeah, well, a good friend of mine has a problem . . .' Lisbeth took a full breath, reaching for her pen, then stopping herself. 'How good are you at solving puzzles?'

88

With the sunroof open and the light rain still drizzling inside, Nico veered off the highway, cutting in front of a white Lexus and following the exit ramp to Okeechobee Boulevard.

'Edmund, what's the address again?' Nico asked, re-adjusting the blanket on Edmund's chest as they approached the red light at the end of the ramp.

8385 Okeechobee Boulevard.

Nodding to himself, Nico leaned forward in his seat, craning his neck past the steering wheel to get a better look at the street that ran perpendicular in front of them. On his right, the light traffic coasted past gas stations and a lawn-mower repair shop. On his left, the open blue water of Clear Lake ran in front of the Performing Arts Center, while a green highway sign pointed toward the beautiful high-rises in the distance. In the photo Nico stole, Wes was broken, shattered, corrupted by Boyle's touch. Nothing beautiful about him.

Tugging the wheel to the right, Nico cut off the same white Lexus, who bitched with his horn for a good five seconds. Not hearing it, Nico pumped the gas and dove into traffic.

'Can you read that one?' Nico asked as he pointed to the address on a nearby car dealership. A droplet of rain whizzed through the sunroof and flicked Edmund on the cheek.

2701.

'What about *that* one?' Nico asked, pointing to a cash-advance store half a block ahead.

That one's, lemme see . . . 2727.

Nico beamed with a beady twinkle in his eyes and hit the gas even harder.

Breathtaking work, Nico. Lord's definitely on your side with this one.

Thinking the exact same thing, Nico reached for the wooden rosary beads that swayed from the Pontiac's rearview. 'Do you mind, Edmund?'

I'd be honored. You've earned them, my son.

My son. Nico sat bolt upright at the words. Surely, Edmund knew what they meant . . . and once Nico heard them, he could smell the black licorice and hickory whiff of his dad's old hand-rolled cigars. Back when . . . back before Mom got sick. When they'd go to church. When things were good. Barely able to hide his grin, Nico nodded over and over as he slipped the rosary beads around his neck and glanced back at the passenger seat.

What? What's wrong, Nico?

'Nothing . . . I just . . .' He nodded again and took another deep breath of black licorice. 'I'm happy,' he said. 'And in a few more minutes, Mom – like Dad – is finally gonna get her justice.'

89

Five minutes ago, I started telling Rogo the story about
The Four, and the note from Boyle, and what Lisbeth
said about Dreidel. Under normal circumstances, Rogo
would've been screaming for a fistfight and stacking up
the I-told-you-sos. But like any good actor, he's well aware
of his audience.

'What's he saying?' Dreidel asks in the background.

'Tell him the Mannings gave me tomorrow off,' I shoot
back through the phone, my newfound anger barely
covering my still-smoldering anxieties.

'The Mannings gave him tomorrow off – just to calm
down from all the Nico mess,' Rogo says like an old pro.
Back to me, he adds, 'You have any idea why he did it?'

'Who? Manning? I have no idea – the First Lady said
maybe they suckered him. All I know is when The Three
recruited Boyle, they were blackmailing him with this
supposed kid. But to get something on a sitting President
of the United States . . .'

'. . . we're talking one hell of a secret,' he agrees. 'Wes,
you're gonna need to be careful.'

'Careful of what?' Dreidel interrupts, clearly frustrated.
'What's he saying?'

'Rogo,' I warn, 'don't give him—'

'Just relax, okay? We're talking about O'Shea and Micah,'
Rogo says, clearly in control. When Dreidel doesn't

respond, I wonder if I'm being too harsh. Even if what Lisbeth said is true – about Manning and Dreidel being ranked the same . . .

'Ask Wes if he wants to meet up,' Dreidel calls out in the background. 'Just so we can compare our notes in one place.'

'Actually, that's a great idea,' Rogo says. For Dreidel, Rogo's tone is completely enthusiastic. For me, his undertone is just as clear: He'd gnaw his own thumbs off before letting that meeting ever happen.

As Rogo continues to hold him at bay, I make a sharp right out of the rush-hour traffic on Okeechobee Boulevard and cut through the wide-open space of the Publix supermarket parking lot. It's not my usual path, but as I check the rearview, the vast emptiness of the lot is the best way to see I'm still alone.

'So when should we meet?' Rogo asks, still trying to keep Dreidel happy.

'I assume you're joking, right?' I ask, looping back through the parking lot and following the narrow two-lane street to the familiar building at the end of the block.

'Ya-huh . . . of course.'

'Fine, then just keep him away,' I say. 'Away from me and away from Boyle.'

'Dammit, Rogo, you missed the turn!' Dreidel shouts in the background. 'The on-ramp's back that way!'

Without a word, I know Rogo understands. By the time they get to Dr. Eng's office, then back to Palm Beach, Dreidel's officially one less crisis I have to deal with.

'Okay, eight o'clock tonight at Dreidel's hotel – you got it, Wes,' Rogo says. 'Ya-huh, yeah . . . of course,' he adds, even though I'm silent. Through the phone, he takes a deep breath. His voice slows down. 'Just make sure you're safe, okay?' I know that tone. The last time I heard it, he was standing by my hospital bed. 'I'm serious, Wes. Be safe.'

'I will,' I tell him as a sharp right takes me up the paved brick driveway that's shaped like a horseshoe in front of my apartment building. Driving past the main entrance, I pull around to the open-air parking lot in back. 'Though I gotta be honest, Rogo – I figured you'd be happy I was finally fighting back.'

'Yeah, well . . . next time try swimming a few laps before you decide to cross the English Channel.'

'I gave my life to him, Rogo. I need to get it back.'

'You're telling *me*? Wes, I fight with everyone. I *love* fighting with everyone – I fight with the snot bagboy who tries to cheap me out by giving me plastic instead of paper. But let me tell you something: You don't fight with people like this. You get your proof, you lock it up somewhere safe, and then you run to the press . . . to the authorities . . . to whoever's in the best position to keep them from knocking your teeth out through your colon. And believe me, when they find you, they're gonna hit back.'

'You still talking about Micah and O'Shea?' Dreidel interrupts in the background.

'Who else would we talk about?' Rogo shoots back.

'Rogo,' I interrupt, 'I *know* how they hit. They're not getting another crack.'

'Good – that's what I wanna hear. Okay, so if you can't go home, where you gonna hide out for the next few hours: that crappy hotel my mom stayed at, or maybe somewhere more out in the open, y'know, like the lobby of the Breakers or something?'

I'm silent for a moment, coasting toward my parking spot in back. 'Whattya mean?'

'Look at the time, Wes – you've still got two hours to kill – so assuming you don't wanna be at home . . .'

I'm silent again.

I swear I can hear Rogo shaking his head. 'You're home right now, aren't you?'

'Not exactly,' I say as the car bounces over a speed bump.

'*Not exactly?* What's *not exactly*?'

'It's . . . it means I'm . . . it means I'm kinda in the parking lot.'

'Aw, jeez! Wes, why would you—? Get out of there!'

'You don't think our security in front can—?'

'That's not security. It's a doorman with a sewn-on badge!'

'I'm talking about the cameras, Rogo. That's what they're afraid of – being seen! And no offense, but until you just blurted it to Dreidel, I probably would've been fine.'

'Just go. Now!'

'Y'think?' I ask, pulling into an open spot for a quick three-point turn.

'Just turn the car around and get your ass outta there before—!'

As I throw the car into reverse, there's a knock against the driver's-side window. Turning to my left, I spot the tip of a gun tapping against the glass.

O'Shea points his pistol right at me and raises his pointer finger to his lips.

'Tell them you're fine,' O'Shea says, his voice muffled through the window.

I stare at the gun. 'L-Listen, Rogo – I'm fine,' I say into the phone.

Rogo says something, but I can't hear him.

'Tell them you'll call back when you find someplace safe,' O'Shea adds.

For a moment, I hesitate. O'Shea tightens his finger against the trigger.

'Rogo, I'll call you back when I find someplace safe.'

I shut the phone. O'Shea rips open my car door.

'Nice to see you again,' he says. 'How was Key West?'

90

'Let's go, Wes. *Out*,' O'Shea says, gripping the shoulder of my shirt and dragging me from the Subaru. As I stumble across the asphalt of the parking lot, I realize the car's still running. He doesn't care. He doesn't think this'll take long.

'Keep going . . . toward the fence,' he adds, barely a step behind. His gun is no longer out in the open. But through the outline in his jacket pocket, it's still clearly pointed at me.

We head toward the back corner of the parking lot, where there's an opening in the tall shrubs that leads to a shaded dog run that runs parallel to the lot. The dog run is narrow and not too long. But tucked behind the shrubs, it'll keep us out of sight.

'So Key West,' O'Shea says, still right behind me. 'Your buddy Kenny says hi.'

I glance over my shoulder just as we reach the two lampposts that flank the entrance to the dog run. O'Shea offers a smug grin, but the way his sandy-blond hair is matted to his head, he's had a tougher day than he's saying. The drizzle of rain looks like beads of sweat across his pug nose.

'I don't know what you're talking about,' I say, turning back to face him.

He doesn't even bother calling me on it. 'Where's the photo you took, Wes?'

'I told you, I don't—'

In a blur, his fist cocks me in the face, jamming into my left eye and sending me crashing to the muddy path. As I skid backward on my butt through the damp grass, my whole eye socket's throbbing, like a just-rung bell.

'I know you have the photo. Hand it over, and you're free to go.'

'It-it's in the glove compartment,' I say, pointing to the car with one hand and holding my eye with the other.

He glances back at the Subaru just as two more cars glide into the parking lot. Their headlights are on, slicing through the early darkness and turning the light drizzle into tiny fireworks that flicker in the distance. Fellow tenants coming home from their day's work. Planting his foot on my shoulder, O'Shea studies the entire scene like he's reading someone's palm.

Without a word, he reaches down, grips the front of my shirt, and pulls me to my feet. Even before I get my balance, he whips me around, and I crash chest-first into the nearest tree. My cheek scrapes against the bark, momentarily forcing me to forget the pain in my eye.

Behind me, O'Shea kicks my legs apart and starts frisking through my pockets, tossing the contents to the ground: wallet, house keys, the folded-up sheet of paper with Manning's daily schedule on it.

'What're you doing?' I ask as he pats my chest and works his way down my legs. 'I told you it's in the glove compar—'

There's a soft crackle as his fingers pat my ankle.

I look down at him. He looks up at me.

I try to fight free of his grip, but he's too strong. Choking my ankle, he hikes up my pant leg, revealing the glossy black-and-white photo that's curled around my shin, the top half of it sticking out of my sock.

Enraged, O'Shea rips it free and shoves me aside. His anger swells as he stares down at the speedway photo of Micah, crumpling the corner of it in his hand – but just as quickly, he finds his calm and catches his breath. Relieved that he's not in it, he locks back on me. The fact I'm still alive means the photo isn't the only thing he's here for.

'Where's Lisbeth?' he asks.

'We had a disagreement.'

'But she still let you use her car? Sounds like she's being plenty helpful.'

'If you want to know if she's writing a story—'

'I want to know where she is, Wes. Now. And don't say *I don't know.*'

'But I don—'

'*Don't say I don't know!*' he shouts, pulling his gun and pointing it directly at my face. Lowering his voice, he adds, 'I know you were speaking to her about the crossword. Now—'

There's a crack of broken sticks and a jingle that sounds like Christmas bells. Behind O'Shea, through the opening that leads to the parking lot, a short woman in a pin-striped business suit shakes a metal dog leash as she leads her fluffy beach-colored cocker spaniel through the entrance of the dog run.

Before the woman even realizes what's happening, O'Shea crosses his arms, hiding his gun under his armpit.

'Sorry,' the woman says, laughing nervously as she ducks down and cuts between us. 'Didn't mean to interrupt.'

'No problem at all,' O'Shea replies, turning just enough that she never gets a clear look at his face. 'We're just waiting for our dogs to come back – they love running down to the end.'

The woman nods, glancing back just long enough to see that neither of us is carrying a leash. Quickly turning away and pretending not to notice, she follows her dog's lead as she's tugged to a small patch of grass about ten feet away.

I'm tempted to run. She's a perfect distraction – and a witness. But as O'Shea lowers his chin and his hazel eyes disappear in the darkness of his brow, I hear the message loud and clear. If I make a move, he'll kill her too.

'Good girl, Murphy – there you go,' the woman says, tugging the dog back between us and reentering the parking lot. For a full minute, we watch her from behind as she crosses the lot and heads for the back door of the building. The woman looks at her dog, at her watch, for her keys – but to her credit, she never looks back. With a faint crack, the metal door to the building slams, and the woman disappears. O'Shea's arms unfold, and his gun goes right back to my face.

'Sorry, Wes,' O'Shea says as he pulls back the hammer of his gun. 'This is gonna sting.'

'Wait . . . what're you doing?' I ask, stumbling backward into a nearby tree.

The light rain taps against his face, but he barely notices. His fair skin shines with a yellow glow in the darkness.

'O'Shea, if you do this . . . the investigation they'll open: You'll never be able to cover it up.'

O'Shea grins as his finger tightens on the trigger. 'Funny. That's what they said to us last ti—'

Pop, pop, pop.

The sound hiccups through the air. My body goes cold.

Not from pain. From the sound. *Pop, pop, pop* – an echo from the past – firing now.

Across from me, O'Shea, a look of angry surprise frozen on his face, shudders and shifts, crashing backward into the lamppost. He slaps his shoulder like he's slapping a bug bite. His knees start to buckle. His head dips slightly to the side. Still, it's not until I spot the blood coming from his shoulder that I even realize he's been shot. His blood looks black in the dim light as it runs down his suit.

'Nuuh!' O'Shea grunts as his head slams back into the lamppost. His gun drops to the muddy ground. The way he's teetering and leaning on the lightpost, he's about to follow. Behind me, there's another crunch of broken sticks. Before I even register the sound, a tall blurred shadow in a black windbreaker races past me, right for O'Shea.

'Move, Wes! *Move!*' the shadow shouts, ramming his forearm into my back and shoving me out of the way. But as I slip on the grass and fight for my own balance, there's no mistaking that voice. The voice from Malaysia . . . from the warning on my phone . . .

Boyle.

91

'Wes, get the hell out of here! Now!' Boyle hisses, his gun pointed at O'Shea. A wisp of smoke twirls from the barrel.

Sliding to the ground with his back against the lamp-post, O'Shea crumples to his knees. Fighting to stand up, he doesn't get anywhere. He's already in shock. Taking no chances, Boyle rushes in and jams the barrel of his gun against O'Shea's head. 'Where's Micah?' he demands.

Down on his knees, O'Shea grits his teeth in obvious pain. 'You finally found his name, huh? I told him this wou—'

'I'm asking you one more time,' Boyle threatens. Moving the gun from O'Shea's head, he jabs the barrel into the wound in O'Shea's shoulder. O'Shea tries to scream, but Boyle puts his hand over O'Shea's mouth. '*Last time, O'Shea! Where's he hiding?*' Pulling back the hammer, he digs his gun into O'Shea's wound.

O'Shea's body shakes as he tries to speak. Boyle lets go of his mouth. 'H-He's dead,' O'Shea growls, more pissed than ever.

'Who did it? You or The Roman?'

When O'Shea hesitates, Boyle twists the gun even deeper.

'M-M-Me . . .' O'Shea grunts, his eyes wild like an animal's. 'Just like I'll do with y—'

Boyle doesn't give him the chance, pulling the trigger and shooting him through the same wound. There's a muffled pop and a splat as a hunk of flesh explodes out the back of his shoulder. The pain's so intense, O'Shea doesn't even have time to scream. His eyes roll back. His arms go slack.

Crumpling like a sack of pennies, O'Shea rag-dolls forward. The instant he hits the dirt, Boyle's all over him, pulling O'Shea's hands behind his back and snapping his wrists into plastic flex cuffs that Boyle's pulled from his pocket.

'Wh-What're you doing here?' I ask, barely catching my breath.

With a loud *zzzip*, the cuffs clench, locking O'Shea's wrists behind his back. If Boyle wanted him dead, he'd fire another shot. But the way he's wrapping him up, he clearly wants something else. What's more amazing is the way Boyle moves – patting down O'Shea's body, working so fast . . . the way his triceps tense underneath his windbreaker . . . he's been training for this.

'Wes, I told you to leave!' Boyle shouts, finally turning my way.

It's the first time I get a good look at his eyes. Even in the dim light, they glow like a cat's. Brown with a splash of blue.

In the distance, a car door slams with a metal *chunk*. Boyle jerks to the left, following the sound. The tall shrubs block his view, but the way he freezes, leaning in to listen . . . like he knows someone's coming.

'We gotta go!' he insists, suddenly frantic as he pulls O'Shea's gun from the mud and pockets it.

'How'd you know I'd be here?'

Refusing to answer, he furiously rolls the unconscious

O'Shea like a log, flipping him on his back. 'Help me get him up!' Boyle demands.

Without even thinking, I move in, grabbing O'Shea under his left armpit. Boyle grabs the right.

'Were you following me?' I add as we lug O'Shea to his feet.

Boyle ignores the question, cutting in front of O'Shea and dropping to one knee. As O'Shea topples forward, Boyle hoists his shoulder under O'Shea's midsection, boosting him up like he's lugging an old rolled-up carpet.

'I asked you a—'

'I heard you, Wes. Get out of my way.' He tries to step around me. I sidestep, staying in front of him.

'You *were* following me? Is that to track them down or—?'

'Are you paying attention, Wes? Nico can be here any minute!'

I stumble at the words. My mouth goes dry, and I swear, every sweat gland in my body opens.

'Now get the hell out of here before you get both of us killed!' Shaking his head, Boyle rushes around me with O'Shea on his shoulder. I spin back and watch as he plows down to the end of the dog run.

'Where're you taking him?'

'Don't be stupid!' he calls out, shooting me one last look and making sure I get the point. 'There'll be time for chatting later.'

In the distance, as he turns away from me, Boyle's black windbreaker camouflages everything but his bald head. Draped over his shoulder, it's the same for O'Shea, whose pale neck shines as his head dangles toward the ground. Boyle yells something else, but I can't hear it. At the clip they're going down the tree-lined path, they quickly fade in the darkness. The sun's already set. And I'm once again standing in silence. In shock. All alone.

Behind me, a car door slams in the parking lot. On my left, a cricket's chirp scratches the night air. The drizzle continues and another twig cracks. Then another. It's more than enough.

Spinning back toward the parking lot, I run as fast as I can. Another car door slams. This one's quiet – like it's on the very far end of the lot. No time to take chances. Scooping up my wallet, house keys, and the photo, I dart between the lampposts, back to the parking lot. As I cut between two cars, no one's there.

After stuffing my wallet back into my pocket – and the photo back inside the ankle of my sock – I run through the lot, searching row by row and scanning the hood of each car. Along every metal roof, the overhead lamps cast a circular reflection that ripples with each raindrop. Still no one in sight. It doesn't make me feel any safer. If Boyle's been following me the whole time, then anyone cou – No, don't even think about it.

Shifting into a full sprint, I plow toward Lisbeth's car, rip open the door, and practically dive into the driver's seat. The car's still running. My phone's still sitting on the armrest.

Flipping open my cell, I frantically punch in Rogo's number and throw the car in reverse. But as I listen to it ring, all I can think about is who Rogo's traveling with . . . and how many questions Dreidel was asking . . . and how – somehow – O'Shea knew I was talking to Lisbeth. Rogo and I were convinced that Dreidel couldn't hear anything from our last conversation, but if we were wrong . . .

Jamming my thumb against the *End* button, I hang up, replaying Boyle's words in my head. *There'll be time for chatting later.* I look down at the digital clock on the dash. An hour and forty-five minutes, to be precise.

As my thumb pounds out a brand-new number and my foot pounds the gas, I tell myself it's the only way. And it is. However Boyle pulled it off, even if he was using me as bait for The Three, by nabbing O'Shea and finding out Micah's dead, he finally gave us a chance. So instead of just showing up at seven tonight – instead of just rushing in blind – I need to make the most of it. Even if it means taking some risks.

As I finish dialing the last digit, all I have to do is hit *Send*. Still, I stop myself. Not because I don't trust her. But because I *do*. Rogo would tell me I shouldn't. But he didn't hear her apology. He didn't hear the pain in her voice. She knew she'd hurt me. And that hurt her.

I hit *Send*, praying I won't regret it. I listen as the phone rings. And rings again. She's got caller ID. She knows who it is.

The phone rings for a third time as I zip through the parking lot toward the front of the building. I don't blame her for not picking up. If I'm calling, it only means trou—

'Wes?' Lisbeth finally answers, her voice softer than I expected. 'That you?'

'Yeah.'

It's not tough to read my tone. 'Everything okay?' she asks.

'I-I don't think so,' I say, gripping the steering wheel.

She doesn't even hesitate.

'How can I help?' she asks.

92

Driving up the curving brick driveway in front of Wes's building, Nico rechecked Edmund's wool blanket and nudged the brakes, reminding himself to take it slow. From the army to the speedway to this, his first goal was never to get noticed. Still, just being this close . . . Nico took his foot off the brake and gave a tap to the gas. The wooden rosary beads seemed to burn against his chest.

Almost there, son. Don't get riled.

Nico nodded, throwing a wave to one of the tenants running out the front door for a jog. As the Pontiac followed the road to the parking lot in back, its headlights stabbed through the dusk like twin glowing lances.

Know where you're going?

'Five twenty-seven,' Nico replied, pointing with his chin at the black apartment numbers painted on the concrete stops at the front of each parking spot.

Within a minute, he'd weaved up and down the first two aisles.

525 . . . 526 . . . and . . .

Nico hit the brakes, bucking the car to a halt. 527. Wes's apartment number. But the parking spot was empty.

He could still be upstairs.

Nico shook his head. 'He's not upstairs.'

Then we should go up there and wait for him.

'I don't think that's a good idea,' Nico said, still studying the lot. Refusing to give up, he took another pass down the next aisle. His eyes narrowed, and he lowered the windows for a better look. To his ears, the rain on the nearby cars sounded like a ten-year-old letting loose on a drum set.

Weaving up and down each aisle, the Pontiac eventually looped back around to the far side of the lot where they first came in.

D'you even know what kind of car he drives?

Slowing down, Nico shook his head and opened the driver's-side door. 'I'm not looking for his car.'

What're you—?

The Pontiac was barely in park as Nico hopped outside, crossed in front of his own headlights, and squatted down toward the ground. On the asphalt, a matching set of curved tire marks formed identical, partially overlapping Vs just outside a parking spot. Like someone left in a hurry.

Standing up straight, Nico looked over his shoulder, rescanning the full length of the lot. Lamppost by lamppost, aisle by aisle, he took in every piece, including the twenty-foot shrubs that completely circled the whole – No. Not the whole lot. Cocking his head, Nico blinked twice to make sure he was seeing it right.

It was easy to overlook – tucked back between the cars and filled with even more shrubbery, the narrow opening in the shrubs practically disappeared in its own natural camouflage. Fortunately for Nico, he had plenty of training with camouflage.

Nico, you got something?

Nico pulled his gun from his pants, tapping the barrel against the rosary beads on his chest. But as he strode toward the cutaway and into the dog run, all he found were muddy footprints scattered like buckshot, and patches of matted-down grass. At first glance, it looked like there could've been a struggle, but with the rain . . . the muddy runoff from the lot . . . it could've just as easily been nothing.

Undeterred, Nico searched the branches (so many crosses), the bushes, the trunks of each tree. God brought him here. The Lord would provide. He squatted down on his knees, peering under shrubs, swishing his free hand through shallow puddles. There were dog prints and footprints under a few overhanging branches, but most of the ground was already too muddy to read.

Crawling through the flooded grass, Nico felt the mud seeping through the knees of his jeans. His heart plummeted. He didn't understand. God was . . . God was supposed to provide. But as Nico frantically searched . . . as he continued to crawl like a dog, pawing through the mud – the proof . . . where Wes went . . . all of it was gone.

'Please – please stop raining,' Nico pleaded to the now-dark sky.

The drizzle continued, falling like a mist from above.

'Please . . . *stop raining!*' Nico exploded, throwing a fistful of mud and wet grass in the air.

The drizzle continued.

Down on all fours, Nico lowered his head, watching the rosary beads swaying from his neck. How could . . . ? Why would God bring him this far? As the rain ran down his face, Nico climbed to his feet and walked deliberately between the lampposts, back to the parking lot.

His head was still down as he approached the Pontiac. He clutched the rosary, trying to say a prayer, but nothing came out. He tried closing his eyes, but all he could picture was the mess of mud and grass and sticks that covered all tracks. His fist tightened around the rosary, pulling tighter, ever tighter. God promised. He . . . He swore to me – *swore!* – that the devil's door would remain shut – that avenging my mother's death would bring redemption. And now to just abandon me like—

With a sharp crack, the rosary necklace snapped, spilling dozens of wooden beads like marbles down on the asphalt of the parking lot.

'No . . . God – I'm sorry – I'm so sorry!' Nico begged hysterically, scrambling to pick them all up as they bounced, rolled, and scattered in every direction. Diving sideways as he scooped them against his chest, Nico lurched for a stray wooden bead like a five-year-old trying to catch a cricket. But it wasn't until he skidded down on his already-wet knees . . . until the bead hopped, hopped, hopped, and rolled beneath the Pontiac . . . that Nico saw the mushy wet pamphlet stuck to the ground. Just in front of the right front tire.

From the look of it – the top half perfectly flat, the bottom half swollen and soggy from the rain – the pamphlet had already been run over. But even in the moonlight, even with the top half of it flaking away and pancaked from tire treads, Nico could still read the big red-lettered restaurant name at the top of the Chinese menu. And more important, the handwritten note at the bottom.

> *You need to know what else he did. 7 p.m. at Woodlawn.*
> – *Ron*

Ron.
Nico read the name again. And again. The Beast.
Ron.
The letters blurred in front of him. Gently peeling the menu from the asphalt, he could barely stop his hands

from trembling . . . trembling just like his mom's head. Half the menu ripped away as he tugged. He didn't care. Clutching the soggy remains to his chest, Nico looked up at the sky and kissed the fistful of loose rosary beads in his other hand.

'I understand, God. Wes and Boyle – the traitors – together. One final test . . . one last chapter,' Nico whispered to the sky. He began to pray. 'I won't fail you, Mom.'

93

The scratched metal door to the old apartment yawned open, and the stale smell of pipe tobacco swirled across Lisbeth's face.

'The reporter, right?' asked a stubby, sixty-year-old man with brown-tinted glasses, a short-sleeve white button-down, and a pointy, crescent-moon chin. He looked no different than the last time she saw him – except for his forehead, where a jagged oval hunk of skin the size of a campaign button had been sliced from the top of his receding white hairline down to his eyebrows, leaving a lump of fresh pink skin in its place.

'Squamous cell skin cancer,' he blurted. 'Not pretty, I know, but – aheh – at least it didn't reach my skull,' he added with an awkward shrug and laugh.

Eve had warned her about this. Like the comic strip folks and the obituary guys downstairs, every crossword designer could use a few lessons in social graces.

As Lisbeth stepped inside, Martin Kassal followed a bit too closely, trying to hide a small limp while trailing her into the living room, where packed bookshelves clogged every wall. Even the tops of the bookcases were stacked to the ceiling with newspapers, magazines, dictionaries, thesauruses, and full sets of the 1959 and 1972 *Encyclopedia Britannica*. Just past the living room, a small sitting area held a white Formica desk that was yellowed from the sun, a two-person beige love seat buried under newspaper clippings, and a freestanding chalkboard that was framed with at least fifty diamond-shaped, suction-cup Baby on Board signs: *Student Driver on Board, Twins on Board, Marlins Fan on Board, Gun Owner on Board, Mother-in-Law in Trunk, Michigan Dad on Board, Nobody on Board,* a bright pink *Princess on Board,* and of course, a black and white *Crossword Lover on Board,* where the *o*'s in *Crossword* and *Lover* intersected.

'June 1992,' Kassal beamed, his moon-chin rising. 'We did a scavenger hunt for the weekend section. Impossible stuff: an old pull tab from a soda can, a baseball card with a player not wearing a baseball cap, and *these,*' he said, pointing to the Baby on Board collection. 'Anything but *BABY on Board.*'

Nodding politely, Lisbeth looked past the suction-cup signs and focused on the actual blackboard, which held an oversize hand-drawn grid. The top half of the grid was filled with words and darkened boxes; the bottom half was almost completely blank.

'You still design them by hand?' she asked.

'Instead of what, some computer program that'll do all the work for me? No offense, but – aheh – I'm obsolete enough as it is. Last thing I need to do is wave the white flag and bury myself, if that makes sense.'

'Perfect sense,' Lisbeth agreed, staring down at the two crossword puzzles in her hand.

'So those the puzzles you were talking about?' Kassal asked, raising his nose and peering through the reading half of his tinted bifocals. As Lisbeth handed him the crosswords, he scanned the top one for a moment. 'Fifty-six across should be *taser,* not *tasks.*'

'It's not the puzzle that's the problem,' Lisbeth pointed out. 'It's the symbols on the side.'

Following Lisbeth's finger to the side of the puzzle, Kassal studied each symbol: the handwritten ⸪, 0, ⚥, and ⸏.

'Sure it's not just doodling?'

'We thought the same – until we found *this*,' she explains, flipping to the crossword Violet gave her.

'Aheh,' Kassal said with his wimpish little laugh. 'Clever buggers. Their own little message.'

'See, but that's the thing. I don't think they made it up themselves . . .'

Already lost in the game, Kassal whispered to himself. 'If the four dots represent the letter *D* as the fourth letter, and the two dots stand for *B* . . . No, no – it's not a cryptogram – not enough symbols for letters. Not an anagram either.' Looking over the tops of his glasses at Lisbeth, he added, 'They could be weather symbols . . . maybe Navajo signs. Who'd you say drew this again?'

'Just a friend.'

'But is it a clever friend, a dumb friend, a—?'

'Clever. Really clever. Head-of-the-class clever.'

'And what do you need it for again?'

'Just . . . y'know . . . just for fun.'

Kassal stared at her, picking her apart like she was the crossword. 'This isn't going to get me in trouble, is it?'

'Sir, the guys in comics – they said you were the best at deciphering these kinds of things.'

'Now you're trying to flatter me, dearie.'

'No, that's not—'

'It's okay. These days, I don't get flattered too often by pretty young redheads. I miss it.' Hobbling over to the yellowed Formica desk, Kassal pulled out a legal pad and copied the symbols one by one.

'So you'll help?' Lisbeth asked.

'Less talking – more working,' he said, once again engrossed in the puzzle.

Lisbeth moved behind him, barely able to hide her excitement.

'Let's start with the four-dot sign you have here,' he said, pointing to the ⁞⁞ . 'If you draw a vertical line down the middle of it, like this:

'. . . and a horizontal line like this:

'. . . the symbol is the same on both sides' of the line, which means this sign is multi-axis symmetric.'

'And that matters *why*?' Lisbeth asked.

'Ever try to look up a symbol in a dictionary? *Four-dots-in-a-square* isn't filed under *F.* But the same way every puzzle has a solution, every symbol has its own classification, which breaks down into four distinct subgroups: First, whether it's symmetrical or not. Second, whether it's *closed* like a triangle or *open* like your four dots here. Third, are its lines straight or curved? And fourth, does the symbol have lines that cross, which opens up a whole new religious can of tuna.'

'And when you answer those questions?'

'When you answer those,' Kassal said, limping to his bookcases and pulling thick, phone-book-sized texts from his shelves, 'then you go to the references.' With a thud, he dumped the pile of books on his desk. *Elsevier's Dictionary of Symbols and Imagery, Encyclopedia of Traditional Symbols, Franken's Guide to Religious Images, The*

Visual Almanac of Occult Signs, *Passer's Handbook of Native American Symbols* . . .

'This is gonna take some time, isn't it?' Lisbeth asked, flipping open one of the books to a section titled *Multi-Axis, Closed, Soft Elements, Crossing Lines*. The open pages contained four encyclopedia entries for ∞ (including its denotations in mathematics, genealogy, and botany) and six listings for ⊗, ◍, and various other over-lapping circles.

'Of course, it'll take time,' Kassal replied, already cata-loging the other symbols from the crossword. 'Why? You got someplace t—'

Lisbeth's cell phone erupted with a high-pitched ring. Flipping it open, she was about to pick up, then caught herself when she saw caller ID.

'Bad news?' Kassal asked, reading her reaction.

'No, just – not at all,' she insisted as the phone rang again.

'You say so,' Kassal replied with a shrug. 'Though in my experience, looks like that are reserved for two people: bosses and boyfriends.'

'Yeah, well . . . this one's a whole different problem.' But as the phone rang for the third time, Lisbeth couldn't ignore the fact that even though her notepad was sticking out of her purse, she wasn't reaching for it. Of course, that didn't mean it was easy for her. But after nearly a decade of trying to turn four-inch stories into front-page headlines, well . . . some things were more important than the front page. Finally picking up, she asked, 'Wes? That you?'

'Yeah,' he replied, sounding even worse than when they watched the video of the shooting.

'Everything okay?'

'I-I don't think so.'

Hearing the pain in Wes's voice, Lisbeth turned back to Kassal.

'Go,' the old man told her, readjusting his bifocals. 'I'll call you as soon as I find something.'

'Are you—?'

'Go,' he insisted, trying to sound annoyed. 'Young redheads are just a distraction anyway.'

Nodding a thank-you and scribbling her number on a Post-it for him, Lisbeth ran for the door. Turning back to her cell, she asked Wes, 'How can I help?'

On the other end, Wes finally exhaled. Lisbeth couldn't tell if it was relief or excitement.

'That depends,' he replied. 'How fast can you get to Woodlawn?'

'Woodlawn Cemetery? Why there?'

'That's where Boyle asked to meet. Seven p.m. At his grave.'

94

Fighting traffic for nearly an hour, Rogo veered to the right, zipping off the highway at the exit for Griffin Road in Fort Lauderdale.

'Y'know, for a guy who deals with traffic tickets every single day,' Dreidel said, gripping the inside door handle for support, 'you think you'd appreciate safe driving a bit more.'

'If I get a ticket, I'll get us off,' Rogo said coldly, jabbing the gas and going even faster down the dark off-ramp. Wes had enough of a head start. Priority now was finding why Boyle was seeing Dr. Eng – in Florida – the week before the shooting.

'There's no way he'll even be there,' Dreidel said, looking down at his watch. 'I mean, name one doctor who works past five o'clock,' he added with a nervous laugh.

'Stop talking, okay? We're almost there.'

With a sharp left that took them under the overpass of I-95, the blue Toyota headed west on Griffin, past a string of check-cashing stores, two thrift shops, and an adult video store called AAA to XXX.

'Great neighborhood,' Rogo pointed out as they passed the bright neon purple and green sign for the Fantasy Lounge.

'It's not that ba—'

Directly above them, a thunderous rumble ripped

through the sky as a red and white 747 whizzed overhead, coming in for a landing at Fort Lauderdale Airport, which, judging from the height of the plane, was barely a mile behind them.

'Maybe Dr. Eng just likes cheap rents,' Dreidel said as Rogo reread the address from the entry in Boyle's old calendar.

'If we're lucky, you'll be able to ask him personally,' Rogo said, pointing out the front windshield. Directly ahead, just past a funeral home, bright lights lit up a narrow office park and its modern four-story white building with frosted-glass doors and windows. Along the upper half of the building, a thin yellow horizontal stripe ran just below the roofline.

2678 Griffin Road.

95

During the first year, Ron Boyle was scared. Shuttling from country to country . . . the nose contouring and cheek implants . . . even the accent modification that never really worked. The men in Dr. Eng's office said it'd keep him safe, make his trail impossible to follow. But that didn't stop him from bolting upright in his bed every time he heard a car door slam outside his motel or villa or pensione. The worst was when a spray of firecrackers exploded outside a nearby cathedral – a wedding tradition in Valencia, Spain. Naturally, Boyle knew it wouldn't be easy – hiding away, leaving friends, family . . . especially family – but he knew what was at stake. And in the end, when he finally came back, it'd all be worth it. From there, the rationalizations were easy. Unlike his father, he was tackling his problems head-on. And as he closed his eyes at night, he knew no one could blame him for that.

By year two, as he adjusted to life in Spain, isolation hit far harder than his accountant brain had calculated. Unlike his old friend Manning, when Boyle left the White House, he never suffered from spotlight starvation. But the loneliness . . . not so much for his wife (his marriage was finished years ago), but on his daughter's sixteenth birthday, as he pictured her gushing, no-more-braces smile in her brand-new driver's license photo – those were the days of regret. Days that Leland Manning would answer for.

In year three, he'd grown accustomed to all the tricks Dr. Eng's office taught him: walking down the street with his head down, double-checking doors after he entered a building, even being careful not to leave big tips so he wouldn't be remembered by waiters or staff. So accustomed, in fact, that he made his first mistake: making small talk with a local ex-pat as they both sipped *horchatas* in a local bodega. Boyle knew the instant the man took a double take that he was an Agency man. Panicking, but smart enough to stay and finish the drink, Boyle went straight home, frantically packed two suitcases, and left Valencia that evening.

In December of that same year, the *New Yorker* commissioned a feature article about Univar 'Blackbird' computers showing up in the governments of Iran, Syria, Burma, and Sudan. As terrorist nations unable to import from the United States, the countries bought their computers from a shady supplier in the Middle East. But what the countries didn't know was that Univar was a front company for the National Security Agency and that six months after the computers were in the terrorist countries' possession, they slowly broke down while simultaneously forwarding their entire hard drives straight to the NSA – hence the *Blackbird* codename – as the info flew the coop.

But as the research for the *New Yorker* article pointed out, during the Manning administration, one Blackbird computer from Sudan didn't forward its hard drive to the NSA. And when the others did, the remaining Blackbird was removed from the country, eventually making its way to the black market. The informant who held it wanted a six-million-dollar ransom from the United States for its return. But Manning's staff, worried it was a scam, refused to pay. Two weeks before the *New Yorker* story was to be handed in, Patrick Gould, the author of the article, died from a sudden ruptured brain aneurysm. The autopsy ruled out foul play.

By year four, Boyle was well hidden in a small town outside London, in a flat tucked just above a local wedding cake bakery. And while the smell of fresh hazelnut and vanilla greeted him every morning, frustration and regret slowly buried Boyle's fear. It was only compounded when the Manning Presidential Library was two months behind its scheduled opening, making his search for papers, documents, and proof that much harder to come by. Still, that didn't mean there was nothing for him to dig through. Books, magazines, and newspaper profiles had been written about Nico, and the end of Manning's presidency, and the attack. With each one, as Boyle relived the sixty-three seconds of the speedway shooting, the fear returned, churning through his chest and the scarred palm of his hand. Not just because of the ferocity of the attack, or even the almost military efficiency of it, but because of the gall: at the speedway, on live television, in front of millions of people. If The Three wanted Boyle dead, they could've waited outside his Virginia home and slit his throat or forced a 'brain aneurysm.' To take him down at the speedway, to do it in front of all those witnesses . . . risks that big were only worth taking if there was some kind of added benefit.

Year four was also when Boyle started writing his letters. To his daughter. His friends. Even to his old enemies, including the few who missed his funeral. Asking questions, telling stories, anything to feel that connection to his real life, his former life. He got the idea from a biography of President Harry Truman, who used to write scathing letters to his detractors. Like Truman, Boyle wrote hundreds of them. Like Truman, he didn't mail them.

In year five, Boyle's wife remarried. His daughter started college at Columbia on a scholarship named after her dead father. Neither broke Boyle's heart. But they certainly jabbed a spike in his spirit. Soon after, as he'd been doing since year one, Boyle found himself in an Internet café, checking airfares back to the States. A few times, he'd even made a reservation. He'd long ago worked out how he'd get in touch, how he'd contact his daughter, how he'd sneak away – even from those he knew were always watching. That's when the consequences would slap him awake. The Three . . . The Four . . . whatever they called themselves, had already – Boyle couldn't even think about it. He wasn't risking it again. Instead, as the Manning Presidential Library threw its doors open, Boyle threw himself into the paperwork of his own past, mailing off his requests and searching and scavenging for anything to prove what his gut had been telling him for years.

By year six, he was ankle-deep in photocopies and old White House files. Dr. Eng's people offered to help, but Boyle was six years past naive. In the world of Eng, the only priority was Eng, which was why, when Manning had him introduced to Dr. Eng's group all those years ago, Boyle told them about The Three, and their offer to make him The Fourth, and the threats that went along with it. But what he never mentioned – not to anyone – was what The Three had already stolen. And what Boyle was determined to get back.

He'd finally gotten his chance eleven days ago, on a muddy, rainy afternoon in the final month of year seven. Huddled under the awning as he stepped out of the post office on Balham High Road, Boyle flipped through the

newly processed releases from Manning's personal handwriting file. Among the highlights were a note to the
governor of Kentucky, some handwritten notes for a
speech in Ohio, and a torn scrap from the *Washington Post*
comics section that had a few scribbled names on one
side . . . and a mostly completed crossword puzzle on the
other.

At first, Boyle almost tossed it aside. Then he remembered that day at the racetrack, in the back of the limo,
Manning and his chief of staff were working a crossword.
In fact, now that he thought about it, they were *always*
working a crossword. Staring down at the puzzle, Boyle
felt like there were thin metal straps constricting his rib
cage. His teeth picked at his bottom lip as he studied the
two distinct handwritings. Manning's and Albright's. But
when he saw the random doodles along the side of the
puzzle, he held his breath, almost biting through his own
skin. In the work space . . . the initials . . . were those—?
Boyle checked and rechecked again, circling them with a
pen.

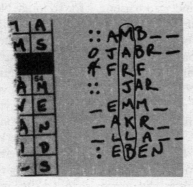

Those weren't just senior staff. With Dreidel and Moss and Kutz – those were the people getting the President's Daily Briefing, the one document The Three asked him for access to.

It took three days to crack the rest: two with a symbols expert at Oxford University, half a day with an art history professor, then a fifteen-minute consultation with their Modern History Research Unit, most specifically, Professor Jacqui Moriceau, whose specialty was the Federalist period, specifically Thomas Jefferson.

She recognized it instantly. The four dots . . . the slashed cross . . . even the short horizontal dashes. There they were. Exactly as Thomas Jefferson had intended.

As Professor Moriceau relayed the rest, Boyle waited for his eyes to flood, for his chin to rise with the relief of a seemingly lifelong mission complete. But as he held the crossword in his open palm . . . as he slowly realized what Leland Manning was really up to . . . his arms, his legs, his fingertips, even his toes went brittle and numb, as if his whole body were a hollowed-out eggshell. God, how could he be so blind – so trusting – for so long? Now he had to see Manning. Had to ask him to his face. Sure, he'd unlocked the puzzle, but it wasn't a victory. After eight years, dozens of missed birthdays, seven missed Christmases, six countries, two surgeries, a prom, a high school graduation, and a college acceptance, there would never be victory.

But that didn't mean there couldn't be revenge.

Fifteen minutes south of Palm Beach, Ron Boyle pulled to the side of the highway and steered the beat-up white van to the far corner of a dead-empty emergency rest stop. Without even thinking about it, he angled just behind a crush of ratty, overgrown shrubs. After eight years, he had a PhD in disappearing.

Behind him, sprawled along the van's unlined metal floor, O'Shea shuddered and moaned, finally waking up. Boyle wasn't worried. Or scared. Or even excited. In fact, it'd been weeks since he felt much of anything beyond the ache of his own regrets.

On the floor, with his arms still tied behind his back, O'Shea scootched on his knees, his chin, his elbows, slowly and sluggishly fighting to sit up. With each movement, his shoulder twitched and jumped. His hair was a sopping mess of rain and sweat. His once-white shirt was damp with dark red blood. Eventually writhing his way to a kneeling position, he was trying to look strong, but Boyle could see in the grayish coloring of his face that the pain was taking its toll. O'Shea blinked twice to get his bearings.

That's when O'Shea heard the metallic click.

Crouching in the back of the van, Boyle leaned forward, pressed his pistol deep into O'Shea's temple, and said the words that had been haunting him for the better part of a decade:

'Where the fuck's my son?'

96

'Can I help you?' a deep voice crackled from the intercom as the man pulled his car up to the closed wooden security gate.

Refusing to answer, the driver pulled his ID from his jacket pocket and shoved it toward the hidden camera stuffed into the tall shrubs.

The intercom went silent. Moments later, a metallic click released the magnetic lock, and the security gate swung open.

Slowly easing his foot against the gas, the man inched the car up the private brick driveway, where three suit-and-tie Secret Service agents turned and stared. When they didn't approach his car, he knew they were getting the news of his arrival in their earpieces. And by the looks on their faces, they were unnerved by it. No one likes when the boss comes to check on things. But with Nico on the loose, they weren't the least bit surprised.

With a tug to the left, he steered his car between the matching black Chevy Suburbans, then readjusted his leather shoulder holster and made sure the strap that held his gun in place was unsnapped. This wasn't like his trip to the office. With the principals here, he needed to be ready. And if the reports were true – that a neighbor had already found Kenny's and Micah's bodies and that finger-prints were already making the rounds – well, this was now about much more than seventy million dollars in payouts and four more years in office.

It was so much easier back when they started. After War College, they spent the first six months doing nothing but running simulations and war-gaming. No need to rush. Better to make it a science. Take no chances, make no contact, and make sure nothing's traced back. Of course, the key to that was creating The Roman, right down to the stolen thumb they snatched from a Tanzania morgue to use with the fingerprint cards required for every informant payout. From there, people would just be chasing a ghost. Once The Roman was 'real,' the true work began.

It was Micah who struck gold first. As a CIA case officer stationed in Khartoum, he received a tip about someone in the Sudanese security agency trying to sell eleven pristine U.S. visas – all of them sterile and untraceable – to al-Zaydi, a known terrorist organization. According to Micah's source, al-Zaydi was paying with its usual mode of untraceable African diamonds – $500,000 worth, which would be delivered in Taormina, Sicily, on October 15.

That morning, to communicate with his fellow members, Micah left piecemeal coded messages in the agreed-upon online chat rooms. Then he wrote up his full official report, which detailed only *one* of the facts – that the Sudanese security agency was rumored to be selling eleven visas. He intentionally left out the rest. That afternoon, O'Shea – in his position as an FBI Legat in Brussels assigned to working with foreign law enforcement officials – took full advantage of the info Micah had sent about the diamonds. Now knowing what to look for, and reaching out to overseas security agencies, he combed through foreign customs reports, eventually finding a

suspected al-Zaydi member traveling through Italy – legally
– with nearly $500,000 of diamond jewelry. That night,
Secret Service Agent Roland Egen – as the resident agent
in charge of the Service's office in Pretoria, South Africa
– put the cherry on top. Calling up his supervisor in the
Rome office, he said, 'I've got a source bragging about
black market U.S. visas for sale – and that he'll give us
the time and place for the drop.'

'What kinda payoff does he want?' the supervisor had
asked.

'Fifty thousand dollars.'

There was a short pause. 'Who's the source?'

'He calls himself The Roman,' Egen said with a grin.

Within minutes, the Service started vetting the tip.
Throughout the community, they called it backstopping
– checking with other agencies to corroborate the source.
After Iraq, it was a necessity. And after the information-
sharing from 9/11, the info came quick. Thanks to O'Shea,
the FBI showed a similar report. Thanks to Micah, so did
the CIA. All three pieces corroborating the same picture.

'Pay it,' Egen's supervisor said.

Twenty-four hours later, Micah, O'Shea, and The
Roman – by simply corroborating one another – split their
first $50,000 payout. Not a bad day's work.

Years ago, it was easier. But that was before they invited
others to join in the game.

'Welcome, sir,' a brown-haired agent called out as the
man left the car and marched toward the pale blue Colonial with the American flag above the door.

Halfway there, a fourth suit-and-tie agent approached
from the front steps.

Well aware of the protocol, the man again handed over
his ID, waiting for it to be looked at.

'Sorry, sir . . . I didn't . . . You're here to see the President?' the agent asked, anxiously handing the ID back.

'Yeah,' The Roman replied as he stepped inside the President's home. 'Something like that.'

97

'Wanna try that one again?' Boyle growled in the back of the van as he dug the barrel of his gun into O'Shea's temple.

'You can demand all you want, it's the truth,' O'Shea said, spitting up blood and contorted by the lightning bolt of pain coursing through his shoulder. As he kneeled in the van, his voice was purposely soft. Boyle shook his head, knowing it was just a trick to bring his own volume down. O'Shea still pushed on. 'I know this is emotional for you, Boyle, but you need t—'

'Where the hell's my son!?' Boyle exploded, shoving the gun so hard against O'Shea's head, it sent O'Shea backward like a turtle on his shell. But even as he worked his way back to his knees, O'Shea didn't thrash, panic, or fight. Boyle couldn't tell if it was exhaustion or strategy. The only thing he knew was that, like a wounded leopard still locked on its prey, O'Shea never took his eyes off Boyle's gun.

Eight years ago, Boyle's hands would've been shaking. Today, he was perfectly still. 'Tell me where he is, O'Shea.'

'Why, so you can wait outside his school – what is he, nine, ten years old now? – so you can wait outside his fourth-grade class and tell him you want visitation rights? You think your girlfriend Tawana—'

'Her name's Tiana.'

'Call her what you want, she told us the story, Boyle – how you flirted during the campaign, how she followed you to D.C.—'

'I never asked her to do that.'

'—but you didn't have any problem hiding her from your wife and daughter for almost four years. And then when she got pregnant – darn! – better do something about that.'

'I never asked her to get an abortion.'

'Oh, I'm sorry – I didn't realize you were a saint.' In the distance, a pack of cars whipped past them on the highway. O'Shea curled downward and lowered his head for a moment, yielding to the pain. 'C'mon, Boyle,' he stuttered as he looked back up, 'you hid the kid from the entire world – insisted that they never approach you in public – and *now* you suddenly wanna take him to the father-son White House picnic?'

'He's still my son.'

'Then you should've taken care of him.'

'I did take care of him!'

'No, *we* took care of him,' O'Shea insisted. 'What you did was send fifty bucks a week, hoping it would buy food, diapers, and her silence. We're the ones who gave her – and him – a true future.'

Boyle shook his head, already agitated. 'Is that how The Roman sold it to you? That you were giving them a future?'

'She needed cash; we offered it.'

'Or, more accurately: You paid her to hide, then refused to tell me where they were unless I agreed to be your fourth turncoat,' Boyle said, his voice now booming. 'So don't make it look like you were *doing her any favors*!'

Pressing his chin down against his shoulder, O'Shea looked up from the floor, his hazel eyes glowing in the darkness of the van. A slow grin rose like a sunrise on his face. 'Boy, we really picked the right push button, didn't we? To be honest, when The Roman said you cared for her, I thought he was full of crap.'

Boyle aimed the gun at O'Shea's face. 'Where are they? I'm not asking you agai—'

Leaning back on his knees, O'Shea erupted with a deep rumbling laugh that catapulted from his throat and echoed through the van. 'C'mon, you really think we kept track after all this time? That somehow we kept them as pen pals?'

As the words left O'Shea's lips, Boyle could feel each syllable clawing straight through his belly, shredding every organ inside his chest. 'Wh-What're you talking about?'

'We killed you, jackass. Or at least that's what we thought. For all I cared, from that moment on, Tiana and her little bastard could've moved right back to that dump where we found them in D.C.'

Hunched over, Boyle took a half-step back. His hand started to shake.

'Wait . . . oh, you . . . wait,' O'Shea said, already chuckling. 'You're telling me that in all the time you spent trying to track us down, that . . . that you never once considered the possibility that we wouldn't know where they are?'

For the second time, O'Shea leaned back for a loud bellowing laugh. Then, without warning, he sprang forward, like a frog, with a ramming headbutt that plowed into Boyle's chin before he even saw it coming. On impact, Boyle's head whipped back, sending him crashing into the bucket seats.

'You feel that?!' O'Shea screamed, his eyes wide with rage. 'This time I'll kill you myself!'

Boyle shook his head no. Slow at first. Then faster.

O'Shea charged forward like a truck. Boyle was already in mid-swing, lashing out with his right hand. And the gun he was still holding in it.

In a blur, the butt of the pistol slammed O'Shea like a ten-pound weight to the head. Colliding with the corner of his brow, it sent him tumbling sideways toward the wall behind the passenger seat. With his hands still tied behind his back, he didn't have a chance. Already off balance, he turned just enough to hit the metal wall shoulder-first.

'That's for my son,' Boyle snarled, buzzing with adrenaline.

O'Shea sank to the floor of the van. Boyle didn't let up, rushing in and pressing the barrel of his gun against O'Shea's forehead. 'And this one's for my daughter, you thieving piece of shit!'

Boyle cocked the gun's pin and started squeezing the trigger.

O'Shea erupted with another haunting laugh. 'Do it,' he demanded, his voice breathless and raw as he lay there, sprawled on his back. His chest rose and fell rapidly as his body twisted on the floor. Between the bullet wounds from the dog run and his current impact, the pain was overwhelming. 'With these metal walls . . . go ahead . . . I-I'd love to see you risk the ricochet.'

Boyle glanced around at the walls of the van. 'It won't ricochet,' he insisted.

'You sure about that?' O'Shea gasped, fighting for air and kicking his heel against the metal floor. There was a loud deep thud. 'Sounds . . . sounds pretty damn solid to me.'

Boyle didn't respond. His hand twitched slightly as he tightened his grip on the trigger.

'That's . . . it's a frightening thought, isn't it?' O'Shea

asked. 'Here you are all ready to wreck the few remaining shards of your life by becoming a killer, and . . . and now you have to worry if you'll shoot yourself in the process.'

Boyle knew he was lying. He had to be.

'C'mon, Boyle – here's your chance to blow my head off. Take your shot!' Defiantly, O'Shea leaned forward, pressing his forehead even harder against the gun.

Boyle's finger rattled against the trigger as a dribble of blood ran from his nose to his top lip. This was it. The moment he'd begged for . . . prayed for . . . the revenge that had fueled him all these years. The problem was, O'Shea was still right about one thing: Whatever else they'd taken from him, whatever cold shell of himself they turned him into, he'd never be a killer. Though that didn't mean he couldn't have his vengeance.

Shifting his arm to the right, Boyle pointed the barrel at O'Shea's still-seeping shoulder wound and pulled the trigger. A single bullet tore through O'Shea's shoulder, taking another chunk of meat with it. To maximize the pain, Boyle kept the gun at an angle, hoping to hit some bone as well. From O'Shea's scream – which faded into a silent breathless gasp as his eyes rolled back and he finally lost consciousness – it was more than enough to do the trick.

Kicking O'Shea onto his side, Boyle knelt down to the splatter of blood on the floor. Underneath the mess, through the metal floor of the van, was a small jagged bullet hole. Sticking a finger in and feeling the musty air outside, Boyle shook his head. Of course, it wouldn't ricochet. Only the President's limo is bulletproof.

Wasting no time, Boyle ducked into the front of the van and wriggled into the driver's seat. Far to his left, another swarm of cars buzzed by on the highway. As he looked down, the digital clock on the dashboard said it was 6:57 p.m. Perfect, he thought as he punched the gas, spun the wheels, and sent bits of gravel chainsawing through the air. One more stop and it'd all be done.

98

'Haven't these people ever heard of a parking lot?' Rogo asked as he drove past the landscaping by the frosted-glass entrance and veered around to the back of the white office building.

'*There,*' Dreidel pointed out as they turned the corner. Around back, a wide lot was dotted with eight or ten cars.

'That's a good sign, right? People still working?'

'Unless it's just janitorial staff,' Dreidel said, eyeing the building through the passenger window.

'How many janitors you know drive brand-new Mustangs?' Rogo asked, parking next to a shiny black convertible Ford Mustang. 'The only thing I can't figure out is why they have all that space in the front of the building and instead put the parking lot around back?'

'Maybe it's a zoning issue.'

'Yeah, maybe,' Rogo said.

'What, you still think it's some kinda mob doctor?'

'All I know is, they're about a block away from the Bada-Bing and the porn shop, there's a funeral home next door, and that Mustang has a personalized license plate that says *Fredo.*'

Dreidel glanced down at the license plate, which read *MY STANG*. 'Will you please stop? It's a doctor's office, Rogo. You can tell it from here.'

'Well, color me a stickler, but I'd still prefer to see it

for myself,' Rogo added, flicking the car door open, hopping out into the drizzling rain, and running for the back door of the building. Halfway there, he looked straight up as a soft high-pitched whistle exploded into a deafening, rumbling earthquake. Another 747 coming in for a landing. Behind him, he noticed that Dreidel was at least ten steps behind.

Rogo finally reached two sliding frosted-glass doors that were almost identical to the entrance in front. Stepping onto the pressure mat, he waited for the doors to slide open. They didn't move.

'Anybody home?' Rogo announced, knocking on the frosted glass, then pressing his face against it, trying to peer inside. Diagonally up on his right, a pinprick of red light revealed a shiny black security camera that was as thin as a calculator with a tiny round lens no bigger than a dime. Rogo turned away, too smart to stare. No way was a doctor's office spending money on high-end tech like that.

'Don't look up,' Rogo whispered as Dreidel stepped next to him.

'You sure no one's—?'

Rogo raised a knuckle to knock again, but before he could tap the glass, the doors slid open, revealing an annoyed security guard with stringy brown hair and a close-cropped mustache.

'Can I help you?' he asked, looking at Dreidel, then Rogo, then back at Dreidel.

'Yeah, we're looking for Dr. Eng,' Rogo said, trying to step inside. The guard stepped in front of him, cutting him off, but Rogo kept going, his short meatball build ducking quickly under the guard's arm and into the salmon-colored marble lobby.

'Sorry . . . it's just . . . it's raining,' Rogo said, pointing outside and flicking excess water from his hands.

The guard didn't say a word, still staring at Dreidel. Rogo noticed that the guard was armed with a 9mm pistol in his belt.

'Anyway,' Dreidel interrupted, 'we're here to see Dr. Eng.'

'Sorry, he left already,' the guard shot back.

'That's fine – if we could just see his office assistant.'

'Dr. Eng is gone. His office is closed for the day.'

Up the hallway, Rogo spotted a tenant directory on the wall next to the elevators. 'Listen, if we came at a bad time, I apologize, but can I just ask one favor?' Rogo pleaded. 'I've been driving for over an hour in tear-your-hair-out traffic. We'll get out of your way – we'll call Dr. Eng tomorrow – but first, can I *please* just use your bathroom? We're talking real emergency here.'

The guard stared at him, unmoving.

'Please,' Rogo pleaded, doing an anxious shuffle with his feet. 'If I wait any longer—'

'Men's room is past the elevators on the left-hand side,' the guard said, pointing up the hall.

'My bladder thanks you,' Rogo said, taking off.

Dreidel took a step to follow behind him. The guard shot him a look, and Dreidel stopped.

'We'll . . . I'll just wait here,' Dreidel decided.

'Great idea,' the guard said.

Without looking back, Rogo cruised up the hallway, which, like the outside of the building, was worn and weary: cracked marble along the floor, cheap art deco light fixtures overhead, and eighties-era aqua and sea-foam modern art paintings on the wall. Brushing past it all, Rogo focused on the office directory next to the elevators.

'Did I pass it yet?' he called back to the guard as he stopped in front of the directory's gold metal frame. Skimming the alphabetical list, he saw:

Eng, Dr. Brian – – Suite 127

But to Rogo's surprise, it didn't list the type of practice or even a business name. Same with every other doctor in the directory. Six in total, but not a single one included their practice.

'Next door down,' the security guard called back. 'On the left.'

Waving his thanks, Rogo ducked into the small restroom, which greeted him with the sharp reek of bleach. Knowing he had to take some time before rushing out, he walked to the sink, hit the lever on the dispenser for a few paper towels, and wiped the rest of the rain from his face. He looked in the mirror to make sure he got it all. That's when he noticed the oak door behind him, just over his shoulder.

Turning back, he studied it carefully. To anyone else, it was nothing more than a storage closet. And to him, on any other day, it would be too. But tonight . . . with everything going on . . . Rogo glanced to his left. There was already a narrow door with the word *Storage* stenciled on it.

Stepping toward the oak door, Rogo gave the doorknob a twist. Locked.

Quick as he could, he glanced around the restroom – the stalls, the urinals, the garbage can in the corner – searching for – *there*.

Next to the sink, Rogo rushed for the paper towel dispenser, slamming the lever as hard as he could. A single paper towel stuck its tongue out. Perfect, Rogo decided, pulling the plastic case off the dispenser and leaving just the lever and the exposed paper towels. He hit the gray plastic lever again, but this time, didn't let go of it, gripping as tight as he could with his fingertips, leaning in with his chest, and putting his full weight against it.

Within seconds, he could hear the damage. There was a loud plastic pop as the dispenser started to crack. Rogo held on, standing on his tiptoes and lifting one foot off the ground to increase the weight. Another pop pierced the air. Almost there. Rogo didn't let up, gritting his teeth and breathing hard through his nose. Don't let go . . . not until . . . With a final short hop, he picked his other foot off the ground. That was it. Plastic shattered with a crack as the boomerang-shaped metal lever snapped free through the bottom of the dispenser. Rogo crashed to the tile floor, and a grin took his face.

As he climbed to his feet, he examined the metal lever, turning the boomerang sideways. Definitely thin enough. Lunging for the oak door, but trying to keep quiet, he slid the boomerang-shaped sliver of metal into the narrow gap between the angled latch and the door's threshold. His forehead and nose were pressed against the door seam as he peered downward and pulled the boomerang toward his belly. Like a child fishing for coins through a sewer grate, he wiggled his hand, trying to jigger the lever against the door's latch. Slowly, the latch started to giv—

Click.

With a frantic tug, he pulled the oak door open. Rogo craned his neck to look inside. 'Hello?' he whispered.

Inside, it was dark, but as the light from the bathroom flooded forward, it was clear this wasn't a little storage closet. The room was deep, almost as big as his and Wes's living room. And as Rogo stepped forward – as he saw what was inside – his eyes widened. It didn't make sense. Why would they—?

'What the hell you think you're doing?' a deep voice asked from the bathroom door.

Rogo spun around just in time to see the security guard coming at him.

99

I know where Boyle's grave is. I've been there before.

The first time was after my sixth and final surgery – the one where they tried to dig the last bits of metal shrapnel from my cheek. Fifteen minutes into it, the doctor decided the pieces were too deep – and far too small, like steel grains of sand – so better to leave them where they are. 'Lay it to rest,' Dr. Levy told me.

Taking his advice, I left the hospital and had my mom drive me here, to Woodlawn Cemetery. Seven months after Boyle was buried on national television, I approached his grave with my right hand stuffed deep in my pants pocket, clutching my newest prescription and silently, repetitively apologizing for putting him in the limo that day. I could hear my mother sobbing behind me, mourning me like I wasn't even there. It was one of the toughest visits of my life. To my own surprise, this one's tougher.

'Stop thinking about it,' Lisbeth whispers, plowing through the unmowed, shin-high grass that wraps like tiny bullwhips around our ankles. As we approach the chain-link fence behind the back of the cemetery, I try to hold the umbrella over both of us, but she's already two steps ahead, not even noticing the light rain. I don't blame her for being excited. Even if she's not writing the story, the reporter in her can't wait to get the truth. 'Y'hear what I said, Wes?'

When I don't answer, she stops and spins back to face me. She's about to say something; most likely, *Calm down . . . take it easy.*

'I know it's hard for you,' she offers. 'I'm sorry.'

I nod and thank her with a glimpse of eye contact. 'To be honest, I didn't think it'd be – I thought I'd be more eager.'

'It's okay to be scared, Wes.'

'It's not scared – believe me, I *want* Boyle's answers – but just being here . . . where they buried – where they buried whatever they buried. It's like a – it's not the best place for me.'

I look up, and she steps toward me, back under the umbrella. 'I'm still glad you let me come.'

I smile.

'C'mon, I got a good vibe,' she says, tugging my shoulder as she sprints back out from under the umbrella. Gripping the top of the four-foot-tall chain-link fence, she stabs her toe into one of the openings.

'Don't bother,' I reply, motioning to a mound of dirt that's piled so high it buries the fence and leads right inside. Despite the pep talk, I still hesitate. That's extra dirt from the graves. Lisbeth has no such problem. Ignoring the rain, which is still a light drizzle, she's up the small mound and over the fence in an instant.

'Careful,' I call out. 'If there's an alarm—'

'It's a cemetery, Wes. I don't think they're worried about people stealing.'

'What about grave rob—?' But as I follow her over the dirt mound, we're met with nothing but the soft buzz of crickets and the thick black shadows of two-hundred-year-old banyan trees, whose branches and tendrils stretch out like spiderwebs in every direction. Diagonally to our left, the eighteen acres of Woodlawn Cemetery expand in a perfect rectangle that measures over seventeen football fields. The cemetery eventually dead-ends, with no apparent irony, at the back of the Jaguar dealership, which probably wasn't the intention in the late 1800s when city founder Henry Flagler plowed over seventeen acres of pineapple groves to build West Palm Beach's oldest and most lavish cemetery.

I take off for the main stone-paved path. Grabbing the umbrella, Lisbeth pulls me back and leads us to our left, behind a tall meatball-shaped shrub just inside the back fence. As we get closer, I spot another huge meatball next to it, then another, then another . . . at least a hundred in total, ten feet tall . . . the row of them lining the entire back length of the graveyard. Her instinct's perfect. By staying back here, we're off the main path, meaning we're out of sight, meaning no one can see us coming. With what we've got planned, we're not taking chances.

As we duck behind the first meatball shrub, we quickly see it's not a meatball at all. Hollowed out from the back and shaped like a *U*, the shrub hides a collection of empty Gatorade bottles and soda cans scattered along the ground. The shrub next to it contains a folded-up piece of Astro-turf that they use to cover open graves.

'Wes, these are perfect for—'

'No question,' I say, finally getting caught up in her excitement. Still, that doesn't mean I'm putting her at risk. Checking to make sure we're alone, I turn left, toward the center of the lot, where a glowing white flagpole is lit up by floodlights and serves as the graveyard's only light source. But from where we are, surrounded by trees in the corner of the far end zone, all its pale glow does is cast angled shadows between the branches and across the path.

'You're slowing down,' she says, grabbing the umbrella and tugging me forward.

'Lisbeth, maybe you should—'

'I'm not going anywhere,' she insists, doubling our pace and glancing to the right, where a skinny bone-white military headstone has a crest that reads:

CPL
TRP E
13 REGT CAV
SP AM WAR
1879–1959

'He's buried near people from the Spanish-American War?' she whispers. 'You sure he's not in the new section?'

We'd seen it when we first drove up. On our far left, past the floodlit flagpole, past the thousands of silhouetted crosses, crooked headstones, and family crypts, was a wide-open field dotted with flat ceremonial markers. Like most Florida cemeteries, Woodlawn learned the hard way what happens when a hurricane hits a graveyard. Nowadays, the newly dead get only flat markers set flush into the earth. Unless, of course, you know someone big enough to tug some strings.

'Trust me, he's not in the new section,' I say. The further we go down the path, the more clearly we hear a new sound in the air. A hushed murmur, or a whisper. Dozens of whispers – coming and going – as if they're all around us.

'No one's here,' Lisbeth insists. But on our left, behind a 1926 headstone with a marble set of rosary beads dangling from the front, there's a loud scrape like someone skidding to a stop. I spin to see who's there. The headstones

surround us. The rain continues to dribble down our backs
and soak our shoulders, its mossy smell overwhelming the
stench of wet dirt. Behind us, the rumble of thunder starts
to – no, not thunder.

'Is that . . . ?'

The rumbling gets louder, followed by the deep belch
of an air horn. I wheel back toward the meatball shrubs
just as the *ding-ding-ding* of the crossing gate pierces the
air. Like a glowing bullet through the darkness, a freight
train bursts into view, slicing from right to left, parallel
with the low fence that runs along the back of the graveyard.

'We should keep going!' Lisbeth yells in my ear,
leading us deeper down the path. The train continues
to rumble behind us, taking all sound with it, including
the rustling and scraping that would let us know
someone's coming.

What about in there? Lisbeth pantomimes as we pass
an aboveground crypt with stained-glass double doors.
The crypt is one of the largest here – nearly as big as a
dumpster.

'Forget it,' I say, yanking her by the elbow and taking
the lead. She doesn't realize how close we are to our goal.
Three graves down from the crypt, the path dead-ends
at the trunk of the enormous banyan tree, which, during
the day, shields every nearby grave from the battering sun.
That alone makes this one of the most select areas in the
entire cemetery. President Manning made the call himself
and personally secured the double plot of land that now
holds the imported Italian black marble headstone with
the slightly curved top and the stark white carved letters
that read:

RONALD BOYLE
TREASURED HUSBAND, FATHER, SON
WHOSE MAGIC WILL ALWAYS BE WITH US

'This is him?' Lisbeth asks, spotting the name and almost crashing into me from behind.

It was Manning's last gift to his friend – a final resting place that kept Boyle out of the land of flat markers, and instead put him next to a general from World War II, and across from one of Palm Beach's most respected judges from the 1920s. It was vintage Palm Beach. Even in death, honchos still want the best seat in the house.

Behind us, the train fades and the sound of crickets returns, engulfing us on all sides. I just stand there, staring at Boyle's grave in the dim light.

'Y'okay?' Lisbeth asks.

She thinks I'm afraid. But now that we're here . . . now that I know there isn't a body underneath this stone . . . and most important, that I never put him there . . . My fists tighten as I reread the epitaph. Like everything in their lives, it's polished and pretty – and a festering tumor of lies. For eight years, Manning – my boss, my mentor – for eight years, he knew I was eating shit, but he never once took it off my plate. He just served it. Day after day. With a perfect presidential grin.

My fists clench. Then I feel Lisbeth's hand on the small of my back. She doesn't say a word. She doesn't need to.

I take one last look around the empty cemetery. For eight years, I've been afraid. That's what death does when it haunts you. But right now, as I stand here in the soft rain and bleeding darkness, I'm ready to meet my ghost. And so is Lisbeth.

We take our separate places, just like we discussed. Lisbeth looks down at her watch. All we have to do is wait.

100

'Outta there! Now!' the guard yelled as he gripped the back of Rogo's shirt.

'Get off me!' Rogo shouted back, tugging free and running deeper into the poorly lit room. Two steps later, motion sensors kicked in, flooding the room with the buzz of fluorescent light. On Rogo's left was a single bed with a beat-up oak headboard, immaculately folded white sheets, and a Bible sitting on a fuzzy, olive-green wool blanket. Rounding out the cheap motel decor was a mismatched white Formica side table and a faux-wood dresser that held a pile of old magazines and a ten-year-old twelve-inch TV. To the right, oak double doors opened into what looked like a conference room, complete with a long mahogany table and half a dozen modern black leather chairs. None of it made sense. Why's a public bathroom connect to a separate bedr—?

From behind, Rogo felt a sharp tug on his shirt. He again tried to pull away, but this time, the guard was ready, yanking him backward toward the bathroom.

'Y'know how much trouble you just got me into?!' the guard shouted.

'I was just – the door was open—'

'Bull . . . *shit*,' the guard insisted, whipping Rogo around and sending him smashing face-first into the room's half-closed door, which slammed into the tile wall as he shoved Rogo into the bathroom.

'Are you nuts?!' Rogo screamed, twisting to break free. The guard held tight, marching him back through the men's room and toward the door to the hallway. A full head taller than Rogo, he gripped Rogo's wrists and held them behind his back.

'I'm a lawyer, you stupid monkey. By the time I'm done suing, I'm gonna own this place and turn it into an Arby's!'

As Rogo stumbled from the bathroom into the salmon marble hall, the guard shoved him to the right, back toward the lobby's white frosted-glass doors.

'Dreidel, tell him who you are!' Rogo called out, his voice echoing up the hall.

'W-What'd you do?' Dreidel asked, already stepping backward, away from the check-in desk.

'Don't move!' the guard warned Dreidel.

Panicking, Dreidel spun around and took off for the sliding doors.

'No . . . *don't!*' the guard shouted.

Too late.

Before Dreidel even registered the words, his foot hit the sensor mat. But it wasn't until the doors started to slide open that Rogo noticed shadows on the other side of the frosted glass.

With a hushed swoosh, the doors yawned open, revealing a thin bald man with chiseled cheeks and a crusted-up bloody nose. Slumped over his shoulder was a fit blond man whose head was drooped down, unconscious. His shirt was soaked with what looked like blood.

'Guess who I found?' Boyle announced as he stepped inside. 'All that's left is—' Spotting Dreidel, he froze. Without even thinking, he let go of O'Shea, who clattered to the ground, splayed out across the sensor mat.

'Boyle,' Dreidel blurted.

'*Boyle?*' Rogo asked.

'Don't move!' the guard yelled at Boyle, pulling his gun and shoving Rogo aside.

'Put your gun away,' Boyle ordered.

'I said *don't move!*' the guard repeated. Turning to his radio, he shouted, 'Fellas, *I need some help down here!*'

Regaining his balance, Rogo couldn't take his eyes off Boyle. It was just like Wes said. The pointy features . . . the gaunt cheeks . . . but still so much the same.

'R-Ron, are you okay?' Dreidel asked, still in shock.

Before Boyle could answer, his brown and blue eyes locked with Rogo's. 'You're Wes's roommate, aren't you?'

Rogo nodded, his head bobbing slowly. 'Why?'

'Is Wes here too?' Boyle asked, his eyes swiftly scanning the lobby.

Confused and completely overwhelmed, Rogo followed Boyle's glance, searching the lobby, the elevators, the check-in desk, almost half expecting Wes to jump out. 'I-I thought he was meeting *you.*'

'Meeting *him?*' Dreidel asked.

'Meeting *me?*' Boyle replied.

'Yeah, no – *you,*' Rogo shot back. 'That note you sent . . . for Wes to meet you . . . seven p.m. Y'know, at the grave-yard.'

Staring at Rogo, Boyle shook his head, clearly clueless. 'I don't know what you're talking about, son. Why would I invite Wes to meet me at a graveyard?'

101

It took him six seconds to flick the four pins and pop the rusted old padlock, and that was with an umbrella in his hand. He knew there was no alarm – that was why he'd come by earlier. Indeed, as the lock sprang open, he quietly tugged the rusted metal chain and unthreaded it from the iron front gates of the cemetery without even looking to see if anyone was coming. With a final push, he shoved the gates open just enough for the two of them to squeeze inside.

'This is where you—? Who would possibly meet you here?'

'Just trust me,' the man said, tipping his umbrella back and glancing up at the ornate stone archway that framed the gates. Sandblasted into the stone, in classic block letters, was the one epitaph that had been on the cemetery's entrance since it was built two hundred years ago: *That which is so universal as death must be a blessing.* 'Wait here,' he said.

'Why? Where're you going?' his partner asked, shielded under a separate umbrella and carefully hanging back. 'You're not leaving me in a graveyard.'

'What I'm leaving you is *out of sight*,' the man insisted, knowing that Wes had to be here already. 'If you want me to clean up this mess – which I assume you do – I suggest you stay here until I tell you it's clear.' Leaving his partner behind, he eyed the floodlit flagpole that bathed the main entrance in light, then quickly cut left and plowed across a plot of graves. Ignoring the stone pathways, he strode toward the south end of the cemetery, using the trees for cover.

Behind him, he could hear his partner following, holding back far enough to stay hidden. But still following. Good. That's what he needed.

Heading toward Wes, he stopped behind a cracked limestone column on the corner of a crypt with a pointed cathedral roof. To his right, across from the crypt, a small gray 1928 headstone for someone named *J. G. Anwar* was engraved with a Masonic and a five-pointed star. Hidden in the darkness, he couldn't help but grin at the irony. How perfect.

Still ignoring his partner creeping twenty feet behind him, he peered around the crypt as the tines of his umbrella scratched against the mushy wet moss that was slowly working its way up the limestone column. Diagonally across the graveyard, at the base of an oversize banyan tree, Wes's single thin shadow paced back and forth, hunched under his own crooked umbrella.

'That him?' his partner whispered, quickly catching up and staying hidden by the crypt.

'I told you t—'

But before he could get the words out, the shadow by the grave pivoted toward him, and he could immediately tell who it was. The ankles were the giveaway.

The man's fist tightened on his umbrella handle. His eyes narrowed, and as he leaned forward, the umbrella tines scratched deeper against the mossy crypt. With a burst, he raced forward. *That stupid motherf—*

'Wait . . . where're you—?'

'*Stay here!*' he seethed at his partner, this time meaning it. All this time . . . All he needed was for Wes to be alone. Half running, he cut diagonally across a row of graves. He knew full well they'd hear him coming.

Sure enough, the shadow turned his way, lifting its umbrella and revealing a glint of auburn hair.

'Boyle, that you?' Lisbeth called out. Getting no answer, she cocked her head, squinting into the darkness. 'Boyle . . . ?'

Barely ten feet away, the man reached into his pocket and used his good hand – his left hand – to grab his gun.

'Boyle, just relax,' Lisbeth said, backing up as the man approached, his face still hidden by his umbrella. For a split second, he ducked under a wayward branch that caught the umbrella and pulled it aside. The instant Lisbeth saw his jet-black hair, she knew she was in trouble. According to Wes, Boyle was bald. 'Listen, whoever you are, I'm just here to—'

Ramming through a row of bushes and bursting from the darkness, he pulled his gun, pointed it at Lisbeth's chest, and stepped in so close, he forced her back against a tall clay-colored headstone with a carved Celtic cross on top.

'I don't care why the hell you're here,' The Roman exploded, knocking her umbrella from her hand. As he moved closer, his skin glowed as gray as the headstones. 'But if you don't tell me where Wes is, I swear to my God, you'll be begging me to blow your face off.'

Frozen in shock, Lisbeth glanced over The Roman's shoulder and spotted his associate stepping between the bushes.

The reporter's mouth sagged open as the final member of The Four came forward.

102

Martin Kassal could read when he was three years old. He could write when he was four. And by five, he would sit next to his father at the breakfast table, eating his raisins and French toast while reading the headlines in the newspaper. But it wasn't until he was seven that he finished his first crossword puzzle. Designing it, that is.

Sixty-one years later, Kassal tapped at his moon-chin, skimming his way through a small beaten paperback called *Myths and Symbols in Indian Art and Civilization*. Even with his tinted reading glasses, he still needed to lean close to see, and as he pulled back slightly to flip to a new page, he was so engrossed in the symbols of the sacred rivers, he didn't even register his phone until the third ring.

'Is this Ptomaine1?' a female voice asked with an accusatory tone.

'I'm sorry – who's this?' Kassal asked.

'*Tattarrattat* is my screen name. Also known as Mary Beth Guard to my friends,' she added with a huffy laugh at her use of the longest palindrome in the Oxford Dictionary, second edition. 'I saw your posting on the message boards . . . about the glyphs you were trying to identify . . . the four dots and the cross with the slash . . .'

'Of course. No, of course. And thank you for getting back so quickly.'

'Hey, you posted your phone number. I figured it was

an emergency. By the way, I like your screen name. Ptomaine. From NPR, right? *Famous historic American. Put his first name inside his last name to get a word.* Ptomaine. Tom Paine. Cute,' the woman said, almost as if she were looking for a date.

'Yeah, well . . . aheh,' Kassal said, wiping his forehead. 'So about those symbols . . .'

'The glyphs – sure – I knew them immediately. I mean, I stare at them every day.'

'I'm not sure I follow.'

'I work at Monticello. Y'know, Virginia? Home of our wisest and greatest President, Thomas Jefferson – and I don't just say that as an employee.'

'These were symbols used by Jefferson?'

'Actually, by Meriwether Lewis.'

'Of Lewis and Clark?'

'Oooh, you know your history, Ptomaine,' she said sarcastically. 'Of course. But what people don't realize is that the main reason Meriwether Lewis was picked to explore the Louisiana Purchase – in fact, maybe the *only* reason he was trusted with the task – was because a few years earlier, he did such an incredible job as Jefferson's personal secretary.'

'Huh,' Kassal said, already scribbling a note to use the info in an upcoming puzzle. 'I didn't realize Lewis was Jefferson's aide.'

'Very first aide to any President. Right after Jefferson was elected in 1801, one of his first jobs as President was decreasing the number of officers in the army. The Revolutionary War was long over, the conflict with France was winding down, and they were trying to shrink the ranks.'

'So the political consequences . . .'

'Very good. Were staggering,' Mary Beth explained. 'You

have the political bug too, eh? Have you ever been to Monticello? I'd be happy to show you around.'

That was always the problem with the message boards. The odds were good, but the goods were odd. 'I'm sorry, I'm just in a bit of a rush—'

'Okay, I get it – you're married. My apologies. I'm just not good at reading these things—'

'Yes, so, aheh – you were saying about Jefferson . . . that the political consequences of firing officers . . .'

'Of course, of course. The politics were tricky to say the least, so to avoid putting his foot in it, Jefferson asked Lewis to secretly rank the loyalty of each army officer. That way, they'd know who to fire and who to keep on board.'

'So those symbols,' Kassal said, looking down at the ∷, *0*, ✢, and ⦂, 'those were . . .'

'. . . Lewis and Jefferson's coded rating system to make sure none of the officers would ever find out what Jefferson's opinion of them actually was: whether they were trustworthy, apathetic, or a political enemy. So when the War Department supplied Jefferson with the list of all the brigadier generals and lieutenants, Lewis took his secret symbols and put . . .'

'. . . a handwritten mark next to each name,' Kassal said, studying the exact same symbols two hundred years later on the crossword. 'To everyone else, it looked like the random blots of a fountain pen . . .'

'. . . right again . . . but to Jefferson, it was a guide to which of his officers were honest Abes. In fact, if you ever do come h— We actually have the original list on display, plus the key that Jefferson used to decipher the codes. It's beautiful to see up close – all the flourishes in the old script.'

'Certainly sounds *tempting*,' Kassal said, making the kind of face that usually goes with biting a lemon. 'But . . . Mary Beth, is it?'

'Mary Beth,' she said proudly.

'If I could ask you one last favor, Mary Beth: Now that I have the signs – the four dots and the cross with the slash through it – can you just read me the cipher so I know what each of these stands for?'

103

'You're telling me you didn't send him a note?' Rogo asked Boyle as he readjusted his shirt from where the guard had pulled it.

'Note? Why would I send him a note?' Boyle asked, sounding annoyed as his eyes flicked between Rogo and the guard.

'I said don't move!' the guard shouted, his gun pointed at Boyle.

'You yell at me again, you're gonna be picking that gun outta your teeth,' Boyle growled back. 'Now I want my contact man, or at the very least, a supervisor, and I mean *now*.'

'What the hell's going on?' Dreidel asked, his hands raised in the air, even though the gun wasn't anywhere near him. 'You said we were meeting at my hotel. Since when is Wes meeting at a graveyard?'

'Dreidel, this isn't about you,' Rogo insisted. Turning to the guard, he added, 'Listen, I know you don't know me, but my friend's life is in—'

'So is yours,' the guard said as he pointed his gun back at Rogo. Turning his attention to his walkie-talkie, he pushed a button and added, 'Rags, we got a problem – I need you to find Loeb.'

'So wait . . . when Wes called . . . you *both* lied to me?'

Dreidel asked, still putting the pieces together. 'Now you have Wes not trusting me too?'

'Don't you dare play victim,' Rogo warned. 'Lisbeth spoke to your old girlfriend – the one with the crossword puzzle—'

Boyle turned at the words. 'You found the puzzle?'

'Boyle, keep your mouth shut!' the guard warned.

'How'd she find Violet?' Dreidel asked, his face paste white as he slowly lowered his hands.

Rogo shook his head at Dreidel but knew enough to stay with the guard, who knew enough to stay with Boyle. Rogo shifted his weight anxiously, barely able to stand still. Every second they wasted here meant that Wes— He cut himself off. *Don't think about it.*

'When'd you find the puzzle?' Boyle added, still trying to get Rogo's attention.

Rogo glanced his way, smelling the opening. Until he could get to Wes, he might as well get some answers. 'Does that mean you're gonna tell me what's in it?' Rogo asked.

Boyle ignored the question like he didn't even hear it.

'No – don't do that,' Rogo warned. 'Don't just— If you can help Wes – if you know what's in the puzzle—'

'I don't know *anything.*'

'That's not true. You went to Malaysia for a reason.'

'Loeb, you there?' the guard said into his radio.

'C'mon, Boyle – I heard Wes talk about you. We know you tried to do the right thing.'

Boyle watched the guard, who shook his head.

'Please,' Rogo pleaded. 'Wes is out there thinking he's meeting you.'

Boyle still didn't react.

'Someone lured him out there,' Rogo added. 'If you

know something and you keep it to yourself, you're just letting him take your place.'

Still nothing.

'Forget it,' Dreidel said. 'He's not—'

'Where'd he find it?' Boyle blurted.

'Find what?' Rogo asked.

'The note. You said Wes found a note. For the grave-yard.'

'Boyle . . .' the guard warned.

'On his car,' Rogo sputtered. 'Outside Manning's house.'

'Since when?' Dreidel asked. 'You never said that. They never said that,' he added to Boyle.

Boyle shook his head. 'And Wes just assumed it was – ? I thought you said you unlocked the crossword.'

'We unlocked the names – all the initials,' Rogo said. 'Manning, Albright, Rosenman, Dreidel . . .'

'These . . . with Jefferson's old cryptogram,' Boyle said as he pulled a worn, folded-up sheet from his pocket. Furiously unfolding it, he revealed the crossword and its hidden code, plus his own handwritten notes drawn in.

⁚⁚	Manning
0	Albright
⚲	Rosenman
⁚⁚	Dreidel
——	Moss
——	Kutz

———— **Lemonick**

⁞ **Me**

'That's the one,' Rogo said. 'But aside from telling us that the President trusted Dreidel, we couldn't—'

'Whoa, whoa, time out,' Boyle interrupted. 'What're you talking about?'

'Boyle, you know the rules on clearance!' the guard shouted.

'Will you stop worrying about clearance?' Boyle barked back. 'Tell Loeb he can blame it on me.' Turning back to Rogo, he added, 'And what made you think Dreidel was trustworthy?'

'You're saying I'm not?' Dreidel challenged.

'The four dots,' Rogo explained as he pointed at the **⁞**. 'Since the President and Dreidel are both ranked with four dots, we figured that was the inner circle of who he trusted.'

Boyle went quiet again.

'That's *not* the inner circle?' Rogo asked.

'*This* is the inner circle,' Boyle said, pointing to the *O* next to Manning's chief of staff, the man he used to do the puzzles with.

'So what're the four dots?' Rogo asked, still lost.

'Boyle, that's enough,' the guard warned.

'This has nothing to do with clearance!' Boyle challenged.

'Those four dots are good,' Dreidel insisted. 'Manning trusted me with everything!'

'Just tell me what the four dots were,' Rogo demanded in a low voice.

Boyle glared at Dreidel, then back to Rogo. 'The four

dots were Jefferson's shorthand for soldiers without any political creed – the opportunists who would give up anything for their own advancement. For us, it was meant to describe who Manning and Albright thought were leaking to the press. But when The Three found a copy and deciphered it, that's how they knew who to pick for their fourth.'

'I'm not The Fourth!' Dreidel insisted.

'I never said you were,' Boyle agreed.

Rogo glanced down at Manning's old crossword, studying the two names with the four dots.

::   **Manning**

::   **Dreidel**

None of it made sense. Wes swore that the handwriting – that all the rankings – were Manning's. But if that's true . . . 'Why would the President give himself such a low ranking?'

'That's the point. He wouldn't,' Boyle said.

'But on the crossword . . . you said the four dots—'

Boyle raked his bottom teeth across his top lip. 'Rogo, forget your biases. The Three wanted someone close to every major decision, and most important, someone who could *affect* those decisions – that's why they first picked me instead of Dreidel.'

'Boyle, that's *enough*! *I'm serious!*' the guard shouted. But Boyle didn't care. After eight years, there was nothing more they could take from him.

'You see it now, don't you?' Boyle asked as Rogo stared down at the page. 'You've got the right name. Even the right reasoning – never underestimate what they'd do for four more years. But you got the wrong Manning.'

Confused, Rogo shook his head, still locked on the puzzle. 'What other Manning is th—?'

A burst of bitter cold seized Rogo's body, as if he'd been encased in ice.

Oh, shit.

104

I know her shadow anywhere. I know it better than my own. I've watched it nearly every day for almost a decade. That's my job: trailing three feet behind her, close enough to be there the moment she realizes she needs something, but far enough that I'm never in the photo. Back during White House days, even when she was swarmed by entourages of dignitaries and foreign press and our press and staff and crowds and Secret Service, I could still stand at the back of the horde, peer through the sea of legs, and find her silhouette at the center – and not just because she was the only one in high heels.

It's no different tonight. Indeed, as I squat down in the shadowy graveyard and hide behind one of the meatball shrubs, as I clamp my eyes into paper-thin slits and try to squint through the braided crisscrossing branches and the nearly fifty yards of headstone-lined darkness, I stare down the crooked stone path and instantly recognize the thick calves, sharp shoulders, and pointed silhouette of Dr. Lenore Manning.

An aching pain swells like a balloon inside my rib cage. No . . . she – she'd never— I shake my head, and my ribs feel like they're about to splinter. How can—? Why would she do that?

At the end of the path, stopping at the tree, she tips her umbrella slightly, and in the light from the distant flagpole, I see anger and annoyance – and even fear – in her face. I can still picture her leaving the White House – the President squeezing her fingertips as they walked to Marine One. She said it herself: When it came to staying in power, they would've done almost anything.

She barks something at the man next to her, but I'm too far away to hear it. She's not happy to be here. Whatever she did, she's clearly regretting it. I pull back, blinking violently. But Boyle . . . If the First Lady's here, and the man next to her, with the bandages on his right hand (is that a gun?), if that's The Roman . . . A rush of blood throbs up from my chest, all the way to my face. I hold my cheek, which burns against my hand, just like when I was shot.

Closing my eyes, I see it all, another black-and-white newsreel. Back at the Mannings' house, she knew I was watching – when she was crying, showing me the letter from Boyle – and then the note on my car. That's why the handwriting matched. She . . . and The Roman . . . oh, God.

I stare back down the path at Lisbeth, who's in just as much shock as I am. It was her idea that we switch places before Boyle showed up: I'd be the lure to bring him in; she'd be the friendly reporter who'd give him more incentive to stay. But Boyle's not coming. He never was.

The Roman steps toward Lisbeth, who straightens up, trying to look strong. But the way she watches his gun . . . and backs up, colliding with the tall clay-colored headstone . . . she knows she's in trouble. We all are. Unless I can get some—

Spinning back toward the fence just behind me in the graveyard, I pull my phone from my pocket and sprint as fast as I can. But before I press a single digit, I slam face-first into the chest of a tall, slim man facing the distant light. He has thin expressionless lips, buzzed black hair, and tiny chocolate eyes that seem almost too close togeth— My cheek burns like it's on fire. I know him immediately. From every one of my nightmares.

Nico snatches my phone from my hand, chucks it to the ground, and buries it in the mud with his heel. Reaching out and seizing me by the ear, he puts the barrel of his gun against my cheek, right against the scars he created all those years ago.

'You've been corrupted by the Beast, Wesley,' he says calmly, almost kindly. 'Now tell me where Ron Boyle is, or you will again face God's wrath.'

105

'You didn't know she was The Fourth?' Boyle asked.

'I said *that's enough*!' the guard shouted, gripping his gun with two hands. He had a build – and a face – like a rhino, but as he stepped closer, Rogo saw the guard's feet shuffle with hesitation. Eight years ago, Ron Boyle was an accountant. Today, he was clearly something more.

'Who'd you think it was? The President?' Boyle added.

'He really ranked me that low?' Dreidel asked.

'Why'd you think you were fired?' Boyle asked.

'I wasn't fired. I got promoted.'

'Sure you were.'

'I'm counting to three!' the guard warned Boyle.

'Listen, please,' Rogo begged, turning to the guard. 'You need to call the police . . . my friend's about to be killed!'

'You hear me, Boyle?' the guard said.

'Didn't you realize who you were up against?' Boyle shouted at Rogo. 'You should've called the cops days ago.'

'We did! We thought we did!' Rogo replied. 'Micah and O'Shea said they were—'

One . . . !' the guard shouted.

'Or at least called in some favors,' Boyle added, turning to Dreidel.

Turning away, Dreidel was silent.

Rogo raised an eyebrow.

'Two . . . !' the guard continued.

Boyle watched them both carefully, then rolled his tongue, more annoyed than ever. He'd worked in the White House for nearly four years. He'd seen that look before.

'You did, didn't you?' Boyle challenged.

'And you did anything different?' Dreidel shot back. 'Spare me the judgment.'

'Wait . . . *what?*' Rogo asked. 'You went for help without telling us?'

Before Dreidel could answer, the guard pulled back the hammer on his gun.

Still locked on Dreidel, Boyle ignored the threat. 'Who'd you run to first? NSA? FBI? Or'd you go to Bendis at—?'

'The Marshals,' Dreidel blurted. 'I went to the Marshals Service.'

Hearing the words, the guard turned toward Dreidel. And took his eyes off Boyle.

That was the end.

Leaping forward, Boyle slammed the guard from behind, wrapping his left arm around the guard's neck and gripping his stringy brown hair with his right.

'Are you—? Get the hell off!' the guard screamed. He reached back to grab Boyle – which was exactly what Boyle was hoping for.

Seizing the momentum, Boyle threw himself backward, taking the guard with him as they plunged toward the floor. It wasn't until they were in mid-fall that the guard realized what he was in for.

'Boyle, don't—!'

Pivoting at the last second, Boyle spun to the left, twisting around so that instead of falling backward, the guard was falling forward. Straight toward the salmon-colored marble floor. At the last second, with a sharp tug of brown hair to steer the ship, Boyle turned the guard's head to the side, so his right ear was facing down.

'Get off me, you lunati—!'

Like a cupped hand slapping water, the guard's ear smacked the ground with a loud hollow pop, followed half a second later by a louder pop as his gun backfired from the impact. Boyle, Rogo, and Dreidel all jumped back as the bullet zinged from his gun, piercing the base of the welcome desk and lodging in the marble wall. Before they'd even realized what happened, the guard's head slumped unconscious against the floor, blood trickling out from his burst eardrum.

'What're you, *on drugs*!?' Dreidel demanded as Boyle climbed to his feet.

Without answering, Boyle motioned to the door. 'We should go. He's got backup coming.'

Still in shock, Rogo just stood there, his eyes hopping from Boyle and Dreidel to the limp figures of O'Shea and the guard. 'I don't . . . I'm not—'

'Dreidel, you don't live down here, do you?' Boyle asked.

'No, but I can—'

'I need you to show me the fastest route to the cemetery,' Boyle said as he turned to Rogo.

Rogo nodded, first slowly, then faster, his eyes eventually settling on Dreidel, who quickly approached to make peace.

'Rogo, before you say anything . . .'

'You made a deal, didn't you?' Rogo challenged.

'Just listen—'

'What'd the Marshals offer you?'

'Rogo . . .'

'What'd they offer you, you cancerous little parasite!?' Rogo shouted.

Dreidel shook his head as his jaw shifted off-center. 'Full immunity.'

'I *knew* it!' Rogo said.

'But it's not—'

'And what was the trade? That you'd spy on us – help them catch The Three – as a way to prove your own innocence?'

'I *am* innocent!' Dreidel snapped.

'So is Wes! So am *I*! But you don't see us running to the authorities, making private deals, and then tattling on our friends *without telling them*!'

'Rogo – both of you – we need to go,' Boyle insisted.

Enraged but well aware of Wes's current situation, Rogo spun back to the main entrance, followed Boyle through the sliding doors, and burst into the parking lot with Dreidel right behind him.

As flicks of rain bombarded from above, Dreidel quickly caught up so they were running side by side, heading for Boyle's van. 'I didn't tattle on you,' Dreidel said.

'So you never told them what we were up to?' Rogo shot back.

'I didn't have a choice, Rogo. Once Wes came to my hotel room that first day . . . I needed the help. They said if I kept my eyes on you and Wes – kept them informed on where you were – they'd do their best to keep us protected as well as keeping our names out of the papers.'

'And that's not spying on your friends?'

'Listen, don't be mad at me for being the only one smart enough to realize that in an emergency, you're supposed to break the glass and call for help. C'mon, Rogo, think for a second. I can't afford—' As they approached the white van, he explained, 'I'm running for State Senate.'

Rushing around to the passenger side of the van, Rogo felt his fingers tighten into a fist. He almost bit through his own lip as he fought to contain his rage. 'Let's go – open the door,' he called out to Boyle.

'I swear, Rogo, I wasn't trying to hurt you,' Dreidel insisted.

As the locks popped, Rogo ripped open the passenger door, reached inside, and hooked his arm around to pound down the lock on the van's sliding door.

'What're you doing?' Dreidel asked. 'Unlock it!'

Rogo didn't say a word as he leaped into the front passenger seat, which was covered with thick piles of cluttered files, photocopies, old newspapers, and a brand-new digital camera. Leaning in Rogo's door, Dreidel stuck his arm behind the passenger seat and tried to open the lock himself. Without even hesitating, Rogo tugged the door shut. Dreidel tried to pull away. He wasn't fast enough. The sixty-pound door chomped down, sinking its metal teeth into his manicured fingertips.

'*Gahhhhh!* Open it! *Open it, motherf——!*'

'Ooh, sorry,' Rogo offered as he nudged the door open, and Dreidel tucked his hand under his own armpit. 'I swear, Dreidel, I wasn't trying to hurt you either.'

Staring downward from his seat in the van, Rogo shot him the kind of glare that comes with an ice pick. 'Don't pretend you're Wes's friend, dickface.'

With a hiccup, the van roared to life, and Rogo slammed the door shut. Dreidel just stood there, pelted by the rain.

'C'mon, we going or not?' Rogo shouted at Boyle.

'Don't bark orders at me,' Boyle countered. 'I didn't shoot your friend in the face.'

'But if you—'

'I didn't shoot him, Rogo. They shot *me*. And if I really

wanted to see Wes hurt, I wouldn't be running to save him right now,' Boyle said as he shifted the car into reverse and jammed his foot on the gas.

Staring dead ahead as they squealed out of the spot and away from Dreidel, Rogo rolled his jaw, forever looking for the fight. For once, he couldn't find it. 'Just tell me one thing,' he finally said as he motioned back toward the modern building with the thermal security cameras. 'What the hell is that place, and why'd they have a bed and conference table connected to the bathroom?'

'Didn't you hear who Dreidel made his deal with?' Tapping the glass of his own window, Boyle motioned to the four-story building that was perfectly located two miles from the airport. 'Dr. Eng's just the name that lets them hide in plain sight. Forget what it says on the front door. That's a WITSEC safehouse.'

'Wit sack?'

'WITSEC. As in *Witness Security.*'

'You mean like the Witness Protection Program?'

'Exactly like the Witness Protection Program – which, along with judicial protection, is run solely under the juris-diction of . . .'

'. . . the Marshals Service,' Rogo said, shaking his head and finally realizing why Dreidel hadn't wanted to come.

'Starting to stink now, isn't it?' Boyle asked. 'But that's how they work. They've got fake offices in every city in America. The only difference here is, it's Witness Protec-tion 2.0. Instead of just putting you in hiding, they make everyone think you're dea—'

Overhead, a 747 shredded the night sky, buzzing down toward the airport and drowning out Boyle.

Rogo stared at the frosted-glass building as the adren-aline from fighting with Dreidel drained away and the dread of his new reality seeped into his system. 'So when the guard called on his radio, he . . .'

'. . . wasn't just calling his buddies,' Boyle agreed as they tore past the front of the building. 'He was calling the United States Marshals Service. And unless we get out of here, we're gonna get a personal introduction.'

106

Lisbeth's elbow scraped against the jagged granite as she backed into the clay-colored headstone with the Celtic cross on top.

'Tell me where Wes is hiding,' The Roman demanded, his gun so close to her head, she saw her own distorted reflection in the tip of the barrel.

When she didn't answer, he asked again, but Lisbeth barely heard the words. All her attention was still focused just over The Roman's shoulder, where the First Lady read Lisbeth's shock for herself.

Soaked by the falling rain, Lisbeth tried to back up even further, but the headstone held her in place.

'Wes?' the First Lady hissed like an angry cat at The Roman. 'You brought me to see Wes?'

'I told you to stay back, ma'am,' The Roman said, never taking his glance or his gun off Lisbeth.

'And I told you to never contact me again – but that didn't stop you from showing up at my house – entering *my home*! Do you have any idea what kind of risk that—?' She cut herself off as the consequences sank in. 'Good God! He's—Wes is here right now?' She anxiously looked up the stone path, scanning nearby headstones. 'You brought him here t— Is that why you had me give him that note?'

The Roman stared at Lisbeth, then glared back at the

First Lady. 'Don't play for the reporter, Lenore.'

'*Playing?* That's not— *Why didn't you tell me!?*' the First Lady exploded, her umbrella jerking wildly with each syllable.

The Roman laughed softly, his sandpaper voice grating. 'No different than a decade ago, is it? You're telling me you really wanted to know?'

The First Lady went silent as the rain tapped on her umbrella. Across from her, Lisbeth stood unprotected, the drizzle slowly soaking her red hair, which flattened and dangled across her face like wet yarn.

'Please tell me they blackmailed you,' Lisbeth pleaded, her voice cracking and her eyebrows knotting.

The First Lady ignored the question, still searching the lot for Wes. Just in front of her, The Roman flashed the smallest of grins.

'And that's it? You just did it?' Lisbeth asked.

'I didn't do anything,' Dr. Manning insisted.

'But you knew. He just said it: Even if you ignored it, you—'

'*I didn't know anything!*' she screamed.

'*That's because you didn't want to!*' Lisbeth shot back.

The First Lady did her best to stay calm.

'They came to me through the Service, saying they could help on security issues – that our senior staff was holding us back by not paying for *Blackbird* and other good tips. Back then, I . . . we needed to show we were strong. *I thought I was helping!*'

'And so you just did whatever they said?'

'Are you listening? They were from the Service! *From our side!*' she insisted, her voice booming. 'I figured they knew best – d'you understand? I never thought they'd – *I was helping!*'

'Until what? Until Boyle suddenly turned up dead and you realized you'd been had?' Lisbeth asked. No question, that could certainly be the case. But it didn't explain why the First Lady had continued to stay silent in the days that followed – or how, when she was first approached by The Roman – when the White House was swarming with an internal investigation of Boyle and the group they started calling The Three – how she could've been so naïve and not even questioned what The Roman was selling. It's not like national security was her pet issue. In fact, that close to reelection – especially when they were down in the polls – the only issue *any* First Lady should've been focused on was bringing home a second ter—

'You wanted to win,' Lisbeth blurted.

'Roman, I'm leaving now,' the First Lady said, turning away, her pinkie flicking the strap of her umbrella handle.

'That's why you never reported him, isn't it? Maybe you wanted to believe it; maybe you just turned the blind eye. But as long as he could help you on security issues – if he could give you the bump in the polls, just this one time—'

'Did you hear me?' she shouted at The Roman, almost crying.

'They learned their lesson with Boyle, didn't they? They approached you with a softer touch. Then suddenly, Boyle got shot . . .'

'Roman, tell her I didn't know! I never knew you'd do that!'

'And now they had it all,' Lisbeth added. 'A sitting President behind in the polls . . . the guaranteed bump from some hired whackjob's assassination attempt. If it all went right and the President hadn't been pulled back by the crowd, The Three would say good-bye to Boyle, while putting you, their unknowing new member with far more inside influence than Boyle, in the perfect spot to pass along your *helpful* new recommendations to your husba—'

The Roman's good hand jabbed forward in a blur, pounding the butt of his gun into Lisbeth's face. Blood burst from her top lip, and her head whipped back, cracking against the headstone. Gasping, she swallowed something tiny and jagged. A lick with her tongue quickly told her it was the tooth next to her left front. '*Hkkkkk!*' As it scraped down her throat, she hunched forward like she was about to throw up, then dry-heaved twice as a mouthful of blood drooled down to her shoes and the soaking grass.

Two miles away, the faint wail of an approaching train moaned.

Staring at the ground as a dry heave flushed all the blood to her face, Lisbeth didn't even hear the whistle. Indeed, as the rain dripped like a leaky faucet from her hair, her chin, her nose, the only thing Lisbeth registered was the squish of The Roman's shoes as he stepped forward.

'She's gonna need an ambulance, Wes,' he called out calmly into the darkness. Reaching down to the back of Lisbeth's head, he grabbed a fistful of her soaking hair, holding her so she was bowed down in front of him.

'Get the hell off me!' Lisbeth shouted.

'Keep hiding, Wes!' The Roman announced, clenching her hair even tighter and taking a half-step back. Almost like he was winding up.

The last thing Lisbeth saw was the flecks of mud on the tips of The Roman's black calfskin shoes. And the ball of his knee as he rammed it toward her face.

107

He smells like hospital antiseptic and hamburger meat gone bad. But as Nico digs the barrel of his gun into my scars, it's not the smell that churns my stomach. I swallow so hard, it feels like there's a brick in my throat.

'How could you help him? How *could* you?' he demands. 'Do you even know what you've unleashed?' His eyes jackrabbit side to side to side to side. He's been off his medication for two days.

'Answer me!' he seethes, forcing me back with a shove of his gun. He doesn't even blink as the rain hits his face.

Stumbling off balance, I crash backward into the shrub. A wayward branch stabs me in the spine, but I barely feel it. Just seeing Nico, hearing him – I'm back at the speedway. The crowd roaring. Manning smiling. A hundred thousand fans stand up, pointing and waving. At us. At me. And the bumblebee. *Pop, pop, pop.* The ambulance doors close on Boyle.

'—ven listening to me?' Nico demands as I blink back to reality. His gun grinds against my cheek, but I still don't feel it. I don't feel anything. I haven't for years.

'Where's Boyle?' he says.

'I don't kn—'

His left hand springs out like a cobra, sinking its fangs into the center of my shirt and tugging me toward him. He pivots to his left, tripping me, and I fall back again, down into a puddle, sending water everywhere. Nico's right on me, straddling my chest, pinning my biceps with his knees, and never moving his gun from my scarred cheek.

'I found your letter,' Nico growls as the Chinese menu peeks out from the inside pocket of his army jacket. '*Where's Boyle!?*'

I want to tell him it's fake . . . that The Roman . . . and the First Lady . . . that I don't want to die. But after eight years of imagining this moment, imagining every minute of finally confronting Nico – what I'd say, where I'd stand, how I'd cross my arms against my chest, even what I'd do if he tried to lash out and throw a punch . . . how I'd duck down at the last instant, how I'd be ready this time, and he'd miss me, and then, before he ever saw it coming, how I'd spin back and clench his throat in my hands, squeezing so hard, hearing him gasp, and still clutching tighter, my fingers digging into his windpipe as we tumbled to the ground and he gasped for mercy – the only words that leave my lips are the ones that have been there since the day he shredded my face. The one question that the doctors, the shrinks, the President, my family, my friends, my parents, and I have never been able to answer:

'Nico,' I blurt. 'Why did you do this to me?'

He cocks his head as if he understands perfectly. Then his brow contracts. He hasn't heard a word I've said.

'I know you've been in contact with him,' he says. 'That's why God steered the bullet your way. The ricochet. That's why you got broken.'

'That's not true!' I shout as a brand-new rage swells within me.

'*It is true! The Book of Fate is written! Everything for a reason!*' he insists in a puff of hot breath that smells like beef jerky. 'You sided with the Beast! That bullet in your face – your fate is written – that's God's will!'

'Nico, they lied!'

'Did you not speak to him? *Did you!?* See . . . it's true!' he shouts, reading my expression and digging the gun into my cheek. 'God gave you your chance at redemption, and you spit at it! That's why He brought me here – to finish His job! To see your blood!' he insists, his finger tightening around the trigger. I try to fight, but he's too strong. All I see is the outline of Nico above me, the light behind him, his head shielding me from the rain, the rosary around his neck swaying like a hypnotist's pocket watch. He pulls the hammer back on his gun. 'This is meant to hurt, Wesley.' He tugs me toward him.

I clamp my eyes shut at the sudden beam of light, but all I hear is—

'Oh, Lord! Y-You have it,' Nico whispers as his hand starts to tremble. I see his eyes glitter in the dark.

'What're you—? *What?*' I ask, confused.

'I couldn't see in the photo . . . but this close,' he stutters, staring at my face. 'It's so clear,' he insists. 'Your scars! The way they intersect . . . jagged in your flesh . . . one cutting through the other. The papers said it was like railroad tracks, but it's really a perfect – a perfect – a perfect – a perfect . . . *cross*,' he blurts. 'Of course! Mother of God, how could I not—? You weren't meant to die on that day, Wesley – you were meant to be born on it!' Craning his head back and staring up at the sky, he adds, 'You transformed him, didn't You? By my actions . . . through Your will. That was his role – *the crossbearer*,' he insists, his head still up as he mumbles a brief prayer.

In the sudden silence, I faintly hear the First Lady's voice in the distance. Lisbeth shouts something back.

They're too far for me to make it out, but with his height-
ened hearing, Nico should—

His eyes pop wide as if he's heard his own name. Slowly,
he lowers his chin, following the—

'That's not true,' he whispers, holding his stomach like
someone put a corkscrew in his gut. I can't hear what
Lisbeth's saying, but as I look up at Nico, it's not hard to
translate. 'No . . . The Three never—'

Nico's knees still pin my arms, but his weight – all the
pressure – is gone, and his body starts shuddering with
his own personal earthquake. Behind us and miles to the
left, a train engine's faint howl pierces the air.

Nico's chin quivers; his eyes swell with tears. Reaching
up to the sides of his head, he clutches the tops of his
ears, tilts his head down, and pulls tight, as if he's trying
to rip them from his skull. 'Please, God,' he begs. 'Tell me
they're lying . . .'

'She's gonna need an ambulance, Wes,' The Roman bellows
in the distance.

Lisbeth.

Jerking wildly, I struggle to sit up. Nico doesn't bother
to fight. Sliding from my chest, he crumbles like a rag doll
onto the wet grass and curls in full fetal position. Sixty to
zero in less than ten seconds.

'Don't say that, God,' he sobs and pleads, his hands
tugging at his ears. 'Please . . . don't . . . don't turn Your
back on me! Help me heed the Book! *Please!*'

'Keep hiding, Wes!' The Roman shouts, even louder than
before.

Scrambling to my feet, I peer through the shrub's
branches, down the stone-paved, tree-lined path, straining
to see shapes in the faint light. Down at the end, at the
base of the ancient banyan tree, I can just make out two

figures as The Roman rams his knee into Lisbeth's face and she lurches backward. Just behind them, the First Lady has her back turned. Seeing her, I should be boiling, raging. But as I study the back of her crooked neck . . . all I feel now is a bitter empty chill. I need to get to Lis—

'*I know you're there!*' The Roman taunts. For the first time, it pisses me off.

Lisbeth's still—

'*She's hurting, Wes!*' The Roman adds. '*Ask her!*'

I tense to run, but there's a tug on my slacks. And a familiar click.

Behind me, Nico rises from the mud – climbing to one knee, then the other – his tall frame unfolding like an Erector set. His short black hair is soaked and matted against his head, while his gun is pointed at my chest.

'Nico, let go of me.'

'You're my crossbearer, Wesley,' he says as he wipes tears from his eyes. 'God selected you. For me.'

'*She's bleeding pretty bad, Wes!*' The Roman shouts.

Lisbeth yells something too, but I'm so focused on Nico, I can't hear it.

'Nico, listen to me – I know you heard them . . .'

'The crossbearer carries the weight!' Smiling sweetly, he points his gun at his own head. 'Will you catch my body when I fall?'

'Nico, don't—'

'Will you catch me when I fall, fall, fall from grace . . . the crossbearer to bear witness . . . ?' He lowers his gun, then raises it up again, pressing it against his temple. I hear Lisbeth moaning.

'God sent you to save her too, didn't He?' He stares at me, transfixed, the gun still at his head. 'Save me as well, my angel.'

Behind us, the train whistle howls, so close it's almost deafening. Nico presses his lips together, trying to look like he's not cringing. But I can see his jaw tightening. For me, it's noisy. For him, it's overwhelming. Wild-eyed, he points the gun back at me to keep me from running.

I don't care. 'I'm innocent,' I tell him as I step toward him. He knows it's a warning.

'Nobody's innocent, Dad.'

Dad?

'Lord have mercy on my son,' he continues, his gun moving from my chest, to my head, back to my chest. He's crying again. He's in agony. 'You understand, Dad, right?' he begs. 'I had to do it. They told me . . . *Mom said to follow the Book!* Please tell me you understand!'

'Y-Yes,' I say as I put a hand on his shoulder. 'Of course, I understand. Son.'

Nico laughs out loud, the tears still streaming down his cheeks. 'Thank you,' he says, barely able to contain himself as he clutches his rosary. 'I knew . . . I knew you'd be my angel.'

Turning left, I glance through an opening in the shrub. The Roman's aiming his gun down at Lisbeth.

'Nico, *move!*' I say as I shove my way past him. All I need to do is—

Blam!

I jump back as The Roman's gun explodes. Down the path, a tiny supernova of light breaks the darkness like a burst firefly, then disappears.

I run as fast as I can.

Lisbeth's already screaming.

108

'You don't believe me, do you?' Boyle asked Rogo as the white van skidded out of the parking lot and swerved onto Griffin Road.

'Does it matter what I think?' Rogo replied, gripping the console between their bucket seats and staring out the front window. 'C'mon, make this light.'

The van blew through the 25th Avenue intersection as Rogo checked his side mirror to see if anyone was following. So far, all clear.

'You still need to hear it, Rogo. If something happens t— Someone needs to know what they did.'

'And you couldn't just write a letter to the editor like everyone else?' When Boyle didn't respond, Rogo shook his head and again glanced in the side mirror. The Marshals' white building was barely a dot in the horizon. 'So all this time, you were in Witness Protection?'

'I told you, version 2.0. *Witness Fortification,*' Boyle clarified. 'Not that they'd ever acknowledge its existence. But once I told Manning what was happening – usually, it takes the President one phone call to make something happen. It took Manning three separate calls to get me inside.'

'And they do this a lot? I mean, c'mon, making families think their loved ones are dead?'

'How do you think the government prosecutes their terrorism cases against these suicidal maniacs? You think some of those witnesses would've talked if the Justice Department couldn't absolutely guarantee their safety? There are animals in the world, Rogo. If The Three, The Four, whatever they call themselves – if they thought I was alive and hiding, they'd slit my wife and kids' throats, then go out for a beer.'

'But to lie to people like that . . .'

'I didn't choose this life. The Three chose me. And once that happened, once they tossed me aside for the First Lady, this was the only way to keep my wife safe, and my kid – both kids – alive.'

'You still could've—'

'Could've what? Taken the family into hiding with me? Put everyone at risk and hoped for the best? The only absolutely unassailable hiding spot is the one where no one knows you're hiding. Besides, The Three have single-handedly compromised our top law enforcement agencies, picked apart our databases for their private use, and collected thousands of dollars in Title 50 money for confidential tips about terror attacks – all without us ever knowing who the hell they were.'

'Until two days ago when they panicked and went after Wes.'

'They didn't panic,' Boyle said as he slowly pressed the brakes. Two blocks in front of them, the three lanes of Griffin Road narrowed into one. Something was definitely blocking the road. 'Is that construction?' Boyle asked, craning his neck and squinting through the dark.

'I think it's an accident.'

'You sure?'

'Isn't that an ambulance?

Boyle nodded as the cars came into view – an ambulance, a tow truck, and a silver car turned sideways from the collision. Boyle glanced to his left, already eyeing the side streets.

'Something wrong?' Rogo asked.

'Just being cautious.' Refusing to lose his thought, he added, 'Anyhow, The Three didn't panic. They got greedy and fat – thanks mostly to The Roman.'

'So what the First Lady told Wes was true,' Rogo said. 'That they started with all these small tips – VX gas in Syria, training camps in Sudan – and then used that to build credibility until they could find the monster threats and ask for the multimillion-dollar let's-all-retire paydays.'

'No, no, no. Don't you see?' Boyle asked, quickly pulling out of the single-file line of traffic and rechecking what was causing the accident. But all was normal. Ambulance. Tow truck. Wrecked silver car. Flipping open the console between them, Boyle checked on a small box the size of a videotape, then closed it just as fast. He tried to hide it with his elbow, but Rogo saw the word *Hornady* in bright red letters on the box's side. Growing up in Alabama, he knew the logo from his dad's hunting trips. Hornady bullets. 'Once they established The Roman as a solid informant, they didn't even need the big threat. Why do you think people are so worried about agencies working together? The Roman would bring his info into the Service, then Micah and O'Shea would serve it again from their outposts in the FBI and CIA. Now, each one's confirmed the other. That's how informants get verified: You check it with someone else. And once all three agencies agree, well, fiction becomes fact. It's like that bombing threat on the New York City subways a few years back – not a single grain of truth behind it, but the informant still got paid. Meanwhile, is this the only way to get to I-95?'

Rogo nodded and cocked an eyebrow. 'I don't get it – they made it all up?'

'Not in the beginning. But once they built that reputation for The Roman, they could sprinkle bad tips in with the good and earn a little more cash. And with the big stuff – you think six-million-dollar tips just jump in your lap?'

'But to make something that big up—'

'It's like making the Statue of Liberty disappear – it's the kind of magic trick you pull off once, then disappear until the dust settles. So when their first attempt . . .'

'*Blackbird.*'

'. . . when *Blackbird* was set up, they had it perfect: hold a fake NSA computer hostage and reel in the cash. It was big enough to get serious money, but unlike promising that a building was about to blow up, there was no penalty or suspicion if the White House decided not to pay. Then when *Blackbird* failed and we *didn't* pay, they were smart enough to realize they needed an inside track at the White House just to make sure the next request went through.'

'That's when they approached and threatened you.'

'When they approached and threatened me, *and* when they tried the softer sell on someone with even more power than that.'

'But to assume that you or the First Lady would go for it – much less be able to pull six-million-dollar strings over and over . . .'

'Y'ever been fishing, Rogo? Sometimes, you're better off throwing in a few lines with different bait and seeing who nibbles. That's the only reason they approached both of us. And though she'll forever deny it – in fact, she probably doesn't even think she did anything wrong anymore – but the First Lady's the one who swam toward the hook,'

Boyle explained. 'And as for making their *next* six million happen, or the ten million after that, look at any White House in history. The most powerful people in the room aren't the ones with the big titles. They're the ones with the President's ear. I've had that ear since I was twenty-three years old. The only one who's had it longer is the person he's married to. Whatever they came in next with – if *she* had a hand in it and thought it'd help them on security issues – believe me, it'd have gotten through.'

'I don't get it, though. Once *Blackbird* got nuked, didn't they at least need *some* kinda results before they could make another big request like that?'

'Whattya think I was?' Boyle asked.

Rogo turned to his left but didn't say a word.

'Rogo, for the snake-oil scam to succeed, people only need to see the cure work once. That's what The Three gave them – courtesy of two bullets in my chest.'

Sitting up in his seat, Rogo continued to study Boyle, who was staring at the open back doors of the ambulance that was less than a car's length away.

'Twenty minutes before the shooting, the Secret Service Web site was sent a tip about a man named Nico Hadrian who was planning to assassinate President Manning when he stepped out of his limo at Daytona International Speedway. It was signed *The Roman*. From that moment on, anything he would've given them – especially when it was corroborated by the FBI and CIA – well, you know the paranoid world we live in. Forget drugs and arms sales. Information is the opiate of the military masses. And terrorist information about attacks on our own soil? That's how you print your own money,' Boyle said. 'Even better, by taking their stealthier approach with the First Lady, they wouldn't've even had to split the cash four ways.'

As they pulled past the ambulance, they both looked to their left and peered into its open back doors. But before they could even see that there wasn't a victim, a gurney, or a single medical supply inside, there was a metal thud against the back door. Then one from above. On both sides of the van, a half dozen plainclothes U.S. marshals swarmed from the tow truck and silver car, fanning out and pointing their guns against the side windows and front windshield. Outside Boyle's door, a marshal with bushy caterpillar eyebrows tapped the barrel of his gun against the glass.

'Nice to see you again, Boyle. Now get the fuck out of that van.'

109

'She's hurting, Wes!' The Roman called out to the empty darkness as the rain ticked against his umbrella. 'Ask her!'

'H-He's not stupid,' Lisbeth whispered, down on her rear in the wet grass. With her back against the Celtic headstone for support, she pressed both hands against her eye, where The Roman had rammed his knee into her face. She could already feel it swelling shut.

Back by the tree, the First Lady stared coldly at The Roman. 'Why did you bring me here?' she demanded.

'Lenore, this isn't—'

'You said it was an emergency, but to bring me to Wes!'

'Lenore!'

The First Lady studied The Roman, her expression unchanging. 'You were planning to shoot me, weren't you?' she asked.

Lisbeth looked up at the question.

Turning to his right, The Roman squinted up the crooked stone path and, as his Service training kicked in, visually divided the graveyard into smaller, more manageable sections. A grid search, they called it. 'Be smart, Lenore. If I wanted to kill you, I would've shot you in the car.'

'Unless he wanted to make it look like – *puhhh*,' Lisbeth said, violently spitting flecks of saliva at the ground as the train whistle screamed of its impending arrival, '. . . like Wes killed you, and he killed Wes. Th-Then he's the hero and there's no one left to point fingers.'

Shaking his head, The Roman stayed glued to the meat-ball shrubs. '*She's bleeding pretty bad, Wes!*'

The First Lady turned toward Boyle's grave, then back to The Roman, her pinkie flicking harder than ever at the strap of her umbrella as she said in a poisonous, low voice, 'She's right, isn't she?'

'She's just trying to rile you, Lenore.'

'No, she's— *You swore no one would ever be hurt!*' the First Lady exploded. She spun back toward the front entrance of the cemetery.

There was a metallic click.

'Lenore,' The Roman warned as he raised his gun, 'if you take one more step, I think we're going to have a serious problem.'

She froze.

Turning back toward Lisbeth, The Roman took a deep breath through his nose. It was supposed to be cleaner than this. But if Wes insisted on hiding . . . Carefully aiming his gun, he announced to Lisbeth, 'I need you to put your hand up, please.'

'What're you talking about?' she asked, still sitting on the ground.

'*Put your damn hand out,*' The Roman growled. 'Palm facing me,' he added, holding up his bandaged right palm to Lisbeth.

Even under the shadows of the umbrella, it was impossible to miss the tight white bandage with the perfectly round, blood-red circle at the center of it. Lisbeth knew what he was planning. Once her body was found with stigmata – like a signature – all the blame would shift to –

Lisbeth stopped seeing the rain. Her whole body started to shake.

'Put your hand up, Lisbeth – or I swear to God I'll put it in your brain.'

Curling both arms toward her chest, she looked over at the First Lady, who again started to walk away.

'*Lenore,*' The Roman warned without turning. The First Lady stopped.

Lisbeth felt the wet ground soaking her rear end. Her hands still hadn't moved.

'Fine,' The Roman said, aiming at Lisbeth's head as he cocked the hammer. 'Have it in your brai—'

Lisbeth raised her left hand in the air. The Roman squeezed the trigger. And the gun roared with a thunderclap that left a ringing silence in its wake.

A spurt of blood erupted from the back of Lisbeth's hand, just below her knuckles. Before she even felt the pain and screamed, blood was running down her wrist. Already in shock, she kept staring at the dime-sized burned circle in her palm as if it weren't her own. When she tried making a fist, the pain set in. Her hand went blurry, like it was fading away. She was about to pass out.

Without a word, The Roman aimed his gun at Lisbeth's now-bobbing head.

'*Don't!*' a familiar voice yelled from the back of the cemetery.

The Roman and the First Lady turned to the right, tracing the voice up the tree-lined path.

'Don't touch her!' Wes shouted, his body a thin silhouette as he rushed out from the shrub. 'I'm right here.'

Just like The Roman wanted.

110

Aided by the glow from the floodlit flagpole in the distance, I study the outline of The Roman from the top of the stone path. He stares right back at me, his gun still pointed at Lisbeth.

'That's the right choice, Wes,' he calls out from the base of the tree. His voice is warm, like we're at a dinner party.

'Lisbeth, can you hear me?' I shout.

She's fifty yards away and still on the ground. Among the shadows and the overhang of the banyan tree, she's nothing but a small black blob between two graves.

'She's fine,' The Roman insists. 'Though if you don't come help her, I think she might pass out.'

He's trying to get me closer, and with Lisbeth bleeding on the ground, I don't have a choice.

'I need to check she's okay first,' I say, as I head toward the path. He knows I'm trying to stall. 'Step back and I'll come forward.'

'Go fuck yourself, Wes.' Turning back to Lisbeth, he raises his gun.

'No! Wait – I'm coming!' Rushing down the stone path, I put my hands in the air to let him know I'm done.

He lowers his gun slightly, but his finger doesn't leave the trigger.

If I were smart, I'd continue to watch him, but as I stumble down the path between the rows of headstones,

I turn toward the First Lady. Her wide eyes are pleading, her whole body is in a begging position. This time, her tears aren't fake. But unlike before, she's looking in the wrong place for help.

'Don't take it so personally,' The Roman tells me, following my gaze.

Moving toward Lisbeth, watching my footing, I keep looking at the silhouette of Lenore Manning. For eight years, she's known I blamed myself for putting Boyle in that limo. For eight years, she's looked into what's left of my face and pretended I was part of her family. On my birthday three years ago, when they were teasing me that I should go on more dates, she even kissed me on my cheek – *directly on the scars* – just to prove I shouldn't be so self-conscious. I couldn't feel her lips because they were touching my dead spot. But I felt it all. Leaving the office, I cried the whole way home, amazed at what a beautiful and thoughtful gesture it was.

Right now, walking past a shadowed stone crypt with red and blue stained-glass doors, I again well up with tears. Not from sadness. Or fear. My eyes squint, squeezing each drop to my cheeks. These tears sting from rage.

Down on my left, Lenore Manning's lips pucker like she's starting to whistle. She's about to say my name.

I glare back, telling her not to bother.

Even in this dim cemetery, she's fluent in reading her staff. And that's all I've ever been. Not family. Not friend. Not even a wounded puppy that you take in to clear your conscience from the other crap you do in your life. Hard as it is to admit, I've never been anything more than staff.

I'm tempted to yell, curse, scream at what she did to me. But there's no need. The closer I get, the more clearly she can see it for herself. It's carved deep into my face.

For a second, her eyebrows tilt. Then she takes a tiny step back and lowers her umbrella so I can't see her face. I'll take it as a victory. Lenore Manning has faced just about everything. But at this moment, she can't face me.

Shaking my head, I turn back to The Roman, who's now forty feet away.

'Keep coming,' he says.

I stop. Diagonally to my right, between two stubby headstones, Lisbeth is down on her knees, cradling her bloody hand toward her chest. In the eerie bluish light, I can see that her hair is soaked, her left eye puffy and already swollen. I'm nearly there.

'I'm sorry,' she stutters as if it's her fault.

'I said *keep coming*,' The Roman insists.

'*Don't!*' Lisbeth interrupts. 'He's gonna kill you.'

The Roman doesn't argue.

'Promise me you'll let her leave,' I say.

'Of course,' he sings.

'Wes!' Lisbeth says, her breathing growing heavy. It's all she can do to stay conscious.

There are no sirens in the distance, no one riding to the rescue. From here on in, the only way Lisbeth's getting out of here is if I step forward and try to make the trade.

The train gets louder in the distance. There's a whisper over my shoulder. I turn back to follow the sound, but the only thing there is my own reflection in the red and blue stained-glass doors of the crypt. Inside, behind the glass, I swear something moves.

'You're hearing ghosts now?' The Roman teases.

As the whispers get louder, I continue toward him on the path. I've got barely twenty feet to go. The rain lightens overhead as I reach the cover of the tree. Its tendrils dangle from above like a puppeteer's fingers. I'm so close, I can see Lisbeth's body shaking . . . and the First Lady's pinkie flicking her umbrella strap . . . and the hammer on The Roman's gun as he cocks it back with his thumb.

'Perfect,' he says with a wry grin. Before I can even react, he turns to the side and raises his gun. Directly at Lisbeth's heart.

111

'*No – don't!*' I shout, already running.

There's a high-pitched hiss. But not from his gun. From behind me.

Before I even realize what's happening, a burst of blood spurts from The Roman's right hand, through the back of his palm, just below his knuckles. He's been shot. At the impact, The Roman's own gun goes off.

Out of the corner of my eye, I see Lisbeth slapping her shoulder like she's swatting a mosquito. I can make out something dark – blood – leaking out between her fingers, like water seeping from a cracked well. She pulls her hand away from her shoulder and holds it up in front of her face. When she sees the blood, her face goes white, and her eyes roll back in her head. She's already unconscious.

'Shit, shit, *shit!*' The Roman yells, bent over, jerking wildly and holding his shattered right hand to his chest. On his right, the First Lady takes off, running back toward the main entrance and disappearing into the darkness. The Roman's in too much pain to stop her. On the back of his hand, the hole's no bigger than a penny. But the signature with the stigmata is unmistakable.

'*You lied to me! He's an angel!*' Nico howls from the back of the graveyard, up by the shrubs. He plows toward us through the darkness, his gun straight out, ready for the kill shot. He's in silhouette. I can't see his face. But his arm is steady as ever.

'Y-You're going to Hell,' The Roman whispers as he anxiously throws his own personal Hail Mary. 'Like Judas, Nico. You're Judas now.'

The way Nico flinches, it's clear he hears it. It still doesn't slow him down. 'God's laws last longer than those who break them!' he insists as he gathers his strength. '*Your fate is rewritten!*' Up the path, he grips his rosary with one hand and aims the gun with the other.

'Nico, think of your mother!' The Roman begs.

Nico nods as the tears again stream down his face. 'I am,' he growls, but as he takes aim, there's a loud whoosh from behind the back fence of the cemetery. Up on the train tracks, a silver passenger train bursts into view, moving so fast it almost appears from nowhere. The clanking is deafening. My ears pop from the sudden vacuum in the air. For Nico, it's fifty times worse.

He still fights it, gritting his teeth as he squeezes the trigger. But the noise is already too much. His arm jerks for half a second, the shot hisses from his gun, and as the bullet zings past The Roman's shoulder and shatters a hunk of bark from the nearby tree, Nico Hadrian actually misses.

A dark grin returns to The Roman's face as the train continues to whip by. Barely able to hold his gun with his right hand, he tosses aside the umbrella and switches the gun to his bandaged left. The way his right fist is shaking, he's clearly in pain. He doesn't care. His shoulders straighten. His knees steady. As he raises his gun and takes aim, I'm already running at him. So is Nico, who's at least thirty feet behind me.

The Roman has time for just one shot. There's no question who's more dangerous.

Bam!

As the shot explodes from The Roman's gun, it's drowned out by the still-passing train. Behind me, just over my right shoulder, there's a deep guttural grunt as Nico takes it in the chest. He still keeps running toward us. He doesn't get far. Within two steps, his legs lock and his too-close-together eyes widen into full circles. Tumbling forward and off balance, his body hurtles face-first toward the ground. In mid-fall, the rosary flies from his hand. He's not getting up.

As Nico crashes, The Roman turns his gun toward me. I'm already moving too fast. Lost in momentum, I collide with The Roman like he's a tackling dummy, my arms wrapping around his shoulders as I ram him at full speed. The impact sends him staggering backward to his left. To my own surprise, it feels like there's a metal plate against his chest. He learned it from Boyle. Bulletproof vest. The good news is, he's already weakened from being shot in the hand. We trip over his umbrella in the dirt. I hold tight to his chest, riding him like a lumberjack on a falling tree.

As we crash to the ground, his gun flies from his hand across the wet grass. His back slams into a zigzagging tree root bursting up from the earth, while his head smacks backward into a jagged rock. The vest helps with his back, but his face clenches in pain as the rock jabs his skull.

Scrambling up and digging my knee into his stomach, I grab the collar of The Roman's shirt with my left hand, pull him toward me, and punch as hard as I can with my right, ramming my fist just above his eye. His head whips into the jagged rock again, and a small cut opens above his left eye. He grits his teeth at the pain, his eyes squeezing shut to protect his sockets. Flushed with adrenaline, I hit him again, and the cut reddens and widens.

The real damage, though, comes from the rock under The Roman's head. With each of my punches, there's a sickening dull *gkkkk* as it drills through his black hair, into the back of his head. Still reeling from being shot, he thrashes his bandaged left hand toward his head, trying to protect himself from the rock.

Refusing to let up, I punch him again. And again. This one's for all the surgeries. And for having to learn to chew on the left side of my cheek. And for not being able to lick stuff off my lips . . .

Below me, The Roman shoves his bandaged hand between his head and the rock. It's not until that moment, with my arm cocked in the air, that I realize he's not protecting his head from the rock. He's pulling it from the dirt.

Oh, crap.

I punch down as hard as I can. The Roman swings his left arm like a baseball bat. He's got the jagged gray rock clutched in his fist. I'm fast. He's faster.

The sharp edge of the rock drills into my jaw like a razor on the tip of a missile, sending me falling to the right and crashing on my shoulder in the soaking grass on the edge of the path. Tasting victory, The Roman's almost up. Climbing to my feet, I scramble as fast as I can, clambering to get out of there before he can—

He jabs me with the rock, his own personal pile driver. It's a solid shot too – just above my neck at the base of my skull. I feel every ounce of it. As I stumble forward, unable to slow down, my vision goes blurry, then blinks back. No, don't pass out . . .

I crash down on my knees and palms as tiny rocks from the stone path gnaw into my hands. The Roman is right behind me. He breathes heavily through his nose. His feet pound at the path, kicking a spray of pebbles at my back. 'You're—!' He grips the back of my shirt. I try to run, but he's pulling too hard. *'You're fuckin' dead!'* he roars, whipping me around like an Olympic hammer throw and flinging me backward toward the polished stone crypt with the X-shaped wrought-iron bars that protect the red and blue stained-glass doors. If I hit the bars at this speed . . .

There's a sickening crunch as my spine smacks against it. A half dozen panels shatter and pop like Christmas lights, one right where my head hits the glass. There's something warm and wet on the back of my neck. If I can feel it, I'm bleeding bad.

As he tugs me forward, my neck goes limp and my head tips back. The rain comes down in slow motion, millions of silver frozen pine needles. My vision goes blurry again. The sky fades to bl—

'Nnnnnnnn,' I hear myself say, fighting awake as he drags me away from the crypt. Still gripping my shirt, he looks around for a moment. Lisbeth's unconscious. The First Lady's gone. Nico's down. Whatever The Roman had planned, he needs to improvise now. His eyes scan the— That's when he sees it.

He yanks hard, and I stumble forward, barely able to stay on my feet. Tucking my head under his arm, The Roman spins around, grips me in a headlock, and leads me across the stone path like a dog being tugged from the dining room. The way his sausage wrist wraps around my throat, it's nearly impossible to breathe. I try to dig in my heels, but my fight's long gone. Still, it's not until we cross the stone path that I finally spot our destination. Diagonally behind two matching husband-and-wife gray headstones sits a small patch of grass that shines a bit greener than the rest of the surrounding mossy plots. At the bottom edge of the patch, a small piece of the grass puckers. Like a carpet. Oh, God. That's Astroturf. He's dragging me toward— That's a freshly dug grave.

112

Tugged toward the open hole, I frantically backpedal, almost vomiting up my Adam's apple. The Roman squeezes the headlock tighter, lugging me toward the hole.

'*Get off me!*' I scream, clawing at his arm and trying to free my neck. He doesn't budge, pulling the leash even harder. As my feet slide from the path, through the damp grass, and toward the husband-and-wife graves, my arms and legs flail wildly – at the ground, in the air – searching for something to latch onto. At the foot of the matching rectangular headstones, I grab a branch from a nearby bush. I try holding on, but we're moving so fast, the sharp woody stems stab into my palm. The pain's too intense. With a final grunt, The Roman yanks me free, dragging me forward.

The freshly dug grave is dead ahead, but as we squeeze between the matching graves, I lunge to my left and clench one of the headstones. My fingers creep like tarantulas across the front, digging into the engraved letter *D* in the word *HUSBAND*.

Enraged, The Roman tightens his vise grip around my throat. I feel my face swell with blood. I still don't let go. He tugs harder, and my fingers start to slide. From the angle he's pulling, the sharp granite corner of the rectangular headstone scratches the underside of my forearm. The Roman yanks so hard, I feel like my head's about to come loose from my neck. My shoulder's burning. My fingertips start to slide. The granite's already slick with rain.

Stretching out his leg to the foot of the grave behind us, The Roman kicks off the Astroturf covering. I look up just long enough to see the seven-foot hole . . . the crumbling dirt walls . . .

I dig my fingers in, but the engraving's only so deep.

The Roman's right hand is soaked in blood, useless from being shot. No doubt, he's in pain. But he knows what's at stake. Leaning forward and closing the vise, he puts his full weight into it. My feet slowly slide across the grass. I try to take a breath, but it doesn't come – he's holding too tight. My arm is numb. My fingers start shaking, skidding from their perch. Darkness again presses in from the sides. *Please, God, take care of my mom and d—*

Blam! Blam!

Small stones spray across my face. The Roman's grip loosens. And I fall to the wet grass, coughing and hacking as oxygen reenters my lungs.

Above me, the top edge of the husband's grave is shattered from one of the bullets. I stare at The Roman, who spins to face me. His blue eyes flit anxiously. There's a brand-new hole in his shirt, at the center of his chest. But no blood. He staggers backward, but not for long.

On my left, just a few feet away, Lisbeth is on her feet and breathing heavily, her own hand bleeding as she grips The Roman's gun. As she lowers it, she thinks she's won.

'Lisbeth . . .' I cough, fighting to get the words out. *'His vest!'*

Lisbeth's eyebrows leap up.

Snarling like a cheetah, The Roman lunges toward her.

Panicking, Lisbeth raises the gun and clenches the trigger. Two shots go off. They both plow into The Roman's chest. He's moving so fast, they barely slow him down. Inches away, he grabs for the gun. Lisbeth pulls the trigger one final time, and as the pistol explodes, a single bullet rips through the side of The Roman's neck. He's so lost in rage, I don't think he feels it. Lisbeth steps backward, barely able to get a scream out. He's all over her within seconds.

Ripping the gun from her hands, The Roman tackles her head-on. As they fall onto the stone path, Lisbeth's head slams back into the concrete. Her body goes limp. Taking no chances, The Roman pins his forearm against her throat. Her legs aren't thrashing. Her arms sag at her sides.

Shaking off my own beating, I hop to my feet and run my hands through the grass, my fingers brailling against the scattered shards of broken granite. On any given day, I'd have no chance against a six-foot, 220-pound, Secret Service–trained steel wall of a man. But right now The Roman's got a fresh wound in his neck and another in his hand. And I've got a sharp hunk of granite headstone clenched in my fist. As I run toward him, he's still bent over Lisbeth. I don't know if I can take him. But I do know I'll leave one hell of a dent.

Cocking the jagged shard back, I grit my teeth and swing at the back of The Roman's head with everything I have left. The shard is shaped like a brick cracked in half, with a tiny point in the corner. It strikes right behind his ear. His scream alone is worth it – a throaty whimpering grunt even he can't contain.

To his credit, as he slaps his hand against the side of his head, he doesn't fall over. Instead, he catches his balance, turns back to face me, and lumbers to his feet. Before he can completely turn around, I take another full swing, cracking the granite block across his face. He stumbles back, falling on his ass. I still don't let up. Stealing from his own playbook, I grip the front of his shirt, pull him toward me, and aim for the cut above his eye. Then I wind up and hit him again. The blood comes quickly.

A strand of drool falls like a silk thread from my bottom lip. He's the reason my mouth won't close, I tell myself as I swing again, driving the edge of the granite into his wound and watching the blood cover the side of his face. Like me. Like mine.

His eyes roll back in his head. I hit him again, determined to widen the wound. My drool sags lower, and I pummel him harder than ever. I want him to know. I want him to stare at it. Each granite blow takes another hunk of skin. I want him to live with it. I want him to turn away from his *own reflection in storefront windows*! I want him t—

I stop right there, my arm in midair, my chest rising and falling as I catch my breath. Lowering my fist, I wipe the saliva from my lip and once again feel the polite rain as it drips from the tip of my nose and chin.

I wouldn't wish it on anyone.

And with that, I let go of The Roman's shirt. He collapses across my shoes.

The granite block falls from my hand, clunking against the concrete. I spin back to Lisbeth, who's still lying on the ground behind me. Her arm is twisted awkwardly above her head. Dropping to my knees, I check her chest. It's not moving.

'Lisbeth, are you—? *Can you hear me?*' I shout, sliding on my knees next to her.

No response.

Oh, God. No. No, no, no . . .

I grab her arm and feel for a pulse. There's nothing there. Wasting no time, I tilt her head back, open her mouth, and—

'Hggggh!'

I jump back at the sound as she violently coughs. Her right hand instinctively covers her mouth. But her left – with the wound – stays stranded awkwardly above her head.

She spits and dry-heaves as the blood rushes back to her face.

'Y-You okay?' I ask.

She coughs hard. Good enough. Glancing sideways without moving her neck, she spots The Roman's body just a few feet away. 'But we need – we hafta—'

'Just relax,' I tell her.

She shakes her head, more insistent than ever. 'But wh— what abou—?'

'Slow down. We got him, okay?'

'Not him, Wes – *her.*' My throat locks as the light rain pats my shoulders. 'Where's the First Lady?'

113

Striding up the block, her umbrella still over her head, the First Lady glanced over her shoulder. Behind her, from the cemetery, two more gunshots exploded. Her ankle twisted at the sound. She didn't slow down. Hobbling for a moment, she quickly found her balance and continued to march forward, still trembling.

She knew it would end like this. Even when things were quiet, even when she first realized whom she'd inadvertently aligned with, she knew it would never go away. There was no escaping this mistake.

Another two shots rang out, then a final one that echoed from behind the tall trees. She flinched hard at each blast. Was that The Roman or—? She didn't want Wes to die. Along with Boyle, Wes's being shot at the speedway was the thing she'd never been able to shake, even after all these years. That's why she always tried to be supportive . . . why she'd never objected when her husband brought him back on board. But now that Wes knew the truth . . . She shook her head. No. She was tricked. She was. And only trying to help.

With a sharp right, The First Lady turned the corner, her heels clicking against the pavement as she entered the small parking lot that ran along the south side of the cemetery. At this hour, it was empty – except for the shiny black Chevy Suburban that The Roman had brought her over in.

Racing for the driver's door, she ripped it open and climbed inside, already rehearsing her side of the story. With Nico there . . . with the hole in Lisbeth's hand . . . that part was easy. America loves to blame the psycho. And even if Wes managed to survive . . .

Playing out the permutations, she reached up to adjust the rearview mirror. There was a sharp hiss from behind. A dime-sized black circle burst through the back of the First Lady's hand as the rearview mirror shattered. At first, she didn't even feel it. In the few remaining shards of glass, she could see a familiar figure in the backseat, his fingers creeping along his rosary.

'I saw you when you drove in,' Nico said, his voice calm.

'Oh, God . . . my hand,' she cried, seeing it and clutching her shaking palm as the fiery pain shot up to her elbow.

'You're taller than I thought. You were sitting during the competency hearings.'

'Please,' she begged, the tears already welling in her eyes as her hand went numb. 'Please don't kill me.'

Nico didn't move, his right hand holding his gun in his lap. 'It surprised me to see you with Number One. What did they call him? The Roman? He hurt me too.'

In the cracked mirror, the First Lady saw Nico look down at the top of his rib cage, where he'd been shot.

'Yes . . . yes, of course,' the First Lady insisted. 'The Roman hurt both of us, Nico. He threatened me – made me come with him or he'd—'

'God hurt me also,' Nico interrupted. His left hand gripped the rosary, his thumb slowly climbing from wooden bead to wooden bead, counting its way to the engraving of Mary. 'God took my mother from me.'

'Nico, you . . .' Her voice cracked. 'God . . . please, Nico . . . we've all lost—'

'But it was The Three who took my father,' he added as he lifted the gun and pressed it to the back of the First Lady's head. 'That was my error. Not fate. Not the Masons. The Three took him. When I joined them . . . what I did in their name . . . don't you see? Misreading the Book. That's why God had to send me the angel.'

Shivering uncontrollably, the First Lady raised her hands in the air and struggled to glance over her shoulder. If she could turn around . . . get him to look at her face . . . to see her as a human being . . . 'Please don't . . . please don't do this!' she begged, facing Nico and fighting back tears. It'd been nearly a decade since she'd felt the onslaught of a deep cry. Not since the day they left the White House, when they returned home to Florida, held a small press conference on their lawn and realized, after everyone was gone, that there was no one but themselves to clean up the reporters' discarded coffee cups that were scattered across their front yard. 'I can't die like this,' she sobbed.

Unmoved, Nico held his gun in place, pointing it at her head. 'But it wasn't just The Three, was it? I heard the reporter, Dr. Manning. I know. The Four. That's what she said, right? One, Two, Three, you're Four.'

'Nico, that's not true.'

'I heard it. You're Four.'

'No . . . why would I—?'

'One, Two, Three, you're Four,' he insisted, his fingers moving across four beads of the rosary.

'Please, Nico, just listen . . .'

'One, Two, Three, you're Four.' His fingers continued

to calmly count, bead by bead. He was over halfway through. Just sixteen beads to go. 'One, Two, Three, you're Four. One, Two, Three, you're Four.'

'Why aren't you listening!?' the First Lady sobbed. 'If you—I can—I can get you help . . .'

'One, Two, Three, you're Four.'

'. . . I can . . . I'll even . . .' Her voice picked up speed. 'I can tell you how your mother died.'

Nico stopped. His head cocked sideways, but his expression was calm as ever. 'You lie.'

His finger slithered around the trigger, and he squeezed it. Easily.

There was a sharp hiss, and a *pfffft* that sounded like a cantaloupe exploding. The inside front windshield was sprayed with blood.

The First Lady slumped sideways, and what was left of her head hit the steering wheel.

Barely noticing, Nico pointed the gun at his own temple. 'Your fate is mine, Dr. Manning. I'm coming to get you in Hell.'

Without closing his eyes, he pulled the trigger.

Click.

He pulled again.

Click.

Empty . . . it's empty, he realized, staring down at the gun. A slight, nervous laugh hiccupped from his throat. He looked up at the roof of the car, then back down at the gun, which quickly became blurred by a swell of tears.

Of course. It was a test. To test his faith. God's sign.

'One, Two, Three, you're Four,' he whispered, his thumb climbing up the last wooden beads and resting on the engraving of Mary. Flushed with a smile even he couldn't contain, Nico looked back up at the roof, brought the rosary up to his lips, and kissed it. 'Thank You . . . thank You, my Lord.'

The test, at long last, was complete. The Book could finally be closed.

114

Ten minutes after seven the following morning, under an overcast sky, I'm sitting alone in the backseat of a black Chevy Suburban that's filled with enough new-car smell to tell me this isn't from our usual fleet. Usually, that's cause for excitement. Not after last night.

In the front seats, both agents sit uncomfortably silent the entire ride. Sure, they toss me some small talk – *Your head okay? How're you feeling?* – but I've been around the Service long enough to know when they're under orders to keep their mouths shut.

As we make the left onto Las Brisas, I spot the news vans and the reporters doing stand-ups. They gently push forward against the yellow tape as they see us coming, but the half dozen agents out front easily keep them at bay. On my left, as the car pulls up to the manicured shrubs out front, and the tall white wooden gate swings open, an Asian female reporter narrates – . . . *once again: former First Lady Lenore Manning* . . . – but gracefully steps back to give us room.

For the reporters and press, all they know is she's dead and that Nico killed her. If they knew her hand in it . . . or what she did . . . an army of agents wouldn't be able to hold them back. The Service, pretending to be clueless, said that since Nico was still out there, they thought it'd be safer to chauffeur me inside. It's a pretty good lie.

And when the agents knocked on my door this morning, I almost believed it.

As the gate slowly closes behind us, I know better than to turn around and give them a shot of my face for the morning news – especially with the cuts on my nose and the dark purple swelling in my eye. Instead, I study the Chicago-brick driveway that leads up to the familiar pale blue house. Flanking both sides of the Suburban, six agents I've never seen before watch the gate shut, making sure no one sneaks in. Then, as I open my door and step outside, they all watch me. To their credit, they turn away quickly, like they don't know what's going on. But when it comes to spotting lingering glances, I'm a black belt. As I head for the front door, every one of them takes another look.

'Wes, right?' an African-American agent with a bald head asks as he opens the front door and welcomes me inside. On most days, agents aren't stationed in the house. Today is different. 'He's waiting for you in the library, so if you'll just follow—'

'I know where it is,' I say, moving forward to cut around him.

He takes a step to the side, blocking my way. 'I'm sure you do,' he says, throwing on a fake grin. Like the agents out front, he's in standard suit and tie, but the microphone on his lapel . . . I almost miss it at first. It's tinier than a small silver bead. They don't give that kind of tech to guys on former-President duty. Whoever he is, he's not from the Orlando field office. He's from D.C. 'If you'll follow me . . .'

He pivots around, leading me down the center hallway, into the formal living room, and past the gold velvet sofa that yesterday held Madame Tussauds' set of Leland Manning eyeballs.

'Here you go,' the agent adds, stopping at the double set of French doors on the far left side of the room. 'I'll be right here,' he says, motioning back to the main hallway. It's not meant as a comfort.

Watching him leave, I bite the dead skin on the inside of my cheek and reach for the American eagle brass doorknob. But just as I palm the eagle, the doorknob turns by itself, and the door opens. I was so busy watching the agent, I didn't see him. Our eyes lock instantly. This time, though, as I spot the brown with the splash of light blue, my stomach doesn't plummet. And he doesn't run.

Standing in the doorway and scratching his fingers against the tiny stubble on his head, Boyle forces an unconvincing smile. From what Rogo told me late last night, I should've known he'd be here. Silly me, though, I actually thought I'd be first. Then again, that's always been my problem when it comes to the President.

Stepping forward and closing the door behind him, Boyle blocks me even worse than the Service. 'Listen, Wes, do you . . . uh . . . do you have a sec?'

The President's expecting me in the library. But for the first time since I've been in Leland Manning's personal orbit, well, for once . . . he can wait. 'Sure,' I say.

Boyle nods me a thank-you and scratches from his head down to his cheek. This is hard for him. 'You should put a warm compress on it,' he finally says. Reading my confusion, he adds, 'For your eye. Everyone thinks cold is better, but the next day, warm helps more.'

I shrug, unconcerned with my appearance.

'By the way, how's your friend?' Boyle asks.

'My friend?'

'The reporter. I heard she got shot.'

'Lisbeth? Yeah, she got shot,' I say, staring at Boyle's

sharpened features. 'The one in her hand was the worst.'

Boyle nods, glancing down at the old stigmata scar at the center of his own palm. He doesn't linger on it, though.

'Wes, I–I'm sorry I had to keep you in the dark like that. In Malaysia, when I was trying to get to Manning . . . All these years, I thought he might've screwed me – that maybe *he* was The Fourth – so to find the crossword . . . to see it was her – and then when I saw you, I just–I panicked. And when O'Shea and Micah started trailing you . . .'

He waits for me to complete the thought – to yell at him for using me as bait these past few days. To blame him for the lies, for the deception . . . for every ounce of guilt he dumped on my shoulders for eight years. But as I stare across at him . . . as I see the deep circles under his eyes and the pained vertical line etched between his brows . . . Last night, Ron Boyle won. He got everyone – The Roman . . . Micah and O'Shea . . . even the First Lady – everyone he'd hunted for so long. But it's painful to see him now, anxiously licking his lips. There's no joy in his features, no victory on his face. Eight years after his ordeal began, all that's left is an aged man with crummy nose and chin jobs, a haunted vacancy in his eyes, and an unstoppable need to keep checking every nearby door and window, which he does for the third time since we started talking.

Suffering is bad. Suffering alone is far worse.

My jaw clenches as I try to find the words. 'Listen, Ron . . .'

'Wes, don't pity me.'

'I'm not—'

'You *are*,' he insists. 'I'm standing right in front of you, and you're still mourning me like I'm gone. I can see it in your face.'

He's talking about the swell of tears in my eyes. But he's reading it wrong. I shake my head and try to tell him why, but the words feel like they're stapled in my throat.

He says something else to make me feel better, but I don't hear it. All I hear are the words that're trapped within me. The words I've practiced in my sleep at night – every night – and in my mirror every morning, knowing full well they'd never get to leave my lips. Until this moment.

I swallow hard and again hear the crowd at the speedway that day. Everyone happy, everyone waving, until *pop, pop, pop,* there it is, the scream in C minor as the ambulance doors close. I swallow hard again and slowly, finally, the screams begin to fade as the first few syllables leave my lips.

'Ron,' I begin, already panting hard. 'I–I . . .'

'Wes, you don't have to—'

I shake my head and cut him off. He's wrong. I do. And after nearly a decade, as the tears stream down my face, I finally get my chance. 'Ron, I . . . I'm sorry for putting you in the limo that day,' I tell him. 'I know it's stupid – I just – I need you to know I'm sorry, okay? I'm sorry, Ron,' I plead as my voice cracks and the tears drip from my chin. 'I'm so sorry I put you in there.'

Across from me, Boyle doesn't respond. His shoulders rise, and for a moment, he looks like the old Boyle who screamed in my face that burning July day. As I wipe my cheeks, he continues staring at me, keeping it all to himself. I can't read him. Especially when he doesn't want to be read. But even the best facades crack in time.

He rubs his nose and tries to hide it, but I still spot

the quivering of his chin and the heartbroken arch of his eyebrows.

'Wes,' he eventually offers, 'no matter what car you put me in, that bullet was always going to hit my chest.'

I look up, still fighting to catch my breath. Over the years, my mom, Rogo, my shrinks, Manning, even the lead investigator from the Service, told me the exact same thing. But Ron Boyle was the one I needed to hear it from.

Within seconds, a tentative smile spreads across my face. I spot my own reflection in the glass panels of the French doors. The smile itself is crooked, broken, and only lifts one of my cheeks. But for the first time in a long time, that's plenty.

That is, until I spot the flash of movement and the familiar posture on the other side of the glass. With a twist, the brass eagle doorknob once again turns, and the door opens inward, behind Boyle's back. Boyle turns, and I look up. Towering above us, President Manning sticks his head out and nods at me with an awkward hello. His mane of gray hair is matted just enough that I can tell it's unwashed; the whites of his eyes are crackling with red. His wife died last night. He hasn't slept ten minutes.

'I should go,' Boyle offers. From what I heard last night, he's blaming his death and reappearance on Nico and The Three. Not The Four. For that alone, Manning'll make him a hero. I'm not sure I blame him. But as Manning knows, I deal with things differently than Boyle.

Before I can say a word, Boyle walks past me, offers a quick shoulder pat, and casually leaves the room, like he's going to lunch. The problem is, I'm the one about to be eaten.

On most days, Manning would simply head back into

the library and expect me to follow. Today, he opens the
door wider and motions me inside. 'There you are, Wes,'
the President says. 'I was starting to worry you weren't
coming.'

115

'I appreciate your getting here so early, Wes.'

'Believe me, I wanted to come last night.'

Nodding soberly and ushering me to the seat in front of his desk, Manning turns his back to me and scans the framed photos and leather-bound books that line the built-in maple shelves that surround us on all sides. There are pictures of him with the pope, with both Presidents Bush, with Clinton, Carter, and even with an eight-year-old boy from Eritrea, who weighed barely twenty pounds when Manning met him during one of our first trips abroad. Unlike his office, where we cover the walls, here at home he displays only the pictures he loves best – his own personal greatest hits – but it's not until I sit down in the antique Queen Anne chair that I realize that the only photo on his desk is one of him and his wife.

'Sir, I'm sorry about—'

'The funeral's Wednesday,' he says, still scanning his shelves as if some brilliant answer were there among the peace prizes, bricks from the Hanoi Hilton, and imprints of the Wailing Wall. Across from him, I also stare – at the bronze casting of Abraham Lincoln's fist that sits on the edge of the desk.

'We'd like you to be a pallbearer, Wes.'

He still doesn't face me. The snag in his voice tells me how hard this is. The way his hand's shaking as he shoves

it in his pocket shows me the same. As President, Leland
Manning buried three hundred and two American soldiers,
nine heads of state, two senators, and a pope. None of it
prepared him for burying his wife.

'A pallbearer?' I ask.

'It was her request,' he says, trying to pull it together.
'From her checklist.'

When a President and First Lady leave the White House,
as if they're not depressed enough, one of the very first
things they're forced to do is make arrangements for their
own funerals. State funerals are national events that need
to be mounted in a few hours, almost always without any
notice – which is why the Pentagon gives the President a
checklist of all the gruesome details: whether you want to
lie in state in the Capitol, if you want a public viewing,
whether you want the final burial at your library or in
Arlington, how many friends, family, and dignitaries should
attend, who should do the eulogies, who *shouldn't* be
invited, and of course, who should be the pallbearers.

Once, they even sent the military honor guard to our
offices at the Manning Library to practice carrying the
casket that would eventually hold him. I tried to keep
Manning from coming to his office that day. But there he
was, watching from his window as they carried his flag-
covered weighted-down casket to the meditation garden
in back. 'I look heavy,' he'd joked, trying his best to make
light of it. Still, he was quiet as they passed by. He's more
quiet now.

'Mr President, I'm not sure that's the best idea anymore.
After last night—'

'That was her own doing, Wes. You know that. Her own
doing. And her undoing as well,' he says as his voice again
breaks. He's trying hard to be strong – to be the Lion –

but I can see that he's gripping the back of his brown leather chair to stand. However it happened, it's still his wife. Looking like a shell of the man I used to know, he sighs and sits down. We both sit there in silence, staring at Lincoln's fist.

'Did the Service say anything about Nico?' I finally ask.

'His fingerprints were all over the car. The blood in the backseat was his. No question he pulled the trigger. But as far as where he disappeared to, they're still looking,' he explains. 'If you're worried he's coming after you, though, I've already asked the Service to—'

'He's not coming after me. Not anymore.'

Manning looks me over. 'So in the cemetery . . . you spoke to him?'

'Yes.'

'You made peace with him?'

'Peace? No. But—' I pause to think about it. 'He's not coming back.'

'Good. I'm glad for you, Wes. You deserve some peace of mind.'

He's generous to say it, but it's clear his mind is elsewhere. That's fine. So is mine.

'Sir, I know this may not be the best time, but I was wondering if I could—' I stop right there, reminding myself I don't need his permission. I look up from Lincoln's fist. 'I'd like to talk to you about my status.'

'What status?'

'My job, Mr President.'

'Of course, of course – no . . . of course,' he says, clearly caught off guard.

'I thought that under the circumstances—'

'You don't have to say it, Wes. Regardless of the end

result, you're still family to us. So if you're wondering if
the job's still yours—'

'Actually, Mr President, I was thinking it's time for me
to move on.'

Our eyes lock, but he doesn't blink. I think he's most
shocked by the fact it's not a question.

Eventually, he offers a small, gentle laugh. 'Good for
you, Wes,' he says, pointing. 'Y'know, I been waiting a long
time for you to say that.'

'I appreciate that, sir.'

'And if you need help finding a job or a recommendation or something like that . . . don't forget, it still says
President on my stationery, and let's hope there're still a
few people out there who're impressed by that.'

'I'm sure there are, sir,' I say with my own laugh. 'Thank
you, Mr President.' The way he nods at me – like a proud
dad – it's a truly sweet moment. A warm moment. And
the perfect moment for me to leave. But I can't. Not yet.
Not until I find out.

'So what do you plan on doing next?' he asks.

I don't answer. Shifting in my seat, I tell myself to forget
it.

'Wes, do you have any plans f—?'

'Did you know?' I blurt.

He cocks an eyebrow. 'Pardon me?'

I stare right at him, pretending they're not the most
awkward three words to ever leave my lips. Steeling myself,
I again ask, 'Did you know about the First Lady? About
your wife?'

Across from me, his fingers lace together, resting on
the desk. I know his temper. The fuse is lit. But as he sits
there and watches me, the explosion never comes. His lips
part, and the lacing of his fingers comes undone. He's not

mad. He's wounded. 'After all our – you really think that?' he asks.

I sink in my seat, feeling about three centimeters tall. But that doesn't mean I'm not getting my answer. 'I saw the crosswords – your ratings – even from the earliest days, you were obviously worried. So does that—? Did you know she was The Fourth?'

At this point, he has every right to wring my throat; to argue that she was tricked and innocent. But he just sits there, pummeled by the question. 'Wes, don't cast her as Lady Macbeth. She was many things – but never a master-mind.'

'I saw her last night. Even in the best light – even if she didn't know who The Roman was when he first approached her – once Boyle got shot, all these years, and she never said *anything*? Doesn't sound like someone being manipulated.'

'And I'm not saying she was. My point is simply that what you found in those puzzles . . . even what you saw first-hand yourself . . .' He cups a hand to his mouth and clears his throat. 'I'm not a moron, Wes. Lenore is my wife. I'm well aware of her weaknesses. And when it came to staying in the grand white castle – c'mon, son, you saw it too. You were there with us – when you fly that high, when you're looking down on all the clouds, the only thing that scared her was losing altitude and plummeting back to earth.'

'That didn't give her the right t—'

'I'm not defending her,' Manning says, practically pleading for me to understand what's clearly kept him up all night. He can't share this with the Service or anyone else on staff. Without his wife, he's got no one to tell but me. 'You know how desperate she was. Everyone wanted that second term. Everyone. Including you, Wes.'

'But what you said . . . with the clouds, and knowing her weaknesses . . . if you knew all that—'

'I didn't know anything!' he shouts as his ears flush red. 'I knew she was scared. I knew she was paranoid. I knew that in the early days she used to toss details to reporters, like the early internal arguing, or the fact she wasn't consulted for redecorating the Oval – because she was convinced that if she could make them like her, they wouldn't kick us out and take it all away. So yes – *that* part I knew.' He puts his head down and massages the front of his forehead. 'But,' he adds, 'I never *ever* thought she'd let herself get dragged into something like this.'

I nod like I understand. But I don't. 'After you left office and it all calmed down, why'd . . . ?' I search for softer words, but there's no other way to say it. 'Why'd you stay with her?'

'She's my wife, Wes. She's been by my side since we were hand-painting campaign posters in my mother's garage. Since we were—' Finally lifting his head, he closes his eyes, struggling hard to reclaim his calm. 'I wish you could put that question to Jackie Kennedy, or Pat Nixon, or even the Clintons.' He looks back at the photos with his fellow Presidents. 'Everything's easy . . . until it gets complicated.'

'So when Boyle was shot . . .'

He stares at me as I say the words. He doesn't have to tell me a thing. But he knows what I've given him all these years. And that this is the only thing I've ever asked in return.

'We knew it might happen, but had no idea when,' he says without even hesitating. 'Boyle approached me a few weeks earlier and told me about his offer from The Three. From there . . . well, you know how fast the Service moves.

I did everything I could to protect my friend. They gave him a vest, stocked his blood in the ambulance, and did their very best to keep him safe.'

'Until I put him in the limo.'

'Until Nico put a bullet in his hand and chest,' he says, turning back to face me. 'From there, they rushed him to the Marshals Office, who patched him up, shuttled him from city to city, and put him straight into the highest levels of WITSEC. Naturally, he didn't want to go, but he knew the alternatives. Even if it wrecks families, it saves more lives than you think.'

I nod as the President stands from his oversize seat. The way he leans on the armrest to slowly boost himself up, he's more tired than he's letting on. But he doesn't ask me to leave.

'If it makes you feel better, Wes, I think she regretted it. Especially what happened with you.'

'I appreciate that,' I tell him, trying to be enthusiastic.

He studies me closely. I'm good at reading him. He's even better at reading me. 'I'm not just saying that, Wes.'

'Mr President, I never thought otherwi—'

'We prayed together before bed. Did you know that? That was our ritual – ever since we first got married,' he explains. 'And during that first year? She prayed for you every night.'

The number one mistake most people make when they meet the President is they always try to extend the conversation. It's a once-in-a-lifetime moment, so they'll say the dumbest things to make it last forever.

I stand from my seat and motion to the door. 'I should really get going, sir.'

'Understood. Go do what you have to,' he says as he crosses around from his desk. 'I'll tell you what, though,' he adds as he follows me to the door. 'I'm glad she made you a pallbearer.' He stops and catches his breath. 'She should only be carried by family.'

Halfway through the doorway, I turn around. I'll carry those words with me for the rest of my life.

But that doesn't mean I believe them.

He reaches out to shake my hand, and I get the full double-hand clasp that he usually saves for heads of state and presidential-level donors. He even lingers a moment, engulfing part of my wrist.

Maybe it was unspoken. Maybe he figured it out. For all I know, she could've even told him outright. But one thing is clear – and it's the only thing he said that can't be argued: Leland Manning is not a moron. He knew Boyle was planning to say no to The Three. So when Boyle went down, he had to've suspected they could've gotten someone bigger.

As I head out through the living room and toward the front door, I spot the huge black-and-white photo of the view from behind his desk in the Oval. Sure, those four years were great. But for him, it would've been even better to have four more.

'Let me know if you need *anything*,' the President calls out from the living room.

I wave good-bye and say a final thanks.

The Cowardly Lion may not have courage. But he's certainly got a brain.

He knows I was running around with a reporter. He knows she's waiting for my call. And most important, he knows that when it comes to political touch, the best touch is when you don't feel it at all.

For eight years, I haven't felt anything. Right now I feel it all.

'Got everything you need?' the bald agent asks as he opens the front door.

'I think so.'

Stepping outside, I pull my phone from my pocket, punch in the number for her hospital room, and head down the red brick path. When Herbert Hoover left the White House, he said that a former President's greatest service is to remove himself from politics and public life. Time for me to do the same.

'You speak to him?' Lisbeth asks, picking up on the first ring.

'Of course, I spoke to him.'

'And?'

At first, I don't answer.

'C'mon, Wes, this isn't the gossip column anymore. What'd you think of Manning?'

Up the path, outside the garage, half a dozen brand-new agents watch me carefully as the closest one tries to usher me toward the Suburban. Outside the front gate, the wolf pack of reporters shake their heads inconsolably as they scramble together video montages to honor the fallen First Lady. With her death comes the inevitable outpouring of sadness and support from commentators who spent their entire careers ripping her to pieces. I can already hear it in their hushed, reverential tones. They loved her. Their viewers loved her. The whole world loved her. All I have to do is keep my mouth shut.

'It's okay,' Lisbeth says. She knows what the press'll do to my life if I'm the one who spills it. 'I'll just tell them to go with the original story.'

'But what abou—?'

'You already fought your battle, Wes. No one can ask any more of you than that.'

I pull the phone close to my mouth and once again remind myself that every opportunity I've had in my life came directly from the Mannings. My words are a whisper. 'Have them send over your laptop. I want you to write it. People need to know what she did.'

Lisbeth pauses, giving me plenty of time to take it back. 'You sure about this?' she finally asks as a Secret Service agent with a flat nose opens the back door to the Suburban.

Ignoring him, I walk past the car and head straight for the tall wooden gate and the swelling crowd of mourners outside.

'And, Lisbeth?' I say as I shove the door open and the firing squad of cameras turns my way. 'Don't hold back.'

116

Two weeks later

A rare Italian snow sprinkled down from the dusty sky as the man crossed Via Mazzarino and lowered his chin toward the lapels of his herringbone wool coat. His hair was blond now – short and barely grown in – but he was still careful as he approached Sant'Agata dei Goti, the fifth-century church that seemed to hide on the narrow cobblestone street.

Passing the front entrance but not going inside, he glanced up at the facade. The relief above the door was an ancient carving of Saint Agatha holding her severed breast on a plate, the victim of torturers who'd attacked her when she refused to renounce her faith.

'Praise Him,' the man whispered to himself as he cut right, followed the signs to the side entrance on Via Panisperna, and quietly marched up the bumpy brick driveway that was blanketed in the light snow.

At the end of the driveway, he wiped his feet on the battered welcome mat, shoved open the brown double doors, and winced as the old hinges shrieked. Inside, the smell of damp wood and rose candles welcomed and transported him right back to the old stone church where he grew up, right back to the Wisconsin winters of his childhood, right back to when his mom passed.

The hinges shrieked again – and he winced again – as

the door slammed shut behind him. Wasting no time, the man scanned the empty pews, eyed the empty altar, then glanced between the Oriental granite columns that ran down the center aisle. No one in sight. His eyes narrowed as he listened. The only thing there was a single hushed whisper. Praise Him. Just like it was supposed to be.

Feeling his heart punch inside his chest, he raced toward his destination, tracing the faded colors of the mosaic floor to the mahogany stall on the far right side of the altar.

As he got closer, he followed the faint whisper from inside. He'd never been here before, but when he saw the picture in the travel brochure – he knew to always trust fate.

Unbuttoning his coat and taking one last glance around, he kneeled in front of the mahogany stall. The whispering stopped. Through a square cutaway in the booth, a small burgundy curtain was pulled shut, and the priest inside stopped praying.

It was only then, only in the screaming silence of the empty Sant'Agata dei Goti church, that Nico lowered his head toward the confessional.

'Bless me, Father, for I have sinned. It's been—'

'Let's go, Nico – make it quick!' the tall orderly with the sweet onion breath shouted.

Glancing over his shoulder, Nico looked past the industrial beige carpet, the cheap oak lectern, and the dozen or so metal folding chairs that made up the small chapel on the fourth floor of St. Elizabeths' John Howard Pavilion, and focused hard on the two orderlies who waited for him back by the only door to the room. It'd been nearly two weeks since they found him in Wisconsin. But thanks to a new lawyer, for the first time in years, he finally had chapel privileges.

Without a word, Nico turned back toward the wooden cross attached to the otherwise bare front wall of the room. Within seconds, the carpet, the lectern, and the folding chairs once again disappeared and were replaced by the mosaic floor, the ancient pews, and the mahogany confessional. Just like the ones in the pamphlet that his counselor gave him.

'. . . it's been far too long since my last confession.'

He took a deep breath of the rose candles – the sweet smell that was always on his mom – and shut both eyes. The rest came easy.

God provided an ending. And brought him back home for a new beginning.

EPILOGUE

The biggest wounds in life are all self-inflicted.
– President Bill Clinton

Palm Beach, Florida

'Just yourself?' the waitress asks, approaching my table in the corner of the café's small outdoor patio.

'Actually, I've got one more coming,' I tell her as she puts a water glass on my place mat to keep the wind from blowing it away. We're at least two blocks from the ocean, but thanks to the narrowness of the street, it always packs a nice breeze.

'Anything else to drink besides w—?' She freezes as I look up. It's the first time she sees my face. To her credit, she recovers quickly, faking a smile – but the damage is already—

'Wait . . . you're that guy,' she says, suddenly excited.

'Excuse me?'

'Y'know, with the thing . . . with the President . . . that was you, wasn't it?'

I cock my head, offering the slightest nod.

Studying me for a moment, she cracks a tiny smile,

tucks a strand of straight black hair behind her ear, and calmly heads back to the kitchen.

'Holy salami, what was *that*?' a familiar voice asks from the sidewalk. On my left, Rogo rushes up to the low wrought-iron railing that surrounds the outdoor patio.

'Rogo, don't hop the—'

Before I say it, he throws a leg onto the railing, boosts himself over, and plops into the seat across from me.

'Can't you use the door like the rest of the bipeds?' I ask him.

'No, no, no – no changing the channel. What was that rendezvous with the waitress?'

'Rendezvous?'

'Don't play dumb with me, Ethel – I saw it – the longing glance . . . the hair tuck . . . the little finger-phone where she held her thumb to her ear and whispered *Call me* into her pinkie.'

'There was no finger-phone.'

'She recognized you, didn't she?'

'Can you please stop?'

'Where'd she see you, *60 Minutes*? That's the one, isn't it? The girls love the Morley Safer.'

'Rogo . . .'

'Don't fight with me, Wes – it's an unarguable fact: A waitress can make the dining experience or ruin it. Read the signal. She's trying to make it. Make it. *Maaaake iiiiit*,' he whispers, rolling his eyes upward as he reaches over and steals a sip of my water. Noticing the menu in front of him, he adds, 'They got fajitas here?'

'It's a panini place.'

'Panini?'

'Y'know, with the bread and the—'

'I'm sorry, do you have a cramp in your ovaries?'

When I don't laugh, he twirls the straw in the water, never taking his eyes off me. Right there, I know what he's really after. 'It's okay, Rogo. You don't have to use every conversation to try and cheer me up.'

'I'm not trying to cheer you up,' he insists. He twirls the straw again as the waitress returns with another place mat and some silverware. He's silent as she puts it in front of him. When she leaves, I glance back at him.

'Still trying to think of a clever comeback to make me happy?' I ask him.

'I was until you just *ruined it*,' he sulks, chucking his straw into his water like a mini-javelin.

When I still don't laugh, he shakes his head, finally giving up. 'Y'know, you're really not a fun person.'

'And that's it? That's your best retort?'

'*And!*' he adds, pointing a finger at me. 'And . . . and . . . and . . . *and*—' He cuts himself off. '*C'mon*,' he whines, 'just put a smile on your face – please. If you do, I'll order an orange juice and do the fake-laugh thing at the waitress where I make it come out of my nose. It burns like the sun. You'll love it.'

'That's very generous of you, Rogo. I just need – just give me a little time.'

'Whattya think the past two weeks have been? You're moping around like it's an Olympic event. I mean, it's not like your life sucks: interviews coming out the ying-yang, you get all the credit for saving the day, *and* semi-hot waitresses are recognizing you and bringing you water with little slices of lemon. You've had the greatest fourteen days of your life. Enough with the woe-is-me.'

'It's not woe-is-me. It's just . . .'

'. . . you're sad to watch them go down in flames like that. I heard the speech yesterday, and the day before, and the day before: *They gave you so many opportunities. You feel like Benedict Arnold.* I understand, Wes. I really do. But like everyone in your office said – the one thing the Mannings *didn't* give you was much of a choice. That castle you were in was built on sand.'

I stare out at the pedestrians walking past us on the sidewalk. 'I know. But even so . . . I've been by Manning's side for the better part of a decade. I was there before he got to the office, and I didn't leave until he headed upstairs for bed. And not just weekdays. *Every* day. For nearly *ten years!* You know what that's—?' I close my eyes, refusing to say it. 'I didn't go to your sister's wedding; I was in the Ukraine during my parents' thirtieth wedding anniversary; my college roommate had a baby, and I haven't even met him yet.'

'It's a *she*, but don't feel guilty.'

'That's the point, Rogo – to go from *every single day* to *never again* . . . I didn't just leave my job. I left – I feel like I left my life.'

Rogo shakes his head like I'm missing the point. 'Haven't you ever played Uno?' he asks calmly. 'Sometimes you have to lose all your cards to win.'

Looking down at my water, I watch the ice cubes bob and crackle inside the tall glass.

'You know I'm right,' Rogo says.

A sharp fissure ricochets like lightning through an ice cube at the bottom. As it splinters, the cubes on top tumble down with it.

'Look at it this way,' Rogo adds. 'At least you're not Dreidel.'

I stab the ice with my straw. This time, I'm the one shaking my head. 'I wouldn't cry for Dreidel just yet.' Reading the confusion on Rogo's face, I explain, 'Don't forget why he got the nickname. He may not be sitting in Congress next year, but mark my words, he'll be somewhere on top.'

'What about Violet, or whatever her real name is? When that came out . . .'

'Dreidel laid low for the requisite week, then strategically started leaking the story of how he brilliantly helped the Marshals throughout their investigation of The Three. Believe me, the moment I saw him and his girlfriend in that hotel, he was prepping his smile for the highlight reel.'

'But with Violet – he hit her – and he's—'

'—the only one of us who made an advance deal with the government. God bless America, I heard he's got a new radio show that's being lined up as we speak, while the book rights sold yesterday for seven figures, plus bonuses when it hits the best-seller lists. And when the paperback comes out, I'll bet good money he tucks in a special addendum chapter with a mea culpa to Violet, just to sell a few extra hundred thousand copies.'

'Wait, so the editor who bought the book rights – is that the same guy who called you last week abou—?'

'Very same guy. Very same offer, including the best-seller bonuses.'

'Oh, God – strike me with lightning!' Rogo shouts at the sky as a few fellow diners and an older woman on the sidewalk turn to stare. 'You let Dreidel *take that*?'

'He didn't take anything. Besides, I promised the President from day one: I'd never cash in on him.'

'His wife almost—' He turns to the man staring from the table diagonally across from us. 'Sir, go back to your soup. Thank you.' Looking back at me, Rogo lowers his voice and leans in. 'His wife almost had you killed, jackass.

And even if you can't prove it, *he* may've known about it all along. So while I'm sure your buddy Dreidel had that same, dumb code-of-honor thing going – and believe me, my momma taught me to appreciate loyalty – attempted *murder* is usually a pretty darn good sign that you can part ways guilt-free and stop sending invites to each other's birthday parties.'

Slightly up the block, a meter maid driving in an enclosed golf cart marks tires with a piece of chalk on the end of a long metal pole. 'Doesn't matter,' I tell Rogo. 'I'm not profiting off them.'

'Bet Dreidel sells the film rights too (though he'll probably only get movie of the week).'

'No profit, Rogo. Ever.'

'And what's Lisbeth say?'

'About the book rights or Dreidel's radio show?'

'About everything.'

I stare up the block at the meter maid, who's writing a ticket for a pale yellow vintage Plymouth Belvedere. Following my glance, Rogo turns and looks over his shoulder.

'I'm only gonna get him off, Richie!' Rogo yells out.

'Only if they're dumb enough to hire you,' the meter maid calmly teases back.

'I think Lisbeth understands where I'm coming from,' I tell him.

'She understand anything else?' Rogo asks, still eyeing the yellow Plymouth.

'What's that mean?'

'You know what it means. You two went through the grinder together – plus you let her write the story as a final gift.'

'So?'

'So I know you talk to her every night.'

'How d'you know I talk to her?'

'I pick up the phone to see who you're chatting with.' Finally turning back to face me, he adds, 'C'mon, what's the story with our favorite redhead? You in there? You counting freckles? You trying to figure out if they make constellations?'

'Pardon me?'

'Don't play naive. You digging for clams, or you still on the beach?'

I roll my eyes. 'Can you please not be so—?'

'Clamdigger!'

'No. Stop. Of course, I haven't.'

'You swear?'

'I swear.'

He leans back in his chair and puts his hands behind his head. 'Okay. Good.'

I pause and cock my head. 'Why *good*?'

'Nothing,' Rogo says.

'Rogo, why *good*?'

'I dunno,' he says, already playing dumb. 'I just figured, y'know, if you're not swimming in that pool, I might try to dive in and – and maybe just – and maybe take my own little skinny dip.'

I can't help but laugh. 'Wait. You? *You're* gonna ask Lisbeth out?'

'Why, you think I don't have a chance?'

'Let me be honest with you.' I pick the words as carefully as possible. 'You don't have a chance.'

'What're you talking about? I'm short and fat; she's a little on the plus size. It's a good match.'

'Yeah, that makes complete sense. Maybe you should just go ring shopping right now.'

He lowers his chin, and his jaw shifts off-center. 'You're not supposed to root against the rabbit getting the Trix.'

'Listen, you do what you want. I'm just warning you – I think she might be seeing someone.'

'Lisbeth is? Says who? Her? Or you just making it up?'

'I'm telling you . . . I could hear it in her voice.'

'Did she say who it—?' His face falls. 'It's not Dreidel, is it? Oh, I'll stab needles in my eyes if he—'

'It's not Dreidel – no way,' I tell him.

'You think it's someone from her work?'

I glance over Rogo's shoulder, where a brand-new lime-green Mustang cruises up the block, slowing as it approaches. 'Kinda from work,' I say as it pulls into the fire lane that's directly across from our table on the patio. The lime-green car bucks to a stop. There's no mistaking the driver's red hair.

'Whoa, paninis!' Lisbeth calls out as she leans out the window of her car. 'Do they actually serve estrogen there, or did you take your shots before you arrived?'

Rogo looks at her, then me, then back to her. '*No* . . . But you said—'

'All I said was I hadn't made any constellations,' I tell him. 'But that doesn't mean I'm not trying,' I add as I reach across the table and pat my hand against his cheek. 'At least you got to slam a car door on Dreidel's hand.' Before he can even digest it, I stand from my seat, hop over the railing, and head for the lime-green car.

'Sweet mother of Harry S. Truman,' Rogo mutters, already following me over the railing. 'Wes, *wait*!'

For once, I don't look back.

At the opening of his Presidential Library, Manning told a reporter that his favorite comic strip when he was little was *Prince Valiant*. The next day, an op-ed ran pointing out that in said strip, Prince Valiant once had a curse that he'd never be content. The op-ed called it the curse of every President and former President. And it is. But it's no longer the curse for me.

Crossing around to the passenger side of Lisbeth's car, I pull open the door and duck down for a quick hello. 'Did I miss the part when paninis became feminine?' I ask her.

'You did the same thing with apple martinis. And Volkswagen Cabriolets,' Rogo interrupts, cutting in front of me and sliding into the backseat. 'You should read *Jane* magazine. That's what *I* do. *Oooh*, new-car smell.'

'Nice to see you too, Rogo,' Lisbeth offers.

Looking side to side in the backseat, Rogo raises an eyebrow. 'Wait, how'd you afford this thing? Did you get a book deal too?'

Ignoring him, Lisbeth turns to me. From the expression on her face, I sniff trouble. 'Good news, bad news,' she says. 'You choose.'

'Bad news,' Rogo and I say simultaneously. I shoot him a look over my shoulder.

'Bad news,' I say again to Lisbeth.

She fidgets with the bandage on her hand, which guarantees it's serious. 'Remember that *San Francisco Chronicle* job I told you about?' she asks. 'Well, they made me an offer – real news too, no more gossip. But they said – not that I'm surprised – they said I need to move to San Francisco.'

'So, away from here?'

'Really away,' she says, staring out the front windshield.

'And the good news?' I ask.

She grips the steering wheel, then slowly turns to face me. 'Wanna come?'

My cheek leaps into the air. Now I'm the one wearing the butcher's dog grin.

'Waitaminute,' Rogo calls out from the back. 'Before we do anything rash, do we know the full picture of their speeding ticket problems out there? Because a man with my particular practice and expertise—'

I turn back to Rogo, and the grin only gets wider. 'I'm sure we can look it up.'

'And let's not forget about lax traffic laws and the slip-shod judicial system that supports it. If they're not there? Those two are deal breakers.'

'You're really worried? It's *California.*'

'Plus,' Lisbeth adds, 'in San Francisco, I bet they have crazy amounts of accidents with all those hills.'

'See, now that's what I like to hear,' Rogo says, beaming as the car cruises up the block. 'Oooh, do me a favor,' he adds. 'Pull up to that old Plymouth with the ticket on the windshield? If I'm gonna pay for this move, we need us some new clients.' From his wallet, he pulls out a business card and tries to squeeze forward and lean out my open passenger-side window. 'Wes, scootch your seat up?'

'Here, try – *here,*' Lisbeth offers, poking a button on the dash. With a whir, the convertible roof retracts, revealing the aquamarine-blue sky and making plenty of room for Rogo to reach outside.

With his stomach pressed against the interior side of the car, he leans out from the backseat and wedges one of his business cards in the seam of the Plymouth's driver's-side window. 'Downwithtickets.com!' he shouts to the few people who're staring from the sidewalk. 'Now go back to your sheltered lives! Go! Flock! Conspicuously consume!'

Lisbeth pumps the gas, the tires bite the pavement, and

the car takes off, sending an air pocket of wind whipping against our faces. With the top down, I watch the royal palms that line the street disappear behind us. Effortlessly, the car roars up Royal Park Bridge, where the polished waves of the Intracoastal are so bright they're almost blinding. As I tip my head back and soak in the sky, the ocean wind knots its fingers through my hair, and the sweet sun bakes against my face.

Nico was wrong. The Book of Fate isn't already written. It's written every day.

Some scars never heal.

Then again, some do.

AUTHOR'S NOTE

History has always been filled with exaggerations – and so, a few words about the Freemasons. In this book, the historical details about Freemasonry are based on three years of research. All the historical figures identified as Masons – such as Voltaire, Winston Churchill, Mozart, and certain U.S. Presidents – have been documented as Masons. Throughout history, Thomas Jefferson has been rumored to be a Mason, but the evidence today, as acknowledged in the novel, does not support that assertion. Nevertheless, Jefferson, Washington, and architect Pierre Charles L'Enfant, while designing the city of Washington, D.C., did build the most famous Masonic symbol (the compass and square) and the five-pointed pentagram into the city grid. There are disagreements over who had the most influence over the final street plan, but I believe the grid speaks for itself. For over two hundred years, those symbols have been hidden in plain sight. It is also true that on October 13, 1792, Maryland's Masonic Lodge Number 9 did lay the cornerstone of the White House in a Freemason ceremony. The same was true during the laying of the cornerstone of the U.S. Capitol Building, where George Washington himself presided over the Masonic ceremony. Washington's Masonic trowel was also used at the cornerstone laying of the Washington Monument, the U.S. Supreme Court, the Library of Congress, the National Cathedral, and the Smithsonian. To be clear, those details are what intrigued me and inspired me to pursue further investigation.

Yet these facts in no way mean that the Masons are trying to overthrow the world's governments, open the devil's door, or unleash secret satanic plots.

So why parse truth from fantasy – especially in a work of fiction? Does it even matter? Well, in this world where fact so easily dances with fiction – and where, for six novels, I have prided myself on my research – it is important to me, as both author and armchair historian, to make sure I don't add even more misinformation to whatever small section of the public consciousness I am so thankful to touch.

So I encourage you to read the historical documents yourself. Any secret fraternity that had John Wayne, Winston Churchill, Benjamin Franklin, Harry Houdini, five Supreme Court chief justices, fifteen U.S. Presidents, and my Uncle Bernie as members just has to be worth checking out. Plus, you should see what symbols they built into the street plan of Sandusky, Ohio. Really. Go to: www.bradmeltzer.com.

Brad Meltzer

Fort Lauderdale, Florida, 2006

If you enjoyed THE BOOK OF FATE read on to find out about Brad Meltzer's other relentlessly paced thrillers. All are available from Hodder.

HODDER

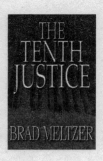

THE TENTH JUSTICE

BRAD MELTZER

Ben Addison had got it made.

He's just finished law school.
He's a new clerk at the Supreme Court.
It's the first step on a golden career path.

But Ben is about to make a huge mistake.
He's about to be tricked into leaking
something he shouldn't.
And he's about to land himself and his three best
friends in really serious trouble.

'Grisham better beware, for there's a new kid
on the block' *Irish Times*

DEAD EVEN

BRAD MELTZER

The marriage made in heaven.
The court case from hell.

Sara Tate had just started as a prosecutor in the
Manhattan District Attorney's office. Her husband,
Jared Lynch, is a defence attorney on the brink of
making partner at his prestigious Wall Street law firm.
They have a golden future ahead of them, and a terrific,
high-spirited marriage – the law brought them together
and it has never kept them apart.

Until Sara and Jared inadvertently find themselves on
opposite sides of the same case. When that happens,
husband and wife are pitted against each other. And
when they're both threatened by parties to the case, the
result is unavoidable.

No matter who wins, one of them will die.

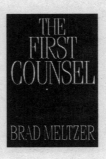

THE FIRST COUNSEL

BRAD MELTZER

JFK Jr. was Lark.
Chelsea Clinton was Energy.
Meet Shadow.

SHADOW is a Secret Service codename for the
First Daughter, Nora Hartson. And when she starts
dating young White House lawyer Michael Garrick, he
starts feeling like the First Counsel. That's what
happens to everyone who lives in her world.

It's a world where you dad's the president, your close
friends wear earpieces and carry guns and a world
where everyone is watching.

On a date, Nora and Michael see something they shouldn't.
To protect her, he admits to something he shouldn't.
And when the problem snowballs out of control, she
may have to do something she shouldn't.

The First Counsel. The President's daughter. You've never
dated anyone like this.

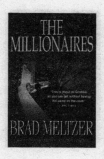

THE MILLIONAIRES

BRAD MELTZER

Two brothers.
Three Secret Service agents.
The world's most exclusive vault.
And millions of dollars there for the taking.
What would you steal if you couldn't get caught?

'White knuckle thriller . . . keeps you hooked from
start to finish' *Irish Times*

THE ZERO GAME

BRAD MELTZER

Come play the Zero Game – you can bet your life on it . . .

Matthew Mercer and Harris Sandler are best friends who have plum jobs as senior staffers to well-respected congressmen. But after a decade in Washington, idealism has faded to disillusionment, and they're bored. Then one of them finds out about the clandestine Zero Game.

It starts out as good fun – a single wager between friends. But when someone close to them ends up dead, Harris and Matthew realise the game is far more sinister than they imagined – and that they're about to be the game's next victims.

'The scenarios are credible, the tension excruciating and the ending slaps you in the face.' *Guardian*